. . .

LINDEN PRESS/
SIMON & SCHUSTER

NEW YORK

LONDON

TORONTO

SYDNEY

TOKYO

SINGAPORE

. . .

THE
LIVES
OF THE
DEAD

a novel

CHARLIE
SMITH

Linden Press
Simon & Schuster Building
Rockefeller Center
1230 Avenue of the Americas
New York, New York 10020

Copyright © 1990 by Charlie Smith

LINDEN PRESS/S&S and colophon are
registered trademarks
of Simon & Schuster Inc.

Designed by Barbara M. Bachman

Manufactured in the United States of America

1 3 5 7 9 10 8 6 4 2

Library of Congress Cataloging-in-Publication Data

Smith, Charlie, date
The lives of the dead : a novel / Charlie Smith.
p.   cm.
I. Title.
PS3569.M5163L5   1990
813'.54—dc20   90-34757   CIP
ISBN 0-671-70531-8

TO
GEORGE
PLIMPTON

I have a feeling that my boat
Has struck, down there in the depths,
Against a great thing.
        And nothing
Happens! Nothing . . . Silence . . . Waves . . .
—Nothing happens? Or has everything happened
And are we standing now, quietly, in the new life?

—Juan Ramon Jimenez, "Oceans"
translated by Robert Bly

The good is evil's last invention.

—Wallace Stevens
"Extracts from Addresses
to the Academy of Fine Ideas"

1. It's just junk down this way in Florida, you have to make yourself look to see, you have to bring yourself to bear on things.

The motel was white, turreted stucco, a beaten, crumbling outpost heaved up across the road from the Atlantic. You could stand in the road if you wanted to—there were hardly any cars—and see all the other motels just like it—like it in ruin—see the pink palaces and the frog-colored forts and the peeling Babylonian chalets and the Moroccan temples; and among them the restaurants and the little stores that stank of gasoline and beer; and if you wanted to you could listen in on the conversations of the local beach wizards, of the touts and idiots washed up here, but why would you want to? Why would you even want to pause in the road that even now, at sunset, shimmered with heat, that burned the soles of your feet through your sandals, that led not to riches and fame, or rest, but only to the next congregation of American lunacy, down there just putting itself together for the evening, beyond the haze and stink of the sea.

The short, limping Englishman who owned the motel came out of the office as I crossed the road and hailed me. I didn't have time to change, I didn't have time to put on the fake beard, to put the lifts in my shoes, to make up a story about Manhattan and my conquistadorial life there, but when he stopped me—Mr. Pogue, rubbing his small, scaly hands—I had enough time to lie. He was lonely in his rumpled clothes, under his thin froth of white hair, lonely keeping this motel that must have been a dream of his back in the fogs and chills of Sussex; he was lonely, I thought, squinting at him, the way many people are after they've gotten what they want. Deferentially, sadly, like a deacon ashamed of his tattoos, he motioned me to join him in folding chairs next to the soft-drink machine and began to tell me about how bad the season had been.

Through the screen door I could see a white-haired woman in a motorized wheelchair moving about. The cranky hum of the chair's motor was punctuated by her whispered curses, as she damned and redamned the machine. Every time it banged against a piece of furniture, she swore.

The old man spoke of banks, of drought, of red tides. From sky, from sea, from land, from the cities, bad times blew. It was like something medieval. I don't understand it myself, I said. It baffles me too.

In the eastern sky the moon was up, three quarters bitten out of it. Beyond the road, beyond lacy jags of piled-up coral boulders streaked with vines, the ocean snarled and hissed. For some reason the beach down here was red; the sand was floury like pulverized brick, hard-packed like rouge left out in the sun, and the strand ran for miles, north and south, straight as a hem, uninterrupted by coves or streams, or anything but distant miragelike white silk buildings hung in the air. You could stand on the piled boulders—thrown up to keep the tide from washing the continent away—and look to the left or the right, look out straight into the sea, and you couldn't help but wonder at how desolate it all was. It was the desolation of deserts, of the waste places where the land gave up on itself and gave itself back to some older notion of earth, to scrub and dust and boulders and to the blank, Precambrian sea; when it didn't care anymore or never cared about prettiness. Or maybe its memory of the old life was so strong, its memory of when everything was ocean, that the ocean—flat, aged, worn by its own rhythms—continued to influence it, like someone who had spent his childhood among the Amish, and kept it—though behind you at night the neon cast its pastel fogs over your shoulders—plain.

The old man rustled beside me, stretching himself, patting a little life into his thighs. Hibiscus bushes, a plumeria with lank white and yellow blossoms that drooped as if they'd all been shocked to death at once— the decorative florals edging the driveway—were covered with pale red dust. Inside the office the woman in the wheelchair whispered curses. "Wretched thing, vile thing," she said. Pogue leaned toward me, touching me with liquid eyes, like someone about to ask for money.

"How do you make your living, sir?" he said.

I'm the director of a small ballet company in New York, I told him; I'm researching a ballet, *Beach Death,* that we want to perform down here, at the civic center in Daytona where they invented car racing.

"You don't mean it," he said.

Yes, of course I mean it, I told him. We want the beach in it and race cars and women in skimpy suits.

"I've never heard of anything like that," he said.

It's going to be on TV.

"You don't mean it."

God's truth.

It was mean to lie to him, and I felt the meanness and thought as I felt it of some other way to live, but the truth was I liked lying better than I liked being nice. It was a movie that brought me here—a film; my last and my latest—the one that heaved in my mind like a team of horses pulling out of mud, that sang in my head like a lunatic tenor lost in the woods—I could see it, flashing ahead of me out of the mirago distances, speaking of danger and wild rides through the night woods and ridiculous deaths, of a woman drawing the body of her lover out of the shallows, of my deadly man, my D'Nel Boyd, my killer, waving from a blood-splashed porch, of dusk and desolation and the wages of love, of the solitude that is inevitable for us all. I could see it—my movie—I could go and snatch pages of it from my suitcase in the damp little room across the courtyard; trembling, beside myself, I could lay it out in front of him if I wanted to, I could tell the story and dance it out and make claims for my actors and my hopes, but I wasn't going to do that.

We're going to set people on fire, I told him, men and women in pale suits, and have them run into the sea. There'll be explosions and sex, dervishes, silk tents, children on their knees barking like dogs.

"My goodness," the old man said, "what a spectacle."

Quite.

"Are you someone I should know?"

No. I don't appear on stage.

"An impresario."

Of sorts.

And famous too. Or partially famous. I was a screenwriter and sometime director, cofounder of Thief Productions, my Lower Manhattan outfit that over the last fifteen years had invented a dozen movies filled with mayhem and disaster (amusing to the Downtown set, titillating to the drive-in crowd), but fame is a slow leak, and the load it carried—me, Buddy Drake—was stalled—as I pictured it—somewhere up an old road—a shale road, as I imagined it, like a country road in Missouri, where I was from—one of those roads that when I was a child you could take from the city—city of St. Louis, where I was born—and ramble on, west maybe or south, following it out beyond offices and factories, past the dumps and the rail yards, out into the country through villages and orchards and farms, on through the tamed countryside of Missouri, until the road began to dwindle, to fade out to a lane and then to a track that finally, miles from the shout and kick of the city, miles from any version you understood, gave out on you, quit, thumped up against some limestone bluff maybe, out in grassy, tree-strewn nowhere of America.

I hadn't had time to paint my face, I hadn't had time to put on a wig, I hadn't had time to build much of a character. Parked in a lawn chair under his green tin awning he could see the shape of me; if he had ever seen a picture of me he could identify me; if he knew me, if he had heard of me, he could tell things about me that I wouldn't want told. No, I said, that's not true; I'm sorry, I'm not a ballet director. I've just gotten out of the hospital; I'm a doctor, a urologist, from New Rochelle. I had a breakdown a couple of months ago, and now I'm traveling around getting my strength back.

He looked at me out of disbelieving blue eyes.

There was a crash—crash of a body falling—inside the house. He sprang up—Excuse me, he said—and dashed into the office, into the white stucco house where he lived. I heard curses, accusations: the woman's voice, execrating and violent.

There was another woman in my mind, a woman living on a movie screen, in the eye of my mind—my character, Molly. She was in my mind, or she was in the world, or she was over there standing with her child—does she have a child?—by the dark blue taffeta waters of the motel pool. A creation, a bright flat figment, she was stepping out from under orange trees, she was singing a ditty, she was pretending to be my mother who one day in early spring took all her clothes off and stood in front of the golden window and looked at me. But it wasn't me, I wasn't there, it was D'Nel, it was the rapturous killer D'Nel Boyd she looked at, who looked back, who stood there in his ten-year-old solitude looking at a woman whose body shone with the light of the sun's fire caressing her breasts, running her small slim hands down her flanks. . . .

But no, there was another picture, an image, of the first time she appeared to me, this young woman with black hair streaked with threads of white: she knelt in sunlight firing a rifle out a window. The whole movie, unreeling from this moment, stood in my mind like a city in a valley, lit up and spread out before me. I could smell the sunshine on the grass and feel the itch of mosquito bites on the woman's back and see her hands holding the silky stock of the rifle, and hear her voice, sweet-tempered and small like the voice of a child, calling to a man who ran through the bushes laughing as she shot at him.

The image of the woman rode in my mind like a yacht. She was anchored there in the blue distance, sunlight pounding off her skin. And at a distance, coming closer, the man D'Nel Boyd, pale and brilliant, cold with fever, gifted with insight, charming, willowy in his dark clothes, broad-shouldered, long-fingered, alien, deadly, strolling out of a past that is unexplainable and only circumstantial, carrying devilment in his hands like kittens. I had only told Van the half of it, and the half of it I told him made him think, as usual, that I was crazy, but he said, as usual, sure, bring it along, get me a script and I'll shoot it. Van had directed, or produced and directed, or produced all my pictures except the first—which won me my place in the pantheon—and he wasn't interested for five seconds in what a story was about, but he could make a picture move like a jet plane and that was fine with me. He was the best person to work with I'd ever known, all tied up with hard knots around a core of calmness—tenderness was another word; it was tenderness—eating pickles straight from the jug and shouting, but the scenes slapped off his hands, he held on to the story line like a pit bull tearing a throat, and he made the movie. I'll make it move, he told me, whatever idiocy you're up to.

I got up and looked through the screen door to see Pogue lifting his wife off the floor. She sagged in his arms like a dead woman hung across a wire; her face, crevassed by age, was streaked redly, and her mouth, brilliant with lipstick, worked furiously, chewing curses. "You need any help?" I asked, cracking the door, but the old man said no. The woman's corroded purple hands floated up; her fingernails were over an inch long. Slowly, almost as if she were waving, they looped at Pogue's face, drifting past his cheek. "You must get that strawberry seed out of my cabinet," she said, or I thought she said. Her voice was dense, crouched in anger. For a moment I saw the mystery and the strangeness of their lives, saw what couldn't be translated. I stepped back marveling, feeling in my chest the quirky fibrillation that comes when we see what isn't to be shown. It was into that space I tried to drive my movies. It is not only that ten times a day we turn a corner and suddenly get a glimpse into people's lives that is as strange as if we are looking at aliens. I think it's obvious that nobody can really understand anybody else; and that is not what makes me wonder. It is the strangeness of what we know laid against what we don't know, which is just like it—which in a way we do know but can't see or describe exactly—it's how close the unimaginable is to what we know as clearly as we know our fingers, or the sugary perfume of our beloved, that fascinates me.

The old gent swung his wife in his arms. His face was tender and loopy and he was humming a tune that sounded like the blues. She clawed in her slow-motion way at his face, twisting her head on her stemmy neck, firing curses. He got his hip under her and leaned her against the chair, but the support plate was in the way and she fell against the arm and slipped down again to the floor. He hoisted her— hands dragging at her hips—and as he did so her dress slid up her thighs so that she was exposed from the waist down. I saw her speckled, lumpy legs, her gray old man's drawers, her soft, drooped belly. She cried out, in shame and anger. The old man thrust her into the chair, dropped her, and leaned over her sprawled body, breathing hard. Then he looked at me, over his shoulder. There was a look in his eyes of such hopelessness, a kind of blind despair that didn't recognize any human brother standing there, that I felt it in my own body. I felt the dead continuous sadness of it. I felt it, like spit on my face. I would have stood there longer, watching them, willing to see what might come next, to see what you do after the next hopeless act, but he didn't want to share it with me. He spun her chair around so that it faced the darkness of the room and then he came to the door. "Excuse me," he said, as he swung it closed, "it's time for Mama's dinner." I smiled at the blank panel and walked away.

So then you are slightly dislocated and it's possible to make up things. I walked over to the pool and watched the woman wade in the shallows with her son. A few thin fingers of scarlet light drifted above the western horizon. The woman looked at me, I said *Sometimes when the sun goes down it looks like the world is coming to an end, don't you think.* She looked away, turning her head; the splash of water on her shoulder, the pulled muscle cord in her neck, made a scar. *My wife,* I said, *my ex-wife, has a scar like that, except it's on her arm. I'm the one who did it.* Why do the heathen rage? Why do those oranges over there, the oranges in those shabby trees in pots, look artificial? Is that a problem? Get a grip, pal; try a little tenderness.

The woman waded away from me, pressing a path through the water with her arms. She shooed the child slowly ahead of her. A dance, a daze, a dalliance. *You will come, sister, in the by-and-by, to admire me.* Someone, one of my movie characters, said that. Just past youth, in the freshening of a more mature beauty, her dark hair streaming down her back, the woman herded the child away from the odd man. The underwater lights—just come on—threw the shadows of their legs along the bottom; the shadows looked like blue fishes feeding on them.

Molly, Molly Picard, my movie's heroine, was another wild girl. In the movies I liked characters who rushed into disaster without calling it disaster. Molly was a mimic and the actress would play her part in voices. Black, French, English, dumb southern, a teenage lisp. If you saw her you would think she was trying to break out of something, but if she was she didn't know it. To Molly, shooting a gun at her lover was a fine thing to do. She wanted to kill him, but it was the way someone wants to kill in a cartoon. In cartoons it isn't death but immortality that's the problem. No one dies, no matter how smashed;

and each is condemned forever to his own maddened pursuit or flight. It's a vision of hell. And always there is an unstoppable energy, no matter which side of the good-and-evil fence the character is on. Molly knew this, she knows this, the way animals know their perfection: through the exercise of it. She rushed through her life—fleeing, yes— wild for conniption.

I stopped by the back fence and leaned my head against it. Just something to stop me and prop me up for a minute. Beyond the fence, where town life began, I could hear the world. A truck shifted gears. A woman's voice called for Richard to hang up his bathing suit. There was the smell of rotting loquats. Once in a while, for no reason, I'll go outside, out anywhere—onto West Broadway, through Little Italy, across the streets of Chinatown—down the rowdy Manhattan avenues, and all I can think of are cocks, cocks and cunts—loose, hidden out there in the street, swinging or vamping under everyone's clothes—and I'll stagger, I'll almost fall down, I'll reel until I have to prop myself against the side of a building, like some exhausted drunk, overcome by the thought that under each pair of jeans, under each soft cotton skirt, under each set of black tights strapped in leather, shines the epicenter of lust and creation: that old fat woman there, tugging at her grocery cart, carries one, balding perhaps now, crusty and singed white; just as that sleek girl in white T-shirt and seamless jeans carries one, dark, polished like an otter's pelt perhaps; as that worn man over there holding a scabby arm out for change carries under his stiffened trousers the shattered pulpit of his folly and his exaltation; as the boy bouncing a soccer ball carries his sweet nubbin, and that slight girl her small plump slitted dove. Leaning against a post, amazed and overcome, I will see in the surging mass of shoppers and revelers all the swinging cocks, all the nestled, plummy cunts, and for a second the mysteriousness of life will overwhelm me, its delicacy and its magic, its wonderful sleight of hand that keeps us all aware and unaware of the feast and the sorrow; how, so close to me—so close I can identify the perfume, so close I can make out the small scar like the nick of God's thumbnail on the neck of that running boy—is indecipherable mystery, that though swinging in my own clothes is the veined and tractile article too—enough like any other cockerel that even the most wayward alien would know me brother to other men—it is hidden, as if it doesn't exist; as all the other cocks and fragrant cunts are hidden, all passing close by, close enough to touch, to fondle, to plunder like sunk treasure, but passing by, never to be known, never, no matter how long I live, no matter how I yearn, to be revealed to me among these thousands, among these millions on earth. God, I would marvel; it was a happy mystery—most of the time; it was a delightful joke, a ribald poke in the ribs, a fabulous conundrum; it reaffirmed that the world is filled with secrets, secrets not of humdrum practicality and logic, but of the imagination, that in some way it is possible to both know and not know at the same time; and that it is imagination's gift—our surrender to the river of it—that is offered to us as a means to fill the gaps, to make the world a whole and holy place.

I smelled the fence's sun-curdled, dried-up paint. Shadows leaned like old, worn-out actors into the courtyard. The white gravel began to fade to gray. The motel's scarlet roof darkened. Sometimes I could smell their skin, these people in the movies. Sometimes I could feel their bodies bumping against mine. That is the way it is when things begin to break down. Everybody—directors and screenwriters included—begins to speak grandiloquently about the personal attention they are receiving from the world; the medium has become their special friend. Now, in the night alone, I could begin to make my claims. I could say: I see the tiny swirl of dark hair just above Molly's buttocks, see her wide hand with its thick generous capable fingers picking at a mosquito bite. See the waxy patch on the ball of her thumb where she'd burned herself on a stove. It was her grandmother's stove, I could say, navy-blue porcelain fired with wood. Sometimes, I could say, she wanted to push a body into it. Sometimes she wanted to crawl into it herself and slam the door shut behind her.

Then I am inside the small room, my own room, bought and bound to me for the night. The photographs in their mahogany frames—of Celest, my wife; of my daughter, Rachel; of Van; of my father, dead and buried; of Bess, my former wife—occupy the table by the bed.

Among other things, I am in Florida to see Bess, to con fantastic sums of money from her so I can make this picture. It was her money to start with, let it be her money again. So often ex-spouses become icons that we pray or dispray to, but not Bess. Not me. Even divorced our marriage is endless. Hello—are you there—damning and capable as usual? Yes—are you there—conning and foolish as usual? Yes. I am here.

But there is a spin, firing through the window at me as I fall into the bed. I was married to someone else now, to Celest, and the father of a four-year-old-daughter. After all this time, after all these years, a daughter knocked about my knees like a pretty yellow boat. And there was Celest, leaning against the door watching me play with our child; Celest, so solemn and impervious and stuffed with wisdom. There she was, tall, willowy woman, vile woman executing me with a glance, whose slightest disfavor stampeded my life. I could see her; she was pasted to the inside of my eyeballs, she was strapped like a pacemaker under my rib cage; her tongue flicked like a snake's out of my mouth. I spoke, I shouted, I screamed, but only in her voice. I touched my skin and it was her skin; I slunk my fingers between my legs to find not a cock but a cunt, the hollow passageway leading to the center of the world. It was no place I wanted to go. I didn't want to get to the center of things, not now, not today in Florida, in a motel room decorated in the worst fears of the Gestapo—Everything Has A Right To Be—I wanted to make movies, to make this movie cackling and clamoring in my head—movies because they exclude enough of the senses and enough of our ability to perceive so as not to murder us, but *include* enough so that we might be thrilled and chilled, catapulted for a time out of the disaster of our everyday lives. Not a small feat, if you ask me.

I took my clothes off and sat down on the bed. My body, white and skinny, looked like something discovered at the back of a closet. The room smelled of old brass and mildew, of ancient things poorly hidden. In the old days, in the days of my travels, I loved motels, but now they were like space stations, empty outposts at the edge of the universe. I saw no reason why I might not open the closet door to find the buttocks of hell pressed against the world, no reason at all.

Sometimes Celest and I would stay up all night. We'd eat odd foods and watch videos and tell lies. Naked, sprawled on the upstairs living room floor of her town house—which I visited but didn't live in—we'd make up stories about our lives. The only rule was that they had to be authentic. They could be outrageous but we had to back them. I loved these mid-life marriages, the ones where there was so much past that it was too much trouble to go into all of it. You could in fact in this country where news came in envelopes that you left on the hall table for days instead of opening, until finally you opened them and stood by yourself in the grainy saffron light trying to understand what was written there on the flimsy blue pages—and even as you read the fourth time couldn't understand—you could in fact make life start over again and again, you could tell it any way you pleased, you could make claims that were the more believable the more outrageous they were; you could, for instance, say I loved a Japanese woman on the island of Okinawa and we lived in a small hut with a thatched roof where each night she would sing songs about the dead fathers, songs that were so humble, so anguished, that tears streamed down my face. You could say I loved this Japanese woman with all my body and spirit; I loved her so much that as she bent over her guitar singing and I watched her glossy hair fall over her shoulders, watched it fall into the light like surprise, that I decided to sell everything I owned and give the money to the poor and go on a long journey by foot into the mountains; that I decided to go on a long walk and I went on the walk, alone, carrying a change of clothes and a spoon and the poems of Basho in a sack over my shoulder; and on the walk I met an old man who taught me to fly-fish, who said one morning as we stood in the black cold water of a stream that wound like a dream out of willows, said: I know the woman of whom you speak, and she is dead.

Celest would tell me a story about wearing a red dress. A sashay story full of night cries and lust. Then she would speak of her years as an artist's model, of standing on the sagging wooden pedestal in a cold room under a wan northern light, contorting her limber body into the alien shapes the painter David Conn requested. She said, My body would lock. Bent, broken into the shape he wanted me, she said, I would feel it lock and then I would feel sensation begin to leave—it felt like small men running down my arms and legs—and then it would be as if I didn't have a body at all, and then I would feel it gone, and then I would feel my emotions, my thoughts, begin to go, feel them tunnel away like moles disappearing into dirt, until my life became a speck receding in the distance. I could get almost to a state in which I didn't exist—I'm only telling you in retrospect; at the time I didn't know anything—and I saw that whatever happened, even if I was about to die of cold and locked-upness there on the pedestal, I couldn't do anything about it, and didn't really want to do anything about it; and then, maybe just before David relented and saved me, as it were, I'd begin to dream, a dream would come like somebody shifting a new panel into view, and I'd see myself standing in a field near some apple trees, and I'd see that the apple trees were old and untended—water sprouts shot straight up off the branches and the flowers were meager—and the look of the trees would frighten me—at first they would—and I'd want to run but I couldn't, the flowers were so naked—so raw—and for an instant it would seem to me that the world was a rank devouring place, a place completely out of its head with proliferation and inges-tion—a maw and a cunt—eating and fucking; and then, without any-thing at all changed, I would see the petals falling from the flower clusters, see the white, pink-streaked petals drifting down, and a feeling like nostalgia, like being in love with your brother, would flood me—I could feel it replacing the coldness and the horror—and just at that moment David's warm hand would touch my shoulder and I would begin to come to. . . .

I wanted to talk to her, but first there was Van, calling from New York.

The phone rang, I picked it up, he spoke, I said, How did you get this number?

You called me from St. Augustine.

That's right, I did. What did I want?

You wanted to talk about the new movie. How's it going?

I can't tell the difference between the movie and real life.

This surprises you?

Of course. Each day is a new day.

I have to retrain you every picture.

You like teaching.

But I'm tired, Buddy, I'm tired.

Why are you tired, Van? You're still a young man.

I've wasted my life.

Are you sure there's any such thing as that—a wasted life? I mean, who's watching?

I see. And I feel it inside me. I feel something shifting inside me, grinding.

Like the continents.

I don't know what it is.

A year ago he'd had a panic attack, a fierce physical and mental assault that struck him like an overlooked bomb going off one afternoon as he rode the camera boom on our last picture. It had been a river shot, a crowd scene taking place on docks the carpenters had constructed beyond a woody place on the Mississippi, just south of Cairo, Illinois. I was down below, arguing with the A.D., when I heard the camera operator cry out and looked up to see Van standing in the chair, clutching his throat. His face was ashen, distorted, and even from a distance of fifty yards I could see that he was in terror. We all watched as the cameraman wrestled with him and watched as the boom cranked down and we all heard him cry out in sobs and shouts; and then I was beside him, reaching for him as the boom swung to earth, terrified myself, calling for Stacey Berg, who was the medico, to get over there; and then with the others, first holding Van and then not holding him, the panic, the attack—whatever it was—released him and left him for dead, so that he lay among us on the yellow grass by the river, wheezing for breath, stiffened and helpless, whimpering, tears like streaks of varnish on his round cheeks.

The doctors said it was physical and common and they put him on medication, but Van, for whom life was a house of many mansions, thought it was much more than a simple physical dislocation; he thought it was spiritual, he thought that the ground sense of his life—whatever that might be—had at last broken through the barrier of work and adulthood to speak directly to him. He would be a fool, he said, if he didn't respond. He finished the picture, which was another failure in a line of failures, and then he scaled back. He was working now on a small project, a documentary about tidal waves, waiting out his life a while, still my partner—mentor, confessor, sidekick, child—but a little more distant now than he had been, a space between us now that had never been there before.

I said, "When are you going to be through with the tidal waves?"

"I'm cutting now. I thought for a while I was going to have to go back and find some more footage, but then I decided what I have is okay. You ought to see it. I got a shot a newsreel cameraman took fifty years ago in Japan of a tsunami breaking over a seawall. There's a man standing against the railing as the wave, which is as tall as a six-story building, breaks over him. It just obliterates him. It's wild, it's like the ocean taking back all at once everything it gave us. Did you know that out in the open sea those waves travel at over two hundred miles an hour?"

"That'd be some ride."

"You wouldn't notice it. The pulse runs down a couple hundred feet, but the wave is so small it'd pass right by without you ever knowing a thing."

"So when will you be through?"

"Eight, ten weeks?"

"I might be ready before that."

"Let's see what Bess says."

"We've already got enough to get geared. I talked to Eddy yesterday and he said I could convert the last of the bonds."

"You don't want to do that."

"Why not? Atlanta and Minneapolis will just have to build their highway bridges without us."

"Didn't your daddy tell you never to dip into capital?"

"What else is it you think we've got?"

"I wish you were better at finding investors."

"Me too. But you know how it is with us artistes; we're sweet as sugar, right up to the moment we turn vicious. It's the terrible wound we all carry; the pain breaks through and we begin to flail."

"Maybe you better take a nap."

"Hell, I'm trying to wake up."

"Yes, don't I know."

Through the half-opened curtains that were printed with gassy purple roses I could see the woman and her young child toweling off beside the pool. Leaning down she held her son's body in both hands under the towel. The boy, who must have been three or four, slipped in and out of the cloth cocoon, his thin arms waving as he struggled. The light from a small street lamp above their heads gave to their bodies a whiteness that was artificial and beautiful. The suppleness of the woman's rounded arms, her soft shoulders exposed by her dark suit, the strong and gentle movement of her hands as she turned the reluctant boy, struck me with a clarifying force, like a whiff of ammonia.

"Are you still there?" Van said.

The woman rose, and reaching behind her head, slowly wrung out her long, dark hair. A brief stream of droplets fell to the pavement. *Molly,* I thought. I could picture her, after the episode with the gun, standing on the dock wringing seawater from her hair.

"If you don't want to talk anymore just bang the phone or something."

I came back to myself, a sharp yank. "I'm sorry," I said, "there's a woman outside."

"What's she doing?"

"Drying off her kid."

"Well, it's always stupefying to get a glimpse of that sort of thing."

"The trouble with you, V.C., is that you've got no imagination."

"That's not trouble."

"I'll call you in a day or so."

"Okey-dokey."

I hung up the phone and let the silence of the room come back. There was a largeness to it, an emptiness, the way it gets sometimes when a connection is suddenly broken. The room was dark, outside it was darkening, but the two were not the same—the interior and exterior—and I felt the opened side of myself, like a side of the body breasting wind, and felt the desire to place that sensitized side against something human, to join some chain of flesh and ordinary life. The woman at the pool bent over her son, then she squatted in front of him and with her fingertips wiped his face. The smooth keel of her backbone was beautiful I thought, and the patches of wet shining on her shoulder blades were beautiful. I had no inclination to go out and speak to her again—I didn't want to know her—but for a second, there in the musty, slightly sea-smelling dark of the small room, I wished she would turn and see me, turn and wave, with an old acknowledgment of a past and a life we shared.

The lights in the bathroom didn't work so I took a shower in the dark. The stall—painted metal that rang when I bumped it—smelled of the ocean, of old iron and iodine and the faint almost fecal stench that I imagined was the smell of the deep-sea vaults where the life of the world creates itself. I closed my eyes so I could feel a darkness inside the darkness. The film began to unwind and I saw her, Molly, in three-quarter speed, as she rubbed lotion into her legs. She sat on the porch, leaning back in an old kitchen chair, her legs propped on the railing, stroking her silky flesh, braced in a shaft of sunlight. D'Nel Boyd, the killer she had run away with, was speaking to her. He was relating his past as an adventure story, one where the rowdy robbers are pursued by cops whom they befuddle and elude. "The way I've lived," he says, "is indefensible, so I don't defend it." He is tall, spare, with dark straight hair brushed straight back, pale, supple skin, and eyes of a blue scorched almost to black. He moves, not awkwardly, but with a slippage in the joints, a cant that gives an almost lurching momentum, as if the energy in him kicks forth, knows where he's going, a split second before he does. It is the movement of some animals, the water riders like otters and nutria, the strikers, the quick runners, that he partakes of, so that for those around him he seems to be moving slightly in another dimension, as if some small percentage of his body and breath were on another, more sprightly plane, which you can see his knowledge of in the dark, bright eyes. Van wouldn't like all the close-ups—he is one for tracking shots, pans, medium-close shots—but I wanted the viewer to be drawn into the mad world of this man, to begin in some way to get stuck, like the rabbit in the tar baby, on the skin and presence of this creature. I could see his wide, long-fingered, knot-knuckled hand rise to touch the silky flesh of her leg, see it drag slowly along the green margin of her bunched skirt until it begins to insinuate itself, formally and irresistibly, under the pale cloth, moving under cover, gently but harshly, roughly, like a stone pushed with a stick, toward the crease of her, into which the cloth drains like a rivulet, the camera moving in at first with the same speed as the hand, then imperceptibly slower, but still moving, until it passes—as the hand closes, as on a pulpy fruit, on the center of her—the sight line flowing silkily on, not rising, but continuing in receding focus as it moves—not just the focus but the camera tracking forward—until we see the evening sky through which sun dogs of pure gold light trail the hammered shield of the sun into the west.

Chilled, my skin puckered, I stepped out into the cold, air-conditioned air, my head brimming, whirling with the frames of this movie. I wanted to call it *Scoot,* but I'd probably change my mind before production was over. We could do it for three million dollars. We'd have to shoot in a right-to-work state, which meant the production would have to move to Alabama or Louisiana; I probably ought to head that way to scout sites. But the sites weren't a problem; I'd found that out long ago. This country, this America, was filled with elaborate hidden worlds, little fabulous culs-de-sac where folks, undisturbed for generations, had thrown together and sculpted wacky paradises and hellholes they might live and knock about in. You could go down to the Gulf and stay with the shrimpers, get the itch on your hands and see the sun rising like a stomped tomato out of the wild blue ocean; you could drift across the high plains and see the cherry trees pioneers had carried in the Conestogas across the wide grasslands blooming like white fire on the hills; you could lie down in a field of blueberries that swept along the edge of granite cliffs in Maine; you could idle your life away among the willows and mossy cypresses of a Louisiana river slough; you could drive your car down the main street of Tucson,

Arizona, straight into the desert. In the country, or in cities—in little parks where azaleas bloomed like secrets finally exposed, down alleys where tombstones had been planted in factory walls, on wide boulevards where at six in the morning, standing alone on the rain-wet pavement, you could feel a form of loneliness like the loneliness of Space— anywhere at all—in the Bronx or in Grosse Pointe Farms, or in a trailer park outside Cornell, Kansas, in a patch of woods behind a miner's house in Blue Creek, West Virginia—you could find sites to make a movie in. I was looking for light this time, for the light that creeps. It was a special light I had in mind, one that moved in contradistinction to the dark; it was not the gray, night-soiled light of New England, nor the crystalline acid wash of the West, nor the mist of Pacific landscapes; it was a naive, untroubled, almost stupid light, the light of fairies and children—a light my daughter would clap her hands to see—of idiot savants, of wading birds and gulls; it was a light that murderers moved through like damp wind slinking through the tops of pine trees, light made by a spoiled and selfish genius; and it pummeled and hated the dark—this light I had in mind—which was its opposite, its black brother, and as powerful and stupid and relentless as it was.

I'd bought a mango at the market. I slashed it with a table knife, split it with my thumbs, and plunged my mouth into the bright yellow pulp of it. In the outrageous sweetness, as always, was the secret taste of a coin hidden, old fine perfect metal, tainting the pure flavor. I was reaching for the towel to wipe the juice from my chin when the phone rang again.

Celest's voice, clear as tap water, came over the wire. "Buddy, are you there?" Yes. I'm here. But it wasn't here; it was Venice, it was the winter we spent sitting under striped umbrellas on the Hotel Marconi balcony, watching the cold raindrops splash like gravel in the canal, waiting for spring. Across the canal, on the yellow side of a building that had once, so the concierge said, been a small pottery shop but was now a patisserie, an aged wisteria vine withered. Its fine lead tendrils plucked at the red rounded bottoms of chimney pots. I thought then that I had the strength and determination to stay in that place, with the woman whose voice leaked from the receiver now, until the vine sprung forth green leaves again, but I didn't.

"I'm right here, Celest," I said, "you got me. Thanks for calling back."

"An Englishman answered the phone."

"He owns the motel. I just came in from talking with him. His wife rides in a wheelchair and curses everything."

"A pretty picture."

"It is. You ought to see it."

"How's the beach? Have you found your dolphins?"

"The beach is beautiful and I'm going to talk to the dolphins tomorrow."

"I called Jimmy. He shouted at me when I told him I wanted to lower the child support, but he's going to let me do it anyway."

"Thank you, dear. Four thousand dollars a month is a lot better than eight thousand." I thought of Rachel, my blond-haired, rowdy child, whom I couldn't afford to keep anymore. I carried my love for her in my pocket, like sugar.

"I know four thousand is still a lot for you, and I know it makes you angry to pay it because you think since I have money I ought to handle it, but you need to accept responsibility, Buddy; you can't spend your *whole* life running around like a wild boy."

"How much of it can I spend?"

"Well, if Jimmy and the judge have their way, I expect the forty-two years you've had so far are going to be your limit."

"But I'm just getting the hang of it."

"Running in the woods and peeing in the creek."

"It's not a bad vocation."

Talking this way put the taste of ruin in my mouth. Three times and I still couldn't get the hang of divorce. I peeled the mango's red skin back. It slipped over itself the way the skin of the face must when the pathologist peels it back so he can carve through the shell of the skull. "Celest," I said, "the majesty and damage and grief of this life are in every move we make, in every gesture, in every smallest moment. You don't have to hurt people to make them know they're alive, or to make yourself know."

"Don't twist what I say, Buddy. Adult life is a pretty simple proposition: if you want to dance, then you'd better bring something to the party."

"That's what you think it's about?"

"Time to pay the piper, sweetheart."

"You didn't used to be so full of these power platitudes."

"You weren't always so reckless."

"Ah, there's where you're wrong. I was always this way, you just used to like it better."

"I suppose."

We both fell silent. Deep in the line somewhere a man's voice said, "Operator, it's either seven-eight-six or six-eight-six. Could you try again?" I thought I could hear desperation in his voice, the noise of a life scrambling to hang on to something. There was such distance! Once we could talk about the weather and be happy. Her voice was once a spill of gold coins in my lap. *What did you do today? Nothing—what did you do? Nothing too.* We'd walk along the promenade at Carl Schurz Park, looking at the lights twinkling on the police boats, and it was as if we were walking on the water, as if we were as complete as trees or fishes, or as the light itself streaking the river surface, we were so bound and merged and happy with each other. But I was not really foolish enough to expect that electricity to vibrate forever. I didn't, but I still missed it. I bent my head and licked the yellow mango flesh; it was both firm and soft, like the skull of a baby. I said, "Sometimes I want to take a knife and stab right through everything that separates us."

"I know. I'm flabbergasted myself at how life moves on. The rope gets pulled out of your hand no matter what you think, or do."

"Ah, we've become old wise ones."

"Not wise or old I think, just foolish so long we've gotten used to it."

Then she giggled, the same bright, silvery sprinkle as always. I said, "Ah, girl, I want you to wear the gold dress again. I want to see you tottering along the edge of a canal in Venice; I want to see you look back at me and smile as if you are about to throw yourself happily off the edge of the world." I want you to die, drown, disappear, never to have lived.

"You're a tired little boy."

"No, I'm not tired, I'm just temporarily deranged."

"What can I do for you?"

"Let me touch you."

"Not in person."

"You won't let me touch you in person."

"You don't want to touch me in person."

"I can't anyway right now."

She was silent a moment. The pump at the pool kicked on, whined sharply and settled into its comatic hum. I pictured the young mother I'd seen, sitting at a table now with her husband and child eating crackers and honey. Molly had someone chasing her: the man who was her best friend from childhood, and the detective he had hired to find her. Her friend was wild with love for her; she was the center of his life, propellant even; he had to make her come back, had to persuade her, charm her back to him.

"Where do you want to touch me?" Celest said, her voice deepening, slowing down. She was blond, like our daughter, limber, long-boned. When I pictured her I pictured her hands breaking bread, the soft whiteness of the bread in her pale, slender hands.

"I want to touch your breasts."

"Yes?"

"I want you to kneel over me and unfasten your shirt, and draw your arm away from your breasts so they slide out free above my face, and I want to reach up and run my fingers along the skin of your breasts."

"That's lovely."

"It's raining outside, gusting, stormy, the rain sounds like sand thrown against the windowpanes, but inside we've turned the lights low, you've put bouquets of peonies and white lilacs in vases on the table; the smell fills the room."

"What are we wearing?"

"I'm wearing white duck pants and a white shirt with the sleeves rolled up. Your skirt is cotton, dark red—alizarin crimson mixed with black—your shirt is white, the same cut and size as mine, though you wear it with the sleeves buttoned at your wrists."

"What do you do?"

"Very slowly I unbutton the cuffs, and push the shirt, which is opened already, off your shoulders, and I take your shoulders in my hands and draw you down so that your breasts press against my chest. We can feel each other's skin, and you can feel the small hairs on my chest and I can feel your nipples pressing into my skin. I lift my face and open my mouth and lick the smooth place under your chin, and I lick your chin, and your face and your lips, and I press my tongue into your mouth and taste your mouth which tastes like oranges . . ."

". . . oranges . . ."

"Yes, and very carefully, but firmly, I bite your bottom lip, and you can feel my teeth pressing into your lip, and I bite until I taste blood in my mouth, until you can taste the blood, too . . ."

I could hear my voice; it was a distant voice, a voice speaking in secret under the sea, and as I spoke, even as the careful, looting words came out of my mouth, I was thinking of Venice again; I pictured myself lying on the gold bedspread in the cold marble room, pictured her slipping the thin straps of her gown off her shoulders as she whistled some totally out-of-place and beautiful country song, something like "Honeysuckle Rose" or "Red River Valley," and I saw the pigeons, even the one with the crooked leg, that had come into the room following the trail of muffin crumbs she had laid from the balcony, and I remembered how strange and wonderful it was that as she stepped naked out of the gown there were birds in the room . . . and the cold rustle of the rain. . . .

". . . and we can feel each other's bodies all up and down the length of us: mine hard and yours soft, and my cock like a bow in my pants pressing into the sweet pool of your belly, into the joining, the opening of you. I slip my hand down, sliding it slowly between our bodies until I can touch the crest of your sex, until my fingers just touch the smooth skin above the hair; and I wind your skirt up your legs and you can feel the cloth pulling against your skin and feel your skin revealing itself to me, to everything in the world. . . ."

I looked into the darkness of the room beyond my bed–circle of light, into the kitchen alcove and the oblong opening of the bathroom, and it seemed, for one second, that there was a tunnel beginning there, a tunnel that was the equivalent, and also the opposite, of the tunnel of light the projector pushes against the movie screen; and it seemed that the tunnel, or projection, the dark blossoming, was unreeling a story so sad and so hopeless that everyone I knew could find a place in it, everyone, including this beautiful and ungraspable woman I was talking to, and Van, and the mechanics and finaglers of my life in pictures, and the young mother drying the drops of chlorinated water from her child's skull, and Molly who stood like casual and permanent freight in my mind, in this movie in my mind, this unveiling; and it seemed that if I wanted to, for just one more second, I could get up off the bed, if I was willing, and walk down that tunnel and disappear into it, and take my place among all the living sorrow and bafflement of the lives that murked out their stories there; and then I thought this was probably what would happen anyway, whether I liked it or not, that it was something beyond anything we could call choice, or an act of the will; and then I heard my voice again, my voice, that, solitary in an obscure room on one of the obscure beaches on the Florida east coast, where the wing of night settled in its long, capacious descent upon movie producers and moviegoers and young mothers and motel owners and the beach and the wide ocean itself, seemed to have taken on some of the sandy vagrant capacity of the darkened ocean, of the fritter and rustle of small sea waves, of the scurrying of ghost crabs that move at night along the waterline. . . .

I said, "I want to curve my hand around your pussy and hold it like I would hold the body of a bird, I want to feel the warmth and the fine feathery hairs, and I want to press my finger into the soft crease and feel the flesh part, and feel how wet and warm it is, and press my fingers into your body, into your pussy deeply, so deeply that you can feel the circles of pleasure rising in your throat . . . and now my pants are down, I've pushed them off and you can feel the hairs on my legs against the skin of your legs and feel my cock pressing against the center of you; and you press your hand down and take my cock in your fingers and guide it into the small sleekness of your pussy; and you draw me into you, slowly, so that your whole body begins to submerge, begins to sink downward as if you are drowning, as if we are drowning in each other's arms, drowning in each other's bodies; and all we can hear is the rub and sluice of the bodies' liquids, of the burned juices sliding and oozing between us; and I am driven now so deeply into your body that you can taste my cock in your mouth, until you can taste it like you would taste your own tongue, until it becomes your tongue that you open your mouth and cry out with, shouting into the room, into the darkness and into the rain banging at the windows, into all the sounds and the silences that are like ivory and salt and gold foil and silk, crushing and killing, and dying in the taste of jism and blood, as your whole body, as our bodies jump like fish, like dolphins, and it kills us and . . ."

"Do you want to fuck me?" she said.

"Yes. Yes I do."

"Oh. I can feel it. I'm shivering. Do you want to fuck me?"

"Yes."

"Say it."

"I want to fuck you. I want to stab my cock into your pussy and fuck you. I want to drive it in so deep it stops your throat."

"Are you fucking me?"

"Yes. I'm fucking you."

"Are you fucking my pussy?"

"Yes. I'm fucking your pussy."

"You're fucking my pussy."

"Yes."

"You're fucking me."

"Yes."

"You're fucking me."

"Yes. I'm fucking you."

"Yes. Oh, *Jesus*."

There was no sound then, only the silence of our masturbation, of her fingers driving the orgasm into her clitoris, of the three fingers and thumb of my right hand pumping the spike of semen into my cock.

Then for a moment our groans echoed each other, our orgasmic moans that were not the noises of animals, but the cries of humans fallen on their faces in the circle of their humanness. There was a long silence through which I could hear the soft chatter of other callers, the hum, I thought for a second, of the wires themselves, some of the planet's energy rebuilding itself between us. I laughed. "That was forceful."

"Strange," she said, "I feel as if my skin is rippling."

"Well," I said briskly, "my night's been washed and dried and now it's ready for storage."

"Don't hang up yet."

"All right. How's Rachel?"

"Oh. She's become a beautiful little sadist. Now she's decided that the way to get me to do what she wants is to tell me I'm bad. If I won't let her go outside in the rain she tells me I'm a bad woman. I never realized how good you've got to feel about yourself before you can bring up a child."

"Don't let her get to you. Just call me, I'll tell you how good you are."

"Sweet man. Sweet . . . and useless man."

"Not useless, girl. I'm just not on your map. Not being on the map isn't the same as useless."

She sighed. I could hear her life in the sigh.

"I wish that was it."

She was rich, an architect and an inheritor of money; she lived in a weathered brownstone in the East Seventies that her father, one of the more successful and less flamboyant Broadway producers, and now dead, had bought for $29,000 in 1938. Her specialty was renovation, a return to the imagined perfection of bygone eras. She thought of herself as a pioneer, clearing a perfected and articulated space amid the debris of the mad American urban forest. I loved her work, loved it the way I loved the afternoons of my childhood when as a boy of twelve I lay on a raft moored among willows along the banks of a Mississippi River slough watching the sun lift the light, bar by bar, off the water. Once she gave me the set of keys that let her into the apartments and buildings her company worked on, and one Sunday I made the rounds, late in the afternoon and alone, of half a dozen of the spaces she had created. I walked through rooms that reminded me of wind chimes and fresh lemonade and rain showers shining in ivy; I climbed stairs that rose

through gradations of light into spaces as open and airy as fields. In a
duplex on East End Avenue I lay down on the rug in a living room
filled with slim ambuscades of color that were like the colors the ocean
takes on in the Caribbean, the translucent greens and blues rocking off
the bone-white beaches of Eleuthera and St. Maarten. The sun lay like
a spoiled cat on the rug and on the rich wooden floorboards and splashed
halfway up the opposite wall, which was the color of young limes. In
a few days, maybe tomorrow, the family would return to their rein-
vented house and I wished that I could see through their eyes this room
of balance and color. I was amazed and humbled that I lived with the
woman who had made beauty such as this, who had fashioned such clean
right angles and such high, creamy ceilings, such mixes of color and
light that you wished you could rub onto your skin, that you wished
you could change your skin into. I wanted to shoot a movie there, I
wanted a woman in a white wash-wrinkled dress to run into that room
crying with joy, I wanted her to cross quickly to the window and call
into the back garden for the man she loved and couldn't love to come
in. And I thought, as I had thought one thousand times already, that
life was in fact this way—if I could only give in to it—that it could
be imagined and made up, created as it was lived, that one thing led
to another through acts of love and intuition, not judgment and control,
that there was in fact a deeper, entirely intended movement we all were
a part of, that we were carried by, singing or moaning—singing,
please—toward the ocean of an infinite dream. A tenderness came over
me then, a tenderness that partook of the green-light-rinsed walls and
the untroubled colors woven into the rug I lay on and the block of fancy
sunlight standing in the window, but in the tenderness, and teaching the
tenderness, was dismay, which was as strong and enduring as tenderness,
and I saw myself only as a man loose in his wife's secrets, a boy playing
with lipstick and high heels; and I got up, without a thought in my head,
but with my body ringing with an energy that was like a knife cutting
inside me, and I took a cab across town to a place I knew on Eighth
Avenue and there I paid a woman twenty dollars to take off her clothes
and sit before me naked—a woman I knew—not to excite me, but to
tell me, as she stroked the sparse hairs of her cunt, about a vacation she

had taken the summer before to an island off the coast of South Carolina. In the early dark of August she had walked with her husband along a beach littered with the bodies of broken trees and with shells washed from the bottom of the sea. She said they knelt at the water's edge, dipped their fingers in the slight tide and touched each other's faces with salt. *The moon shone on the water and it shone on us,* she said. *The light was the color of pearls, and it turned us, and everything near us, white.* As I listened to her, watching her small fingers draw a cold fever into her body, I could see, not replacing her, but becoming another version of her, the image, the features, the body and face of Molly Picard, who leaned into a rectangle of sunlight placing a bright capsule of brass on a window ledge; could see her raising a rifle and sighting along the rust-picked barrel and firing at a form fleeing through the half dark under the sweet-apple trees. She was firing at someone she loved, and it was a game she played, mad and conscientious, the shots slapping bark off the trees; firing at a man, or at emptiness.

I couldn't hear what Celest was saying. "What?"

"I said don't run when the officer comes to deliver the papers."

"What if it's somebody pretending to be an officer?"

"You'll know by the signs," she said teasingly, but I was too tired to play.

"I'm making a movie, Celest."

"I know," she said. "You're always making a movie."

2.   I got up at dawn the next morning, went down to the beach, and swam in the rich, cool, unleavened Atlantic. Cleansing myself, I wallowed like a whale. I knew a man once, an actor, who took twelve baths a day. In even the palest light his rubbed skin glowed with a luminosity like fox fire, but he didn't glow in the dark. In the dark there's only the light of the movies. Celest glowed though, when she was pregnant, not because of the pregnancy. I would come uptown—it was during the time I tried to write down everything I remembered about my life—and we would sit in the large dressing room off her bedroom—a living room actually, figured in gold and ocher—and while I wrote she would lie naked on the green chaise across the room. The lamp, her condition, whatever it was, made her skin glow. In the tower of the Russian Orthodox church across the court, the bells would let off the hours with a clear finality, as if it owned them. I would look up from the green blaze of the desk and see her and my mind would leap across the room to touch her. There were moments when she seemed some knobby, polished animal, and I thought how little it takes to make life into a dream, how little it takes to make us turn it around into something else that it may or may not be, and how the dream is so like life—may in fact be life—that we can lose our place and begin to speak—sometimes in the world, sometimes in dream—of creatures and places that are figments.

The sea washed me, it stung my body with its salt. The beach was empty, no strangers lurking. Up shore, toward the pier that was lifting out of mist, there was an empty place, a small empty spot where yesterday I had seen something. Now another man moved slowly along, near the tide line, sweeping a metal detector over the hard red sand. The world penetrated me, I couldn't—wouldn't—hold it off. I opened my arms and cawed, I barked, I growled. The sea threw itself over my head. The movie in my mind—the actual movie, not the lie of a movie—stepped out into the world. I could see it walk forth, or I couldn't see. Molly, her tiny suitor Banty Jakes, D'Nel Boyd. I wanted them to take over my life.

In a flat-roofed brick diner set at a slant to the main road, at a table where someone had put, oddly, for it's not a table flower, a few sprigs of crepe myrtle blossom—the heavy, candy-pink flowers emitting a fragrance like fresh pine sap—a wide woman in culottes and a steely hairdo served me breakfast. She was friendly, garrulous; we talked about the slack season, beach sewage problems, houses for sale, the drought.

"I don't know what's to become of us," I said, trying to speak her language. "The little man has a hard time getting a foothold in this country." She looked at me down her long nose, which reminded me of the English nose of an actress I knew that was pinched in just above the flare, and sloshed a cup of coffee in front of me. "We've spread ourselves too thin," she said. "We need to concentrate." She continued to talk to me as she brought the parts of my breakfast, moving almost in a rhythm with her own speech, as if the talk was part of the breakfast too.

"Everybody's got scared," she said. "That's what the trouble is. Where you from?"

"New York," I said, "but I was born in St. Louis."

"St. Louis," she said, "I don't know that place."

"You know New York?"

"I don't know New York, neither."

Behind the counter a black-haired man—her husband, she said—argued with himself and banged his spatula against the side of the stove as he cooked. He banged the spatula against the stove as if it were a horse he was urging more speed out of. A couple of bedraggled homeboys came in panhandling and he shouted them out the door, charging around the counter waving the spatula at them. It was too much commotion this early.

The waitress sat down across from me. She looked around wildly and then sighed. "I'm the restless type," she said. "I want to keep moving." She leaned toward me, her brow wrinkling like crepe, her large hand moving among the condiments. "Serving all these tables all day long cuts some of the itch, but I swear I wake up in the night wanting to buy me a bus ticket long as my arm." She laughed, a laugh like aluminum foil crumpling. She was just a waitress, joking with a customer.

Then an old woman carrying a can of root beer came in. She was short and wrinkled about the eyes and mouth, with bright gray tousled hair like a flare she was sending up. She strode to the counter and rapped on the Formica with the bottom of the can. "How about letting me have a paper bag," she cried in a voice someone else might use to tell his commander he was finally ready to lead the charge. "I opened this can and it poured out all over me. I need a paper bag. Can you give me one?"

The waitress—proprietress actually—got up, rummaged under the counter, and gave her a small sack.

"It spilled all over me," the old woman cried. "I got it on my arms and all over my pants. I don't know why they make these cans like this. Look, you see where it stained me."

"Let me give you a napkin," the waitress said.

"I don't need no napkin, I need to sue these sorry people. They been in business a long time. They ought to know how to make cans by now."

I guess the cook—the husband—had had enough of the old woman's chatter because he charged around the counter waving his spatula. "You want a sack?" he shouted. "Let me get you a goddamn sack."

He reached over the counter behind the register and pulled out a grocery bag. "Here's a sack," he said. "Give me that drink."

He snatched the sacked can from her and thrust it roughly into the bag. This was happening right beside me. The waitress leaned against the counter—the sunlight streaking the speckled Formica—her hands slid into shadow.

"This sack'll do great," the man shouted. "It's just the goddamn sack you need."

The old woman had drawn back, appalled, a dumb smile fixed on her face. Her skin, where it wasn't wrinkled, looked waxed.

I touched the man on the arm. "Ease up a little there, friend," I said. "We don't have kings in this country."

I meant *you don't know more than anybody else,* but I meant it in a friendly way, which I guess he didn't get, because he spun around and slapped me in the face with the spatula.

Though I jerked my head with the blow, it still stung like fire. I thought, Jesus, it's only seven-thirty in the morning. I got up and laid my napkin beside my plate. Then, with joy in my heart, I laced a punch at his head. He ducked, swung the spatula again, missed, and then I caught him with the same right hand in the sternum. He went down on his butt and sat there coughing, holding his chest with both hands. The old woman scurried for the door.

I leaned down to help the man up. "I'm sorry," I said.

"Get away from him," the proprietress cried. She had the telephone in her hand. In the other hand was the top half of a sawed-off baseball bat.

"Look," I said, raising my hands, "no guns."

"I'm calling the police."

"I'm leaving."

I dashed out the door as behind me I heard her call her husband *sweet darling* and out of the corner of my eye I thought I saw tears start in her face. Everybody can be touched by something, almost everybody. Maybe, I thought, we don't want peace at all; maybe drama is what we're after, some kind, any kind, some hard nip on the skin that wakes us. Maybe we don't even know it.

The old woman toddled on down the side of the road. Some old raider, broken down now, the mission complete. She made her way slowly, lifting her feet as if each step was a new adventure, through the sandspurs and the chokeweed, in the direction I'd come. I let her go.

Some mornings the clamor gets up with me. It's there by the bed banging a pot. Celest would get out of the bed and, naked, do squats and stretches. The morning light in her room would be pale yellow, touched with the first hints of violet shadows. Sometimes Rachel would come in, skipping across the patterned floor in her pink pajamas with the attached feet. She'd crawl into bed with me and we'd watch Mama doing her exercises. Celest's body slipped through the sunlight like a body gliding through water. I'd take my daughter's hands in my mouth, I'd taste her skin. "Are you going to eat me up, Daddy?" she'd say. "Yes," I'd say, "yes, I am." She'd pull my lip back, run her finger under my gums, press her small nails into my tongue. Past her—it was once this way—I'd watch the shadows begin to dry beyond the bookcase and at the foot of the closet; they left a residue of dust, of stain on the parquet floor, the way a body would if it had been left there a long time, the way logs lifted off the woods floor reveal darker earth. "Don't let anything get me," I'd whisper to my daughter, smiling a not so big smile. "I won't, Daddy—I'll protect you," she'd say and press her small blond head against my chest.

The day had blown up fair, dry and static, as all the days had been this droughty summer. A few small clouds, like puffs of cannon smoke, blew along in the south. Across the road sunlight gleamed and sparkled on the ocean like scattered treasure. I flexed the hand I'd hit the cook with. It hurt. I felt sorry for him—some guy life was eating alive—but the truth was, I had wanted to drive my fist through his skull.

3.   This woman was tall and wide and her hands were hard and large, streaked with sun stains as white as white paint, and her nails were cracked. She got up from behind a desk that was piled with books and messed papers and carved fishes and one three-foot-long inflated rubber dolphin, and shook my hand. She had her dark hair pulled back and tied in a ponytail, like a teenager from the fifties. Her lips were thin—like the lips of people who never marry—but her high forehead was smooth and intelligent, and her eyes, which were a startling, brightly lit hazel, were long-lashed and risive. In her left hand she twirled a pair of sunglasses.

"I bought these yesterday," she said, tilting the glasses away from her and squinting through them, "paid twelve dollars, and now I can't wear them."

"Why not?"

"They make my brows sweat."

"What are you going to do?"

"Give 'em away. You want 'em?"

"Sure."

She handed me the glasses and I put them on. Green-tinted, made for aviators, they brought a slight, intense color magic into the room. The reds in the U.S. map behind her head jumped. The blue book on her desk gained weight. Large-bottomed shadows settled.

To a secretary I had spoken my errand, explaining that I made movies and that I was making one that had dolphins in it and perhaps I could meet with the Atlantic Kingdom curator to get some information. Now I offered my credentials, but the woman, whose name when she said it sounded like Katie Jess Willard, didn't bother with them. "What do you want to know?" she said, slapping her hands together.

My little man Banty Jakes, who loved Molly Picard with every cell of his body, adored dolphins, even if I did not. He had a dolphin ranch in his backyard, or in the cove beyond his backyard, where he kept a male and a female bottlenose he'd saved from the fresh water on a Willihaw River slough—after a hurricane—and turned into pets. He swam with them and fed them fish from the market and from nets he ran in the tidal streams during the mullet and mackerel runs of late fall, and he taught them tricks that he slowly worked them toward, one move at a time. Often, at night, he would walk out onto the dock where under the capacious starry sky he would whistle them to him like two dogs.

I said, "Will a dolphin come to a whistle? Like a dog?"

"Sure," she said, "they recognize people. They'll come to whistles or calls, or even hand signals, or to the sight of someone they know."

The room was concrete-floored; it smelled of stale coffee and fish, and preserving fluid, and, oddly, of gardenias. Through the single window next to her desk I could see a raggedly flowering oleander, the white stucco corner of the main office. From time to time bits of breeze thrapped the oleander branches against the window.

The doctor—she said she was a veterinarian—sat down on the edge of the desk and began to relate dolphin facts.

They eat fifteen to twenty-five pounds of fish a day, she said, almost any fish.

Such as?

Mackerel, sardines, herring, blue runner, mullet, capelin, butterfish.

What do they do if you touch them?

The same things humans do: get closer or move away. It depends on how they feel about you.

About *you?*

They have their favorites.

How are they organized?

A hierarchy. Smartest and strongest first, then on down. Often a female's at the top.

I like that.

They're often larger. And stronger.

How do they communicate?

They rub, they poke, they make noises.

What kind of noises?

Clicks, whistles, barks.

No speech?

Whatever might be called speech is only mimicry.

They can mimic speech?

Some.

What do they say?

Hello. Pretty ball. I love you.

They can say I love you?

They can mimic it.

That's better than some people I know.

Haw. That's the truth.

Can they feel it? Love, I mean.

They're almost totally sensual.

What does that mean?

They touch and rub and play physical games. They're bisexual.

In mating season?

All the time.

Guys making it with guys, women with women?

If they like.

How do they go about it?

She kicked her leg out, as if at something. Her plain white sneakers were worn the gray color of Spanish moss. Her ankles were trim.

Well, they don't have any hands. And they're in the water.

I could imagine it; I could imagine the long gray creatures rolling body against body, tumbling in a sea fall—I could imagine myself, arms strapped to my sides, or without any arms at all, falling through the green water with Celest, or with Molly, or maybe not me, maybe Molly's lover, the pale man, the murderer, the capricious killer D'Nel Boyd, the two of them bumping and nudging, poking each other with their long smooth noses, falling like depth charges into the heart of the dark ocean.

I said, They seem so obvious, so popular. Is there anything sad about them—lame? Are they always happy?

No. Not any more than you or me. Sometimes they're angry or sad. They get frustrated and ill-tempered.

What happens?

Sometimes fights break out.

I thought well maybe in the ocean they could just swim off and calm themselves down, which they couldn't do in this place. As I had come in I had seen the huge concrete tanks, like white bowls rising among the cabbage palms, that the fish lived in. The tanks were the largest water-holding receptacles I'd ever seen, but they were still tanks, cages—but since this wasn't my gig, and I needed information, I wasn't going to make any remarks about setting the fish free.

How long do they live?

We don't know for sure. The oldest dolphin in captivity is thirty-five years old and she's not senile, so we don't know yet how long they live.

Bess, my former wife, had once told me the same story about orchids. She said they had only been domesticated for a hundred and thirty-five years, and, so far, the oldest orchids hadn't yet shown any signs of senility—they prospered still as flamboyantly as the young—so nobody knew what their life span might be. The story had charmed us both; we were thrilled that there were still such mysteries on earth.

And I thought, well, I am imagining a wild woman and her murderous lover and her mad ex-lover, and I will show on a screen thirty feet high their faces and their hands as they rend the life out of a few helpless people, I will show them sneaking across a porch at night, climbing unlighted stairs under the chime of a grandfather clock, show them pushing open a bedroom door to find a sleeping couple whom over the space of an hour they torment, sexually torture, and kill. But, and here's the mystery for me, the itch that keeps me moving, I want something loving and admirable and compassionate to come out of this. It's a conundrum, as my father might have said, who found life so full of conundrums and paradoxes that he was choked to death.

I said, Why do you think people love dolphins the way they do?

They're pretty; they seem to be friendly; they respond to us.

Like children.

Something like that maybe. But also that they're different.

Which makes them mysterious—that they have these qualities we recognize, but they're also foreign, swimming down there in the deep and all.

Which, I thought, is also like children. Often my daughter, who had my mother's sky-blue eyes, my wife's nose, my own wobbly and ambivalent mouth, would at the table, as she lifted the first spoonful of dinner to her lips, break into song. Like some wild, buoyant, fizzing creature from another world.

Do you ever get in the water with them?

No.

Why not?

We might not get along.

I thought I might josh with her then, touch a human chord, but I didn't. I felt tired, weary even, as if—which wasn't true—I hadn't slept last night. Maybe it was Celest's and my performance on the phone, the sad spirit of our human love winding down to lust and its vapid scenarios. Maybe just the wrench of dismemberment, of six years of marriage come down to the inventories of partition, to *this is yours, this is mine,* and our poky bundles heaved onto our shoulders, then farewells, and then a toddling on down the road. My hand still hurt from hitting the bone in the counterman's chest. When I reached down to help him up he raised a face of such baffled simplicity that I thought I could forgive him no matter what he'd done. What can we do against the confession of our humanness, except forgive?

I said, Will you let me get in the water with them?

I don't know if that's a good idea. They're not used to people swimming with them. She raised the plastic dolphin and stroked its side, swung it away from her as if making it dive. You won't need to actually; they'll come right up to you.

Which was true, as I found out a few minutes later when we walked across the road to the main tank. We went through the back doors, along walkways out of sight of the tourists, and climbed a ramp that was shaded by large hibiscus bushes to a green wooden gate that let us into the arena. The space, centered by a pool half as large as a football field, was painted green and white and raised off the ground; over a low white wall I could see the ocean, chipped now by a light breeze that flickered and faltered among the tiers of the metal canopy that covered the viewing stands.

She called for Welchel to come out, and he did, a squat man in a white uniform, emerging from a small structure like a bathhouse, carrying a bucket that he showed me contained a couple of pounds of herring. They took me over to a circular pool a little larger than the rubber children's pools you can buy at Sears and showed me their number-one dolphin, a female named Delphie, who was thirty years old and had been born at the Kingdom. The animal moved in the water like someone pacing at a bus station, the flat, faintly striped top of its head lifting regularly to sip air. Welchel knelt beside the pool, clapped his hands, and called the dolphin's name. Nothing happened. The dolphin continued to swim around and around, ignoring us.

"She's a smart dolphin," Welchel said, grinning at us with crooked, stained teeth. His uniform shone as if the cloth were polished. "She won't work for free."

He groped a fish out of the bucket and held it a foot off the water, just back from the lip of the pool. The dolphin made another circle, its flat scythe flukes barely flexing, idled down as it approached, and in a single clear and fluid pulse, rose from the water like a man standing up, snapped the fish, with a curiously tender, sideways move of its head, and back-sheathed into the clear water until it lay with its chin on the lip of the pool. I saw when it opened its mouth that its tongue was grayish pink and long, narrowing at the tip, and very muscular. Its teeth, in single rows, gleamed like wet orange seeds. It clicked and trilled, making a running sound in its throat like Velcro unsnapping. It slid its head away, sank, circled the pool, and returned. Welchel offered another herring and it rose to place its head again on the pool's rim. This time he took the dolphin's head in his hands, patting in a commonplace way the browed forehead, chucking it under the mouth; then, his thick fingers curling slightly, he gently stroked it along the jaw, as gently and precisely as a man would caress someone he loved. The dolphin made a series of rapid clicks, swung its head back and forth, slid into the water and back onto the rim. "May I?" I said, stretching out my hand.

"Of course," Dr. Katie said, "just don't touch her eyes."

"Looka here, Delphie," Welchel said, holding out a fish. As the dolphin took the fish I placed my hand on top of her head. I remembered as a child reaching to touch a policeman's horse and the horse brusquely swinging its head to nip skin off the bottom of my arm. But Delphie ignored me; she suffered the touch. Her wet skin felt like the paint job on a fine new car, though underneath, unlike on a car, I could feel the slight resilient give of underflesh; an inch of blubber, Dr. Katie had told me. The dolphin slid into the pool and came up again. I ran my fingers under her chin. She didn't respond but she was looking at me all the time. Her eye was a round dark disk ringed in tan, very bright under flexive lids that squinted and opened wide; passing along, it seemed to me, expressions of disdain, sagacity, and glee. She shook her head, slapped my hand lightly with her cheek; my hand jumped back.

"Is this dolphin kind of ironic?" I said.

"She's a sport," Welchel answered, laughing a little *ki-ki-ki* laugh that was very like one of the sounds the dolphin made. In my mind I saw D'Nel Boyd standing at the end of the dock as Banty Jakes called the dolphins in. I watched him lean his slender body—in the strong hunched shoulders, the narrow hips offering the constant hum of menace and shamelessness—over the dolphins, who stood on their tails in the water, their heads risen above the surface, looking around like two gents on Sunday promenade. It came to me, a little click in my mind, that what D'Nel was put on earth to do was to eliminate the helpless.

The dolphin slid away and began to circle. She moved under the water, which was as clear as the water in a swimming pool, with a fluidity and grace that no human I'd seen had ever approached. Watching her glide I thought—the only thing human that came to mind—of swans I saw once in a ballet my father took me to in St. Louis—how at a certain moment in the production, with arms thrust forward and crepe skirts flared, the ballerinas had all slipped backward, for an instant, for seconds, becoming birds in flight, so completely and apparently effortlessly, that I, a child of four, cried out in recognition and glee. So this strange, sleek underwater bird streaking along the circumference of a child's wading pool, moving almost in a stillness of self, a completeness so perfect that it seemed, if you looked only slightly slant, that it was not the dolphin, this Delphie, who moved, but the water—the world itself—that rushed by; as if, I thought, with only a little self-charming, perfection of being included movement without movement, that completeness was a stillness in which eternity became the flow of images and action that passed by; that you didn't need to swim. Ha, I thought, it's like the movies, it is what they are about, too. When I was a child my parents had complained that I spent too much time locked up in movie houses where for thirty-five cents—a quarter for the double feature, a dime for a box of salty popped corn—I could watch transfixed, for four hours, as the seamless profusion of images streaked by. They moved, but I didn't. There I discovered it wasn't necessary to gavel myself into any action; what was necessary was that I supply a rapt and charmed attention to what occurred before me, that I give myself—which I was glad to do—to the hustle and spark of light and sound unrolling before my eyes. That, I thought, was what movies were supposed to teach us pontificating to myself now as the dolphin slipped the surface to snatch small breaths through her blowhole that opened and closed like a thin-lipped mouth—that within all movement, and essential to it, was an irreducible stillness, that it was the stillness itself that created and sustained the movement. Christ! I felt like Emily Dickinson refusing to go to church because, she said, she could already see from her bedroom window Jesus prancing in the grass.

Yet this dolphin moved. She was made for the water; the water was made for her. I said, Is the water salt?

Yes, Dr. Katie said, smiling indulgently.

How do you get it so clear?

We filter it.

Then I began to ask Welchel how he got the dolphins to do tricks. There was no mystery to it, he said. They are playful creatures; you throw a ball into the water and they'll bat it around on their own; they're interested in the world, all you have to do is direct them a little.

How do you do that?

With what you see in this bucket.

They work for pay.

They're professionals, he said laughing. Welchel was a country boy, I could see that. The cracker sauciness, the lank black hair battened right back showing comb tracks, a looseness around the waist, coarse-skinned face puffed now by middle age but still showing the hard angles and slim bone of the Saxon field hand. These darlings, he said, will do just about anything you want them to do if you stick with them.

Such as?

They'll put a basketball through a hoop, do flips, tow a dog around on a board, catch a football. He slapped the water with the flat of his hand, and waved at the dolphin, as one might wave a child in. The dolphin ignored him.

"How long have you been working with her?"

"Fifteen years. Come on, Delphie. Come here."

He sniffed his fingers, plucked another fish and swung it over the water like a small silver dinner bell. The dolphin stood up in the water and smacked its jaws, emitting a series of running liquid clicks. Welchel swung the fish. "Come here, sweetheart."

The dolphin slipped under, swung to the right and began to circle, picking up speed. She circled the rim, a foot under water, running so close to the white concrete side that it seemed she might graze herself. She made me think of the chimps I'd seen at county fairs when I was a child, riding motorcycles around the inside of a huge barrel, held up by speed and centrifugal force. Welchel continued to hold the morsel of fish over the water, a few feet above the surface. The dolphin sliced through the sparkling pool, turning on her side slightly so I could see the pearly gray underbelly, hurtling at effortless speed.

"What's she doing?"

"I don't know."

I looked at Dr. Katie, who leaned over the pool, shading her eyes with the flat of her hand. Her lips poked out slightly, like a teacher's who was about to put a stop to this foolishness.

"Delphie, Delphie," Welchel cried, almost under his breath, his voice gentle and a little hesitant, like one who didn't quite want to interrupt. The dolphin surged on, turning its jet fuselage of body away from the wall, zagging through the water, churning the surface. She swung to the far end of the pool, kicked hard—the tail springing like a switch-blade knife—and rushed toward us. At the final instant she slid down-ward and to the side, stabbing away, shot her tail up and popped the fish out of Welchel's hand. The herring tumbled like a bright coin high into the air and fell, as the dolphin rose wholly out of the water, standing, for one second, like a waxed icon six feet high, caught the fish in her long, constantly smiling mouth, and fell with a watery crash full length into the pool, drenching us all.

For a couple of seconds, like someone posing for a photograph, Welchel remained stalled in his position, kneeling with outstretched hand, as bright beads dripped from his face. Sheepishly grinning, he wiped the saltwater from his eyes, touched his shirt with his fingers. "Lord," he said in fake tremolo, "you are an extravagant beast."

"Looks like you got her trained all right there, Welchel," I said.

"Yeah, it took me about six months to teach her that. But hadn't she got it down good?"

He laughed his small dolphin laugh.

I thought, my friend, they don't make pictures about you. Or if they do, they make you stupid or noble, or in some other way ridicule who you are. I was one who might do that. My killer man, D'Nel Boyd, Molly's lover, who in his ruthlessness, in the completeness of the evil impulse he embodied, might claim a certain dark obverse nobility, would be to you only a meanness, a gross smudge that ought to be wiped away. D'Nel would laugh at the thought of someone doing away with him. He would reach from the shadows, from an alley or a tree line, and pull you into the dark place where life smelled like the negative of itself, and in a small tittering voice he would speak to you of what you couldn't understand, of what you never wanted to know. He would say in his lazy voice *Look, here it is; it exists.* And what would it matter that you had dressed in your formal suit, in your red wig and your bowler hat, what would it matter that your flesh stank of perfume and sex, that you practiced the rituals of hope or despair, that just two weeks before you'd stood on the foreterrace of Carl Schurz Park waiting for your wife to pass with her new lover, while up the long rising street, up Eighty-sixth Street, wide open under its frail stoplights all the way to Central Park, you could see the massed residue of sunset flaring above the trees, yellow as gold plate; what would it matter that the hand reaching suddenly through your shirt to grip your heart was not the hand of love or forgiveness but of rage and terror, not of conversion or conjury, but of entitlement? And what would it matter then if at your back the soft summer breeze lifted itself tier by tier through the dogwood trees and the honey locusts and the elms with their broken branches hanging down like damaged television antennas, and the rats lurked under the benches, and a solitary man strapped into a black wheelchair labored up the steep slope from the promenade— what would it matter that you fought against this knowledge, this feral claim, this investiture; what would it matter that the one who spoke to you then was not real, or was real?

Kneeling beside the trainer, I stuck my hand in the water. The dolphin came to me, as easily as a dog. Hovering, balancing in water, she nuzzled my fingers and rubbed her lower lip against the side of my hand. For a moment, through the thin frictionless skin, I thought I could feel the warmth of her body, the mammal burning that she carried like the burning of life itself through all the cold waters.

I didn't want to see the show, so I excused myself ("Come back to the office," Dr. Katie said, "if you have any more questions") and took a walk around the complex. It had evolved and wound around itself in a series of tanks, passageways, and covered terraces, like a huge mollusk shell. Tourists in light clothes wandered about in groups, drawn steadily toward the large aquarium in the center and toward the show, from which soon I heard their shouts and laughter.

I have never been offended by the antics and enthusiasm of tourists; on the contrary, I enjoy their dumb questions, their amazed or worn-out faces, their relentless adventurism. They are a comfort to one who has felt always, outside of the studio or the movie house, that the world was a baffling, glorious, terrifying place. Their willingness, burdened with cameras and adipose tissue, to board rafts for journeys down rivers that once took the lives of some of the world's most courageous men, to climb mountains that for thousands of years were reachable only in dreams, to cross deserts and venture out on the grassy veldts still populated by the remnants of the greatest animal kingdoms on earth, are to me feats of courage and spirit equal to those of any Vasco da

Gama or Daniel Boone. These are not Cortez's hardened soldiers, born for battle, not the perseverant, salt-leathered sailors Columbus drove across the unknown Atlantic; they are neighbors, churchgoers, sufferers from sciatica and athlete's foot, common voyagers, grocers, and the managers of auto-parts stores; and thus, for me, the plucky forays they make along the high-ridge pathways of the Sierras, into the lighted underground cathedrals of Mammoth Cave and Silver Springs, no matter how well roped and led, are the journeys of heroes. I am always happy when, on the street near where I live above Canal, or on some back road where I am scouting scenes for a movie, they stop me to ask directions. I am unfailingly courteous and I will gladly go out of my way to show them the street or address they are looking for. To do so makes me feel stronger in my own life, more comfortable in the surroundings that haunt and confuse me, for a few moments connects me to the wandering human band we were all born heir to and remain part of; murderers and saints and fools, carrying on.

I stopped to eat a hot dog at a little stand built under a shelter of winged concrete near a small grove of queen palms. The palms sprouted like celery, their tractor-tread bark shredded and shabby under the tousle of slim fronds. On stalks under the crowns were bunches of orange, plumlike fruit that looked good enough to eat, though I knew from my reading that the fruit was in fact sour and puckerish, impossible to tolerate. From a newspaper someone left on the counter I learned that the drought, which had descended upon us this year like one of the plagues of Egypt, was in its 114th day. This close to the ocean, on the east coast of Florida at least, it was not so apparent. This section of the Atlantic coast is in fact a desert, home of prickly pear and yucca and the drought-thriving yaupon, so it was not so easy to see the effects of the rainless season, especially for visitors. But I believed the effects were there. I had noticed that the concrete along the edges of driveways seemed to crumble more profoundly, that the leaves of the spindly hibiscus plants were streaked with dust, that the sour rattling of palm fronds was huskier this year, more hopeless. The paper said the city government had begun to ration water, that it was now a crime to water your lawn between the hours of noon and midnight, and that all other

times were legal only on alternate days. I had noticed the burned
branches in the live oaks; and the sycamores and the tulip poplars, which
are the first trees of fall to shed, had begun to lose their leaves earlier
this year. It was only July and already, drifted into gutters, and scattered
on unswept back porches, the yellow leaves had appeared, though the
forests that you could see to the west rising beyond the tallest dunes
were still heavy with the green mirage of summer.

Last week on television a reporter interviewed a young couple whose
lawn had become a baked patch between two houses. The couple were
the winners of the weekly prize for having the most desiccated yard.
They said they had stopped watering their lawn in May and now, as
the reporter in his sparkling white shirt pressed his microphone under
their chins, they laughed at the brown expanse of dried grass and
parched bushes that surrounded them. The prize was a hundred-pound
sack of grass seed and a length of garden hose, which, snorting a laugh
that sounded like a cry, the husband said they would put to good use.
For some reason, watching this I was scared to death. Maybe I had been
making movies too long, maybe the wild fantasies of destruction and
horror that Van and I had created had begun to get to me; maybe, as
Van told me, it was simply that I had a hard time telling the difference
between fact and fantasy, but it seemed to me that behind the rouged,
smiling faces of the young householders, there shone a terror that could
not be dissolved by the ruggish antics of the TV reporter; as if instead
of grass seed the couple wished he would hand them an icon and bless
them and promise them, so they could believe it, that their lives would
be all right.

Molly, D'Nel, and Banty Jakes—who found them, through his
detective, living in a sea-breeze house on the Gulf a few miles from the
town of Ernestina, Florida—were not the sort of people who would
notice or, if they did notice, would care whether the country was going
under for lack of water. I was aware that in recent years I had set my
pictures in places and times where there was little contact with or
interest in the usual accoutrements of modern life. I didn't do historical
pictures but neither did I fill my pictures with the images and names
of momentary fashion. I had the idea that objects should have signifi-
cance through their use, through the application—antic or murder-

ous—the characters put them to, and not because of some predetermined understanding between the audience and the picture. Of course this was impossible to do to perfection since even scenes that took place on an obscure city street, or in a lost town, or even in the wilderness itself, contained the signatures of human involvement—at least of a recognizable human perception—and so were tainted, but I did my best. Having said this I could admit that I had written a scene in which my three maniacs drive forty miles up the coast to the resort and shopping complex that has sprung up in what ten years before was a sleepy fishing town. Usually, as my characters drove deeper into the darkness of their fate, there was a shedding of the few treasures of contemporary life they might have accumulated—like beggar lice shedding from pants legs—but this time I wanted to take them out of their fate's character as it were, into the lights of ordinary human lives, to propose a contrast. By this time the audience would have seen the first killing, and would have sat through the meeting—or remeeting—of Molly and Banty Jakes at a funeral in Ernestina, would have been introduced to the breezy seaside house—shot through a green filter—in which D'Nel and Molly rest between their murderous jaunts, would already have watched the early morning light come up over the Gulf that is gray, then opalescent, then blue, and seen the breeze in the gray dawn begin to rouse itself among the sea oats, and seen the purple martins from the gourd house in the yard soaring and diving at the sea (in a scene completely empty of human life in which light and the sounds of the natural world—the windspatter in the citrus leaves, the churn of cicadas—step in quietly like the notes of an orchestra); they would know already that these folk were not ordinary townspeople out on a spree. So, the three of them drive around the gaudy, high-bounding resort like small-town folk—which is what they once were—out to see the Christmas lights. They stop at a giant hotel to walk around the lobby where native fish swim in a turquoise pool, drive to a mall where they race through shops selling fine leathers and woven goods and chocolates with the name of the manufacturer written on them in gold sugar; they try on silk jackets and English shoes, finger caps from Nepal and shawls from Guatemala—all done in the spirit of samurai on a weekend pass—until, sated, exhausted, their lips stained with the juice of cherry drinks, they stop

on their way out of town at a fancy sweet shop. Behind them is the
resort—which the camera draws away from—shining in a squall of
colored lights, and before them—the camera dollying back until it is
shooting over the car's headlights—the dark tangle of sea woods they
have come from. They step onto white gravel and enter the shop, which
is like a confection itself, all pastel colors and plastic, and though Banty
is still somewhat naive, or he is attempting to remain naive, about how
his companions confront the life that opens at their door, the audience
can see in D'Nel's eyes that the restraint he has practiced on this
jaunt—and it is restraint—has begun to crack. In his eyes, and in the
harsh vertical lines of his face, in the hard gleam of the lights on his
watered hair, they will see that he cannot keep himself much longer
from hurting someone. He is an alien here in his white buttoned-up shirt
and black, creased trousers, in the way he walks—as if there is a metal
in the joints of his hips that he has, through will and grace, overmas-
tered—in his air of remorseless exuberance. As Molly and Banty, chattering about the adventure, move toward a booth, he tacks slowly to
the counter where a girl in a uniform the color of lemons waits. She
looks up at him. Their eyes meet, shy away, and lock; abruptly, her face,
which is very fine, rosy with the glow of summer and teenage health,
begins to collapse—like a child's who has just discovered the lies of
someone she loves—and the collapse is like the draining of some essential fluid, which is soaked up and shines on the skin of D'Nel's face, and
in his expression, which for a moment is the expression that might
appear on the face of a bully on Christmas morning, when all around
him he sees arrayed the fine and intricate toys of children he is the terror
of.

   It is a powerful moment. It is the moment when—with the girl—the
audience realizes—intuitively, in an itch that jumps in the blood—that
in this world there is no protection at all.

I decided I better call Bess. In my mind the phone rang, she picked it
up, and I began to talk a hundred miles an hour. What a feast it was
to talk to her, this bright, rich countrywoman who had given me the

heave-ho. Bankers thought the new movie was too risky, but Bess wouldn't; she'd be glad to invest.

I refolded the paper, handed it back to the girl behind the counter, and thanked her. She nodded the blond bell of her hair at me. In the center of her forehead, in the place where Brahman women wear a spot of rouge, she had a star-shaped scar. I couldn't help myself, I said, "How did you get that mark?"

"Which?"

"The mark on your forehead. I think it's beautiful."

She turned her head slightly away and touched the scar with her middle finger. "It was an accident."

"I've got several myself; that's why I ask." I lifted my leg, pulling my pants away from the V-shaped gouge on my shin. "I got that one when I was four years old and I fell off the car while I was trying to hit the cat with a broom."

She giggled.

I raised my head, poking my chin toward her. "See that slice? That comes from the bottom of the Mississippi River in Bar Etienne, Missouri. You'd think the Mississippi would be safe, wouldn't you? Not for me. I dived off one stump and hit another. They had to give me ten stitches."

"It must have hurt."

"The stitches didn't—they were only scary—but when I hit it felt as if I'd jammed my face up inside my head. I was ten."

She giggled again, a high tremulous sound, again like the sound of dolphins.

"So where'd you get that mark?" I was nearly dancing with energy and exuberance. I didn't want to embarrass this girl, but I couldn't stop talking.

"I got hit."

"Oh, that's too bad."

"My brother hit me."

"You're kidding."

"He stabbed me with an oyster knife."

"You were fighting?"

"We were really young. He didn't mean to exactly."

"That's good."

"He was trying to open some oysters. He was too little to do it and he got mad when I poked fun at him."

"Well," I said, "I think it's a beautiful mark. It's like the sign of beauty on your forehead."

"Shoot." She laughed outright, this time at me, a grown man trying to charm a girl.

"I mean it."

"You go on." She was forgiving me, and shooing me away at the same time.

I turned to go. A heave of wind shook the tops of the palms. The ground was littered with orange fruit. From the stadium across the way came the shouts of tourists and the splash of the dolphins.

"Well . . ."

"Don't let the fish bite you," she said.

"Okay."

I hurried away to find the phone. I couldn't wait to talk to Bess. It is wonderful the way time and the natural buoyancy of our hearts will sometimes rescind the pain of disasters. When Bess left me I thought there'd never again be enough bone and fiber in my body to hold me upright. I was trying to get a picture financed then too, and I moved about the city, from office to office, in a storm of tears. In a new suit, spanked and shining like an ambassador, I laid out my plans to my potential backers, speaking in ornate offices firmly and seriously, but not solemnly, tossing off a manly joke, raising the lid, as it was required, of a cogent humility, restraining the energy and brightness as if they were fine horses ready to race, charming, describing my well-laid plans as crisply as a general—doing everything I thought I had to to get grown men to part with money—but when I hit the streets again where the early storms of fall had stripped the leaves from the ailanthus trees and the air was clean and smelled of the sea, my hearty composure cracked and before I had gone ten steps I was sobbing like a heartbroken child. All the way across town, into and out of cabs, on the street, crossing the cathedrallike lobbies of Downtown office towers, rising in gleaming brass elevators, I sobbed, dashing tears openhandedly, like a countryman, from my face. Stained, nearly obliterated by the loss of her, I would stagger into the men's room, wash my face and construct from the remains an apparition that could pass financial muster, and then make my way briskly, smiling broadly, into the next office, where I would prance and perform, only to find myself, minutes or hours later, back on the sidewalk with tears streaming down my cheeks.

It took years—it seemed like years—to hoard enough acid to dissolve what we had built up between us. To erase it and clear ground again and build something new. Ah, now green wheat grew luxuriantly and bright flowers hung from the trees and liquid tones of easy laughter were heard in the glades. Now she supported me lustily in the very efforts she had once tried to drag me away from. I had refused, after her father's death, to return with her to West Florida to run the family enterprises. I wanted to stay in New York and make movies, which she no longer saw any point to. It's amazing how disaster can locate itself in a moment. The events of our lives, the turning points, have to do heavy duty. Going to Florida meant nothing, but we let it stand for everything. What it stood for we didn't talk about. Not the failures, or the losses, or the attack. It was all long ago. Now we were as sweet as cherubs. On the phone—we talked regularly—we roared with laughter, capering on the flights of each other's fancy, pleased as punch with our new lives. It was the best of endings, the best of sequels, and an ordinary lie.

Flying toward the sound of her voice, I got lost. It was a detour really: down a flight of aqua steps into a darkened corridor that smelled of the sea bottom. Shadowy figures moved about and pressed their faces against small windows cut into the left-hand wall. Beyond the windows, through which seeped a green and chalky light, was water. The water was not clear; it was green-gray, murky, sun-slashed, and filled with tiny bubbles like storm water. Through it swam all the fishes of the sea. Like horses on a merry-go-round, they swung in a great circle: groupers, bluefish, yellowfin, sharks and barracudas, sawfish, eels, and brightly colored schools that soared and plunged. I paused only a moment to look. The tank was jammed with fish.

Beside me a man in Bermudas gripped the sill of his portal as if it were the railing over an abyss, struggling, it seemed to me, with vertigo.

The fish swam so close that one or two brushed the glass. A shark, its mouth set in a frown, nudged along the bottom. A school of blue-and-silver mackerel twirled by. I wondered how they fed such a crew, how they kept the fish from being torn to pieces.

Down a ways the corridor swung away from the windows into darkness. I followed it, into a deeper sea smell and the trickle and plink of water, toward what as it turned became a dim light. The corridor opened into a small room. Here too were windows, as small as windows in a playhouse, and set at different heights along a wet concrete wall. The only light in the place was the foggy light that fell from them, but it was enough for me to see the pay phone clinging like a crab to the opposite wall.

I punched her number, recited my card number, and waited for her voice to come on the line, squatting to see through the nearest window. The tank appeared to be empty.

A brisk voice said, "Appel Nursery and Orchards."

"This is Buddy Drake. Could I speak to Bess."

"I'll see if she's here."

The line clicked softly and music rose from it, some tune from the sixties, transmogrified by time and a studio orchestra into a concoction as strange as music from space. I listened with pleasure. This substratum music emanating from elevators and held phones and dentists' offices was something else I was grateful for. It was another example of life becoming like the movies, all of us struggling or prancing through our lives to a sound track scored by modern masters. When my father caught the stroke that would kill him, it was as he walked through the Embarcadero Mall on the river in St. Louis, the conniption in his brain knocking him to his knees as above him the speakers played "Light My Fire."

The music blinked out. "What are you doing calling me in the middle of the day?" Bess asked in her husky cracker voice.

"I couldn't stand not talking to you for one more minute."

"Where are you?"

"I'm in a tunnel looking through windows at some fish."

"You're at Silver Springs?"

"Not a glass-bottom boat, a tunnel. Atlantic Kingdom. I'm tracking down dolphins."

Now the water boiled, a curtain of bubbles bulged forth out of which streaked four small dolphins, running head down. They veered abruptly away and up again out of sight. "Jesus, it's the show."

"What show?"

"A flight of dolphins just went by. They looked like the Blue Angels."

"Why are you chasing dolphins?"

"A guy in this new movie I'm working on keeps them."

"You're making a movie about dolphins?"

"No, just a character in the movie has a dolphin ranch. I'm on my way over to see you."

"I don't have any dolphins."

"Van sends his love."

"Likewise."

Bess affected a toughness of speech and a cynicism that were part of a ruse she had developed for herself. She had the idea that a businesswoman—which is what she was—should—the way a gunslinger might casually draw back the skirts of his coat to reveal revolvers—make sure that everyone caught glimpses of her toughness, the deadly metal under the fine cloth. She was in fact tough—or what passed for it—but we had both learned years ago that any toughness will shatter, like any other shield, and you better have something else going for you because in this life that day of reckoning was bound to come.

I said, "I have a proposition for you."

"I don't want to hear one of your propositions."

"Of course you do."

Out of the murk, from nowhere, the dolphins—six this time— roared past the window, flashing like race cars. They were the gold muddled color of the yellow grape wine my grandmother made each summer. I had never seen anything under water move so fast.

Bess made a sound like a cough, or some harsh clearing of obstruction. The coughing—harsh, grating—went on for several seconds, followed by panting. "We've got enough trouble over here without your business," she said.

"What kind of trouble?"

"R.B.'s upset again."

R.B. was her brother, a strange and delicate character. Like many of us, he occasionally found life too much. Once in a while, in the middle of breakfast, in the potting shed, raising himself on his elbow from a dock-house chaise, he would begin to bark out a complicated and accusatory madness, an arrant figuration that, if you didn't know him, if you didn't know his gentleness, his helplessness, might frighten you. Another's pain—the fractured life of some cousin in Kansas, the sadness of priests, flowers broken by hail—would set him off down a loopy track that might not end until he was fetched up, harassed and rumpled, blind with pity and exhaustion, out in the woods somewhere, or far down the beach in a bayou cove among the cypresses and the saltwater ponds, where, leaned against a tree or on his hands and knees above the brassy, stinking water, he would croak like a crane, groan, whimper, sigh, thrash feebly until someone came to bring him home. These episodes had begun during his teenage years, but they were infrequent. He went long periods with no disturbances at all, content within the golden net of his family to pursue his researches into the daily lives of Roman citizens and the home life of princes. I had always enjoyed talking to him.

"What's the matter?" Beyond the windows the tank boiled.

"He took it into his head to go around and fire everybody."

"He's done that before." A single dolphin sailed by, pursued by two others.

"He started threatening people physically. He scared the girls in the kitchen and they quit."

"What's the matter—they lost their sense of humor?" Like the click of a switch, from the opposite direction two other dolphins—or the same dolphins—dashed by trailing twisted streams of bubbles. By bending down and craning to the length of the phone cord I could see the surface: chopped, clear, shaking glass.

"I'm tired of it, Buddy."

"Is that why you called me last week?"

"I guess. I wanted to joke and light farts and cut up with you for a while. Forget for five minutes this damn business. Celest said you two are getting divorced."

"She says that all the time."

Her cough puffed along the wire. "Is it true?"

"Yeah."

"What's the matter with you, Buddy?"

"How come you hear we're getting divorced and you automatically think it's my fault?" A dolphin skidded by on its tail.

"Whose else could it be?"

"The lawyer calls it misalliance. He says that's the term."

"More like mis-species. You know we have a human race going here. You ought to give it a shot."

I slapped my wrist. She couldn't hear it, but I slapped it anyway. "Flesh is what I am." Scattering bubbles, a dolphin fell through the water on its back, twisted upright, and streaked away.

"I know," she said flatly.

"Don't you want me to come by?"

"Yes, of course I do. I'm just feeling a little distressed and argumentative. I don't know how good company I'll be."

"Good enough I'm sure." A pod—five or six, that was the veterinarian's word—tumbled loosely down, split like a star burst, and vanished into mist.

"What is it you want?"

"I've got another movie in mind."

"I'm not putting any more money into your movies."

"Did I ask you anything like that? What do you take me for?"

"A cunning liar."

"Well, besides that." A dolphin spiraled by, falling obliquely. Out of the shadows another spurted forth and rammed it hard just above the right flipper. The struck dolphin kinked its flukes and streaked away.

"A general fuck-up, I guess."

"How can you say that?" There was just the slightest edge in my voice; this touched, if only faintly and in memory, on the old clamors. She heard the edge and deflected it.

"I'm sorry; I don't mean that. You just roost in a different tree."

"And a fine perch it is." The whole group flashed by, disappeared, and, in a few seconds, flashed by again. They seemed to be picking up speed, racing now around the inner edge of the tank. My pulse was racing. I pressed the hand holding the receiver against my heart. Her voice said my name, and again, "Buddy?" I squatted and skewed the receiver against my ear. "I have to go, Bess. I'll be there soon."

"What was that thumping?"

"My heart. I'm watching the dolphins. They're wild. I have to go."

"I'll keep a lookout for you."

"Fine."

I threw the receiver at the hook and ran to the window. Where were those creatures? I'd never seen such speed, such slippery perfection.

The tank was empty. Pressing my cheek against the glass I could make out above the surface a shadowy white contraption, a thin cranelike arm suspended over the water. Then I saw them, dark shapes, bending in a diffused arc above the arm. All this in a second. They fell and the water broke as if a bomb had dropped—two, four, six small slim forms crashing through the boiling mist. They rolled, split, tumbled, skidded through the green water.

I could be Molly or D'Nel or Banty Jakes. Molly would want to absorb these creatures, to take them into her and be transformed by them and transform them; Banty Jakes would love them, he would want to shower them with kindness, to protect them; D'Nel Boyd would want to stab them. Molly and Banty would touch the slick bodies with awe and glee. D'Nel knew that the only way to deal with excellence was to kill it.

Wherever I went now, he followed me. Wherever I was, he spoke to me, this D'Nel. It had become a nuisance, a distraction, a horror. When I told people about this movie, this piece, this bright tale I had to tell, I didn't mention that he was alive, this man, this D'Nel Boyd. Was he alive? Wasn't he the one I met in the Dakotas? Or was that too just a dream?

Last week—or last year—I had walked out late onto Lafayette to get a soda at the all-night deli. Just this side of the corner, in the middle of the street, the police had strung their orange tape in a triangle around some cones, marking an accident. I hadn't heard it happen. There was a pool of something between the cones. I walked over to it: it was blood, a slick of it six feet across, in the middle of the pavement. Beside the pool, next to one of the cones was a pair of shoes. Loafers, the stitching ripped on the right one. There was nothing else around, no wreckage, not even any cops. I stood there looking at the blood, in the empty street. Then a voice behind me said, "That's right, lean over close. Take a look. You can see your face in it." I turned, quickly, my hands raised, but it was hopeless; there was no one there.

Backstage now, the show done, the dolphins nipped and butted each other. They lazed and twirled in the murky water, nudging each other, kicking at someone getting too close, lolling. Pressing my ear to the glass I could hear their streaming clicks, their fierce, bickering chirps. They were just like actors everywhere.

4.   The hand pressed into my face, suffocating me. I woke with a start. The air was broken into pieces, like a jigsaw puzzle, each piece shining, the puzzle irretrievable. So the darkness and the evil came on. The world couldn't keep itself. Walking around corners, crawling, slithering, it pressed itself into our lives. There was no such thing as help. As my father, the ruined river trader, had believed. *Do something,* he had whispered on his deathbed, *do something,* but there was nothing to do. It was damaged beyond repair.

The throbbing thunderstorm I had pulled over to let pass was gone. In the north and west ragged denim clouds piled against a light blue early evening sky. The storm was a feint, a dodge; this deep in drought the brief scattering of rain would strike and run off the surface without penetrating, like water off a shield. Out on the road leaf sprigs and wisps of moss lay tossed about. Puddles that would be gone in an hour shone on the pavement. My panicked breathing slowed. Settle down, I thought, settle down.

But how can I deny—and so settle down—that I love the pornography of this life? I love its rough trade, its stink. Every time I leave New York I wish I were back there, back on the streets where any moment somebody is seconds away from the opening notes of a scream. You tell me it's too much and I'll tell *you* it's too much. Some girl, some actress I know, goes from office to office in Midtown, giving blow jobs to executives. In the cleansed bright airs, among the polished credenzas and the ferns, she kneels to take into her mouth the washed, rubber-encased penises of men who buy and sell. At night she sways on a vertical stage suspended beneath the Williamsburg Bridge, reeling in fake drunkenness through the six acts of a production that says life is unmoored, impossible, only a bauble careening through the stars. And my pal Jacob Drue, who, in a tight skirt hiding the world's smallest operational cock, lounges among the azaleas outside the entrance to the Holland Tunnel, offering his charm and the stunning beauty of a face so given to pleasure and performance that it is no longer a human face at all but simply a creation, to whoever might roll down his window and ask. And I am there beside him in a liquid purple vest, my hair oiled, wearing lipstick, grinning and honking, taking notes. I am there under my red wig, in my silk suit, brandishing my warrior's strong arm, ready to tussle, ready to break heads; maybe I am filming, maybe I am reliving my youth, maybe I am a conjurer myself, one for whom performance is life, one for whom the lie is the truth; maybe I am a missionary, searching the faces of the exhausted commuters, the revelers, for one who is so lost he is ready to give in totally, ready to give up, ready to say *All right—if this is next, then let it happen.*

An engine coughed, sputtered, and died. Across the ditch, fifty feet away in a fenced pasture, two men leaned over an open truck bodice. "Fuck you," one of them said to the other.

"Fuck you sideways," the other answered. I was west of Ocala, on the edge of the Florida horse country, the last open ground before the fifty-mile-deep border of wild woods that sheltered the coast. Live oaks prospered singly here and there in the wide field. Under low, flattened crowns their massive branches stretched out from the trunks like the wings of heavy birds, expressing, as Bess had put it once, the free will of trees. As if, she said, released, their deepest desire was to spread out, to *cover* the earth, not rise up off it. In the distance half a dozen thoroughbreds grazed. Water gleamed like patches of polished silk on their flanks.

"Get off of there," the first man shouted. He wore a red shirt. His tea-colored hair was shaved high along the sides of his head.

"Fuck you, asshole," his companion answered. They didn't pay any attention to me, stalled out on the other side of the fence.

A swell of cricket song rose and subsided. Wisps, tendrils of mist shambled along above the wet grass. My head throbbed.

The man in the red shirt pushed the other away from the hood. The struck man staggered back, whirled around unsteadily, reached into the cab, and came out with an ax handle.

"I'll snap your head off," he cried.

The red-shirted man ignored him. He leaned into the engine well, so far that his feet came off the ground. He was wearing cowboy boots the color of limeade.

"Lookahere, Burt," the man with the ax handle said.

"Get in there and start it up," the other man said.

The man slapped the side of the truck with the handle, got in, and fired the engine. It barked, wheezed, and caught in a roar. "Aye, good dog!" the red-shirted man cried and slammed the hood. He stood back grinning and rubbing his hands together. His hands were black with grease.

The man behind the wheel slid out, bringing the ax handle with him. He ran his hand up and down the yellow wood. "Hey," he said, "you got no right to call me an asshole."

The red-shirted man looked at him and laughed. "I got right enough—asshole." He glanced at the truck, which was a mistake. The ax man swung, catching him in the belly and doubling him over. The man—skinny, with a sucked-in mouth—raised the ax handle again and brought it down across the red-shirted man's shoulders. The man fell face forward, his breath whoofing out of him. "Got you now," the ax man cried.

The red-shirted man lay where he'd fallen. His companion poked his head with the tip of the handle. "Got you now, Burt," he said. Burt didn't move.

The man raised the handle as if to strike again, then he let it swing down. He dropped it in the grass. Then he turned and looked at me, straight at me as if he had been conscious of my watching him all along. I had an urge to speak, I had an urge to get out and take my licks, too, but I stayed where I was, upright in my seat, staring at him through the window. The man looked at me hard, a long look as if he were memorizing my face. I stared back, welcoming the scrutiny, wanting it to trigger something. Once, in a fit of erotic excess, Celest and I stood naked at one of her tall living-room windows. It was night; the hot track lights showed our bodies off like white sculptures. We stood there until a man stopped in the street and looked at us. He grinned, and we grinned, and we let him look as long as he wanted. The club-wielder, the skinny man with the narrow face, stared at me hard, and then his face relaxed and he smiled, showing his empty mouth. I smiled back and tipped my hat. Then I watched as he dragged the loose body of his companion up and muscled him into the truck bed. Through the window I could hear him grunting. He tossed the ax handle in the bed, got into the truck, and drove slowly away across the misty field and out of sight.

I thought of Rachel, my child, the small blond connipted beauty. Celest told me she took her to church last week. Probably to someplace elegant and architecturally profound. It was the first time in her life, in Rachel's life. Celest said when the opening hymn began Rachel was surprised but then she began to sing too. She sang the only song she knew, "Take Me Out to the Ball Game," which I had taught her last summer, as we sat behind first base at Yankee Stadium. I saw it as a movie, my blond child belting out the old song under the high vault of a Manhattan church. I saw the camera dollying in from the choir loft, passing like the wing of God over the raised singing faces; I saw it find my handsome wife and dally there a second, touching with the full hand of light her fine aristocratic face; and then I saw the camera touch my daughter, sniffing her out like a bird dog, feeling its way up her slim, yellow-frocked body to her face, which shone with the full light of innocence and morning. I saw it touch her and caress her, saw it brush her throat and her sandy brows, saw it find her eyes, which were the dark, burned blue of D'Nel Boyd's eyes, and then I saw it begin to penetrate, begin to reach through the temporal fascia into the heart of her, into the life of her being, into the delight and trust and vigor of her; and as it reached, and found, the moment, the pure perfected expression of her passing life, it became no longer a camera, no longer whir of film and speed, but the very living eye of the viewer himself; it became the need and the love and the hope of the one who watched—homage and theft—a conjuring, a dream fully realized, breathing and singing, filled with love, on this planet and in this life that was passing, that we would not escape from, or outlive.

I. It was an old house, a hundred years old, I guess, with two fronts and no back, sprawling white-winged like a pigeon flopped down in the grass, tricked out with a green iron roof and porches sporting trellises of morning glory and firecracker honeysuckle. The big bang of the blue-throated Gulf sang away behind, and the pinewoods started up like a shout way off past the manicured grass on either side. The woman who divorced me ten years ago sat on the steps eating a peach.

We embraced and clucked at each other and she swept me into the house where immediately servants I had known for years brought bowls of fresh green salad and plates piled with breaded pork chops and then a baking bowl filled with banana pudding. I thought, bending to the food, that no man could be happier than to come on something like this as she stood beside me in fawn-colored jodhpurs and a white shirt with the sleeves rolled up and the collar open showing the sun-flushed skin of her throat; thinking: I planned all along to shoot the movie here, it wasn't just the money I'd come after, or what sweet presents she might offer, but to find the *location* I could use from which my tough sports would rove forth to hack and hew. Just because she laughed out loud when I told her this and poured me another glass of elderberry wine— yellow as sunshine—there wasn't any reason, I figured, why she wouldn't do it.

"Let me tell you about this movie," I said, and she laughed again and said she didn't want to hear about any movie, especially any movie I might be making, but I started in anyway, telling the tale that yipped in my mind like a wild dog.

I had brought my briefcase in with my bags and I fumbled in it and drew out the pages I had scribbled on. "Look at this," I said. "You're going to love it."

She was thirty-eight years old, childless, bronzed by a life in the sun, beautiful as a country prize. Her sun-streaked chestnut hair was tied back with a silver ribbon.

"I don't want to know anything about your famous movie," she said, chuckling. She leaned against the counter, settling her fine bulky ass against the inch-wide metal strip bordering it. She waved her hand as if at a fly. I felt a little of the old singing inside me.

"No, no," I said, "you're going to love this."

I wanted to read the section about Molly and D'Nel's first murder journey. They have spent the afternoon fishing on the beach outside a small town, after which they have dinner in a dockside restaurant, then drive to a large house on the edge of town. In the house is an older couple, roosted up in their elegant bed, whom they break in upon, rob, and kill. It was a very dramatic scene, one played against the grain of what they were doing, filled with casual talk about their pasts, with a game they play with a garden-spider web and Molly's astonishment at the opulence of the old house, its furniture and paintings that she runs through the hall barefoot touching, like a child playing tag.

I began to read but a thumping began upstairs and then there was a cry.

"What the hell?"

"That's R.B. I told you he had gone off."

"What is he doing?"

"Pounding things into shape. He says. On this side of reality we call it breaking up the furniture."

"I'll go talk to him."

She sighed and looked out the window to where, on the back porch, a gray heron stood, still as a garden statue. Beyond his spindly form the sun hurled itself onto the grass. The chopped tops of Gulf waves looked like hands waving. "Don't upset him," she said.

I found R.B. sitting on his bed with the dismantled pieces of a rocking chair in his hands. He was a tall thin man with a bony forehead and large, green, rheumy eyes.

"Hello, Buddy," he said. "I figured you were coming."

I looked for a place to sit down but the two other chairs in the room had been dismantled too. There was a head-high pile of something in the corner covered by a gauzy white cloth. Honeysuckle vines shrouded the windows, letting in a dim, greenish light. The high ceiling was dark and dusty looking. R.B. was barefoot. I sat down on the foot of the bed.

"What's with the broken furniture?"

He looked at the ripped sticks in his hands—black-painted yellow wood—and hawked spit into his throat. "Ah, my friend, I'm doing ridiculous things here. I can't seem to stop myself." His voice was naturally high-pitched. Now it almost squeaked.

"What's bothering you?"

"I don't know. It was the Perseid meteor shower that set me off."

"A meteor shower?"

"Yes. You know, the time every summer when the falling stars come. It got to me."

"Little too much of Miss Infinity and her boys."

"Yeah. You get it. It's like looking at somebody you love singing, and all you see is the back of their throat. That they're nothing but delicate flesh." He raised and lowered the pieces of his rocking chair—a chair I myself had sat in; it had belonged to his grandmother—and cradled them in his lap. "I mean this world is too fragile for any of us to live in."

"So what should we do?"

"Wear paper slippers. Move very carefully."

I understood him. He was one of us, too. You realize that everything is finite, that it's going to pieces before your eyes, so, in grief and horror, you reach for the end, you break up the furniture. D'Nel Boyd would love this. He would get pleasure out of R. B. Appel.

I said, "I'm working on another movie."

"Oh, that's good. I enjoyed your last one."

"You saw it?"

"Oh sure. It came to the drive-in up at Belle Haven. Bess and I went up to see it. I liked the part where the sled went out of control."

"I liked that part too. I thought it was going to kill us trying to get it filmed." Stuntmen arguing. Artificial bodies sprawled everywhere, falls, Van screaming, near breakdown.

"The thing I like about your movies is even though you make sweet tidy endings, with all that's gone before nobody can believe them."

"You think so?"

"Yessir. You hit too hard for anything to be solved."

"You're probably right. I have trouble with structure. And Van gets carried away too."

"Van's the director?"

"Yeah. He's the one who gets all the momentum into everything."

Outside this house, right now, I could see my lovers move. I could see the sculpture of wires and steel cables D'Nel had swung between two big oaks; I could see D'Nel and Banty, his adversary and biographer, climbing in the swaying cables—at this distance like two spiders—rising to the top that was seventy feet off the ground, and I could hear their conversation in which D'Nel, the killer man, taunted and frightened Banty Jakes, drawing him into his web of horror, opening, as a man would open his hands, the presence of a new world, a world of damage and death, enticing the little man in. It was from this sculpture that Banty would fall—not to his death, but to his awakening—fall twice: first by D'Nel's hand and then by his own and wake naked in bed with Molly, carried there by D'Nel, who sat at the foot of the bed watching them, his hands fumbling lightly at the bedclothes, as if for a key misplaced.

I pushed up to my feet and went to the window. "Damn, R.B., I'm glad to be here."

"You are?"

"Hell yes. This is a fine place."

"I'm here all the time, so I wouldn't know."

Two men in white coveralls crossed the lawn carrying between them a large coiled garden hose. The grass sparkled with water; it shimmered. Breeze jumped and danced in the tops of cabbage palms and in the tops of the live oaks and the sweet gums. The old windmill, aloft above a steel tower like a derrick, creaked and turned its tan wings. The glass roof of the long greenhouse below it was smeared gray-white with lime wash. Out in the Gulf the grass islands gleamed like the risen hairy backs of sea beasts.

I said, "Bess is worried about you."

"She is?"

"She thinks you're having another breakdown."

"Well, Bess always did have a genius for the obvious."

"She says you caused the kitchen help to quit."

"I fired them. They were a bunch of strangers. I could tell they were getting in Mattie's way."

"Mattie the cook?"

"She's been here since I was a baby. That's important. You've got to have some form of continuity in your life or the world will eat you up."

"That makes sense." But then I thought, What if you can't get any? What if the message the world shouts is that there is no place of rest? There was a scene, which I wasn't sure I would put in the movie, in which Banty Jakes confronts Molly's father, an old farmer holding on for death. In it, accompanied by Tubby Wells the detective, Banty tries to get the father to support or at least bless his search for Molly, who has been missing for a year, but the old man, who at first won't even come out of the house to speak to the men, doesn't want to know about it. Banty yips and capers, tears springing into his eyes as he describes the danger Molly is in, seeking from the worn gentleman one word of approval and hope, but the old man stands firm. "I don't know who you are talking about," he says, "and I don't want to know."

Banty begins to describe what Molly means to him, he speaks of how as a teenager he pedaled his bike up the river road to help Molly water the mules, how he stood with her under the shade of the old capacious oak trees listening to the mules suck water from the trough and how in those moments with the smells and sights of farm life all around him and this girl standing limber and sweet-smelling at his side he felt love pour out of him, love for all the creation. But the father—I had only written this as story, not as script—isn't listening. He is thinking—I had not put this into movie language—how long and complicated life is and how few real resting places there are in it and how maybe all the effort of his lifetime that had gone into subduing and harnessing this five thousand acres of north Florida river land has been nothing more than his attempt to clear a small space where he might rest in peace, and that space is cluttered yet. He wonders if he is at last old enough and defeated enough to give in to the true bitterness and he wonders if there are enough kicks left in him to resist the relentless encroachment of decay, and he doesn't know the answer. His eyes are filled with grains of weariness, like sleep; he looks around at the two men—the detective, the tall Tubby Wells, who stands, thin as cane, leaning against some form that cannot be seen but which holds him up perfectly well, and he knows that there is a cruelty in the man that he cannot understand and that frightens him, and he knows that the other man, this Bantling Jakes, whom he has in fact known all the boy's life, as he has known his scamp of a father and his stolid, perseverant mother, does not see the cruelty, or if he sees it he does not take it seriously; and he knows, as if someone he loved stepped out of a prison and told him, that he cannot muster the resistance necessary to prevent these two from pursuing what they are bound to pursue, and that this quarry is his daughter, and that now more than ever he does not know what will happen to her.

These were only told words now; I didn't know yet how to film them—they would be spoken—but I knew that I had to make this come across, I had to plead and push Van to make this come alive on the screen. We had to know that it was possible that even a father—one of the last anchors—out of grief and hopelessness, to save himself, could turn his back on his child, and let her go on her way to the devil.

R.B. slewed around on the bed and pressed his face against the pillow. "I have to rest now," he said. "Will you come back later?" His watery eyes swam toward me, touched, and moved on.

"Sure."

"Would you take that away?"

He indicated the chair pieces. I scooped them up and carried them downstairs.

2.   It has come to my attention that I am living, right now, in my time. When I was younger, for my whole life in fact—through my twenties and, I think, well into my thirties—I thought of my time as something that was about to come. The heroes of my youth—Willie

Mays, King Oliver, Elvis, Buñuel, de Kooning, Haystack Calhoun: the long string of them—the events, the *routine*—were all factors in an extravaganza I was not part of, though I yearned to be. They were out there, these makers, charging the world with their grace and energy, while I ran through my exercises in the wings. It is only a few years that I have been among them, and only recently that I have realized that the greats, the near-greats, and the mediocrities I move among are the men and women of my own time, that I am now in the midst of something that is neither the past nor the future but the present. Those I work with, and the gentlemen who run the country, the artists and ball players, the studio executives, the police commissioners, the depressed Iranian who operates the newsstand on the corner, are my coterie, my comrades; we are riding on the raft of our time together, making our passage up as we go along or cribbing it out of manuals, trying to please the memories of our parents or to placate the future, singing or moaning, making it or losing it, going down in glory or defeat, in lights or nameless—all members of the same tribe, living in our time.

I find it very disappointing. Unlike Rip Van Winkle, I have awakened into a life that has not changed. The discovery I have made—that this man at my elbow who is making the movies of our era, this beauty whom all adore, this diplomat shuffling between warring factions, is only another like myself—has brought down with it the fantastical structure I built on the lights and names of past and future. We are, after all, only human.

I am not alone in this realization, for Bess knows it too. She discovered it in New York, years ago, when she realized that New York was like every other place. She saw me sprinting about, trying to get into the movies, she saw all the others charging down the chute of their dreams, and she was not flummoxed by this into any sort of grandizement. She knew that when all the adventurers returned to their penthouses or their lean-tos, soon—even amidst the caviling or the praising—would arrive the simplest and most human of moments, when, with tea mug or wineglass in hand, the posturer sat alone with his own small self, desiring nothing like peace on earth or the cloak of gods, but only a little hot water or a bowl of strawberries or a moment's attention from someone he loved.

This knowledge made her conservative, in the oldest sense of that word, as one who sought to preserve and enhance what sustained. It slowed her down—me, it sped up—turning her face toward the place and enterprise that had shaped her. She decided to return to Florida, to the practices and beliefs of her people, to run the nursery and manage the shade tobacco allotment and take care of her brother, who, after the death of their father and, two years later, their mother, had begun to stray from the palaces of reason.

So I wasn't surprised when as I came out onto the back porch she asked me if I was going to the reunion. And I wasn't surprised that she meant the reunion of *my* family.

She had changed into her old black tank bathing suit. The worn bottom hung off her ample ass in a single shined swag. She was chasing flies with a swatter, smacking them against the screen.

"Do you want to go this year?" she said, speaking to me over her shoulder. There was a fatigue in her broad back, a slackness, like a whiff of stale urine, around her hips, a new angle of sorrow in the way her hands connected to her wrists.

I hedged.

"You ought to."

"I'm not sure that's true."

She was red-tanned as farmers are tanned: face and neck, wrists and forearms. Her upper arms were creamy white, smooth and finely rounded—except for the welted scar along her right forearm, the arms of a delicate beauty—but below her elbows, enhanced by the sunburn, they took on a massivity, a ropy thickness that bespoke her calling. Her wrists were thick, and flattened like the wrists of athletes, and her hands were sinewy and broad with small, tapered fingernails nearly filled with white moons. Her legs reiterated the scheme: slender thighs, hard and muscular calves, paddle feet.

She moved around the large room briskly, snapping the swatter at the heavy, iridescent Gulf flies.

"I think you ought to go this year," she said.

"I'd just feel lonely."

"No you wouldn't."

She had been a submanager of the reunions for fifteen years. Will-

ingly, with great vigor, she had taken on the task during the first year
of our marriage, calling and writing to cousins and aunts and uncles,
cajoling them into appearances at the events, which were held on the
river a hundred miles south of St. Louis every two years. Five years ago
she told me she was writing a history of the family—or she was
collecting information toward a history. Since then I would receive
every spring—as did a hundred and twenty-five other members of the
Drake family—a manila envelope from which spilled Xeroxed sheets
detailing the wriggling historical line descending from the loins of one
of the original Drake brothers.

Four generations ago—or maybe five, I'm never sure—Samuel
Drake—a young handyman, apparently—journeyed from northern
Kentucky down the Ohio to Cairo, Illinois, where he took a right turn
upriver, traveled only fifty miles before he got off the paddle wheeler
for good at the town of Bar Etienne, a small farm shipping village set
on a grassy rise between two shale bluffs on the Missouri side. There,
by a process that has remained obscure, he came to own some ten
thousand acres of Missouri woods and grassland upon which he raised
beef cattle and took out timber for the construction of riverboats. He
didn't marry until he was well into his forties, at which time he plucked
from the bosom of her upright family a black-haired girl of sixteen
who, over the next twenty years, bore him eight sons. It is these sons
whose trails Bess follows. It is a typically American story, the journeys
of these folk. In Europe, maybe, there would be a continuity of enterprise and creed, but in this country, at least among the Drakes of
Missouri, there has been none such. At these reunions, which I attended
with some regularity before and after our marriage, I met professors and
crooks, a railroad engineer, a swimming-pool attendant, a couple of
lawyers, salesmen, a fifty-six-year-old biker, an orchard man, a few
farmers, a buyer for Saks, a former ballerina, three newspapermen, a
handful of ne'er-do-wells and hard-faced country sports, a doctor, the
president of the largest advertising agency in Pittsburgh, an oyster
shucker from New Orleans, a drag queen, a charter-boat captain, an
architect, a wilderness fishing guide, and the assistant chief ranger of
Yellowstone National Park, among others. Some were tall, some were
short; there were the skinny and the fat, the pale-skinned and the

swarthy; some voted Republican, some Democrat, some had never voted; some were city dwellers, some swore by the country life, some were travelers, some had hardly ever left the county in which they were born. There were the honored dead, the missing, the lost sons, the wayward daughters, the ones with evil hands whose names weren't mentioned, the handicapped, the pure of spirit, the suicides. Francey Jameson, a cousin from Cincinnati, whom I had never laid eyes on before, spent two hours one August afternoon haranguing me about the Air Force's callous and blockheaded treatment of her love life—apparently she had been booted out after an affair with an officer at Eglin—a recitation of such complicated and relentless misery that by the end of it I was so exhausted I had to go in the house and lie down, but which my Aunt Eleanor told me later was entirely a figment of Francey's mad and permanently twisted imagination. And she wasn't the only one.

Bess thrived on these gatherings and on the satisfaction and security she found in being part of a familial chain. She and my mother spent hours on the telephone exchanging stories about the goings-on of the Drake clan. During our married life I would come on them sitting head-to-head in the front parlor of my mother's house on Bonny Richard Street in St. Louis, cackling over some farfetched family tale, their dark eyes shining, like the eyes of a couple of terrorists, with merriment. I myself was affected by all this; I took the story and the setting of my first movie from these gatherings—a violent tale of a backslapping midwestern family reunion that veers off into a bloodbath; shot in four weeks for a budget of $276,000—but as I always pointed out to them, there was nothing especially interesting about the Drake family, unless you were willing to jack their commonplace experience into the realm of movie glamour, a process which chewed up and swallowed the initiating facts—if there actually were any—leaving a residue that it was not fulfilling to return to. When I tried to tell her this Bess would roll her eyes and hoot, assuring me, as if she hadn't heard what I said, that what I *really* wanted was my own small, neat place at the family table, just that.

It was something else I had dropped from the argument, so that now as she reached, her strong calves bulging, to swat another grinding fly, I attempted to slip the noose of confrontation.

"Maybe I will go this year," I said. "Maybe that would be a good idea."

"You're just humoring me."

"No, no. I haven't been in a long time. Some of those people are pretty interesting."

"Those people?"

"Drakes. My blood and kin."

She gave me a long look, her dark eyes opening wide so that I felt for a second the old tug toward her heart—circumscribing tug that had once driven me crazy with resistance—and laughed her sunny barking ironic laugh. "The great appeaser," she said. "All you want is for us life-living folks to leave you alone."

"I guess," I said a little glumly.

She picked a magazine off the sofa, fashioned it into a scoop, and began to clean up the flies. As she squatted, pressing forward slightly over one knee, she emitted a small rosy fart.

"Such a country girl," I said.

She shook out a smile over her shoulder for me. "You've lost touch with the natural world."

"I never had that much anyway. I'm a city boy."

"Not by disposition."

Though I was the one fourteen years ago who had turned cartwheels when we discovered the two-story garage off lower Broadway that had been my home ever since, she always maintained that what I really wanted was a country home—what I needed, at least—gardens and work in the fields and the rhythms of weather. "Not by disposition or practice."

"By nature."

"You've always seen things I don't. And things nobody else sees."

She shook the flies into a wastebasket that had a color scene of running horses painted on it. She was panting slightly, a sheen of sweat on her forehead. The porch, screened with green wire, was furnished like a room: flowered sofas, cane tables, heavy brass and green glass lamps, heavy, cotton-clothed armchairs, a small Persian rug richly patterned in green and red. Books and magazines, unsheathed newspapers from Florida's major cities as well as Washington and New York were scattered about. Against the house wall was a fireplace. On its sooty floor were scattered a few bleached shells from the last oyster roast.

She held the wastebasket up, peering nearsightedly into it, then carried it to the fireplace and dumped the flies. She balled a piece of newspaper, dropped it on the small carcasses, and lit it with a kitchen match she took from the mantel. "I see you pretty well," she said, gazing at the quickening lick of yellow flame.

"What amazes me is that I am one of the world's easiest people to read, and you, who were married to me for five long years, have never for a minute gotten anything about me right."

She cocked her head and looked at me fully. "You think so?"

"Yeah," I laughed.

"What'd you think of R.B.?"

"He seems to be in one of his spells. They pass. Don't they?"

"Usually. This one's worse though. Actually he's been getting worse for some time."

My mind had wandered from the movie. Get along, little dogie, I thought, prodding it back. What was Molly up to? Where was D'Nel? There was a funeral, a village affair. Banty, wandering around in the village, where he has stayed for two weeks with the detective Tubby Wells, meets Molly and they go to the funeral—of no one they ever knew—together. It is their first encounter.

Here, it was late afternoon. The shadows of the live oaks released long pools onto the watered grass. The clack-clack of a stemming machine came from the greenhouses. Sprinklers, set in metal rosettes sunk in the lawn, came on, spurting tall fans of fresh water, subsided, and came on again. They emitted a steady shussing sound. Over the Gulf, sunset touched pink to a few thin streamers of cloud.

She rubbed her palms and opened them absently over the smoldering paper.

I said, "I don't think he's really different from people in general. We all go in these cycles of flight and fall. R.B.'s arc is just a little wider than the rest of us—us's."

"Buddy, you ought to get somebody to pay you to be an idiot, you're so good at it." She set the wastebasket beside the sofa, tapping it into perfect place.

"What?"

"R.B. is not a movie problem. Explaining how some people just swing out a little farther than others is no help when it's your brother and he's come apart in front of your eyes."

"But, Bess, he's shagged out before."

"I'm telling you it's worse. He's in trouble."

"What do you want me to do? I'm not a doctor."

"I don't know. Spend some time with him. He's always loved you. Why don't the two of you go out fishing."

"Fishing?"

"He likes to go out with the sponge divers. With the Greek boys."

"I didn't know that."

"Why don't the two of you go. Take him out and get some charge in his blood."

"I suppose that would be all right."

She flicked me a short-lipped risive smile. "You are a generous soul."

"I thought you said *I* was the liar."

"I just want you to feel at home." She looked me up and down. "Go get your suit and let's swim. Gulf water is just the ticket for you grimed-up city boys."

"Yokey-dokey."

She grinned and feinted at me, lunging close so that though I didn't grab her in my arms I could feel the energy off her body; and I could smell her, a bitter frictiony smell, like the odor of rotting leather.

3. I would do almost anything she asked me to do. It was no hardship to take R.B. on a fishing trip, or almost any other kind of trip. I had always enjoyed his company. He was a bright man and generous in spirit, and it had never bothered me that he could not find anything in this world to do that suited him. He was like my father in that way, who though he worked a public trade all his life couldn't keep from getting crushed. My father tried as hard as he could to make a place and a motion in the world that would keep him—and us—from harm, and he tried to fulfill the requirements—as he saw them—of manhood in this country, and he failed. But when I think of him I don't think of the wan man shuffling down the corridors of his warehouse or directing the stevedores as they unloaded a shipment of metal toilets come down the Ohio from Cincinnati, or of him rushing to file the papers of incorporation in a last-ditch effort to stave off the stranglehold the corporations had him in; I think of him sitting one afternoon in the walled garden behind our house on Bonny Richard Street. It is Sunday afternoon in late spring. The big crepe myrtle by the gate has just broken into blossom and the masses of ruffled pink flowers pull the branches down, making it look as if the bush is trying to bow. We are sitting there in the old lounge chairs, as my father liked to do on Sunday evenings, him talking to me a little about the river life—which never included anything about how hard it was to make a living off the river but instead was a recitation of hunts and treks, of early-morning duck flights, and herds of deer slipping down at dawn for a drink—when over the wall bounces a white tennis ball. In a minute there is a knock on the gate, and a small voice calls out. "Come right in," my father cries. The gate eases open and a small face pokes around the edge. It is the face of a young woman. "I'm sorry," she says, "but I believe my tennis ball came in here."

"Yes it did, my dear," my father answers, and gets up and retrieves the ball from under the mock banana bush.

The woman slips in shyly and stands on the walk just inside the gate. She looks to be in her early twenties. Her soft blond hair is tied back with a red ribbon; she is dressed in tennis whites and is very tan. I think her shyness odd and stare at her, but my father, if he does, makes no sign. He brings the ball to her.

"Here you go, my dear," he says.

She thanks him and turns to go, but my father touches her arm. "Won't you stay and have a glass of tea?"

I can see he is charmed by the young woman and, for some reason, this embarrasses me. I turn my head and see my mother looking at us through the kitchen window. There is something in her eyes that shocks me. The girl, flipping her ponytail, turns that way, and I guess she sees it too because her face clouds. "Thank you for your generosity," she says in a small formal voice, "but my friends are waiting."

My father sighs and smiles. "Another time, I hope."

"Thank you," the woman says and slips out through the gate, latching it behind her.

We sit down again on the lounges and my father is silent for a while, gazing at the closed gate. My mother calls us brightly from the kitchen. Her voice is rosy though it is only the usual Sunday supper she calls us to. My father looks at me and I see that he is smiling a smile of such sweet sadness that I think he might be about to cry. Then he pats my hand fondly, rubbing for a second the place on my wrist where a dog bit me the year before. "You have to remember," he says chuckling, "that Ulysses, when he had his sailors tie him to the mast so he could hear the sirens sing, regretted his foresight."

I was eight then, small for my age, desperately in love with my parents. I don't know when my life was more intensely lived or of brighter prospect than in that year, or in those years, of young childhood, so it is odd to me now, even this far away in my forties, that those few words of my father's and the look on his worn face of mingled loss and desire, have remained, when so much else has faded.

4. Rinsed and refreshed by the green Gulf waters, we ate supper at the long pine table in the kitchen. At the Appel table everybody was welcome, not only Bess, R.B. and me, and the relations, but the servants too, the maid and the houseman, the driver, the two yardmen, and the farm and nursery foremen, as well as anybody else who might drop by. There were times I remembered when twenty-five people bellied up to the old scarred table for a supper of country delights. Judges, road tramps, lost relatives, local fishermen, the winners of the Occasion Babe Ruth League pennant were all welcomed and accommodated. Nobody within reach went hungry.

R.B., in a sparkling white African bush helmet that in moments of distress he pulled down over his eyes, sat at one end of the table, and Bess, with me to her right, sat at the other. Only the cook and a server refused to sit, hurrying through the prestidigitations of the courses with a fierce and committed concentration. There were calls for this and that, for more Tabasco, for more iced tea, for another helping of stewed corn, as Bess, regal in a red silk robe, presided over the mayhem, offering tidbits and delicacies to all within reach, pushing the fine food at us as if it were a ticket to paradise. Her dark amber, sun-raked hair, still wet from the shower, was combed back from her forehead and held with a flat gold clasp behind her neck. Between courses she tapped out with the blade of her knife a quick rhythm on the honey wood, barking directions to a reluctant gorger, recommending the chutney or the pickled green tomatoes, conducting with relentless verve the symphony before her.

I was happy to muscle in; I always had been: this Appel approach allowed any and all to let loose their demon's appetite, and we were grateful. Judge Horace Jennings and his wife, Felice, a tidy woman in yellow bangs, were there, as were Uncle Porto Lefebre and his wife, Estelle, and a scattering of cousins—some of whom, over their mother's protests, ate the crisp wild duck with their hands—along with the two foremen and their wives, and a few other small children, anonymous to me. A vast gurgling and crunching came from the table as James Willis, the black servant, moved among us in a spotless white jacket, sliding the platters—teetering, both James Willis and the platters, as if about to crash—between us, and gathering the refuse of duck bones and crab shells and soup plates and dropped cutlery.

"I never had it so good in all my life, Bessie," the judge crowed, smacking his tuberous lips. His wife seconded him with a series of quick bird bobs that dislodged a small bead of duck grease from her chin and sent it arcing into the gravy bowl.

Uncle Porto Lefebre, snugged like a bus passenger at my right elbow, pumped me, between mouthfuls, about the movies, which I was glad to speak about, for the benefit of Bess, in detail. "How do you get those fellows to do those stunts—jump off buildings and set fire to themselves and all that?" he wanted to know, and so I began to explain about air bags and false heights.

"No," he said, "I mean how do you get them to do it, how do you convince them?"

"Well," I said, snapping the crushing claw off a large blue crab, "there are certain people who like to do that sort of thing, and we pay them well, too."

"You'd have to pay me an awful lot to get me to let somebody set fire to me," Aunt Estelle put in. "Whoo, I don't think any amount of money would make me do that." Chunks of crabmeat shone like extra teeth as she spoke.

"They wear suits," I told her.

"What kind of suits?" Uncle Porto wanted to know.

"Asbestos."

"You'll wind up with a lawsuit on your hands with that asbestos," Judge Jennings said from across the table. "And I can tell you, if they brought the lawsuit you would lose it."

"They're all expert," I said. "It's their craft."

"This day and time, expert or not, when something goes wrong, people want to sue."

"Buddy," little Judy Lefebre called from down the table, "Buddy, Jerry wants you to put him in the movies, would you put him in the movies?"

"Quit it, Judy," her little brother Jerry cried, slapping her arm with his spoon. "Buddy, don't listen to her, she's got a crush on you."

"Mama," Judy cried, "tell Jerry to hush up. Hush up, Jerry."

"I will not, 'cause it's true. Mama, you always told me to tell the truth."

"Yall eat quietly," Uncle Porto said, "or there won't be any dessert."

"Mama!" the children cried in unison.

"That's fine," Aunt Estelle said absently, shaking out her napkin. "I think we're having banana pudding for dessert."

Judge Jennings began a pungent discourse on a gang of punkish boys who'd come before him that week, charged with murder, but attempting, he said, as a ploy, to split the venue, so they could get separate trials and, he figured, blame each other. "They were cunning as rat snakes," he intoned, slathering a biscuit with dark slashes of cane syrup, "and there wasn't a thing I could do to prevent them from getting what they wanted."

He went on about the need for judicial reform, the biscuit grasped between thumb and forefinger, stabbing it softly at the air like a plug he was sticking in a breach, as the meal swirled around us. Mattie, the cook, a large woman in fawn trousers and a neon blue shirt—with collar buttons, I noticed—worked her equipment like an organist, pumping and riffing, beaming and frowning as the audience shouted its approval.

R.B., secure in the solitude of his large round hat, ate steadily; Bess tapped her rhythm on the wood, and my mind began to slide.

Beyond R.B. I could see, through the dining room and the hall, the living room, where a light left on cast a tender radiance, touching with soft regard the green silk sofa and the knobby chairs, the edge of the gold rug and the latticed fireplace screen. Something could bound softly forth across that room. Someone could be waiting there. Then Celest was in my mind, spread out naked under me as I sat hunched over her ankles, running my hands up the smooth blade of her yellow shins. She looked at me down the flagged-out length of her body, touching herself delicately, as if in discovery. *One and one make one,* she said, *and one and every other number make one too.* She meant—and I had heard her say this—that it was only in sum, one added to another, that anybody made a whole. Divorce is not freedom, she said, it's only separation, it's exclusion—no one survives alone. We had briefly argued over this, as outside the tall bedroom windows the linden trees surged in rain, me taking the part not of hermits or lonely conquistadores, but of indifference, of the life lived so energetically that no attachments mattered. *But you're crazy,* she had said. *It's not something based on choice; we simply can't live that way.* But I couldn't hear; my mind was aspin with the fleshy reality of her, a reality so profound and delicious I couldn't take my hands off it. *Magnify,* I said, *pump it till it's huge; then you don't have to worry a minute about who or what you're joined to, or if you're joined at all.*

Liar! she barked and pulled me down on top of her.

Bess's fingers found my wrist, half touching me, half tapping out the rhythm of her thoughts.

I dipped my head and kissed the back of her hand—scarred from work, thinly, bluely veined—lightly. "It's like going to a party every night," I said, looking at Uncle Porto shaking his fork at one of the children, who giggled and made monkey faces in return.

"Or a dogfight," she said.

"R.B. seems calm."

"He's just building up some steam."

"Hey, R.B.," I called, "how are you doing?"

He cocked his hat back with one bony finger and looked at me, for a second, without recognition. Then he smiled, a thin greasy smile. "Have you noticed," he said with mock gravity, or what I took to be mock gravity, "how humankind can think and even speak with wisdom, but then turn around and *act* so childishly?"

"Yes," I said, "I have. I'm a well-known perpetrator."

He smiled in complicity. "Good. Me too." He raised and opened his hand. "Now look at all these folks. They confuse gluttony with passion. But pull anyone of them aside"—he flipped a meager grin at Estelle and Porto—"present a problem, and they will speak to you with all the concern and wisdom gathered through a hundred human generations. They will speak of God's will with more than a passing understanding. They will find a platform for your hope, for generosity. They understand loss, and are familiar with the wages of grief. In their hearts and sometimes in their mouths is the knowledge that they fight a war to survive that they can never win, that no matter what they stack up against the army at the gates it will break through and carry them off into the darkness. Even the dumbest—look at the judge; look . . . at his wife" ("Now, R.B.—*iy, iy iy,*" the judge proffered) "look at the two of them snorting and slurping—even those two would, anytime you asked, draw aside with you to listen for a moment to your sorrows; and they would speak of the glory in each day's journey—with humility!—of the weakness of human powers, and of our need for direction from a higher, wiser source." He picked up his spoon—fine, heavy, grooved silver—and looked at it. "It's a miracle. And it leads me to believe there is a God who acts on this earth. You watch these numb-skulls move around, crashing through the furniture, and then they speak, and it's as surprising to hear as it would be if a hog stuck his face up out of the wallow and said a few words to you." He spat out a small burred laugh. "Only God could make such a joke. Don't you agree?"

"Sure."

In his fine white broadcloth, his silk Harvard tie, with his small, round, handsome head, he looked like the young assistant minister of some elegant urban church.

"Yes. We confront God through his miracles—there's no other way to faith—but we have lost our understanding of what is miraculous. We discard the old tricks—the water into wine, the Red Sea parting, Lazarus rustling up from the dead—because we sense that in this particular arrangement of object and space they are impossible, but if by that rejection we think we have done with miracles entirely we're mistaken. Look at Estelle there," ("R.B., pshaw, you coot") "as absent and craven a specimen as any you might find." (She didn't respond to this, only smiled, not ignoring him but living in the midst of him as background.) "You might wonder how such a one could have the ability to get herself dressed in the morning, much less fare forth into a world in which she encounters such wonders as auxiliary verbs, flush toilets, and the racks and hierarchies of government, and much, much less any gathering of ideas, any tramp of logic or creative speculation—but this"—he held his hand out, palm up as if her image danced on it—"this lady, this collection of guts and wind, not only dresses herself but has borne and raised a small brood of similar creatures." ("Now, R.B.," Porto said genially as he drove his knife into the thigh joint of a mallard, "don't start in on the children, *huph, huph*".) "She has raised them, scattering them forth like bright candles on the earth, she keeps a house, reads, tends her husband, sells real estate—*real . . . estate*—on the side, and would, if you asked her, speak with verve and assurance on any number of topics—more, in fact, than probably the most scholarly monk in any Benedictine monastery could come up with—she would dazzle and rout him in fact—and we sit here in her presence—I don't mean to single you out, Aunt Estelle, anybody would do—unable to see the miracle of her."

He took his hat off and set it like a bowl beside his plate. His dark rich hair was wet. A spasm passed over his face, twisting the mouth, dragging through and jamming his eyes. Sweat sprang out on his forehead and upper lip.

Bess, who had been watching him intently the whole time, said, "R.B., why don't you go upstairs and lie down."

R.B. looked at her with the wan simplicity of an exhausted child. "You think I should?"

"Yes. I think you've worn yourself out."

"I'm very tired."

"I know, darling."

He rose, pushing up straight-armed, as if his body were a weight he was lifting. "If you folks will excuse me, I think I will toddle off."

"Perfectly all right," the judge intoned, rising slightly with his napkin pressed like a truss into his lap.

"Take care, son," Uncle Porto said. The others murmured felicities.

He made his way, with the gravity and delicacy of an old man, through the unlighted dining room into the hall, where he stopped, musing into his palm. "Left turn, R.B.," Bess called. He lifted a soft wave and tacked into the living room, stopping again. Bess craned toward me—scent of salt and light florals of her perfume, her harsh breathing—to see.

"What's he doing?"

"Standing."

"Go see about him."

"He's all right."

His right hand lifted, vaguely, touched something out of sight, and fell back. He turned slightly, picked up a small object from the reading table and looked at it—a paperweight or knickknack—turning it in his hand. He put it back and picked up another, a small bowl that he upended, staring at the bottom. Bess didn't say anything else, but I caught her glance of mingled fear and disgust. R.B. brought the bowl to his face and sniffed it. Then he put it back and began to walk slowly around the room touching objects here and there, running his fingers carefully over bright surfaces. This went on for several minutes until finally Bess got up and went to her brother. She took him gently by the arm—he didn't protest—and led him upstairs, a man too dazzled by the shining variety of this world to find his way by himself.

5. Now it is late and the stars tack the blank sheet of the sky onto the face of heaven. Now the sea that I walk beside following my ex-wife is a mix of darkness and phosphorus, of chipped starlight and its own small sounds. Far out the lights of shrimp boats shine, touching the edges of the world. I follow her tracks and then I follow the shape of her body moving ahead of me in the darkness. She walks along the tide line, her heels sinking deep, scattering the small flights of ghost crabs before her. A night bird calls from the trees. Beyond the tide, ranges of shell trash, of skate eggs and snarled weed are heaped as if someone carefully raked them; beyond the debris patches of grass rise, like beds or thickets for mice, and then the dunes lift off the level of the strand, their smooth surfaces stippled with sea oats and clumps of pampas grass, run through by strings of sea grape. My ex-wife leaves the water and begins to cross the beach in a slow, rising diagonal, angling toward a fleet of dunes beyond which the tall pines rise straight and narrow and dark. She disappears beyond the crest of a dune. When I reach it I see her two dunes away. She enters a grove of dead cypress trees between the dunes and the pinewoods. The spiny gray trunks hold up sprays of naked branches. I follow into the grove, walking carefully, as noiselessly as possible across the ground bed of dead moss that crackles under my feet. For a moment I think I have lost her, but then I see she has stopped. She stands next to a tall tree, leaning against it. She coughs. I hear her harsh, powerfully drawn breaths. She stands there a long time; I wait, watching her. Then a soft moaning, a whispery keening, begins. She coughs, cries out softly, and sinks to her knees. I hear the sound of retching. The sound goes on for a long time. I wait, fascinated, terrified, unable to approach. The retching stops; she rises slowly. An owl presses its soft, silky cry into the night. The wind stirs in the pinewoods beyond. Maybe I look away, maybe I don't, but now she is gone. The darkness around me, the slap of surf, the whiskery frets of the wind, seem for a moment about to enter me, but they don't. I am alone at the edge of the woods. There are so many voices I never hear, there are so many meanings I never get.

6. The phone, in Van's voice, said, "I'm not home, but if this is a call from anybody in the movie business—except those in financial services—you're wasting your time. I don't like hearing from you and I won't call you back." God bless him. They were after him to direct, even the majors wanted him. And they knew a dying duck when they saw one. Our first picture made money, and a small but definite impact, as did the next few, but then one died squealing and the next was no better, and now, as we heaved toward the latest, nobody wanted to play with us. Van had directed and produced, with my help—at least my company—all the pictures, except the first, and now, though nobody wanted to back us again, they wanted Van. But Van didn't want to be a star.

Silence. A dying beep. "Listen," I said, "things are a little twisted down here. You remember Bess's brother, R.B., well, he's not doing too well, in fact he's come apart, so Bess is pretty distracted. I haven't talked to her about money. Did you check on that new arrangement Mitsubishi's got, that little outfit they spun off to handle small projects? Why don't we give them a try? That is, if you can get away from the tidal waves. I know all a moviemaker needs to know about dolphins. And I've had one fight and watched another. I think I may have seen a guy get killed this afternoon. It was like a dream, I mean I woke up and saw it, out in this field. I don't know if I was dreaming or not. It looked real but who can tell? Are you doing all right? Listen to this scene. . . ."

I began to read the scene in which D'Nel and Molly break into a house and torture and rob and eventually kill an old couple. It was a scene of some power, I thought, building from a candlelight dinner on the wharf, through a trek across the moonlit backyards of the town to the mansion—during which they discuss the most mundane subjects—to the upstairs bedroom where they wake, like Mom and Dad come to rouse the children for an early trip to the beach, the sleeping couple. It was graphic, and it didn't shirk; in it, for the first time, the audience saw the dark place D'Nel Boyd lived in—thrived in—the place he had brought Molly to, and what she had become.

There was only five minutes' message space on Van's tape, so I had to call back five times to get it all in. I finished the last scene, in which we are outside the bedroom door with Molly, as D'Nel, still inside, fires the ending shots. She hears the shots, then there is a silence in which she listens to the grandfather clock strike the half, sees a pool of light on the floor before her, and wades into it up to her hips. Dark above the waist, she seems to be sunk in a tank of light, a ripped body still standing. Then she presses her hands slowly down the front of her dress. Her hands are bloody. Then she sinks forward and down into the light until we can see her face. It is the whited face of an angel, but an angel who has bitten into flesh. Her lips are smeared with blood. Her mouth opens and we can see the blood on her teeth, blood like a pool of red in the hollow. The camera moves in until all we can see is blood.

"Well," I said, "that's it."

"Finest kind," said Van, "finest kind, but don't you think we ought to stay in the room a little longer?"

"When'd you come in?"

"I think it was the second reel. They'd just seen the spiderweb in a tree outside the house."

"You liked it?"

"I thought their conversation was a little discouraging—you're getting too digressive again—but once they got into action everything zipped right along."

"I want to have them just talking, lull the audience a little, show that human beings are doing this."

"It's a little awkward, especially how you're getting across that deal with the web—how's it supposed to hang from the tree?—but there's nothing that can't be fixed. How's Bess?"

"She's upset about R.B. I don't know if it's serious or not."

"Are you at her house?"

"Yeah."

I was in a white room—white wicker furniture, white walls, white rug—in a corner on the second floor. Night bugs tapped on the screens and I could hear the faint flop of surf.

"I can't find anybody up here who wants to give us money. Even the Japanese aren't interested."

"What are you going to do?"

There was a moment of silence. "I might be able to get something if I promise to direct for Metro."

My heart kicked. "What's the deal?"

"They're having trouble with one of their kiddie pix and they want me to take it for them."

Above my head a fan turned in steady slow circles. "What about us?"

"If I do their show they'll put some money up front and do a negative pickup on us."

"But that puts us twelve months out, maybe eighteen. I don't want to wait that long. I don't think I *can* wait that long."

"I don't want it either, man, but nobody wants to give us anything."

"We could go out to California and crawl."

"There's no need to do that. Crawling around here works just as well. It's the same guys anyway."

"Ah shit."

"Yeah, I know."

"Are you going to do it?"

"I don't know, Buddy."

"Jesus, Van, you can't run now."

"I'm not running, but I can't think of any other way to get the money. What does Bess say?"

"I've only been here a day. I haven't talked to her yet. Like I say, her brother's having trouble and I didn't want to bother her."

"You're afraid she'll turn you down."

"Yes I am."

"Some of that money she has is yours. She's still living off *Blood Tie.*"

"Well, I don't believe she thinks of it that way. She thinks the money's hers outright—I gave it to her—and anything added to it is what she's made herself."

"Maybe that's a place where begging'll work."

"You can't beg Bess. She thinks it's praise, and she doesn't like praise."

"Then tell her you have to have some of your money back."

"There's got to be somebody up there who'll finance us. What about Teague? He's close to all those Broadway guys."

"Teague's been indicted."

"He has?"

"Yeah. He was setting up dummy companies that these guys were using to launder drug money. Some kind of auxiliary affair, I don't know what it was. He says he's out of the business, at least until next year."

Once in a while somebody would walk up to you and hand you money. Every lifetime had a moment like that. Everything in your stars lined up—like that moment at a traffic light when, out of nowhere, for a minute all the turn signals blink in unison—and out of the spiffy sunlight stepped a benefactor, come across continents to find you. It happened once—everyone had a moment—and then you had to live with what it did to you. Then the test of character and purpose came. Would you take it in your stride, accepting the gift as incidental, not meant to prove your superiority, and so press on as energetically as ever? Or would you take it as a sign of arrival, of privilege, and loose your stays and begin to wait for the next gift, until you became one of the begging gentry, unable, on your own, to initiate the simplest act? Or would you, in some combination of the two, press on, nearly as usual, but now carrying the wound of awareness dripping in your side, a man who understood as well as anyone the necessity for continued effort, and who gave himself to it as best he could, but who could not forget ever that once, the portals of being had opened wide and freely, and had given him, for no reason of his own making, everything he wanted?

I said, "Do you ever think about beggars?"

"Which beggars?"

"The guys on the corner, in the subway. Do you ever think about them?"

"Just to the extent that once in a while I'm scared I might wind up like that. Why?"

"I think they're proof of the possibility of ecstasy."

"I think they're proof that the government's not doing all it could."

"No. The government can't help them. They're a spiritual proposal, not a political one."

"You've been out of the city too long."

"I know I sound like an idiot, but listen a minute: you stand on the corner with your hand out and every once in a while somebody comes by and puts money in it, somebody you don't know or have never seen before." Christ, I thought, you sound like R.B. "You get a gift—grace, something free that you couldn't make for yourself. That's ecstasy, right? I mean, it's out there, it's happening all the time."

"What are you suggesting—prayer?"

"I don't know, does it sound like it?"

"It sounds like something ecclesiastical."

"R.B. keeps talking about grace. He asked me once if I had ever thought that maybe the world was a place designed to get us into a position where there was nothing left for us to do—nothing we *could* do, he meant—so that we can learn that our only hope is grace."

"I hope you threw some cold water on him."

"Have you ever considered anything like that?"

"No."

There was the small, starchy crack of night bugs banging against the screens. Breeze bellied the curtains, like bodies falling into the room. A night bird called, a single high-flown note that trailed off in a series of diminishing eighths.

"Well," I said, "I've got this script here, treatment actually, story actually. But it's a virgin pining for a suitor."

"I'm looking for a man in need."

The small mortal clutch gripped inside again. "This is pretty important, Van. It's going to be a good movie."

"I know, brother."

I didn't want to ask him, I didn't want to beg him not to take the Metro job. He knew I didn't. He sighed. "A good picture that needs money."

"Maybe I can find something."

"I'll call David in California and see if he has any ideas."

"Okay."

I was silent for a moment. Outside the world carried on, heavy with the freights of summer. "Are you still with me?"

"I'm always with you, kiddo."

You fall in and sink, you scrabble for purchase, clawing at the rocks, you think your chest will burst, it's dark, the rocks are slippery, *you are under water,* you don't know how you got there, you don't know what to do, it hurts and there is no method or light, you thrash, you cry out, there is nothing; you swim.

"Don't worry, Buddy."

"Okay."

"Good night, pal."

"Good night."

Good night good night good night.

7. She said, "I lie there in my bed and listen to you talk to Celest on the phone."

It was early on the beach, the water blue-gray like the back of a seal, the pines behind shaggy and still dark with the remnants of night. The sand was littered with writhed driftwood, dotted with burned stumps, the hoofprints of cattle. There was a boardwalk from the house, but we had walked down on the grass; you could see the thin lines of our tracks in the dew. A few yellow flares of sunlight rose tentatively in the east.

"Our marriage has been a long circular discussion."

"I like tangents."

She wore the same black bathing suit. Her hair was pinned up under an old green shower cap.

"Which ones?"

"The ones that are sexy."

"You listen to us make love on the phone?"

"Yes."

It didn't make me angry.

"You enjoy it?"

"I do. It's so human . . . and sad."

"It's what we've come to. It's all we do now, in that department. The sex, you know, the sting of it, I like; it's thrilling, all imagination and wickedness, all the stops out. We say crazy things. But when we're together there're too many layers between us. We can hardly speak."

"It's like that, isn't it?"

"For us."

She gave me a long look, waded a few steps into the surf—which was no surf at all actually, only yellow-green lakelike waves rustling over the smooth, hard sand—and squatted so that her ass was in the water. She sank her arms, leaned forward, and dipped her face in. I had waked out of a hurtling dream, one in which my body rode in some unknowable vehicle at great speed, rushing and swerving through cityscape and woods. Faces fled past, the gray edges of buildings, a large fountain, an enfilading line of sycamores that I recognized as a section of path that curved by the lake in Central Park. It had all gone so fast that I wasn't able to be frightened, but then my arm caught, on a stair post or on a branch, and I felt a sudden shock of pain that woke me. The blow in the dream was physical, but in the early light seeping through the muslin curtains, it was emotional, all inside. My life was a waste, dumb, ridiculous, and at an end. The pain inside me said this. By end it meant more of the sad same, all downhill from here. *Celest,* I said, *oh damn, Celest,* but in the wan light speech seemed silly and so I got up, pulled on my clothes, went out, knocked on Bess's door, and asked her if she wanted to come for a swim. Downstairs I could hear the servants stirring in the kitchen.

"Sometimes," she said now, water running off her face, "it's hard to think about the next phase."

The water on her sunburn made her skin look slightly boiled.

"The truth is things overlap. It's pretty rare that everything comes to an end at the same time."

"But sometimes that's the way it is."

"I want you to give me some money for this movie."

It was the first time I'd said anything about it. For a week we had talked of other things. I wandered the house, sat out on the beach, followed her as she made her rounds of the nursery, put my feet up on the railing of the second-story porch, and talked to R.B.

"You know I won't do that."

"No, I don't know it."

"You should. Nobody's more careful with money than me."

"Then why don't you carefully invest in my movie. The way you got most of your money was by being the one married to me when I made it, off a movie."

"Yes, as the original investor. It's my money now. And besides I've tripled and quadrupled what you gave me."

"All the more reason for you to invest in me now."

"No, Buddy, it wouldn't work. We'd be tied together in a way that would hurt us. You'd come to hate me. And I would come to despise you. We tried it before."

"What makes you think I won't come to hate you now?"

"Because when you think about it you'll see I'm right. You'll see how good this is for you."

"But, Bess, I'm going under. I can't get anybody to finance the picture."

"Then you'll just have to face what's next."

"Jesus, girl."

She slid over onto her belly and swam a few choppy strokes. The water beyond the surf line was smooth, oily in the low swells. It looked worn out to me, like used-up water. The grass islands poked out like the sprouted heads of submerged giants. I dived at her feet, went under and caught her ankle.

"*Woof,*" she said coming up and skeeting a handful of water at me. "I thought you were a shark."

"I thought you *knew* I was."

"Don't start feeling sorry for yourself. You're much more attractive when you're bold and enthusiastic."

"Would you let me show you some of the screenplay?"

"I don't think so."

"Bess."

"It might upset me."

"You'd like it and then that would make you feel bad about turning me down."

"It *would* make me feel bad. I'm not a callous woman."

"You are a hard one though."

A hurt look swam into her gray eyes. She had always been easy to hurt. "I'm not a hard woman either," she said with a simple humility that touched me. I rubbed her shoulders with my knuckles. "Steady?" She laughed. "Okay, steady."

I thought I would wait and try again. Bess could hold a position, but I—as she knew—would keep coming at her.

"Isn't this drought something?" she said.

"It doesn't look too bad around here."

"That's because we run the water all the time. It's bad though. The squirrels are eating the figs and the pears. I've never seen that before."

"I've never even heard of it. I thought they favored nuts."

"They do, but this year it's so dry I think they look for moisture in the fruit."

"There're cattle on the beach."

"They come down at night."

"They probably like to come down here and look out over the ocean and imagine what a wonderful world it would be if you could drink salt water."

She laughed. "You never were much of a farmer, were you?"

"I'm a pretty good moviemaker though."

She gave me a wise look, smiling the same benevolent, understanding, possessive smile she had offered me through the years of our marriage. There was something so obvious, and vulnerable, and carnal about it—like the child who says that piece of pie looks lonely when she means she wants to eat it, and she knows and everyone knows what she means.

Above our heads, in the gray light, a scattering of purple martins—set free by the dawn from the gourd houses on the lawn—chased mosquitoes, diving and sliding. They seemed to be diving at the sea.

8. All the windows were flung wide—as was always the case in Bess's house—it was after midnight, the best time to work. The pages were loosed from my briefcase, spread around me on the old deal table I had dragged in from the hall, littering the floor. In the dark, when I got up to take a leak I stepped on them, a sensation I liked for what I took as its hominess. The breeze rubbed its face against the curtains, the old house creaked. There was the tap of footsteps in the hall, then silence as they met the rug, then tap again: R.B. moving about, looking for a safe place. As was Banty Jakes, come now this afternoon to the village of Ernestina, Florida, to find the woman he loved. I was moving backward in the story again, returning to the first meeting of Banty and Molly after the detective Tubby Wells had found her. Wandering away from lunch with Tubby, Banty walks about the town, half looking for her, but mostly wandering the sand streets looking at the shabby fisher houses, thinking about the lives led in them. He comes, at the dead end of a narrow street, to an abandoned house and climbs the porch to look inside. As he peers into the rooms that are vivid and disheartening in their emptiness and decay, he hears her voice, Molly's voice, speaking to him. It is her real voice, speaking in real time, but it is ghostly, pealing out disembodied from among the empty rooms or from the shadows under the live oaks. She speaks to him of the first time they made love together, when they were teenagers, on the beach behind her father's house. She tells the story vividly, filling it with incident and emotion, but it is not the story he remembers. He begins to object, to correct her, but she rolls over his words, turning them, laughing as she accuses him of taking advantage of her. He knows she is lying, but as he listens he begins to believe her, and the story, which is violent and damning, begins to become the story he remembers. She excites him, driving him through the tale until he is nearly breathless. He wants her, he wants to touch her, wants to sink to the ground in her arms—as he hasn't for years—and lose himself in her, wants to slide into her body and become her.

But as the tale ends, it is still afternoon in a village on the Panhandle, the wind lifts the strands of gray moss hanging in the trees.

Far down the street, beyond the state road, Banty sees a small crowd gathered. Men and women dressed in church clothes stand in groups talking. "What are they doing?" he asks her.

"Let's go see."

"Wait a second."

"Come on."

She starts up the street, swinging her hips; he hesitates and then begins to follow, a few steps behind. The houses they pass are small, screened in front, painted white or soft shades of green or yellow. Yuccas flower in sunlit spaces, live oaks streaked with moss hang over dark, grassless patches; here and there mallows bloom redly. The morning sun has lifted the smell of brine and the ruggish odor of the river flats into the air. The sand is fine and slippery under his feet; he would like to take his shoes off. A set of raccoon prints trails across the street and disappears into some cherry laurel bushes off to the left. He notices again that Molly is barefoot.

"Wait," he says, raising his voice slightly. "Let's see what's going on."

She stops at the high road and looks back at him. "Come on," she says, "don't lollygag."

He says, "I thought we would go somewhere and talk."

"We are somewhere. This is a place. Look at those cedars. Look at the way the highway ends down there: not many roads you know of, I'll bet, that you can come to the verifiable end of. Nothing beyond Florida Highway 72 but pelicans and high water. You've been talking to me."

"You've, as usual, been talking to *me*."

"That's what you miss."

She weaves in her tracks, bends low like someone looking under a wash line, and peers at the assembled. They are two houses away, standing in the yard and out in the street in front of a small yellow

cottage. There are skiffs laid across sawhorses in the yard; one of them
is half covered with a new coat of navy-blue paint. Across the keel of
the other someone has slung a nylon mullet net.

"What do you suppose it is?" she says.

"Camp meeting."

She makes a face. "They don't have those in town."

"Reunion."

"Maybe. But everybody's too finely rigged for a reunion."

"Why don't you go ask them—no, I didn't mean that. Let's just stay
here."

She grins at him. "Bold and fearless as always, I see."

He is standing next to her. Her elbow brushes his. She smells of
sunburn and lemons and sweat. "This is difficult," he says. "I always
figured I'd have to come get you from somewhere, but I still wasn't
prepared."

"You've been dreaming of it all your life. I'll bet you've got a
thousand scenarios."

"Not *one* like this."

She purses her lips, looking at him in a way that is common between
them: sharply assessing, on the verge of laughter. The gesture makes her
nose, which is broken and slightly knobbed across the bridge, stand out
more sharply. "I want to follow some footsteps," she says.

"Whose?"

"The ones that lead to that house."

They walk up the road toward the cottage.

There are mostly men in the yard; a few stand near a kumquat bush
drinking from a pint bottle they pass among themselves. Others carve
slices of orange cheese off a quarter hoop on a folding table at one end
of the porch. "It's a funeral," he says, lowering his head as they come
up the walk.

"You're quick," she answers, smiling at him.

She takes his hand and leads him through the front door into a
parlor where men and women sit on straight chairs and on a brocade
sofa pushed against the wall under a large hanging bucket containing
a massive asparagus fern. There are candles on the walls, pitchers of
iced tea and cakes and a melting pile of brownies on the bench of an

ebony upright piano. A coatless man with a green tie pulled askew
approaches them and tells them he is glad they could come. The man's
long face is pulled into austerity by what Bantling assumes is grief.
He is nervous, as always, among strangers; he wants to retreat, but he
is caught—you can see in his face that he is caught—in fascination.
He moves behind Molly along the edge of the room, half bowing at
the settled mourners who, he overhears, are members of the Cantrell
family, mourning a son (cousin, nephew, playmate) who drowned the
day before. A large man in a pressed khaki suit, who as he talks turns
his hands like puffed biscuits on his knees, says to a thin woman in a
shiny blue dress sitting next to him, "I remember how one spring all
that boy did was carry a box kite around with him everywhere he
went. He told everybody he was going to use it to fly away from
here." From behind a closed door off the parlor comes the sound of
a woman weeping. It is muffled and distant, like noise from a turned-
down radio.

"We shouldn't stay here," Bantling whispers to Molly, lifting himself to her ear. She raises her face and holds it high, as if she wants to
push it through something. "We're fine," she says. "Everybody's welcome at a funeral."

"I have more persuading to do."

"I don't want to be persuaded."

"I know, but you'll enjoy my trying."

"I enjoy the tricks you can make animals do. I enjoy your devotion
and how accurately you retell the stories of the books you read; that's
about it."

"Folks don't know how much they love somebody until that somebody's gone."

"So country music tells us."

"Not music; I just made it up."

"Everybody makes that up—once or twice in their lives. Even if it's
true you won't die from it."

As they talk they move—she leads him—toward an open door on
the far side of the room. Above the door hangs a small painting of the
Sacred Heart. Ruby drops of painted blood drip from the heart that is
red as a valentine and bandoliered with thorns. She ducks her head as

she goes through the door, though the lintel is not low; he wonders if it is in avoidance of the painting.

They enter a small bedroom. A large double bed takes up most of the space. There are half a dozen people in the room, mostly women. A bouquet of white lilies droop from a green vase on a Parsons table that has been pushed against a tall upright dresser from which the blue paint has mostly faded. He can see the grain of the oak wood, stark as veinal cordage, where the dresser has been partially sanded. In front of the dresser, beside the table which has the same proximity to her as a doctor's stand might, a woman with loose, thick blond hair that falls in a stiff mass against her cheek leans over the bed. Beside her, the table between them, a man in a dark suit hovers, his left hand splayed open on the table, the fingers arched like a pianist's bridge. The bed is stripped to sheets. The sheets are washed to a soft and brittle white. They are so thin he can see the striped blue mattress underneath. On top of them, his head propped on a soft white pillow, lies the body of a teenage boy dressed in a white Sunday shirt and black trousers. The trousers are loosely cinched by a narrow brown belt with a small rhinestone buckle shaped like the head of a snake. The snake has ruby eyes and a green jaw. It is the sort of belt children wear with cowboy suits. The boy's face is pale and has the rinsed, scrubbed look of a child's fresh from rain or a bath. The features have the look of carvings. The rims of the ears are purple and there are streaks and shadings of gray and purple under the jaw and flaring in the neck, which is so dark where it presses against the pillow that it looks as if you might lift him to find a smear of his blood underneath. In his ears and nose are stuffed wads of white cotton. His smooth, featureless hands are laid on top of each other on his stomach.

Only the attendants move about, the woman bending to press a blue washcloth against the dead boy's ear. The thin man leaning on his fingers—the human activity around the stillness of the body—makes the scene eerie to Banty.

Through a half-curtained window beyond the attendants he can see a withered garden in the side yard. Lank brown tomato vines writhe among torn yellow stalks of corn. Beside the garden a wooden coffin lies across two chairs. It is only a box, hammered together out of yellow pinewood, like a fish box, except longer. The blue sky above the oaks is speckled with small white clouds.

No one asks why they are there. The women talk briskly of cooking and of their children. He looks at Molly. She is staring at the man on the other side of the bed. Her lips move; she speaks silently to him. The man straightens up, brushes his fingers that are long and knobbed like roots against the front of his suit jacket. Bantling nudges her with his elbow. The face she turns to him is delighted; her eyes sparkle. He looks again at the man and sees that he has begun to lean over the narrow bed toward Molly. She places her hand on the side of the bed and leans toward him. The body moves slightly with her movement; the blond woman draws back and looks at her; she places her hand lightly on the man's wrist, to caution or prevent him, but he doesn't seem to notice; he leans, thinly and gracefully, toward Molly, whose face lifts toward his.

The moment before their faces touch, stretching toward each other as two parents' might meet each other above the body of their sleeping child, something seems to distract Molly. Her hand lifts brokenly to her hair as if to fix a strand of it, her face collapses, and she begins to turn toward Banty; he sees dumb bafflement appear in her eyes. Slowly, as if in lazy fatigue, she begins to turn in a circle, crouching slightly, or falling, as a dog would turn to make its bed, and then she pitches suddenly to the side, toward him, so abruptly that he can't catch her, and falls to the floor. Sprawled on her back she shakes and flaps on the floor like a caught fish, her hands and feet curling like rigid claws. As the hiss and grunt of her wrenched breath begin to fill the room a commotion starts—all draw back—Bantling sees one man slip quickly out the parlor door—and a woman cries out, and another woman begins to weep. As Bantling drops to his knees beside her he sees out of the corner of his eye the man in the dark suit vault onto the bed and leap off it, nearly knocking him over as he lands beside them. He sees—and he doesn't think anybody else does—the man step on the ankles of the dead boy; he sees the chalky outline of the man's shoe on the bottoms of the boy's black trousers. He looks at this, and he looks at the way the body surges briefly from the man's passing—the clasped hands shifting minutely as if a last jolt of life rushed through—and at the way the blond woman reaches quickly to place her hand on the dead boy's shoulder to steady him, and for a moment he doesn't notice the man kneeling beside him to cup Molly's head between his hands. Then he comes alive with urgency—he has been through this times before—and as the man holds her head, bending it back slightly, shoving the flat of his hand between her jaws, he pins her arms, or at least holds them, and calls out for someone to hold her feet—"Loosely, please, so she can move"—and the two of them, and then a third—a large black woman in a black dress—ride her under them as she thrashes and moans. Her lips are drawn back fiercely from her teeth, her face gleams with sweat, her eyes under half-open lids have turned up into her head, her neck is bridged so that he can see the knot of her Adam's apple and the muscles that stand out like cables. He feels new strength, marveling, and shoves his hand sideways into hers; the sharp grip, spasmodic and merciless, almost makes him cry out. He has an erection. He bends down and whispers to her now, saying any soothing word he can think of. He has no idea if she hears him. As he speaks—"Yes, darling, you're doing fine. You're lovely, so good"—the thrashing slows, the body's panic and surging begin to subside. He sees the dark seepage on the rug where she has pissed herself. All the while the man holds her head, staring at her. He is not frightened, there is no hesitation in him. His black hair falls over his forehead that is high and white and as smooth as polished stone. Then he lifts his head, as a rower might from the oars, taking a breath, a single assessing glance, and Bantling sees his eyes that are sunk deep behind thick Cossack cheekbones; the eyes are blue, but so dark they seem almost black, and they are merry.

Around them the mourners watch in dismay. He has never seen anyone at ease amidst this kind of violence. Even doctors sweated, their faces contorting in imitation of hers as they sustained themselves with activity and instructions while she thrashed under them. There is no part of her that is not owned and battered by the spell. What contorts her face—the expressions of horror and bestiality that rush across it—is never seen in daily life. Nobody could make themselves look like that. The running figurations are pictures from the darkness, facsimiles from a world nobody in his right mind would want to know about. Here only the boy on the bed is unaffected, riding easily on the waves of commotion like driftwood—the boy, and this man, whose hand bleeds where she has bitten it before he could strike it deeply enough into her mouth to paralyze her. The blood leaks down her cheek; bright drops of it shine on the waxed pine floor and on the man's wrists that are smooth and polished like the wrists of a girl. He looks at Bantling and he grins, showing large, even, perfectly white teeth, like the teeth of a movie star. It is as if they are riding a wonderful roller coaster, some invigorating romp that they are both doing awfully well at.

Then he feels her give way, feels the spell relax its grip as she begins to drop away—he always thinks of her as falling—and the moans become not the cries of the damned, but the moans of a hurt child, whimpers from troubled sleep. To the blond woman on the other side of the bed Bantling says, "Go get a rag and soak it in cold water." To the others, to those peering now through the parlor doorway, he says, "It's all right. It's just a spell; she's coming out of it, it's nothing serious."

The woman returns with the rag and he presses it to her forehead. The man pulls his hand from her mouth and touches her lips with the tips of his fingers. "Thank you," he says and takes the rag from Bantling. Angry, Bantling sits back on his heels, about to say something. The man touches his hand—the touch is cold—and again thanks him. "I can see you've helped her before," he says. "I can tell I would have a lot to learn from you."

For a moment Bantling is confused, then he realizes this must be D'Nel Boyd, the bad one she has run off with. But what is he doing here? Bantling begins to straighten her clothes: her skirt that has pulled up around her thighs; gently he tucks her white shirt back into the waistband. It is like an emergency in a bus station: you do what you have to do no matter the strange faces. Which, he thinks, produces a special intimacy that maybe only kings or movie stars—or the crazed— know, this intense living in full view of others. Or the bereaved. They know it. Who shuffle about now, who cough out loud, whose hands stray to touch their clothes, their attention shifting between the corpse of a boy and the slender woman sprawled on the floor.

Bantling rises with her hand in his—which has gone limp now as she passes into the sleep that always comes after—and between his fingers he softly presses her cold fingers straight, smoothing the back of her hand, rubbing his thumb across her knuckles. She is as helpless as a child—unwakeable like a child—and he knows well the part in himself that loves this, this moment of her defenselessness that she protects herself from through every waking second. Her hair lies swirled around her head like the hair of someone drowning.

Out the window two men lift the coffin from the chairs, another holds the lid under his arm the way one would hold a plank. The wind whips in the tops of the pines at the edge of the yard; he hears the four ascending notes of a redbird's call, the cry of gulls.

The man—Boyd, that is who he is—slips his arms under her shoulders and waist and lifts her lightly. Bantling steps unwillingly back, wanting to protest, wanting to snatch her from him. "She needs to sleep now," he says. "When she wakes up she won't know . . ."

"I know," the man says, "and sometimes she's wild as an animal. I ought to get her a helmet so she doesn't bust her head."

For a second Bantling holds on to her hand; for just a moment, that hardly exists, there is a tug-of-war between them—that he sees, to his dismay, the man will win: he wouldn't give up—and Bantling sees how easily one could pass on to the next configuration, moving from the place you have finally learned to be comfortable in to another where the rules have changed and more will be required of you than you have in you, and how this is not always under the prod of high drama but can come in a moment when you are really intent on something else, and not thinking of change—he is not willing to make a scene here— and he lets her hand go, watches fascinated as it seems to slip in slow motion from between his fingers, still feeling the ridged and callused palm, his fingernail almost catching, in his mind, on the fortune lines, the descendant frayed lifeline that twirls at the bottom of her hand like an unstrung broom, the stunted heart line, the head line deep as a cut, the star.

He looks at the man whose face lifts as he looks back at him; the same cold merriment is in the eyes—ultramarine, that is the color—and a slight, fanciful smile plays about the corners of his thin mouth. "Follow me out," the man says, shifting Molly's weight, stepping back and turning to go through the door.

Bantling starts after him, but the man turns back. His eyes play over the mourners, settle on the blond woman who holds the washcloth against her chest. "All my condolences and sorrow are yours," he says. "The boy is with one who will look after him now." He pauses and looks at Bantling. All the risiveness has slipped from his eyes. They are two blue stones. "As I will look after this one," he says.

Bantling bows at the woman, at the others, aware as always, in some part of himself, of his small size, of his thin piping voice that in moments of stress, even at thirty, becomes the strangled, skinny voice of a child. "He's very beautiful," he says, nodding at the dead boy, and follows D'Nel Boyd through the parlor and out of the house where he stands aside to let the men carrying the coffin bring it up the front steps. The open box is unlined; someone has strewn a handful of pink rose petals in the bottom. The men nod at the onlookers as they carry the coffin by them. They carry it delicately, as if it were a fine piece of furniture. Boyd is ahead of him, making his way slowly but without hesitation down the front walk that is lined with a few late-flowering Spanish dagger plants and a couple of rosebushes that look like wind and hail have nearly taken them. Wind skitters in the cabbage palms and in the oaks, and as Boyd passes under the outflung bough of a large, dying live oak, a scarf of moss blows loose and falls across Molly's breast. Bantling skips up behind him and scoops the moss off, throws it away as if it is nasty. As he does so he sees Tubby Wells standing across the sand road under a mimosa watching him. He has half a coconut in his hand from which he scoops with his pocketknife slivers of the meat and nibbles them into his mouth. "He eats like some insect would," Bantling says under his breath, "some mantis or beetle, or maybe a horse chewing up a carrot." With the knife blade Wells motions to Bantling, calling him over. Bantling waves but continues to walk beside D'Nel Boyd, whose hand caresses Molly's cheek with an insistent intimacy that infuriates him. He shakes his head no.

Wells calls his name, in the tones of one who has unexpectedly come on a friend. Boyd looks at him. "Is that man calling you?"

"Yes, but never mind."

"Somebody you don't want to run into?"

"Not right now."

Wells steps into the road, folding his knife against his pants leg. "Let me speak to you a minute," he says. He nods coldly at Boyd.

"I'm busy right now," Bantling answers. He doesn't want to be interrupted. Something small and wheedling in him says take it slow, but he doesn't want to listen. He hears the cry of a jay and then the cry of a mockingbird that is harsh and peremptory, some other bird trying to stop a robbery.

Wells stops in front of him, barring his way slightly. "You want some coconut?"

"No, thanks."

Boyd has walked on a couple of steps. Now he stops and looks back at Bantling. "I'll put her in the truck up here and wait on you," he says, as if everything between them has been settled.

Wells takes Bantling's arm, his thin yellow fingers closing gently around his sleeve. He inclines his head toward him. His hair is thick with pomade. "You don't want to do it like this," he says.

"I thought you told me to come up with something."

"This is too risky for you."

"Molly had one of her spells. Epilepsy. I'm just going to make sure she's all right."

"Did you talk to her?"

"I did but it wasn't long enough."

"Long enough I'll bet for her to tell you to mind your own business."

Wells shakes himself suddenly; he seems to quiver in his clothes, so that Bantling thinks of him blurring, like a figure in the rain—though he doesn't blur—and he steps back, away from the touch on his arm that has grown more insistent. "I don't have to stay here," Wells says. "I've done already what you paid me to do."

"Then why are you hanging around?"

"Because it's a fascinating case." With his little finger he picks out a gob of coconut from the space between his large front teeth. "You are totally helpless against a character such as D'Nel Boyd. You are like a piece of flit he will brush from his coat sleeve. What amazes me is that you have no idea what his sort of meanness is like."

"I have an idea."

"You have a dream. That's all."

"It's necessary. I can't do without it." He meant to say her, but he stops himself.

"It's the woman. She's beautiful. I get it. But you are a fool." Wells shakes his head, laughing silently to himself. A soft whining sound escapes his lips. "You have no idea yet how alone everybody in this world is. Or maybe you have an idea, but you can't believe it. D'Nel Boyd knows that the way you know how to take a shit. He's teaching it to your play-pretty girl over there. From what I can tell, she's glad to know it."

"I don't care what you say."

"But you do care. You care what I say and what everybody else says. You can't help yourself. You pay attention to everything. That's why you stay to yourself so much. So you won't *have* to listen."

"I don't know what you are talking about."

Wells spits a milky gob on the ground. His head bobs on his stringy neck. Yellowed leaves from a chinaberry in the yard litter the sand. They look like doubloons. Bantling is thinking of the maple leaves on the water at home, and the dolphins bursting through them, red wet leaves clinging to their backs. Inside the house they were loading the boy into his coffin. The blond woman must have been his mother. Her face was pale and drawn with grief. Drowned, someone had said, the boy drowned. She had pressed the cloth so very gently to his ear from which seawater dripped.

Wells touches his arm again. "I've made a study of these cases," he says. "There are certain common factors." He seems to chew the words out of his mouth.

"This is a special situation," Bantling answers.

"Each one is, but each one has certain characteristics like all the others." He runs his free hand down his long face, squeezing the cheeks so his mouth purses. "People become what they get up next to. That's not the problem. The problem is why they choose to rub up against what they choose to rub up against. That's what you got to look at. It's how you can find them if they're lost, and it's how you know whether you want to go looking for them or not."

"You looked for her."

"It's how I make my living. I'll look for anything if the money is good. But that doesn't mean I'll recommend the grieving party follow up the sighting. Sometimes it's just better to push on."

Bantling sighs. He looks up into the oak above their heads. The ferns that grow like a hairy mat on the branch sough in the breeze. "You're getting me confused," he says. "I thought you were helping me with this."

"I am."

Molly had once claimed that everyone had a sickness of the mind, some obsession. Find out what it is, she told him, and you know when they're telling you the truth. And you know how to get around them when you need to. Sometimes he would seem to wake from a dream, stumble out of a blackout as he walked down the street, and notice suddenly a young woman whose hair had gone wholly gray, and a boy in a red shirt crying on his mother's shoulder, and a man brushing a bee off his sleeve—he would notice these people, and life would seem for a moment a brilliant conjuring feat and a mystery, and he would picture the gray-headed woman sitting on the side of the bed at one in the morning, and the young mother getting up in the dawn light to comfort her child, and the man out in the backyard watering the azaleas with a hose as he thought of another life he could have had somewhere else that would have been better than this one; and in these moments, which seemed to come out of nowhere—they were like Molly's spells, his version of a spell—he seemed so close to the heart of life, to some kind of identification, or merging with it, that all necessity for thought and reason, for understanding, vanished, and he was completely comforted.

"I'm afraid," he says, "that I'm going to wind up ashamed. I'm afraid that's what's going to happen—that I'm going to shame myself." But he is speaking to something Wells hasn't said. He smiles, he feels a tenderness toward the tall, bony man who watches over his shoulder as what will come next approaches. "We've spent a week down here living in that houseboat behind the hotel. I hadn't done anything but wander around and mope. This is a little village. Nothing goes on here but fishing and complaining. You got business to tend to. I know I paid you for another week, but if you need to go it's all right with me. You told me you'd find Molly and you did. I'll take it from here."

Wells nods his head as Banty speaks, as if he agrees with everything he says. His hazel eyes darken. "Life's not in how the likenesses fit," he says, "it's in how the contradictions do. You ever had pepper ice cream?"

"No, sir."

Wells holds up the coconut. He looks at the husky shell. "Hairy as a pig's back. Inside soft white meat, pretty as Rachel's bosom. Curious, ain't it?"

"Only a little."

"You're right—only a little bit. The truth is, nearlybout everything's that way. We act surprised when we find out ferocious lions are gentle with their young, or oysters taste good, but we're not. Or if we are, it's the kind of surprise we expect and welcome. It's just the kind of thing we like. That's what's curious." With his fingernail he scrapes out a sliver of coconut meat and puts it into his mouth. "Now what's curious about Mr. D'Nel Boyd is not how he's so different from what he seems. He was gentle with you, wasn't he?"

"I guess."

"He's like that. But what's curious is not that under his courtliness he's a killer—any killer with enough brains and lack of conscience can be courteous—what's curious is that he doesn't care about hiding anything. And he doesn't, really. He's always acting like he wants to kill you, and he always does. A cat isn't being kind to the mouse it plays with. It's exciting itself. If you look it's obvious. Life ain't no parlor show, my friend. It's no trick. You might think there's magic there but there ain't a bit of magic in this world." Banty is silent. The world moves in slow motion.

He waves his hand, lightly, dismissive but without rancor, at the older man, who chews on the meat of coconut, his thin nimble fingers touching his cheeks, and turns to look down the street at D'Nel Boyd, who is covering Molly with an Indian blanket in the back of his pickup truck. Above them the massed leaves of an aging pecan tree shift in the sunlight, throwing down their own version of cover, dark to light and back again, coins and streaks appearing and disappearing on them. The area around the truck is sprinkled, salted with shifting particles of light, brighter it seems than the rest of the day, than the tunneled-out road gray-white under oaks, than the sandy yards pocked with sandspurs and the knobby prickly pear, than the worn facade of the yellow hotel rising in its three tiers like an old paddle wheeler beached on the marshy shore, than the Gulf itself, roughed and frayed by slim breeze, blue and blue-green, dully sparkling. Then, as if he senses his eyes, Boyd turns and looks at him. The light falls gracefully in a slender band across his face, shading and brightening it, gleaming on one cheek like polish, darkening an eye. It is the sun, the sprinkled light and shadow, that makes his face, for one moment, look like the shattered, smirking face of a devil.

9.

It was two-thirty in the morning when I put the pen down and got up lame, rigid with rage, my mind filling and emptying, filling with pictures of a burning girl, of sorrow, of a man raising the bloody stumps of his hands, of the fires that wouldn't go out. I heard the usual voices speaking in the night, I heard them amid the wonderful civilized smells of tea olive and cedar berries and resiny citrus, above the smell of fresh earth, heard them shouting down the tunnel, calling out warnings. I couldn't make out words. It was always the same: the voices started—*in medias res*—and I couldn't understand what they were shouting though I could understand the tone—danger: run—and always, behind the voices, like a warm flood banked, was something else, a balm, a promise, a peaceful place like a shelter under old trees after rain. My mind fled to Bar Etienne, to my grandmother's house, to the river curving out of Illinois, to the long frothy banks of willows, to the grassy fields above the town where the shale poked through the earth like the leaves of giant stone books left out in the weather; and I could picture—I didn't know it was a picture—I could picture my father walking along under the streetlights of his hometown, I could picture him as he stopped at the corner and stood there on a summer's night baffled and outraged by his missing life, and I saw him bend down to pluck a rose off a trellis and bring it to his nose and smell deeply of it, and saw him raise his head and stare into the blank darkness of night beyond the rosebush—standing there, my father, lost in the world, without a clue—and then I saw the tears begin and saw them slip down his cheeks and fall, saw him standing in the dark of the town he was born in, crying. . . .

I got up and went out onto the porch. The pale salts of the Milky Way were scattered toward the south; the gnawed moon descended beyond the line of woods in the west, pushing a faint yellowed light toward the tops of the tall pines. Out to sea the red and white lights of shrimp boats were small explosions on the black of the sea, small articulations and promises, and it didn't seem craziness to picture the other one out there, not my father now but this X, this D'Nel, this bombardier and impresario, this one, this tallish, slender man who walked up a driveway in the Dakotas to speak a few smooth and helpful words to a movie director. *My mind is your mind,* he had said, *we're together on this.*

And I thought, *Together on what? What could you possibly do for me?* And I thought, You are not real, or if you are real you are only a man in a charcoal suit walking up a driveway in the Dakotas on a frosty morning in September; you are only a particle of my imagination that I may or may not use, that I have no use for this moment at all since I am in the middle of one more goddamn movie, one more last-ditch effort to save my life of moviemaking. How could you know how terrified I am, how confused I have become, how I am willing to repeat the old successes, to sell myself down any and every river just to keep going? How could you know what I would do to save my own life? But he only laughed, this figment or apparition, this actual human leaning against the station wagon fiddling with the antenna, there under the last hickories in North America, there on the edge of the wheat fields that ran almost forever into Canada where soon we would rig the stuntmen in harnesses that would make it possible for them to fall off a silo and live, where a young actress, her face smeared with blood, would slip into an empty room in an old house and begin to play at a scarred upright piano the opening passages of "Jesu, Joy of Man's Desiring." *Together on what?* I said.

And then I am no longer in the Dakotas, I am out walking, alone,

late at night on a street near the Manhattan Bridge. The street is empty
except for a couple sitting on a stoop down the way. The man is singing
softly to his beloved, a small Caribbean song of love and fidelity; her
head leans against his shoulder. I nod as I pass them, looking away for
an instant upward toward the soft spittle strings of light hanging above
the bridge, and then I look back, smiling, to see the blue fiery glow of
hatred in the man's eyes, which are staring at me, straight at me from
the darkness; and in my chest, down toward the lockers of my bones,
I feel my helplessness, my feeble, hopeless humanness—and I begin to
turn toward them, as if I might in some way explain this to the fiery
eyes, at least to the woman who is small and nearly shapeless in the
apartment house shadow. I want to tell her that finally I am ashamed
of myself, that finally I am sorry for the way I have lived, as we all
must be someday; I want to tell her that her partner, this dark one with
the burning blue eyes, is not the one she supposes him to be, that he
is another entirely and doesn't love her, only uses her for a momentary
sordid purpose, but as my mouth opens, as my mouth opens and I begin
to speak, I hear a voice cursing, a voice making claims and speaking of
love, and it is my voice, and the woman is in my arms and these are
my teeth biting her throat.

I slicked dew off the railing and washed my face; down the way,
where the porch crooked out in a short ell from the body of the house,
the light in Bess's window was still on. I took a step toward the light
and stopped, thinking how the world was a place where you could make
up anything you wanted, and give your whole life to selling yourself
on it, and lean your shoulder against the world to make it believe too,
and how sometimes you, and the world too, gave in, or seemed to give
in, and believed. I had always loved the rank array of America. It was
a country made up of crackpots, where any moment the guy next to
you on the bus might begin to shout out, with total conviction, some
wholly arrant nonsense that his fellow passengers, despite themselves,
despite their sore feet and their wicked children, wrenched from the
clatter of their own madness, might at any moment begin to applaud.
I knew that my job wasn't to convince an audience that D'Nel Boyd
actually walked the earth, but that he, and the earth he walked, were
real: and I knew how you were supposed to go about doing this, knew

the avid detailing and cross-stitch of purpose and action, the thrust of sudden emotion, the midnight cry, the lost child waiting out the rain under a box elder tree; I knew how you could mask a camera so that it would find and reproduce a light so similar to the light of dreams that the field and patch of wind-wrinkled cove it spied upon would seem the place you had longed to come to all your life; and I knew how from the crystalline shadows reaching into the weary light you could draw forth the figure of a man, a darkness moving first amid a darkness and then into light, and how the shape of his body, the bend of his arms as they rise to sink a pole that will push his boat free of grass, could evoke a memory that was finer than any memory in any life actually lived, but which, for that fabulous and original moment, became a memory that was as deep as any other—this figment, this lie—and that would, maybe only for a second, sustain the weight of disorderly and sorrowing breath, of the life of the one who perceived it.

There was a striking in my chest, and a snapping figure of pure demand began to shape and unshape and shape itself—in a blink—inside me. A rage like madness surged in my body, a rage against all that prevented me, all that harried and taunted me. I pressed my body against the rail. From the lawn and from the flower beds came the shussing sound of the sprinklers. In the corner of my eye I caught movement in Bess's room—how could she tell me no?—and I headed down that way. The rage popped in me, crackling in the skin beneath my hair, sparking in the backs of my hands. Hardened conquistadorial rover of rage, it goaded me, it leapt like a monkey through my body, swinging from my nerves and veins. I shook myself as I walked, dashing it off me as if it were sweat. The porch floor squeaked under my feet; a night bird called lamely from the woods, pretending it was lost. There were lights on in two of the greenhouses.

I had thought to raise the screen and push inside to force her someway to give me money for my picture—I didn't think I might kill her, but then I didn't think I might not—but when I reached the window I stopped. She stood beside the bed—a large white corseted expanse—and though she wore only a faded green T-shirt she had the air of one who had just rushed in. Her buckeye hair was loosened and it hung down her back in corrugated waves, hiding her shoulders. As I watched she raised one foot to the bed—her back was three-quarters to me—reached down, and took something shiny from a small box. With her free hand she reached behind, pulled the hard cheek of her ass aside, and inserted the object, a suppository. For a moment I could see the crinkled burrow of her anus. From a pale blue tube on the bedside table she pressed a drop of gel onto her finger and smeared it into the opening, grunting, then sighing slightly, bending forward over her knee, the long gracilis muscle under her thigh tightening to a cord. Then she leaned over the knee, as a dancer might, and stretched her long, sun-roughed arms before her and opened her hands. The soft bole of her breast swelled against the top of her leg, she closed her eyes and hummed a slip of something, rested there. My rage subsided; I felt a tenderness like desire; I wanted to softly kiss the shiny smear of unguent, to feel on my lips the kinked slick hairs.

I must have made a noise because she started and snapped a look of surprise and fright at the window. "It's me, Bess," I quickly said.

"Doggone, Buddy, goddamn," she cried and leapt under the covers.

I stood where I was, silent.

In a minute she craned around the table lamp and looked at me. "Well?"

"Under the circumstances I don't want to come in without permission."

"So come in, you spy."

I raised the screen, stepped through, and sat down on the edge of the bed. She held the knobbed white spread to her throat.

"I wasn't spying. I was coming to throttle you."

"Well, that's nearly as bad."

The rage sputtered, spat, and faded. It was human presence—her presence—that deterred me.

From the table she took a tissue and wiped her fingers, pressing outward along the length of them, studiously cleaning herself. Her fingers were squared and bony, and long, and her palms were wide, as thick along the edges as coarse yellow biscuits.

"So, why are you getting divorced?" she said.

I'd scared her, so she had to snap at me.

"You've been through it with me; you ought to know why. Hasn't Celest told you?"

"She says you won't talk to her. She says when you come over you go into your room and lock the door." Though we had been married six years, I had never given up my garage off lower Broadway, and though we had been married six years, it was only at my place that we shared the same bedroom, Celest and me, happier and safer when we knew we could retreat to separate strongholds.

"I've drawn a blank."

"You've drawn a life, you mean, and you still won't get going with it."

"I get exercised pretty good."

"She told me you stopped making love to her. She told me you'd go six months—before you stopped entirely—without touching her."

She flounced the covers so they belled up from her body and slowly, like a collapsing tent, descended; I caught a glimpse of the patch of thick dark hair at her groin.

"That's true."

"What's the matter with you?"

"I was distracted."

From the woods an owl called, a sweet, mewling, wholly undefended cry; as if the owl were claiming that the forest was a bad place but even so you could let yourself go in it, weep publicly and fully, as if it had come to that. For a second I thought of the shadows gathered under the pine trees, the darkness of the deep woods, a desire—someone's desire—to turn away from the world and go walking in. I had come on Celest in the maid's kitchen, as she leaned in the half dark over the wiped white counter while Jamie Sellars, an actor who at that time was playing at a theater in the Village the gay brother of a woman dying from AIDS—a careful and poised fellow capable of sudden outbursts of emotion—rummaged one-handed deeply in her ass. Seeing this I had stopped—I had only been looking for a piece of cloth bought years ago on a beach in Africa—stunned and fascinated. There was something so fastidious, so clinical, about it that I thought for a second to ask him what the problem was. They didn't notice me. Celest gazed as one gazing out a window at the closed cabinets before her; she could have been daydreaming. But then she moaned, and her head dropped, and on her full bottom lip gathered a small bulb of liquid that gleamed in the hall light. The bulb hung on her lip, gathered, slowly separated itself, and fell, trailing a string of silver to the countertop. I wanted to rush in and lick it off the tile. For a moment I wanted to rush in and kneel there and beg them to smear the juices from their bodies over my face. But I didn't do that. With my breath trapped in the soldered coffin of my lungs I retreated, carrying before me into the bright rooms my scrap of alien cloth wrapped around my hand like a bandage.

Bess balled the tissue between her fingers, lifted it, her hand falling back onto her wrist, and snapped it into a wastebasket at the foot of the bed.

"Good shot."

"So what's up?" she said. "Why don't you make love to your wife?"

"I make love to my wife."

"Over the phone."

"It's very exciting over the phone. It's a pure act of imagination; or mostly pure."

"But it's not good if you can't touch."

"Are you sure?"

She blushed slightly along her jaw. "Gosh, Buddy, of course. I *know* that."

The truth was it had been more than a year since I had touched— except incidentally—anyone.

She pulled at her long bottom lip. "It'd be a lot harder life than it is if you couldn't once and a while snug up with someone."

"Who do you snug up with these days?"

"I have my fellows."

She said she did, but I knew she didn't. I had been without too long myself not to recognize the signs, the dense and fractured light that skittered through her eyes, the cement stains at the corners of her mouth. . . .

There were a hundred ways to approach her and any of them could work; she was just human, a thirty-eight-year-old dark-headed woman, a sucker for attention and humility, a businesswoman and a farmer, one like the rest of us who had spent days and nights rigging some weave of love and effort to keep her safe from terror. But if I said *There's this reason, there's that reason*—reason why you should help me now—she would tell me that I should be glad we were sitting in this room together after all these years, talking as the wind ticked against the pawl of the world. *Look,* she would say, *come to the window,* and out there, riding the silky waters of the Gulf of Mexico, would appear, as if she had called them, a sea flight of dolphins, traveling west in the moonlight, rising and descending and rising again as their stainless bodies flattened out the molecules of salt rushing past, carrying them away on an errand indecipherable to us, but which, in its very unknowableness, uplifted and celebrated our lives. She would have me know this, she would say this to me and have me say it back to her in the same words, as if she understood, like St. James, that what issues from our mouths is who we are. And I would say what she told me to say.

But now there stood a figure in my life, this man D'Nel Boyd, who for no reason gave in to nothing.

I said, "There's someone I want to introduce you to."

She swung around, punched the pillows propping her three good hard strokes, and settled back. "Who is it?"

"A man I met. A few years ago. He's very strange. He's a man who kills people."

"For true?"

"Yes. I've known guys before who've killed people—there was a one-armed man who worked for my father on the docks in St. Louis who had killed his wife, and I've met a couple of people who've manslaughtered their boyfriends or their girlfriends—but this is a man who kills people because he likes to."

"Where did you meet him? In prison?"

"No, ha ha," I lied, "I met him through somebody else, a woman I stopped in the street because I thought she might look good in a movie."

"You're still doing that?"

"Sometimes it works out."

She slid down in the bed and turned on her side, drawing up then extending her legs. Under the covers they looked like the sapped legs of a paraplegic. "I was thinking," she said, "do you remember how you used to get in fights?"

"Yes. Sometimes I still do."

The breeze had fallen off. I could hear the sawing of crickets. In the room the single bed lamp threw shadows like dark suits over the backs of the upright chairs and over the old gray velvet sofa. On the walls were faded prints of upland scenes: hay mowing in the mountains; boys walking under large beech trees; a flock of dark birds—crows maybe—swooping into a narrow valley. For some reason the pictures had always reminded me of Missouri, of the downriver shore where old Eustace Drake had made his landfall. There were no mountains in that country, but the rise and fall of terrain, the sandy bluffs marshaled under oaks and sycamores, the long defiles of grass pestered by rain, the shape and length of the light casting through the leaves of a weathered orchard contained some of the same mystery and solidity that were in the paintings. We had made love in this room many times and it had seemed always a sweet finish to me to wake from the plunderings of orgasm to the sight of these pictures, their humanless, autonomous landscapes that were peaceful in themselves. Like the memory of any loved place they said yes the world is savage but here it's not; rest awhile.

She said, taking a sip from a glass of lemonade she raised from the table, "You never meant to get into fights, but you always did. You always found a reason why you had to."

"It's curious isn't it? But let me tell you about D'Nel. You would like to meet him."

"I don't know. He sounds dangerous."

"He is, but you like that. You're always reading those books about psychopathic killers, those guys that murder households and throw babies against the wall and walk out grinning."

"Hmm, yes; I love that. But in real life it might be scary."

"Well, it's not really real life if I only tell it to you as a story. To me it might be real, but you are only hearing it, so to you it's just imagination and a fairy tale."

"Okay."

So, as the night ticked away on the clock of the world, I began to tell her the story, taking her back beyond the scenes Van would film

into the deep past of D'Nel Boyd, who was born among vagabond
farm-worker folk to a vanished father, and to a mother who was already
old and worn by long hot days in the fields. She carried him with her
across the country, from farm to farm, from the wheat fields of north
Texas and Kansas to the celery and tomato fields of Southern California
and to the apple orchards of Oregon. He lived his childhood in the
world of the camps, which is a world apart and a world complete in
itself.

All his life he remembered the dark dewy mornings when he would
walk outside into the California—or the Nebraska or the Oregon—
dawn. On the morning I was thinking of, it was California; he could
see down the way a woman with a baby wrapped in a Mexican shawl
as she pumped a basin of water from the cistern. From the eucalyptus
above the woman's head a flock of redwings surged into the sky, rising
and falling above the tree in what seemed to him the same rhythm as
the rhythm of the creaking pump handle. The dust underfoot, damped
by dew, smelled of the sourness of rotted almonds. The woman's arms
were scratched and cut—by brush, by the sharp branches of almond
trees most likely—but the welted cuts seemed to him the residue of
some ritual, some dark and purposeful practice that he couldn't fathom
the reason for. He could see the weariness in her ocher face—he too
had lain awake listening in the shack next door to the baby crying (It
isn't just the work, or the long hours, or the rejection, he would say
later, that kills the poor, it's the noise)—and he could see in the bent
peculiarity of her bones an image of his own mother's body, see the
creep of age like a wearing tide, and the stains of the tide and the slow
erosion of the bodyscape beneath it. As he watched the woman shift the
baby onto a less raw place on her hip, his mind curved back—as the
universe in the great myth curves back on itself endlessly unchanged,
pressing still forward, if the story is true, through new fields of Space
toward what it has left behind—to his mother reared above him naked
in the shabby bed, to the arch and shine of her body which though he
had seen it unclothed at least one thousand times seemed now, as she
rose above him, the body of invention, of conjuring.

In the midnight underwater light of a coal-oil lamp his mother raised
herself above him, straddling him. Her skin was clammy and the dead

white of it was underlain by a darker color like the stain of sediment left in the tubs after they washed up. It was smooth like the cold flesh of a river fish, and it squeaked under his fingers that she drew into herself. Her hair, which had once been a rich red-gold, was shrieked and graying now, coarsed by sunlight and age—what was age to him; she must only have been in her late thirties—and age had stripped and pummeled her small hands, carving the thin veins into relief, scuffing and grooving the knuckles, scarring. Her breasts were small, and though fallen they were as soft as cotton, and they gave and then didn't give like cotton pressed into as she held his hands on them and pressed his hands into the flesh as if she wished he might reach through into her heart. She swung her face close so he could smell the sour wine on her breath, and the smile on her thin lips was a smile of lunacy and desire, like the smile one might see on a face peering out of a jail window; he was not repelled, though he was terrified, as one might, on seeing the imprisoned face, respond not with aversion but with the desire to tear down walls and release it; so something in him gave way—it was as common and natural, he would say later, as catching a ball someone has suddenly tossed you—something in him welcomed her, and, awkwardly—he did not have the practice of a man—but with force—he was a child, he understood force—he stabbed his hands past her face, laced his fingers around the back of her head (feeling the cool, worn wolf coat of her hair), and wrenched her down on top of him. She cried out—in glee or pain he couldn't tell—and began to beat his face with kisses. She smelled of age and rotted sweat and bitterly of wine, and pungently of the sugary perfume she doused herself with; the mix to him was not foul but simply her, this concoction of bones and flesh he knew best, loved best, in the world. Her hand snaked between them, it closed like a claw of fire around his penis, dragging it, the sudden stiff wand at the center of him, into the wispy hair at her groin, grooving him there like a plowman driving a furrow through grain, then arching, and cruising back upon him so that he slid abruptly into the slick tear of her cunt, deeply, buried to the hilt. He cried out then, in surprise and terror and joy, thrusting upward into the new hot territory of her body that was suddenly—incomprehensibly, like a jungle in Africa—opened to him; and she herself, barking, drove down on his body so that for a second he thought the opening in her might be a passageway opening into the stars—it seemed a tunnel into space—pulling something so deep and securely fastened in a rush out of him—as something in him wildly, like a dead man brought back to life, leapt from the floor of his being, screeching and capering. He raised himself, or his body jerked up, like someone struck from the back, and grasped her, clinging to her—small monkey—plunging his hands down the deeply grooved plain of her back to the deeper groove of her buttocks, clutching at the flesh there, parting it, peeling her with his small fingers so that for a moment that drove as sharply as a nail into his skull he touched the raw slit of her anus, and then, farther, an inch beyond it, the slimed conjunction of their bodies—well and stake—touched the heat, the engine of their union.

He never knew, that time, if he came—he must have, he thought later, since his exhaustion had been so deep—because he fainted—that was a word he used in telling the story, lightening it sometimes; to him it was obliteration, a momentary erasure of everything that was D'Nel Boyd—and waked in the sallow half-light as she held him across her lap, cooing small, soft sounds that she blew like feathers across his face. There was a horrible, volumic sadness about her. Around him, the objects in the small room—the clothes spilling from the broken suitcases on the floor, the small candlesticks and the strings of dried red peppers, the mangled shoes—seemed to glow with immanence, polished, delicate, and profound, as if each were the original prototype of all its successors, of all the other life-worn objects in the world; as if the room—small, square, webbed in the eaves—were the one room left in the world, and its collections of objects, the loved objects and the incidental, were now become—the light like a coat of brass or resin on the back of a hairbrush, on the pale red sweatshirt his mother wore in the fields, on their bodies even, on the streaks of sweat between her toes—objects of ritual and worship, to be faithfully preserved. He thought, I will remember everything, I will hold all this in my heart for as long as the world lasts, I will die with the picture of it in my eyes. For a moment, a moment that passed, he knew how a life could be changed forever in an instant, he knew that he would not be again who he had been, that the world had lurched into another shape. And further, and much more important, he knew that the making of the new world had not killed him, had taken place in fact while his attention was elsewhere; and he looked at her hand, which moved like the hand of his destiny across his clean chest, picking faintly at the skin as if to pluck small loose bits of it, and he saw the three raised cords and the trickle of veins, and the large scar where she had burned herself last week on slopped grease, and he thought that it was entirely possible for that hand—or anything material—to press without resistance through the wall of his chest—it was no denser than the amber light—and close around the muscle of his heart and hold it and do with it anything the hand might desire: kill him or caress him or shape him into some new being entirely; and this knowledge, which flooded him with no resistance on his part, seemed to him the one piece of knowledge that was essential—that could be touched, and shaped, at the center of himself— the one piece, the small kinetic granule, that in itself was able to—that would, that did—propel him toward that place that was not only a future but a past and present too, the well universal, where one drowns, as a man fallen off a ship into the sea drowns into infinity and salt, into idea and object, both at once, both the same, interchangeable, and everlasting.

These thoughts were not thoughts really, they were not what a man like D'Nel Boyd, incipient killer though he was, could think, but they existed, as the smell of a mountain fire exists for a man walking in a distant valley, as the sun exists behind the evening clouds, behind the darkness, so that in himself, as the moths beat against the screens and his mother shifted her slight weight under him, as dark tongues began to lick at him from the corners of the room, he saw the shapes of the dead, he saw his father who had never been anything but shadow, rise before him, and saw the long line of his kin stretching back unbroken to Adam; and he saw the faces of strangers, of people struggling to cross a street in the rain, to plant vegetables in small city plots; saw the orchards of the world heavy with fruit, and the contrails of jets, and the curled orange inner skin of a peach; and saw a handful of rusted nails and saw a knife pierce the temple of a child, saw priests running across a stone courtyard in China, saw the bed of a river dried to quilted yellow sand, saw a herd of horses galloping across a brushy plain; saw, in a finality that startled him, his own hand rise, clutching the rock fragment his mother had pulled from the wall of a pueblo in New Mexico, and kept with her always, saw the hand flash downward, saw it rise and fall, saw the blood. . . .

All of this in the early sway of stained light on a California morning, as a woman carrying a baby filled a bucket at the pump. He smelled the sweet scent of loquats, thinking that he was thinner this year, wondering where he would find breakfast. The woman turned away from the cistern. She raised her free hand and rubbed her nose with the flat of her palm. He heard the loose squish of wet membrane. Then she looked at him and smiled, an easy smile, as if they were not trapped in a migrant camp in the San Joaquin, as if the seven dollars and change that would be placed in their hands at the end of the day were nothing that one should get upset about. He smiled back at her. His belly growled faintly. Hell, he thought, I don't care where I am. I'm the king.

I told Bess this in the late night of Florida, as the breeze kicked the screens, lying half curled on the bed listening to the creaking woodwind of her breathing. She was silent for a long time. I bent down and smelled the covers over her thighs. They smelled strongly of laundry soap, and faintly of gardenias. Her hand moved lightly, a little reflexively, to touch my ear.

"Some story," I said, "isn't it?"

"Don't talk for a minute."

I fell over, clownishly, I thought, and crawled up beside her. She shifted her body, giving me space. Her collarbones stood like handles half hidden in the opening of her T-shirt. I snugged up, cloth between us, as the night breeze drained the room and refilled it with itself, rattling papers on the desk pushed against the wall, lifting the curtains, probing for assassins.

The story was already more than I wanted to know about. Already I was losing the line of it, allowing—or giving in to—certain cracked and wayward elements that would divert the hard thrust of it into something murky and indecipherable. The formula of movies was a simple one, the three acts, the rising action, the clear resolution. It did not take a genius to write one, though it often took the perseverance of a zealot to get one made. I could hear Van as he turned the pages of the script: Well, he would say, we don't need to know this, who cares about who he thinks he is, stop trying to make him think. I had become excellent at building movies that were hard and fast and conclusive— limited though they were—but it was only by staying close to the community, to the others who believed in and had learned to follow the prescribed and settled routine. It was true that the evidence was already there—see my late features in which the straying, in which the sharp line of action had begun, *sacrebleu,* to fray like a blasted drug deal—that a murkiness, a diffusion had begun to occur. The critics had remarked on this; in their way they had attempted, by gentle then not so gentle chiding, to redirect me toward what I could—with Van's help—do well. It was only with the last movie that the adjectives *stupid, offensive, confused,* and such had been applied to my work. Such wrongheaded pretentious drivel, they cried. Such waste of talent, a romp reduced to a crawl, who does he think we are? Well, I understood. It was not only my movies that were confused. How many times I had wanted to call them up on the telephone to speak openly, one human being to another, to say, Frank, David, Margaret, I understand why you write these things and I want you to know I am not offended. I find what you say instructive and supportive, and I want you to know that I have come to my senses, I will do better next time, I promise. How I wanted to please them, how I wanted their eyes to light up as my images flashed across the screen before them. I wanted them to invite me into their homes, out for weekends to their vacation cottages in the Hamptons and in Mirabar; I wanted them to offer me food, to name their children after me, to encourage me to sleep with their wives. David Sample, the critic for the *Times,* was the most damning—though I noticed, perhaps I was the only one who did, a strain of friendly concern—cranking the hot machine of his prose into a white-hot excoriation that would blister. He had, he said, hated *Blue Gun*—my last picture—so much that he left the theater in a state of profound nausea that took him two days to recover from. He went through, he said, a prolonged period of involuntary spitting in an attempt to get the taste of it out of his mouth. It was (he said) like something dredged up from beneath the seats—did he mean seas?—so foul and shapeless that it would take a team of experts—no, not experts: convict volunteers possibly—to perform the exploratory necessary for any cogent analysis. It would take, he claimed, someone stronger than the heavyweight champion of the world to punch any hole of sense through such foul matter.

Van suggested we purchase a howitzer, haul it to the top of the condominium high rise shadowing Sample's brownstone, and shell the shit out of him, but I demurred. If you want to know the truth, I thought he had a point. Anybody could tell you I had become a haunted, mixed-up man. People will claim that they are able to separate their personal lives from their work, but I don't believe it. Not only don't I believe it, I believe that our personal life *is* our work. As the life goes, so goes the work. It was Einstein who pointed this out to modern man. Einstein and all the great ones—Darwin, Proust, Freud, Joyce, Stieglitz, Renoir *(fils),* and old Joe Conrad—knew, whether they could prove it or not, that the unified field does in fact exist, that everything and its brother are in fact so interwoven that we can't twitch our slightest nerve end without setting off corresponding reactions in the world around us. Kick a dog and a man falls to his knees in India. Shout at your wife and a Little Leaguer in Kansas misjudges a fly that allows the winning run to score. And conversely, let me add, press a penny into a beggar's hand and suddenly someone stepping into a Dublin street breaks into a smile.

Thus I knew that it was no mystery why my feature films had, in the critics' eyes, become occluded. The critics were not fools, they knew what they saw. I appreciated their kindness and circumspection in not commenting on my personal life. I saw them, often enough, in New York mostly, and occasionally, though I rarely went there, on the West Coast, and they were for the most part ordinary and well-meaning fellows, worried about their children's education and about the difficulty of finding excellent workmanship in the products they bought. They too had troubled marriages and moments of intemperance, they too respected the simple equation of hard work and good pay, they too had to discover a way to rub enough peace into their hearts to make a good job possible. If they raged at me it was not because they had woken up one morning transmogrified into psychopaths, but because, to them, whether they knew it or not, my disorderly life had begun to appear untransformed in my work, forcing them, good shepherds that they were, to remind me, with sharp words or a crack of the staff, about what it was we were all doing here on this cloudy hurtling planet. I was grateful, chastened, willing to change.

I looked at my ex-wife, who seemed to be listening to music in her head. Her mouth was partly open, showing a slim glistening rind of teeth, her fingers lay loosened, slightly curled on the coverlet, her toes pointed straight up. Often, in the days of our marriage I would come on her lying just this way, dreaming like a child, alone on the bed, a late night lamp throwing a soft and inarticulate light on her strong face. What are you doing? I would ask her, and I could see the question penetrate her reverie, I could almost follow the syllables of it as they ribboned their way into her brain, absorbing and replacing the thoughts that swam there. She would look at me, not as one startled, but as one stepping out of sunlight into a cool darkness, her happiness not broken but augmented by my presence. To see the light of recognition and welcoming appear in her eyes was a profound experience for me; I had never felt so loved, so approved of, so raised up. Her eyes would lift to my face, as if rising above the edge of something, some childhood wall she peered gaily over, and a light would come on in them; her hand would light vagrantly, in a small half motion of opening, she would pick from the blue china bowl on the table my souvenir baseball— Official Approved National League, *Chub Feeney,* Pres.—and begin to squeeze it lightly and slowly (afraid she lacked stamina and strength, she worked steadily to improve her physical prowess) like a pitcher preparing to throw. She would smile, and hand me the ball, which I would toss behind my back and catch in front of me, then roll down my arm and catch again (as likely as not dropping it and comically flailing into a routine of awkwardness and dismay) and pass back to her. Our fingers would meet around the ball, we would hold it between us, touching each other's most obvious flesh around the scuffed leather and the red, frayed stitching, enclosing it, trying in mutual consent to cover it entirely, to conceal it, to make it disappear. Then it *would* disappear, as our fingers crossed, interlocking as in the child's game of church and steeple, joint grazing joint, grazing phalanx, bits of skin rubbing against equivalent bits, the small glue-colored nail of her index finger scratching at the heel of my palm, tapping the carpal bone. Shyly, slowly, with patience, with a steady taking of pains, she would tap for entrance, and I would respond, sliding down beside her, sending my hands on careful, awe-struck errands up her arms and across the evolved terrain of her collarbones, finding the soft flesh at the base of her neck, dipping into the hollow there as into one of the mysterious pools worn into the surface of rock, to her face where I would touch the corner of her long mouth, the small, slightly upturned nose, brush the edge of the long lashes that were as black as if she inked them. We would move, carefully and steadily, as travelers moving through a wood at night, peering into the familiar unknown of each other's bodies, lifting a hand to touch the warm recognizable flesh.

But now nothing like that at all. I leaned over her, whispering about a movie. "Do you want to hear more?" I said.

"This late at night I think it might be too much for me."

"Is the story too crazy for you?"

"It's terrible and I can tell it's going to get worse."

"But you love the terrible stories."

"I guess I do, but this one sounds mean. Is D'Nel actually a person? Or is this just something you've made up?"

"No, he's alive. I met him when we were filming *Dakota Mercy*. It was when we were on location, out there—you remember—in North Dakota."

"I remember. . . ."

"Yes. It was only early September but already there was frost in the mornings and the wheat fields looked like places where battles had been fought, and there were all those little towns with their silos and those stores with the blank fronts that made you think of corpses with their backs turned, and some little kid, the only juvenile delinquent in town, roaring off on a sloppy little motorbike he's painted airplane silver, yelling some curse that wouldn't shock his grandmother."

"How did you meet D'Nel—what is his last name?"

"Boyd. I met him there in town. He was there—just hanging around. He was a strange figure, completely out of place—you could see it instantly—but completely at home, as if he didn't notice—like some guy who's obnoxious without knowing it"—"Like you"—"Yeah, but he wasn't obnoxious at all; he was weirdly elegant and completely composed, this guy in a little North Dakota wheat town wearing very well tailored gray suits and rep ties—I thought at first he was somebody from one of the eastern papers, some guy from the *Times* or *The Washington Post*—just hanging about at the edge of the set watching us. I noticed him and I asked Barney Gelb, the publicist, about him, but he couldn't find out anything either, except that he wasn't from the media, and then I forgot him—the picture was a mess; I'd gone off the deep end with all kinds of stunts I wanted the actors to do, and Van and I were arguing it all out—until one morning—I was staying in a little studio cottage in the backyard of this lady whose family had owned the local grain-elevator business (a real dowager queen who would serve me fox-grape wine on the screened porch in these heavy crystal glasses that looked like they'd been hacked out of a block of glass with a pickax)—I came out and the car wouldn't start." "You've suffered for lack of limos." "Yes, I have—terribly—but what I was telling you was that I came out and the car wouldn't start—it was another frosty morning, white and wet glitter shining on the grass and on the tumbled old mess of a garden—and there he was, standing under this big red oak beside the driveway, as if he was waiting for me. I ignored him, I really didn't pay attention to him, I tried to start the car and it wouldn't even turn over and then I looked up and he was standing there beside the door. He had on a dark gray suit and a red tie, very elegantly tied, and he was standing there looking at me with this composed look of concern on his face, very slowly running his hand up and down the radio aerial.

" 'Thing won't start,' I said. 'I don't know what the matter is.'

" 'Change of season,' he said. 'It affects automobiles the way it does people.'

"I had the walkie-talkie with me, so I tried to call Van to come get me, but it wouldn't work either, just a bunch of crusty static. He had his hand on the upright in front of the window, rubbing it a little in the same motion he had used touching the aerial, and he leaned down a little—I'd rolled the window down when I got in—and smiled. His face, which was narrow, and bony around the high forehead, was as white as the face of someone who has lost blood, but his smile was very gentle, and good-humored, like, well, aren't we all just bozos from time to time. I had been up half the night going over script changes with Van, and you know how it is on a movie set—like being in the army of some confused and self-absorbed Third World country (though for us it was always a little better since we were so small and under-financed)—and I was just about to ring a few changes on the theme of how goddamn crazy everything was getting, and at the same time holding it in a little before a stranger"—"Which you've never been able successfully to do"—"Yeah, I know, but then, not earnestly like a groupie or some such at all, but like one good fellow offering another good fellow assistance, he offered me a ride in his car. I did look harder at him then and remembered that he was the fellow I had asked Barney about, and remembered that I saw him every day standing around by the trucks, or off just out of the scene talking to one of the wranglers—he was familiar, so I said sure, thanks, got out, and followed him to his car.

"He drove me to the set, which was out at the edge of town near the river, talking in this good-humored and easygoing way, about pheasant hunting. It was interesting, the way he described the snowy emptiness of the fields and the way the dog would point a little tuft of hay grass you couldn't believe a bird as large as a pheasant could be hiding behind, and then how you'd take a step forward and the bird would snap up in an explosion of snow and wings like some furious little haywire engine just that second created. I remember he used that word, *created;* he said, *The birds are like little beings spontaneously created for the pleasure of your killing,* and he grinned, the same effortless grin as before. I was a little charmed. You know how I am making a movie, how I don't want to think about anything else"—"And you're always making them, aren't you, scamp"—"You're right—and can't really think of anything else, but there was something about what he was telling me, something really interesting and uncluttered, and something in the sound of his voice—it was pitched very low, and there was a windiness in it, a slight chafing in the consonants, as if he was re-creating for me the ambience of the Dakota steppes, and it was very clear, well articulated, and completely unaccented, as if he had brilliantly and wholly learned the perfect dictionary pronunciation of every word, not by rote or dumbly, but as if he believed in it, if you know what I mean, as if he had been converted to it—that was soothing to me. . . ."

"This is the man you were telling me about, the one who did it with his mother?"

"Yes. But I didn't know that then. He was just an interesting fellow who had saved me some time on a worrisome day."

She raised her head, pulling at her neck so that the skin tucked slightly above her collarbones. "R.B. wants us to get air-conditioning, which I can't see the benefit of. It's much better to get real air, as much of it as you can."

"If you had air-conditioning you could build fires in summer."

"Is that so? But what a waste it would be."

"You could still have fires."

"I know that is exactly what R.B. wants to do. He pictures himself sitting in an armchair, with his feet propped up on the fender, staring profoundly into a crackling fire."

"Many people do."

"I have enough fires with the orange groves. Last winter we had to run fires seven separate times, night after night, and the last time we lost the fruit anyway; the frost just *burned* it up."

"There's something wrong with the weather."

"You don't have to tell me. I *know* there's something wrong with the weather."

She bounced on as she did always, her mind flying to the world of her work and her place, to the things of her hand that she had turned to long ago to gather to her and build a life with. The New York years—she had come there to study music—were a dream now, and like the bulked yellow curtains that had shape only because of the passing intrusion of wind, had shape only because of my own continued presence in her life—mine and Celest's and the few other friends with whom she exchanged occasional energetic notes; we were the fitful breeze giving continued—shifting—shape to what was in itself diffuse and ungraspable and passing, maybe only intrusion now. At forty-two I knew already that the world doesn't change us, that it can't, that change is not what we are here for, that the possibility of change is only some fey notion attractive to preachers and poets, to those artificers who are fretted by the claustral contrivances of this world to the point where they must demand something greater, something different, something flashier or more peaceful somewhere else. I knew that she believed this too, that her life was representative of it, snugged down here on the Florida sea edge with her plants and her family and the Gulf shuffling its feet like a bored bodyguard.

On a long narrow nut-wood table edging the other side of the bed were stacks of seed catalogues and farm magazines, a few dismantled gadgets sent to her by salesmen and inventors who sought to improve, for a fee, the lot of the nurseryman, and separately, in leather bindings stacked neatly under a small blue-and-gold glazed pot containing a shedding bonsai juniper, half a dozen of my screenplays. I leaned across her, shifted the plant, and pulled out the top one. It was my first movie, the violent, high-speed, totally nihilist epic in which a large middle American family murders itself at a summer reunion on the banks of the Mississippi River. My father, an appreciator of fantasized paybacks in blood, had laughed all the way through it. He and my mother, along with Bess and our New York friends, had accompanied me to the premiere, held at a West Village theater one June evening when the sky between the buildings was lit with the rampant red fire of summer's first sunset. Looking down the street I had seen the scarlet light climb onto the second-story windows and rest for a moment there, washing the blank panes and the ledges with what seemed to me a blaze of promise. When we walked out two hours later, charged and rinsed by the applause, the city seemed to sparkle before us like a sea of diamonds; and for a moment, it was ours, a fabulous possession that no future conceivable could snatch from us.

As I crossed back over her body to my side of the bed—former marriage side—her hand lifted and she stroked the brass-colored leather. The touch was quick and shy, the way one might reach through wire to touch a bird, but it startled me, not because of its tenderness, or even its humility, which was part of it (even if crusted around the edges with her gentle mockery), but because of its familiarity. There had been many times when she reached into the center of some action to touch me. I might be climbing a ladder, or working on a screenplay, or scrubbing between my shoulder blades when her hand lightly and fondly would reach through the concentration to stroke me softly back to this world. She was like some goddess, some Athena, who in the midst of frenzied fight offered quiet words of direction. I loved her for this, now that I had distance from it. At the time, mad to pursue my obsession of the moment, I had raged against interruption, flinging her affection from me as if it were a snake. "Don't you understand," I would cry, "I can't get done what I have to get done if you keep interrupting me." Baffled, bitten to the quick, she would retreat, only, good heart that she was, to return another time, soon, to slip a caress through the thorny mesh of my concentration. It had taken years to make bitterness root in her.

Now I stopped, turning the flat sheaf of pages toward her, careful, in that way only the aristocrats of missed chances can be, to *allow* her. We looked at each other—brown eyes; gray eyes—out of our separate energy and our separate weariness, fondly, not for one second letting go of the resolutions concerning each other we had made long ago, but with great understanding and tenderness, and—which as much as anything was what kept us close now—forgiveness. "Do you remember," I said, "the first time I visited you after we were divorced?"

"Two years after—yes."

"It was down here. I was passing through, chasing another movie. It was the year of the rain, when all the tobacco beds got washed out and you had to replant."

"I remember."

"We slept in your old bedroom, the one you slept in when you were a child."

"In those little tiny beds with honey-bear coverlets."

"Do you remember in the bathroom the next morning?"

"Yes."

"You had put flowers in there, all different kinds of lilies."

"In buckets."

"That's right."

We had woken early, snapping to like children, or like the old, rising stiff-eyed into the gray salty light of Gulf summer dawn, staring at each other, at the strangeness of our renewed proximity. Beyond the windows the last bullbats dived at the sea which still had some of the night left over in it, gray and worn to pieces on its surface. Circumspect, trivializing somewhat our past together—so I thought—we had, the night before, undressed carefully out of sight of each other, neither turning in the small pitched room to see what new time had done to the well-known bodies, though I was curious, as I thought she was. We had talked late, avidly, like two thirsting for intimate talk, yucking and juking as the tree frogs chimed their brass pipes in the yard, and the pet crane out on the porch croaked in troubled sleep, admitting to everything, forgiving everything, glowing with complicity and fine fellowship, our hands beating the childish covers, our bodies jerking involuntarily at a particularly salient point, all the while our glances sneaking at each other like the glances of gamblers, assessing chances. It was a wonder we didn't start doing back flips we were so delighted to lie easily in each other's means.

"I was taking a shower," I said, "and you came in the room."

"Yes, I remember. I couldn't help it."

"You were naked, but you didn't say that."

"No, I was laughing."

"We were like little kids running around at the beach."

"Except aware."

"You knew that?"

"Of course."

Over the top of the milky shower glass I had looked at her as she fumbled through perfumes and unguents set out on a silver tray beside the sink. The orange, black-stippled petals of tiger lilies were scattered over the cream marble and collected in small piles, where she had swept them, around the bases of the silver buckets; the yellow, yellow-crowned stamens hung nakedly down. Her body, turned half toward me, was the strong, working body of a woman in her thirties, slack at the breast, filling in perceptibly at the waist, the rectus muscles on the tops of her thighs and the rounded calf muscles protrudent, the skin at the back of her neck creased just where the sunburn ended, the wrists bony and strong, the hands corded and muscular, work-chapped, with the broad fingernails cut back to the quick. She looked to me like some frontier wagon master, hard through necessity and through years of work and years of holding on through weather and disappointment to the lines of destination, someone who had not given in. But this was only the reading of enthusiasm and distance, a coda of sorts whereby I could replay the concluded revisionism of our past life, and so set myself free from it. Because on her body that was pale where sun didn't reach, and still, though strong, softly rounded, gleamed, starting just at the crook of the elbow and worming six inches down her forearm— bright as if she buffed it—the scar where four years before, on a night in which my life had crashed about my head like black, splintering ice, I had, with a chisel picked up off the floor of a destroyed loft, ripped her sweet flesh to the bone.

I had intended to kill her, and I would have killed her—which is something that only she and I knew, a secret unmentioned to lawyers, best friends, and new lovers—if she had not prevented me, first with the fending blows she struck me and then by running away down the stairs of that damaged place I had lured her to, and out into the convulsion of a TriBeCa night. We had not spoken of that time all through the cavalcade of the previous night's jabbering, had not mentioned it when she picked me up at the small grassy airfield the Piper pilot had set me down on late the afternoon before, nor on the ten-mile ride through the tall forests of pine and cabbage palm, nor as we turned down the long palm-lined driveway to the house, nor that afternoon as we lounged on rafts in the Gulf, plucking strands of yellow seaweed off the surface with our toes, nor later at dinner when Uncle Porto Lefebre, after his half-lit rendition of a one-legged Scottish reel, asked us, leaning over the murky puddle of roast beef gravy collected on his plate, why it was two such fine specimens as we two fine specimens hadn't been able to get along—"What a shame," Aunt Estelle murmured into her napkin, "what a shame . . ."—any better than we had; nor later, after drinks in the library with R.B., who played for us the Scarlatti variations he had just mastered that week, nor when we climbed the wide heart-pine stairs to the bedroom—"Stay here, with me, let's sleep in my baby room so we can stay up and talk"—nor any time during the four—five or six—hours when as the noises of family community converted gradually to the creaks, snaps, soft burrs, and snatched songs of the exfoliate world, we jabbered like caught wild birds, telling every story but that one, remembering every act but that one, plunging our faces recklessly into every one of memory's cisterns, but that one.

Now I said, "Seeing you naked was like seeing you naked for the first time. It made me wonder if the only reason the monks deprived themselves was so they'd get a bigger kick when they hit the streets of heaven and got their goodies. I guess that *is* what they're doing. But it was more than that, seeing you. Because you were the same old gorgeous self, but you were also changed, had been changed, so your presence was in a way amplified."

"I wanted you to come out of the shower. I wanted to see what you looked like naked. I wanted a look at your cock."

As she had reached for the tap I saw the scar fully; it stretched like a rope drawn taut, disappearing along its outer length into the matted silver hairs on her forearm. For me, the bright rip of it burned in my mind like a permanent wound, wound not only to her, but to me, so that it seemed the harsh point of the spike had drawn across my brain this cut, which hadn't healed. She herself was only intent with washing her body—though I can't speak for her—which she began to do with a large yellow sea sponge, dabbing her shoulders, her neck, and her breasts carefully, the clear water runneling between her breasts, fanning over her belly into the dense sooty hair in her groin. She didn't know what trapped me in the shower stall, amid the smell of soap and sulphur water and the faint but permanent iodine smell of sea life; she couldn't know; there was no way to make knowledge spring from my mind into hers; which seemed suddenly curious, even amazing, to me. I thought of sex, of its gathering, its soothing of anxiety that would allow the mutual humanness to find its companion each in the other, but I knew that even this wouldn't be enough to strike a deep enough connection between us. No matter how deeply I looked there was still a mystery, and there always would be.

Then she saw me watching her, saw me peering over the shower wall, and she turned more fully toward me, exposing her body to me, generously and without shyness, without thinking of exposure. Or so I thought. Thought until her left hand drifted across her body, fingers fully extended, to touch, then smooth, as one would smooth out a mussed pleat, the scar. She scratched it, and smoothed it again, and then she smiled at me. She saw me looking at it too.

"I used to hate you for this," she had said then. "I felt so impure, so ruined. My body was always something to me to be protected, to be saved and kept from harm. I was careful with it, shy of it, I wore it like a new dress you wear to church, careful against spills. When you did this to me I thought you had destroyed something so essential that in some way—much deeper than just the physical—I was maimed permanently, broken. I thought inside me I'd be limping forever."

"I hate that I did it."

"I know. I knew that all along. But I hated you so much I didn't want you to get over it either. I wanted it to burn like radium in your head, until it burned a hole and your brains fell out."

"I'm sorry."

"No—don't; you can't be sorry enough, and I don't want you to be sorry. It isn't sorry that heals and I don't care about it. I need your forgiveness as much as you need mine, and I ask you for that—please forgive me"—"I do"—"but what heals is time and the greater good you have to find and surrender to. Silly as that idea is, maybe it's all we're offered."

She had raised her arm then, bending to meet the flesh, and kissed the edge of the scar. Lifting her head, she said, "Do I sound pompous to you?"

"Earnest, but not pompous."

"I can never tell. So much of life down here is done alone, and I'm always talking to myself—out loud, it turns out, these days—and mostly I can't always tell anymore whether I'm making sense or not. I listen to Uncle Porto and the rest of them and I know they're not making sense—R.B. is quick but he's wan—and then I start wondering about myself. You know how it is, you're walking in the pasture and suddenly you hear a voice and you turn, really surprised—maybe a cow has broken into speech—and discover it's you. Life is pretty strange."

"I know."

"What was I saying?"

"The scar."

"Yes. Dear wound." She licked it, rubbed hard down the glistening rubbery length of it. "You didn't exactly do me a favor, but good has come of it."

"What do you mean?"

"I'm not scrupulous anymore. Fastidiousness has flown. I was orderly and circumspect as a child, now I'm reckless. Maybe not reckless, but brazen. I go forth boldly."

"What do you mean?"

"All that false fanciness, that self-protectiveness I labored at is gone. I don't watch over myself anymore." She cocked her head at me. "You know, you could have killed me. Sometimes I think—just the edge of the thought slips into my mind   that you really were trying to murder me; which is to say I came very close to dying   you were, after all (I think), stronger—I chanced, in the middle of my life, into the death house, and death, that nasty spike you found, struck me."

"Agh."

"It was like electroshock. I came to muddled and weak, but after a time, life began to bloom again and I found out I could go forth into it without dragging around the stupid load of the past—whatever it was—that had tangled me up until then."

"Hell, if that's the case you ought to be thanking me."

"No. It's not something you thank somebody for. I'm grateful—life is bright now—but it's not what I intended. I wouldn't have made this choice, and I had good reason, as I saw it, to live the way I was living. It was good too."

"I thought you said you were freer now."

"I am, and it's good, but being free isn't always the best thing in the world."

"You're confusing me."

"I know. It's all right. I confuse myself too. What I do now to live with the confusion is go very boldly and stubbornly toward what I want. I'm a good damn farmer—nurseryman—a woman who's an asset to her community, who supports her family and provides jobs and who turns out a product that's useful to others."

"My stabbing you turned you into a Jaycee?"

She sputtered with laughter. "I guess so, and a sure enough energetic and devout one."

But there is always more than speech can carry. She had turned then toward the bathroom window, which was wide and fully curtained, but through the muslined surface of which we could see the shadowy, distillate Gulf. Out there life ran its variations, and it was a life where gulls shrieked, accusing everyone of robbery, and amberjack drove the silver bait fish in a frenzy toward the shallows, where on a winter morning you might come on a calf lying dead of exhaustion beside its mother, where any day someone you loved might step out of the shadows with a knife in his hand.

She was lying; I saw it in her face, saw it in the bulge of muscle collected at the bottom of her cheek, in the cords that stood in her neck like stretched taffy as she turned her head, in the way, for a second, she drew her thin lips between her teeth; and I felt for her then, as I had not been able to feel for myself, a rush of pity—I do not mean that I was somehow better or brighter, in any way absolved—pity, and what could pass for tenderness, gratitude, and a kind of sudden fealty, of association, as if the long process, so humanly, awkwardly carried out, of converting suffering and terror into faith was—so I thought in that passing moment—the true work of our lives, and she—this sturdy, scuffed naked woman in front of me—had somehow become one of the good knights of the enterprise, here on the wilderness coast of Florida—ordinary America—where despite knowledge and pain you got up anyway in the morning and roved forth into difficult day.

Here in Florida, years later, I said, "Do you remember that scene?"

"Yes," she said slowly, "I remember. And I remember what we did afterward, there on the floor, on that blue rug that stuck to our skins."

"Yes."

It had been as if I was murdering her twice.

IO.

I am not alone anymore. My movies crowd around me, and they are my companions. My characters, who are not actors but real, stand by my bed at night, and they speak to me. Nellie Mock from *Blue Gun* tells me of her life in the distant mountains, of the child she lost and mourned two whole winters, of her husband who is slow but loving, of the wheat fields and the abundant skies. Bert Willis, who took two bullets in the face in *Destiny,* whispers about nights on the river fishing for shad; I see him standing in the moonlight—that is like light created for the occasion, cold and profound and white—lifting the silky nets that are heavy with fish, the writhing whiteness of the nets rising slowly from the black, estuarine waters. Davey Conner, who, in the last reel of *Flyboys,* drove his scout plane into the side of one of the red, scarred mountains above Khe Sanh, talks earnestly, desperately, his hands cutting figures in the air, about the summer in 1957 when he lived with his grandparents in a tall white house perched above the banks of the Mississippi, of how each night, like a commando in training, he would sneak from the house, untie the small skiff hidden among willows, and push out into the river, riding out into the massive stream where great black barges stacked with coal and ore, pushed by the slight river tugs, moved slowly by him in stately migration toward the heights of Memphis. Patricia Bass, frail murderess lost in the streets of *Death City,* from her corner, stiffly hunched above the crushed white petals of her wedding dress, speaks airily, and wholly to herself, of what she calls the Eglantine Mysteries, some concoction of death through delight, that will save us all.

Like fireflies that rise wavering from the park's luxuriant summer grass, these shapes tremble and sway around me. I love them with the whole heart of gratitude and forgiveness. I have given my life for them as they have given their lives for me. Slipping for a moment across a screen filled with light, they turn toward the breathing world to lift in their hands the feeble truths and horrors of their lives, undefended

and without refuge, spinning out over the course of a couple of hours
tales of misalliance and confusion, practicing before bathroom mirrors
the phrases that they hope will open the door into the hearts of those
they love, challenging, like deranged samurai, the forts of their despair,
or surrendering meekly, begging for sufferance, calling out to their
damaged gods, to their missing families, to cracked hope fluttering away
like an anonymous bird through the trees—all those who have learned
that beyond truth and righteousness and death there is either mercy or
there is nothing at all.

But one lives who does not slink through shadows or stand beside
my bed explaining himself. He does not sneak into the orchard to sit
in the dark under the peach trees heavy with fruit wrestling with his
own mind. He does not stand at the edge of the lathering sea to shout
out his misery. He does not pull his friend aside to explain his latest
bargain with God, nor does he stay up late drinking his pain into
oblivion, stuffing it like a strangled baby into a sack that he will
heave over the ferry rail and be done with; he doesn't complain, he
doesn't live on memory or hope, he doesn't make scenes, he doesn't
offer false modesty or false pride as a means for surviving in this
world; he sells nothing, seeks nothing, does not return after a long
evening of pleasure to cry at your knees; he does not whimper or
defend himself, or seek a better world, or take this one seriously
either.

Ah, D'Nel, what did you mean when you said energy is a curse, that
hopelessness is the only happiness we can know?

II.   In the old days sometimes I stayed up all night. I would sit up
working, rushing my loose hand across sheets of light blue paper,
kicking characters to life, placing cameras, fiddling with the lighting,
seeing in my mind's eye the flash of the strobe, watching the actor step
from shadows into the circle of light and begin to play. I remember the
mornings, the dawns when I would rise creaking from the tailings and

curds of labor and the creations of labor, leave my desk, and go to the window where in the street the day would just be getting to its feet. Tatters of mist would lurk around the base of the furniture warehouse across the street, and the flat dark green side of the Tattnall building— windows painted over as if the inhabitants had given up on light— would shine with dew like something rinsed by the sea. Patches of wet would gleam on the roughed cobblestones, mica grit just beginning to faintly reflect light in the seams between them. There would be a salt smell in the air and the frailest of breezes would carry the slight stink of ailanthus flowers from the park up the street. From the market would come the crash of carts, and the grainy shouts of vendors as they began to heave their lives into the day. On such mornings it was easy to believe I lived on an island, even to conceive that it was one not nearly landlocked but a heap of land and construction far-flung into the Atlantic upon the shores of which strong tides smashed and whose weather was gift or sentence offered wholly by the ocean. On such mornings, exhausted, the swirl of papers littering the floor like crushed flowers behind me, I stood before the unpeopled light of early day as a feeling of promise and capacity came over me—not vying with fatigue, but accompanying it—maybe, through the open bedroom door, I would hear Celest, who every shared night of our married lives spoke long phrases of accusation and welcoming in her sleep, moaning interrogatories into her morning dream; from the kitchen would come the creak and whirr of the refrigerator starting into life; shifting my feet I could make the old green boards beneath me crackle a little and groan, from the roof next door would come the slap and rattle of the empty rope attached to the pole up which one of my neighbors ran the French tricolor each day. I would lean out the window, too tired to shout, and study the fire escape on the warehouse across the street, which some former tenant had painted a mussed blue and white so that it looked like stairs made of water. For a moment, work-drained, I would imagine myself climbing the stairs, making my way slowly from the seabed toward the daylighted surface, climbing through the tons of water, one slow fathom after the next, breathless, spent, nearly prevented. Above me, far away, I could see the chopped freedom of air. It was then, and only then, in Manhattan dawn, that the panic would strike me.

. . .

"So, partner, you've come after your friend." Boyd holds the wheel with the fingers of his right hand, caressing it, rubbing the black plastic with his slender thumb. His other hand lies in his lap. With it he cups himself, squeezing, tugging a little at the apparatus. Bantling looks away out the window. Pinewoods give way steadily to marshes beyond the far reaches of which he can see the blue glittering line of the Gulf. They are traveling east and south.

He says, "I told her I would."

"You told her. Yes. She said you were coming." Boyd begins to speak, making conversation at first, then shifting to stories of his life with Molly. Each one is more earnest and detailed than the last. There is a begging tone in his voice, an imploring tone, as if he wants simultaneously for Bantling to forgive him and leave him be. His voice, accentless but silky and rich with inflection, wheedles steadily so that Bantling begins to grow embarrassed for him and wishes he would stop. "I just never had any sweetness in my life," Boyd says, "nothing you could speak of until she came along. I don't mean to say *she*—this woman's not a pronoun—I mean to say Molly, Molly Picard—until Molly came along. Molly's all those wonderful ways you can describe a woman." He touches Bantling's shoulder, a touch Bantling shies from. Boyd doesn't seem to notice. "Let me tell you what she did. God, it made me cry. One afternoon I had come out of the shower. I was sitting on the edge of the bed drying my feet when she took the towel out of my hands, knelt down, and began to dry them for me. On her knees she did this, with a peach-colored towel. She touched me as gently as if I were a baby, and all the time there was this look of wonder and gentleness in her face, like someone worshiping. She dried each toe, and each foot, top to bottom. It did, it made me cry. Nobody had even come close to doing anything like that for me. I lay back on the bed with that sweet woman touching my feet and I cried I was so happy. It was the same as heaven, I'm sure of it."

And now, in the bright sunlight of full afternoon, there is a tear sneaking down his face. With his forefinger he wipes away the line of it. They are driving slowly, maybe twenty-five miles an hour. Molly is on a mattress in back, covered with the striped blanket. Every thirty seconds Boyd swivels his head to look at her. "You think she's all right?" he says anxiously.

"She'll be fine. After a spell she's always woozy and exhausted, and sometimes she doesn't know for a while who she is or what's happened, but she always slides on out of it."

"Slides on out, huh? You're a good man. You must have loved her for a long time."

Bantling says nothing to this. The country they ride through is country he has hunted and fished in. Still wild, as wild nearly as the Gulf, in its way, it has for him the freshness of a new place and the familiarity of an old one. His first long fishing trip—when he was five—left from the dock at Ernestina. Thirty-five miles out, as he watched a sailfish jump, he had put a fish hook into the ball of his thumb. In the woods they passed he had fished for perch and bream in the sinkholes, sat by a hickory fire at night listening to the cries of owls and panthers. In these woods his father had told him the story of the One-Sided Man, a man born ripped in half who when he turned sideways was invisible, and whose pleasure was to tear children in two. He could trace the pulse of his life back to those moments of terror, when he felt the presence of that man running through the woods.

Boyd places his hand on Bantling's knee. "My name is D'Nel, D'Nel Boyd," he says. "Did I tell you that? It's a nigger name, I don't know where it came from, but I've gotten used to it."

"I don't know. I'm Bantling Jakes."

"I know that too. Look," he says and points out the window, "that's an osprey—sea hawk. You don't see many of them anymore."

Bantling watches the great brown-and-white-flecked bird wheel over the near pines, soaring above the sun-shined salt ponds.

"This is the best country in the world," Boyd says. "I've seen a lot of territory and this is just about the best. It's clean still, and you can get lost in it, and it's intricate and full of surprises." He places two fingers at his temple and presses. "And I like a place where the trees come right down to the ocean."

Bantling likes that too, but he doesn't say anything. He is wondering, and his heart picks up as he wonders, how he is going to move next, what he will have to do to take Molly away from this situation. He looks back at her. She lies on her back with her hands drawn up under her chin. Her dark hair half covers her face, which is mottled and drawn. She snores. He feels breath on his cheek; Boyd has leaned close to him, glancing back at her too. He pulls away as Banty does. Boyd gives him a quick, searching look. "She's a Madonna," he says. "To me she's the whole mystery. A red-lipped Madonna. You know what I mean?"

"I don't know. What do you mean?"

"I don't mean like the Virgin, I don't mean J.C.'s mother, though I'm sure she could handle that sorry job too. I mean there's something true and real about her, some picture of the world that she makes that you just can't put together with your mind. It takes faith."

"Whore and Madonna," Bantling says. "That's a cliché."

"Is it? I didn't know. They're just words to me. Part of the whole inadequacy of talking."

In the dark water filling the ditches along the road the purple flowers of hyacinth bloom. The clouds are white puffs, as mysterious and specific as smoke signals. Bantling can smell his own sweat, which is sour like the smell of old apples. And he can smell the marshes that run along beside them, the foregrounds of mud the color of cigar ash and the green and gold reeds supplely bent by wind rushing toward a jagged wing line of dark pines. It is the smell of old boots and unwashed corners, wet webs, salt and decay, crushed things. Under his breath he says, "No, it's not the wildness, it's the order, it's the perfect fit of the pieces of this world that enchants me: water and grass, grass and trees, trees and sky, sky and water. One man couldn't hurt it." Boyd pays no attention.

"She's my best friend," Bantling says louder, blushing suddenly.

Boyd pats him on the knee. "She's a pip," he says. He begins to hum. Some stripped and patchy tune Bantling doesn't know. The sound is sweet, and, Bantling thinks, oddly shy.

They turn off the highway onto a dirt road that runs through the pinewoods. The pines gradually give way to groves of cabbage palms, interspersed with pines and stands of live oak. Cypresses grow in ponds, their feathery, burnishing crowns overreaching the trees around them. Understories of yaupon and myrtle swell beneath the tall trees. The road

narrows to a single lane, grass-tufted in the middle. In the distance a
white tower rises among the trees. As they draw closer he realizes it is
a windmill. The fan blades are stripped to spokes, so that the rotor looks
like a propeller. The windmill is wooden, and it leans to one side so
far that it looks as if it is toppling. They bump over a one-lane wooden
bridge separating two grassy fields, come around a bend through a patch
of mossy oaks that gives way to a small grove of orange trees among
which rise a few tall palms, and more grass, and there is the house: white,
two stories with a screened porch running all the way around it, a
decrepit garden off to one side near a tumbledown unpainted garage,
and beyond, the Gulf, hard and blue and bright. Behind the house is
a structure like a bunch of crossed steel wash lines hanging between two
big tulip poplars. Bantling sees it and doesn't understand it. It shears him
loose a moment from what he knows. The world seems strange and
indecipherable. The feeling only lasts a moment. The branches on the
cable sides have been lopped off. The cables gleam in the afternoon
sunlight as if they are polished. In one of the trees someone has tied
pieces of red cloth. The cloth flares and spits in the breeze.

   Boyd lets the clutch out, coasts around the side of the house, and
comes to a stop near the back steps. Brown, limp gardenias hang in
bushes growing against the porch.

   "Is this your house?" Bantling says.

   Boyd laughs. "No. We're just going to break in and stay awhile.
Yeah, sure it is. That is, we rent it. From an old lady in Ernestina. The
house and the island that goes with it. You want something to drink?"

   "I want to know what's going on here," Bantling says. The words
surprise and scare him. He wants to pop them back into his mouth.

   Boyd looks at him. The scorched blue eyes are dark. The light sinks
into them and stops. Like a false bottom. His lips narrow; then he grins.
He places his hand flat on Bantling's cheek. The hand is cold; it feels
good.

   They carry her into the house that is sun-washed and smells of Clorox
and dead lilies and sunburn, and put her in bed. She wakes as they carry
her, but it is the waking of dream; for a moment she struggles in their
arms, twisting, so that Bantling thinks they will drop her, but then, just

as quickly, she goes limp, her hand rises to her face and swipes her hair, she moans, repeating a word that sounds like *cholera;* the blanket trails off her, dragging on the waxed wooden floor.

Boyd holds her while Bantling pulls the yellow roiled sheet back. "Maybe we ought to change the sheets," Bantling says.

"You think? Yeah, I guess"—Boyd grins sheepishly—"we forgot to do that. Sometimes we get overrun. Neither of us is a very good housekeeper."

"Where are they?"

"I don't know. In the closet in the bathroom maybe."

"I'll be right back."

He hurries into the hall and into the bathroom that is awash with clutter. A crab trap lies in the tub; a pair of muddy rubber boots, their tops fallen over, stand on the closed commode. There are streaks of rusty grime in the sink. When he opens the closet door, flakes of plaster fall on him, like dry snow. The sheets he pulls out are covered with dust that he shakes off, coughing. Carrying them in a bundle he runs back to the bedroom. Boyd is sitting on the bed with Molly in his arms. There are tears in his eyes. Maybe he is a killer, Bantling says under his breath, but he can sure pump up the emotion. The walls are painted very light green and hung with maybe a dozen paintings, all of farm scenes— mowing, apple picking, milking, hands returning home after a long day—as if, Bantling thinks, somebody is crazy with nostalgia for some other life entirely. Unlike any that could be lived here, he adds to himself looking out the window at palms, the blue glittering Gulf.

Boyd gets up and Bantling spreads the sheets on the mattress. "It'll make her feel good when she wakes up," he says. They tuck her in. Boyd places a frayed teddy bear in the crook of her arm and leans down and kisses her gently on the lips. "Sleep well, darling," he says. Bantling leans down after, but before he kisses her he wipes her lips with his forefinger.

"Let's let her sleep," Boyd says, "let her rest."

"Okay."

Bantling follows Boyd out, down the hall that is dim and cool, into the kitchen. Half a dozen sweet potatoes froth out of jars on the windowsill. Their white roots seem to writhe in the water, their spade leaves hang voluptuously over the sill, trailing into the sink that is filled with unwashed dishes. On a long pine table in the center of the room are jars of tomatoes and okra and cucumber pickles left randomly. A black wood stove hunkers next to a modern gas range that is smeared with grease. "You want something to eat?" Boyd says. He unscrews a cap from a pickle jar and pulls out a big cucumber. "You've had Molly's pickles?"

"Yes."

Bantling says he doesn't want anything. He is restless. He doesn't want to stay there.

"Come on," Boyd says. Bantling follows him out of the house across the yard to the dock that juts out narrowly into the water. He stops first under the cables and looks up into them. They sway in the breeze like a hammock, the angles shifting, forming and reforming in a stately succession. Light gleams on the steel, winks away, and catches again. There is a brutal and dense heaviness about the assemblage that troubles him. He steps out from under it, afraid that it might fall on him. Boyd, who has continued on to the dock, comes back toward him. "You like it?"

"What is it?"

"My sculpture. Molly helped me make it."

"It's very vigorous, but there's something scary about it."

Boyd frowns. "It's a net," he says. "For catching big things."

"What things?"

"Whatever's big and hasn't been caught yet." Boyd gazes up at the sculpture, admiring it. "I got the idea from space stations," he says.

"From space?"

"Listening stations. Platforms out in space. You want to climb it? That's what we do."

Bantling suddenly wants to. "Yes," he says, "yes, I do."

"Great."

Boyd shows him how to climb the big poplar, bouncing quickly up the notches he's chucked into the trunk, pulling himself up the knobs of the lopped-off limbs until he can swing into the cables. His walk sinks and rises, the cables tremble as he moves, holding on to one above his head like a man crossing a rope bridge; Bantling feels a touch of the fear one might feel swinging on ropes above a chasm. The lowest cable is maybe thirty feet above the ground, the highest another forty feet above that. There are junctures, resting places where several cables cross, and he follows, swaying, reeling nearly upside down, until he reaches behind Boyd one of the highest spots, a little fret of lines off a jutted wing of branches in which the tulip leaves are turning brown. Boyd lies down in the cables. Bantling slides in beside him and sits down on two crossed lines, leans back against another. He can see a long way out into the Gulf, beyond grass islands and the blue line of pines pressing out from the west, into the channels and the open water. A few shrimp boats, white figures against the pale horizon, ply their trade far out; they don't seem to move at all. "It's spectacular," Bantling gasps.

"Yes it is. It's the best I've done."

"You've made other things like this?"

"Sculptures. Yes, similar ones, something like this; not as expert or as big."

"I wish I had one."

"Anybody would."

Bantling looks back at the house. Its green roof shines as if it has been rained on. "Molly has come into a strange world."

Boyd smiles without showing his teeth. His lips are smooth and thinly rounded. "How old are you?" he says.

"I'm thirty. The same age as Molly. Except she was born on the first of February and I was born in November."

"You've been friends all your lives."

"Rare and true."

"I envy you. I don't think I've ever really had a friend, not someone I could count on, or who could count on me." He says this without self-pity, socially, as one might speak of the clouds.

"I don't guess I'd know what it is to be without one—since Molly's always been there."

"Until recently, ay?"

"They say you're bad for her."

"They say?"

"Those I've talked to. They say you are a dangerous man, who hurts people."

Boyd laughs. It is a small gurgling sound, like water guttering in a sink drain. "I have no defense against the accusation," he says with some dignity. "But then, I'm not looking for one either."

"I don't know you, but I do know I miss Molly."

"It's brave of you to come after her. And foolish maybe."

"I can't help myself. I've got no choice."

Boyd studies him. There is a hint of gaiety in his dark eyes. "Times come," he says, "when we can't prevent ourselves. We wake up in the night and we feel what we fear coming toward us. It's like some ancient beast with blue stone eyes that we can't resist. We think it's going to eat us, and we're terrified of the pain, and flinch from it, but what is worse—and we forget it and rediscover it each time—is that it doesn't want to eat us at all; it wants to become us, which is what it does. We are picked up like a puppet when the hand thrusts into its body and begins to move it. We nod, we bow, we wave our arms. When it's finished it throws us down."

"Mostly, where I live," Bantling says, "it's quiet. I get up early and go out and feed the dolphins. They're as happy to see me as puppies. They chirp and splash. Sometimes I think if they could they'd like to jump out of the water and play with me in the yard. But they can't. I have to go in with them. I used to be scared but now I'm not."

"Molly told me about your dolphins."

"I caught them in the river. Or I saved them, I don't know. Hurricane Ethel scared them out of the Gulf. It was five years ago. They had swum two miles upstream, so far up that they were in the clear part—the river's spring-fed—so you could see them swimming underwater, just streaking along all silver and sleek, running along above the reeds. They'd gotten trapped in a cove. The water wasn't more than three feet deep. I came on them in my boat; I was seining for mullet—there's some good mullet fishing sometimes in the fall after a storm—and I caught them in the net. They thrashed so I thought they would kill themselves or drown—which they almost did. I dragged them behind the boat all the way to the bay and I put them in the cistern we used to use when we raised fish, until I could build a pen. Now they live out there and I put on shows with them. I've got a little set of bleachers I bought when they tore down the American

Legion park over at St. Luke's, and people come to see them jump and swim."

"Nobody told you about letting what's already wild stay wild."

"Yeah. They did. And I'm usually somebody who respects that. But this time I couldn't resist. Something in me had to have those dolphins in my life."

"It's a fatal error. Common, but still fatal. We go along like fish, drawing the water in and letting it out, but then one day we decide to hold it in. Just this sweet mouthful. We hold it and it turns sour, it turns to poison, and it kills us. I think that's your story, Little Person. You sowed your doom with those dolphins. Because you did that you're here now."

"What is going to happen?"

"Everything you've dreaded."

"I just want to get my girl back."

"Sure you do."

Boyd waves his hand dismissively, and he may have pressed with his foot against the cable Bantling sits on, because as he—he isn't sure—moves slightly in response to the wave, he feels himself dropped then pushed forward slightly so that he starts. He stands upright, his foot slips, he scrambles for a place to stand, finds none, and falls. He drops through the cables, bouncing against them, grabbing for purchase as he drops, panic whistling in his mind—he cries out—wincing from the slap of the steel, until he hits on his knees against a strand fifteen feet below, bounces backward against another strand and catches with one hand a cable above his head and hangs there, swinging slowly, gasping, dizzy and unsure of where he is. He manages to grab the cable with his other hand, but he is too weak to pull himself up. Boyd peers down at him from his high perch. The poplar leaves, crumbled brown as if they are burned, stir behind him. Boyd looks like a bird peering over the edge of its nest. "Hold on," he says calmly.

Bantling watches him descend, as agile as a cat, springing from cable to cable, sliding in closer, slipping the strands, until he eases in beside him. "Here," he says. He leans his back against one cable and pushes another with his foot so Bantling can step onto it. Bantling catches it with his foot, lurches forward, and falls, like a sack of grain thrown over a fence, across the strand Boyd leans against. Boyd holds him around the waist. "There," he says, "you're safe." He holds him while Bantling climbs back into a sitting position. They sit side by side, forty feet above the ground. The grass beneath them is yellowed, stippled with patches of sandspur and billygoat grass. Bantling takes a deep breath; he feels a little faint, light-headed.

"Close call, ay?" Boyd says.

"Close enough."

Banty leans forward and spits between his legs. He looks at Boyd, who is studying him with a look of curiosity and delight in his eyes. The skin of Boyd's face is smooth and very white, like skin never touched by sunlight. Long vertical creases run down the cheeks, as precisely cut as if by a scalpel. The lips are long and thin, mobile, smiling now. The wide-set, blue-black eyes are large and very round, filled not with understanding but with knowledge. They are the eyes of someone who knows exactly what he is doing, and what others are doing. "I come out here at night," Bantling says.

"Yes, you do."

"I tracked her down, but I was afraid to come directly to her. I didn't know what was up, and people told me to be careful of you, so I sneaked out here at night and spied on her from the woods. I was so mesmerized by watching her that I didn't even notice this sculpture. I guess I need to say I'm sorry for spying."

"You can if you want to, but I don't mind it."

"What do you do?"

"With my life?"

"Yes."

"I rearrange things."

"What things?"

"Whatever looks like it would do better somewhere else. There's no plan. I just respond to the need as it arises."

"And Molly?"

"You mean what have I done to her, or what has she done to herself?"

"Either."

"She's just taken the next step."

"Running off with a stranger?"

"I'm not a stranger anymore."

"She's got a whole nother life that she's abandoned. In the other life—which I don't know if you know about—she gets up in the morning and goes out into the good fields and works them, and she comes over in the evening and we sit out in lawn chairs on the dock and talk about life and listen to the dolphins jumping and tell each other stories about the constellations, and lie about our childhood. It's quiet and spectacular in its way; and I miss it so much it makes me want to lie down and die."

"Don't do that, partner."

"Don't do that, huh?"

Bantling is a small man, thin. When he was a boy people said *He's so skinny the wind's going to blow him away.* There are voices in his head. The wind seems to have hands and the hands touch him about his body, tugging at his clothes. The Gulf, where the sun is rubbing its body clean on the blue surface, seems tilted at the far end as if the sea is slowly rising toward them, as if the world, stately as a king, is falling toward them. He stands up, shaking in the wires. "You think you do things that nobody else will do," he says. "Watch this." There is a trembling in his legs. The cables surge and sway. He thinks of them for a second as harp strings he might pluck a tune from. Then he lets himself go.

He falls through the cables, bouncing against them, rebounding off one to the other; for a few seconds it is as if strong arms are throwing him, the way his uncles threw him when he was a baby—throw and catch: *Boy, we might just throw you away*—but then there are no more cables and he is falling through the bright air, faster than he has ever fallen before, plunging downward on his back so that for one second he can see above him the body and face of the slim man hanging in the wires above him, the head leaning off the stalky neck like a strange white flower, the eyes watching him with shock, but with interest too, excitement, steadily watching him, until the ground rushes up behind him and slams him hard in the back, so that the breath—and nearly the life, he thinks—is knocked out of him. He is completely conscious and he is aware of his body fully—though there is nothing he can move and no pain—so that he lies in the grass that comes up around his ears like a straw hat, drifting, as if in a grassy sea, looking up. As if at a great distance, in slow motion, he sees the thin, strong man slipping down through the webs of cable, sliding gracefully and steadily down from strand to strand, as, behind him in the blue sky, the clouds move like another planet's portable white statuary, and the breeze, stooping low, licks at his face. He thinks that there is nothing in his life he isn't making up, that it is a mystery without meaning beyond the fact that he is alive in the middle of it; and oddly, since he is one who worries the oddities of his existence like a penitent would worry his sins, this thought does not bother him, he wants in fact to leap to his feet and tell it to someone, to Molly, who, he remembers, slumbers in her dispassionate sleep, lost, as she always is after a spell, to the life of this world—as if there is no world—he wants to shake her awake, as he used to when they slept together as young children, to speak of some suddenly realized and fantastically interesting thought, to say to her that he has just made the discovery that what life is about is the living of it; but as he thinks this, the words forming like bubbles on his lips, it doesn't seem such a remarkable thought after all, maybe it is a thought others—even Molly—have had many times before, have had and moved on from to the more stringent thoughts of adulthood, whatever that is, and so he lets it slip away from him as he continues to watch D'Nel Boyd, who is already remarkable to him, and who is as real as any boat or dolphin or metaphysics, descend through the maze of cables—he seems to leap, to spring from strand to strand—he reaches the bottom strand—it looks as if he isn't going to climb down the tree—and then—maybe Bantling blinks—he is crouched beside him, touching his forehead with a hand that is cool and gentle. "Easy, boy," he hears him say, "easy. You've had the wind knocked out of you." And maybe I have broken bones, too, Bantling thinks, but he is unable to speak. Then Boyd gets up and takes a step away from him and in a moment Bantling hears the fizz and splatter as he pisses against the side of the poplar tree. "I think you're only stunned," Boyd says over his shoulder, "but it's a miracle you're not hurt." He turns and Bantling sees the white rope of his penis drawn quickly back into his pants, and watches the dip of his hips as he settles himself. Boyd gazes at him, studying him, and then he comes back and sits beside his shoulder. He looks up at the maze of cables that swing slowly in the afternoon breeze. "Yes," he says, "that's a long way to fall. I guess the reason you didn't get hurt was because you have some kind of protection." Yes, maybe that's it, Bantling would say if he could talk, but he can't and he lies in the grass, oddly, he thinks, unfrightened—he could be paralyzed—and, in fact, content. Boyd leans down and brushes the hair away from Bantling's forehead and places his forefinger against his neck. "Your pulse," he says, "is fine." He looks away out into the Gulf where the breeze moves in the reeds near shore and flicks at the tops of the thin, sunny waves. "She told me about what life was like up there where you two come from and I guess I have to say it doesn't sound like too much to me. I don't expect I'd be satisfied working a farm and sitting on the back porch evenings watching the chickens get ready for bed."

Bantling wants to protest, but he still can't speak.

"I need a little more movement, you know? You ever play dodgeball? You're in the middle of a circle of kids and they're throwing a ball at you trying to hit you. At first there's not too much to it because there're a lot of other people in the circle with you, but pretty soon they're weeded out and then you look around and you're by yourself with everybody else out on the rim throwing at you. That's what I like best." He lifts one haunch off a slow fart and settles back. "I like to be out there . . . dodging."

There is a soothing tone in his voice, very gentle, as if the words are drawing over a bed of cool green leaves. He dips his head between his legs and sniffs himself. His laughter crackles. "You know you love someone," he says, "when you like the smell of their farts." He waves his hand. "Sometimes I'm such a coarse fellow. You'll have to forgive me. Sometimes I have no control at all. I just blunder on." He plucks a strand of sandspur and whips the clustered head against his pants leg. The sandy burrs stick to the cloth. He leans over his knees and looks at Bantling. It is as if, Bantling thinks, still floating, he is peering over the top of a wall. "You ever think about suffering?" Boyd says. "You ever contemplate it much? Sometimes, huh? I think about it a lot. It's obvious that everybody suffers, it's obvious that that's the human condition, so it's not the suffering per se that's important, am I right? Sure. What matters is what we use to represent it. What dance it jigs us into. We name it: we call it drink, or lust, or the Boss, or race, or our twisted foot, or even this hot, devilish day that is too much for us—we call it something so we can use it. We say, *I have this grief because my brother died,* so our friends will feel at home." He thrusts his hands out open-palmed, turning them this way and that, looking at the nails. "People ask me, I say I'm just a nice Jewish boy from Baltimore, which makes them feel fine, except I'm not Jewish and I'm not from Baltimore. I say, Yes, I lost my brother too; he fell from a boat and drowned, and I see their eyes light up with sympathy. Ah, the government, I cry, why won't they treat us right—and common souls gather around. We all know pain, we live in it all our lives. Don't ever pretend it isn't so. But make sure you find some way to describe it that other people can connect to. Then you're okay. You can go ahead and suffer according to your lights. You don't have to be afraid. It's a tool like any other. This world's not so baffling if you stop and take a good hard look at it."

Bantling has lost the train of what he is saying. He discovers he can move his head, just slightly. It creaks on his neck; he is afraid to try any other part of his body. He looks toward the Gulf, where the wind wrinkles the surface of the water. Then the wind shifts slightly and the creases smooth and the water begins to take on an oily sheen, as it does late in the day, and the sun-glitter sets a scattered trail of chipped light that gathers as it recedes from him toward the peninsula in the west, until it fills the horizon nearly with a yellow shattered skirt of light. People talk about oceans as permanent and unchanging, but nobody who lives by one would say that. In thirty years he has almost never seen the Gulf the same two days together. There are always elements that are the same—maybe whitecaps two days running, or two weeks running—but the light has changed, or the wind that had been steady is fitful now, shifting into another quarter, and a storm off Cuba has pushed a new pulse into the swells, shortening them, staining them with the color of itself. He was an idiot to have come here, to have followed Molly to this place where the irrepressible D'Nel Boyd preached on about life and suffering, but here he is, stretched out in a shady yard where above his head green damselflies skitter and sail, and off in the side yard a couple of white sheets on a wash line flap, making stiff, popping sounds like the sounds of distant gunfire. And then he hears the heavy buzz of a horsefly, and then he sees it, squat and heavy-headed, stumble onto his arm, take a few steps among the brindle hairs, and then dip forward, like a man sinking his head to drink, and he sees the sharp plunger of its beak strike his flesh and he feels the sting that is more like electricity than a needle, and he flinches, involuntarily, and brushes it away.

"See," Boyd says, "you can move. Nothing's broken. We just had to wait for you to come back to yourself. I know that feeling," he continues. "It's like for a minute your body's been tossed out of itself. It can be frightening, you feel so empty, and sometimes you panic. I've seen guys broken all to pieces who jump up and try to run away, like maybe they could escape their fate . . . or maybe catch it. Yeah, maybe catch it—the former fate that has just been whacked out of them. Here, let me help you."

He bends down, and carefully, squatting, thrusting his arms under Bantling's shoulders and back, begins to lift him.

"Ah, go slowly," Bantling cries.

"Don't worry, partner."

He lifts him in his arms—whisks him, Bantling thinks—carries him into the house and through it to the bedroom where he lays him down on the bed beside Molly. She sleeps on her back with her arms tossed above her head, snoring lightly. White flecks of spittle have collected at the corners of her mouth. Boyd's hand snakes under Bantling's throat and begins to undo the buttons of his shirt. "What . . ." Bantling starts to say, but then he doesn't have the strength to resist. Boyd unbuttons and pulls the shirt off him, then he slips him out of his trousers and then out of his Jockey shorts. He stands over him, looking down at his slender naked body. "You're a pretty boy," he says. "You're a lot prettier than I imagined." Bantling feels the small web of his sex stir, but that is all. Boyd leans over Molly and begins to undo her clothes. Gently, he undresses her until she is naked too. "Twins," he says. "You'll do fine together." Bantling might have stopped him, but something in him wants this. He hasn't seen her naked since they were teenagers.

Everything he remembers about her body has changed. She isn't anything like she had been, like the picture of her he has carried for fifteen years in his mind.

"You are letting me do this," a voice says. He doesn't know if it is Boyd. He looks at him but his lips aren't moving.

Molly's hips are bony; they hold up, like the rim of a bowl, the taut tawny well of her belly. The black hair in her groin is thick and shines as if it has been buffed. Her breasts are small and slack, two brimming pools in which the red, turgid nipples float. "Dear heart," he murmurs, "dear heart."

Boyd stands over them, but apart, gazing at their bodies. They lie on their backs. From the chair by the bed he picks up a bow-tie quilt, flaps it open above them. "You both need rest," he says. "It's all right with me if you take it." Bantling watches the quilt flare and descend over their naked bodies. It is like a tent set loose by breeze. He feels the wind it makes pass over them, picturing in his mind the dead boy on the bed and Boyd leaping over his body to reach Molly. He sees Boyd's foot press into the dead white flesh above the boy's ankle. Now he feels his coarse breath. Then he is asleep.

What I wanted to say to Bess when we came upon each other, as two deer might chance on each other in a rainy wood, that time in the bathroom, that time years later after forgiveness and time had begun to heal us—after we had begun to pretend they had—was that when I looked at her from the shower and then came forth naked to stand in front of her undefended nakedness, it was the scar, the bright sprung worm of it, that seemed most alive to me, that made life jump in me; this brand, eternal tattoo, that I had fastened to her body, that would burn on undiminished into the grave, until flesh itself dissolved. What I wanted to say was that I loved it. But there was no way to say that. There was no way to tell the truth and ask for forgiveness too.

1.

R.B. came up beside me and stood there, haunting me for a few minutes without my knowing it. I lay on my back on the old mohair couch in the back hall, on the Navaho blanket Bess had bought on a dirt street in a village not far from the Grand Canyon—thirteen years ago, I guess it was, I guess it was that long ago, a summer's day when we put down from the car like two exhausted voyagers, put down out of anger and resentment and grief, and thirst, and she disappeared into the red adobe shop like someone vanishing into the next scene, to come out a few minutes later, smiling, a Coke tipped straight back glugging down her throat and the blanket tossed over her shoulder. Through the french doors I could see the sky and the Gulf partially. The fleecy heads of pampas grass waved at the edge of the yard; a breeze snapped at the tops of the cabbage palms. I was thinking about the wanderers, I was thinking about the men who travel the country—the salesmen, the homeless, the migrant workers, the long-haul truckers—all the ones for whom America is not a place but a passage, and I was thinking about the way, in Manhattan, the night sinks down among the buildings, on a dark street, say, on the Lower East Side, how the light sinks and settles so that the buildings, which are helpless, deanimated, become relicked and strange, and about the play Celest told me she attended that was put on by friends of hers in a narrow street space between night buildings—down in the Financial District, where the buildings are so close together that their tops seem about to sew themselves closed, and the oldest are the color of soot—and how the players, dressed in black, struck postures of grief and loss in the darkness under the buildings, and how dark she said it was—the stage (the street that was the stage) unlighted, the street unlighted—so that the audience standing slightly apart and the players moving slightly apart seemed episodes of the same story, simultaneously told, until the shadows moving—the players— seemed to take on the quality of thought, as if they were the thoughts of the spectators living partially and apart, wordlessly for a while, or with only the faintest and most incomplete of ejaculatory noises, and how when, silently and swiftly, in the silence beyond the hum of Manhattan, in the dark street, one of the actors, a woman in a long black gown, squatted, raised the gown above her waist, and pissed slowly and eloquently, profoundly, on the raw pavement, and how the noise of it, of her pissing, of the siss and splatter of it, in the silence, was like, so Celest said, a flower bud opening out of season, or the hand of your beloved touching you in the darkness, a sound of humanness and comfort (as when one of the continental wanderers, stranded somewhere on a low night outside of Topeka perhaps or Cheyenne, Wyoming, will take from his pocket a small pouch wrapped in tinfoil and unfold it to gaze a few minutes again at the small travertine stone given to him six years ago by a waitress from a roadhouse outside Birmingham, Alabama, after she spent the night with him in the small half-burnt-out motel near the river, riding his body, riding the pommel of his meager cock as if she actually believed him to be the raw and magnificent mustang that he, on nights of drunkenness, dreamed he was, so that now, since it was so long ago, and since the stone, only slightly larger than the ball of his thumb, is not the image or picture of memory but the container, he raises it as his eyes wander across the landscape of patchy weathering grass and across the stands of aspen, which are whispering their own indecipherable secrets to the night and themselves, to the mountains like piles of dark laundry heaped in the distance under the blank and indifferent sky, and taps the stone gently against his teeth, *tok, tok, tok,* remembering, dreaming it alive again . . .), and how, at that moment as Celest watched the stream of piss splatter the woman's ankles and flow between them to collect in a pool in front of her that in the darkness took on the sheen of an unidentifiable light, and watched as the woman bent slowly down over her knees, tipped down and licked the piss, and then slowly raised herself, smacking her lips, and raised her hand, groping with her fingers at the darkness, she felt her own breast open, helplessly, and felt the emptiness under her heart that began to hollow itself more deeply into the cavity, and did not fight this, but welcomed it, as one in fever will, after days, begin to welcome the fever, as one who is lost in a wood will, finally, begin to praise her solitude.

For a moment, for a moment just before R.B.'s hand touched me on the shoulder, I thought I was about to come to something, and I felt something in me begin to rise up, as one will get up from a bed to answer the phone, and I remembered waking in my bed in the long upstairs room of my garage on the Lower East Side, and how there was often a moment when the sun and shadow shapes standing in the tall windows were not simply shapes of weather, but beings, sojourners who had been waiting for me, and one in particular waiting, one I was tracking now through the wilderness of reality and imagination—not a brother or a father or a lost love, but something like all of these—this D'Nel Boyd, connipter and liar and murderer—and I thought to myself as I began to hear the rustle of his body behind me, You are one strange moviemaker, my boy, you had better put your foot down through the clouds and stomp around awhile in the dirt. . . .

R.B. touched me, I started, he laughed—the bristly, familiar, distracted laugh of the psychically damaged—and he said, "One more, doggonit, with a pox eating him up."

I laughed—distractedly myself—and hoisted my body upright. "You mean me?"

"You were concentrating like a baby squatting over his doodoo."

I said, "Do you know that phrase, nervous as a dog shitting razor blades?"

"Yes. I often live it."

"That's how I feel sometimes. It's not like I'm about to jump out of my skin, but like something else is about to jump *into* my skin."

"I know exactly how you feel."

He grinned and I grinned back. I was glad to see him.

I said, "Bess wants us to go out fishing together, out on the sponge boats, which actually I'd like to do since I've never seen how sponge fishermen work."

"Anytime you'd like to, just let me know. I have many friends in the sponge business."

His black hair was sleeked down with water. It looked weighted, as if something invisible were pressing on it, and it made his cranium seem a little squashed. He was dressed in rumpled white—white trousers, white linen shirt—and had knotted a red bandanna around his neck. He smelled richly of cologne.

"Are you too busy," he said, "to come with me? I have a little project
I'd like you to see."

"I'd be delighted."

I hadn't seen much of him since the first night when Bess led him
upstairs by his sleeve. Occasionally I had heard the metal taps on the
heels of his loafers clicking by in the hall, and, once or twice, the ragged
sound of an old piano had wafted from under the eaves of the third-
floor porch, outside the suite of rooms where he lived. From the yard
I could see the string of maritime flags he'd attached to the roof fascia,
snapping and twirling gaily in the afternoon breeze. Just before sunset
he would amble down the boardwalk in his big-belled hat and scuffed
maroon robe for a dip in the surf. My feet propped on the second-story
rail, I would watch him carefully, with a slowness that was like the
slowness of drugs or a dream, unfold a striped blanket, place four
smooth stones at its corners, align books, capped glass of brown whiskey, pillow, and the black wooden rosary—blessed, so Bess told me, by
the pope himself—shrug off the robe, which he neatly folded and placed
under the hat, and walk solemnly down to the surf for a puffing swim.
Finished, he would return, walking nearly in the same tracks, towel off,
climb into the robe and hat again, and lie down on the blanket, where,
hands folded on his bony chest, he would remain for half an hour as
still as a corpse. Although he had been born on the Gulf, his skin was
so sensitive to sunlight that he never exposed himself to direct rays. If
ever he went out in midday it was only under cover of trousers and
long sleeves, under a broad-brimmed hat and dark glasses, often with
a towel or scarf wound around his neck to prevent the slightest sliver
of sun from sneaking through. His skin under his clothes was a smooth
yellowish white, like pancake batter, and soft to the touch; it dented
like a baby's.

Now he touched my wrist lightly and directed me to follow him,
which I did, through downstairs corridors whose open doors let out the
calls of servants, the noise of daily bustle, through bright streaks of
white July sunshine, west through the long house to his study, a darkened room behind a tall white door. Inside, under the high, yellow-
stained ceiling, were bookcases stuffed like immigrant satchels with
weathered volumes and yellowed papers, with bundles of manuscript

tied with brittle binder's twine, small artifacts placed here and there among them; around a large table pushed under a window that was curtained in heavy blue velvet drapes, plump torn striped armchairs, casual tables, and green-shaded lamps from the necks of which dangled small icons were arranged as if for a seminar that had long ago been abandoned but not cleaned up after. On the stained pinewood floor was a large scuffed Persian rug that gave off a faint seaweedy odor.

I followed him to the table—he walked straight to it—and we stood above it as if it were the lip of a pool we were about to dive into. Or, I thought, as minutes ticked by while we gazed down on stacks and scurries of typed sheets and green cardboard folios from which pages protruded like bits squashed out, as if it were a corpse we were viewing. It was all right with me to stand there, not talking, without designation of the moment; his quiet was calm, self-absorbed but generous; his left hand moved diffidently through the papers, touching them lightly, as if to assure himself all was in place, the expression on his face one of slight bafflement, almost awe. I thought of my daughter, of Rachel, who would sometimes perch on the other end of the couch as I worked over a lapboard, lifting her head from time to time from the complicated undressing and re-dressing of her favorite doll to study me; in her face would shine a sweetly defenseless look of fascination and wonder, as if somewhere far back in her being, something wholly primitive and untamable helplessly asked her what in the world she was doing here, in this place, in this world. Such a look was in the face that R.B. lifted to me in the dim, lamplit room, a sweet bafflement in his smile, his hand moving slowly among the papers.

"I'm compiling a new dictionary," he said. "I think it's going well."

"That's what all these papers are?"

"Yes. Notes and completed entries. I have five hundred pages done, over a thousand articles."

"That's quite a lot."

"Yes, but then it's a big world."

He was so solemn, so childlike that I nearly laughed out loud. "Would you show me?"

"I want you to see it."

He shuffled through a slanted stack, pushed it aside, opened one of the large folios, drew out a small sheaf, and handed it to me. The paper was heavy and white, the type soot-black and smashed into the page, as if he hit the keys with his fists. It was an entry entitled *Success,* which was, so I read, "The ability to walk humbly under the will of God, to serve, to wholly seek a usefulness in the world of God and our fellows; to abandon all, as one would abandon a child, without looking back to see that it is fed and cared for, and step forth into the light and circumstance of God's will; the love of what is and the releasing of it; a tenacious tenderness; the ability to see oneself in others and so forgive; a constant mimicry; wanting what you've got; harmony; a casual deference; the ability to give from our poverty rather than our riches; the realization that there is nothing God won't forgive; the ability to love all creation which includes maimed children, rats in the palm trees, the spirochete, hail, lost love, Ethiopia, men who love money, cold women, spit on the sidewalk, etc.; acceptance of the indivisible harmony of all creation, its necessity . . ."

The entry ran on for another page, the wild moral words chiseled into the thick paper, all the phrases claiming some order of acceptance and surrender as the only definition of the word. I glanced through some of the other sheets; there were entries for concepts and things, for activities, for body parts, for stones and shapes. There was one on babies that began, "You see how small they are . . ." and another—*"Amethyst:* They dig up stones out of the earth . . ."—that ran on for five pages; each entry was as wild and coagulant as the next, each as filled with moral imperative and cracked wisdom as the first.

As I read he hovered beside me, nodding and bobbing, rising on the balls of his thin feet and letting himself drop with a sigh. From beyond the draped curtains came the faint crash of machinery as tractors heaved to at the end of the fruit rows for an exchange of plows. Bess had told me she was putting drain tile in the groves, in anticipation, she said, of winter rains, which she believed would come this year to end the drought. I had knelt down at the end of the rows and taken the sandy, ash-colored soil in my hands and pressed my face into it, a soil like the planet's dirt waste, useless for anything beyond pines and palmetto and the twisted low brows of blackjack oak, but which she, following her father, had raised the destiny of, as a queen might lift a peasant out of his poverty, kneading peat, horse manure, sewer sludge, and compost, as well as the lighter commercial fertilizers, into it, until in places in some of the fields it shone with the dark deep friable richness of Midwest ground. In here, R.B. had blocked all that out. Someone cleaned—there was no dust anywhere—but no one rearranged. This was a life he had made for himself.

I shook the pages and put them down. "This is wonderful," I said, looking him in the face.

"Thank you. I have great grandiose plans for it that make no sense in reality, but mostly I just like doing it."

"How far will you go?"

He pressed a finger into his long bottom lip. "Until I get everything into place."

"How long do you think that will take?"

"All the time I've got. I hope. Actually I'm almost through."

"Then what?"

"It either works or I'm ruined." He chuckled, offhandedly, like someone who knows much more about the case than anyone else but is being nice about it.

"I know the feeling," I said.

While he made tea in a dented tin pot he set on a hot plate in the corner, I wandered around looking at the books. Shelves on two sides of the room went up at least twelve feet to the ceiling. He had everything in them you could want. There were thirty feet of encyclopedias, hundreds of novels, works of history, a book on the coloration of butterflies, books of journeying and exploration, a history of underwear, a book on the development of torture instruments, a boxed set of books on the symbols of Japanese culture, dozens of books on the natural world, on birds, on flowers, on soil. It exhausted me to look at them. I retreated to an armchair and eased myself down. He brought me a cup of thick dark tea that smelled of anise and faintly of tea-olive blossoms. "Something I mixed myself," he said when I looked a question. "I think it's good."

As he moved about the room he began to talk about his life, about his struggle to stay alive on the wilderness coast. I didn't mind listening to him. It was my practice to listen to strangers. Having done it all my life—son of a river man, taught from an early age to listen to the stories travelers told—I had begun to learn, I thought, certain things. All stories were about struggle. All contained the seeds of triumph, but most often they were about failure, about the missed chance, about the attempt that fell short, about the lover who didn't show up. Many men wanted to tell you they had pushed through, breaking barriers of adversity, but even these, once the imaginary wreaths of triumph began to fade, would fall back, settling, as debris dropped into river mud settles deeper each season, into the common bed of bafflement and loss. A railroad engineer spoke of how, twenty years before, he had hit a car stalled at a crossing, killing a woman and her child; a lady in a yellow-feathered hat told of the time she fell in love, on a ship crossing the Pacific, with a man who turned out to be a thief. An aging lawyer, his eyes seamed with years of laughter, told of the year in West Texas when tornadoes roved across the plains like robber bands, destroying towns and farmhouses, destroying the house he was born in, and returning two months later to knock the back porch off the house his father had built with his own hands and the help of his neighbors to replace it. *Look at what the world has done to me,* they cried. *Can you believe it?* Hands open, eyes wide with surprise, or shaking their heads and slapping their legs, kneading themselves under the ribs with pointed knuckles, they would whisper or exclaim, shaking their heads in bafflement or grinding their teeth, drawing back cloth to show the wounds.

I was always impressed, always amazed. I listened as one coming out of a prison might listen to a man suffering the ordinary starvation of American life, afraid to be useless, so paying attention; and as I listened I discovered that I loved best the bitter raconteurs, the blinded plumber who had turned on life, the housewife with one arm who hated every-one, the aging haberdasher who could not forgive God for taking his wife. I knew about the sly ones, the ones who told the stories that disgusted and frightened me, but who, when I peeked through the fingers of the hands thrown over my face, I could see were smiling, smiling because after all it was *their* story. But it was to these others, the unforgiving ones, the ones who, by God, were not getting over it, that my heart opened. They were never going to appear in any testimonials about the human spirit triumphing over adversity. They had nothing to say about triumph; they were too busy down on their knees banging their withered fists on the floor. Unreconciled Jobs, they didn't care about prosthetic developments, about gadgets that produced vibrations in the eyeball to simulate sight; they didn't want to know that many thalidomide dwarfs lived productive lives. Fuck productive lives, they cried, I am filled with hatred and shame. You think that I sit in this wheelchair dreaming of the time when I could dance, they cried, but you're wrong; I sit here dreaming that I could leap up and strangle you. I loved the murder in their eyes, the pure menace. I loved the stories about the quadriplegic begging for somebody to smother him, praying twenty-four hours a day for thugs to come kill his parents so the doctors would turn off the goddamn machinery keeping him alive. They were the ones who cried *I will not be appeased;* and I thought, Christ help us, they should be worshiped.

Now my ex-brother-in-law, skinny and disturbed, leaning into life as one might lean into a gritty wind, tacked toward me with a pot of honey in his hand. I scooped a dowel full and plunged it into the dark tea. "Local product?" I said smiling.

"Yes. From the hives. It's probably a little more bitter than you're used to."

"That's okay."

He eased himself down, as one who still does not trust gravity, or furniture, onto the sofa opposite me. He lay back, then pulled himself forward, out over his bony knees. "What I meant," he said, continuing, "was that I don't seem to be able to get past anything these days. That's a way of putting it. Everything has an equal glamour."

"A holly sprig means as much to you as a baby."

"Yes, like that. It began to happen two years ago, one spring when the tides were really high. They came in over the beach all the way up into the yard. They drowned the fig bushes, and flooded the yard so you'd go out in the morning and find starfish and sponges and old corroded pieces of man-of-war jellyfish strewn among the flower beds and tangled in the trellises. And what was even odder to me, they'd undercut the banks—you'd look out and see flower sprigs and tufts of grass floating in the surf. It was like one of those exchange programs where the Balinese come over in their dresses made out of leaves and flowers, while your team's over there in their suits, and each community stands around gawking at the other. I mean I'd seen the work of storms—though as I'm sure you know, there hasn't been a real tearing hurricane around here in forty years—but a storm is quick, it doesn't last long enough for you to get a feeling that the world is changing. . . ."

"Just that it's powerful . . ."

"Sure, but it passes. It's not like the long work of the tides. And that spring it was a long work, six weeks maybe, each day some new chunk of alien debris thrown up in the yard, each day some other bit of the ground you'd been standing on all your life out there floating away in the waves. It was curious and unsettling, and it made me look hard at things, in a way I hadn't done I guess since I was a child, and apparently—at least according to Miss Bess—it affected me so profoundly that I have become as nearly unfit as is possible down here for human company."

"She worries about you."

"She worries about anything that's not in the place where she's used to seeing it."

I chuckled.

"Anyway," he continued, pausing to sip a short sluperation—as Uncle Porto called it—of tea, "I became excited—agitated, Bess would say—I began to handle these objects, these starfish and Japanese fish floats and pieces of shark hide that were replacing the lawn I had turned somersaults on when I was four. I began to look at them, turn them over in my hands and study them, and I began to sense a strangeness in them that disturbed me."

"They were from the ocean."

"Yes, but that wasn't it. I've heard of the wild sea life—two-hundred-foot-long squid, sharks with human bones in their bellies—but living down here I've already seen it; that's not what I'm talking about. These creatures—this flotsam, whatever—weren't strange because they were from the ocean; they were strange because of themselves. It's what seeing the chunks of grass bobbing around on the salt waves showed me. Not strange to see grass out there, but strange to see *grass*. It took my breath away. It came to me that everything was distinct and alien and unexplainable. Which, as you might imagine, cracked my mind. I had a breakdown."

"Bess said you were hauling the stuff into the house. She said she couldn't get you to stop."

"That's true. But she only saw the surface, the act. I went into a frenzy, like one of those fellows who build an altar in their front yard out of glass and concrete and bottle caps and bits of tin they've picked up off the road; I worked like a slave—long hours, I can tell you— picking up and carrying in every piece of flotsam I could find. They were stacked on the porch so high you couldn't move among them. Everybody complained—the stink was terrible, though I tried to pre- serve what I could—but the worst problem, at least for me, was that I got so caught up in it I forgot to sleep, or rest in any way, eat. The enterprise wore me down. I began to collapse. I'd fall down on the lawn and come to with sea horses in my hands, looking up into the stars. This is a crazy household, I will tell you that—I guess you know—so they let me go on with it for quite some time, and I can be a bit ferocious myself when I have to"—"Yes . . ."—"I don't blame them for taking so long to come to my rescue—I didn't *want* to be res- cued"—"No . . ."—"and when I finally did get rescued—or stopped—I wasn't glad *or* sad about it, not either one."

"How did it happen?"

"I was hauling the wheelhouse of a shrimp boat up the boardwalk when I passed out and it fell over on top of me. They told me later that I was trying to drag it, even though I was under it. I was still moving, heading for the porch. It was actually pretty funny, I guess, in a twisted way—which is our favorite down here—me on my back with this sea-greasy gigantic board on my chest, trying to pull it like a blanket up over me and into the house. It was another time I alarmed the servants. Bess and a couple of the hands came out and lifted it off me; and then they picked me up and carried me into the house. Appar- ently I wasn't coherent. I do remember a smell like crushed ants, and somebody—one of the servants, I guess—whistling under his breath, a church song, one of the sweet lilting ones that I couldn't quite remember the name of, about the church being the bride of Christ, all that. And they had the doctor come and give me a shot and a transfusion—I was, in my feeble way, quite violent—which kept me under for three days—an experience, by the way, I can remember vividly, the knocked-out time, I mean: it was like a big black foot standing on my face, crushing and choking me"—"Yes . . ."—"and then I was groggy for most of a week, stayed in bed, with Mattie bringing me soup and milk toast as if I were a little kid with the chicken pox, all of them nice as you please so that I wouldn't notice that they had me locked in, which they did, with a padlock and buckle fastened to the other side of my door—can you believe it?—until finally I could get up and around and they saw that I wasn't going to attack anybody and the fit seemed to have passed."

"Were you okay?"

He stretched his hands out, opening his thin fingers. When he spoke his voice had lost some of the cultured inflection he had taught it through the years—and which by bearing and learning was natural to him—softening toward the rifts and hollows it was native to. He didn't seem to notice.

"I was all right physically. I passed a few grins around and I began to eat with the usual heartiness, and I even played a few pieces on the piano for everybody, but the truth is, it was only for show. The truth is, I was traduced."

"What is that?"

"I was like Saul on the road to Tarsus. Stunned by light. Changed entirely."

"What did it feel like?"

"As if I were living in a body carved out of white stone. With the same fixed and eternal perspective that a statue has. This permanent immobility of gaze. Like a fakir or a game-show contestant. I knew what I had to do—as they say in the movies"—"Yes"—"I knew what I was supposed to do, what I was going to do, and I knew that it didn't matter what anybody thought of it; I knew in some curious way that nobody would even notice."

"So this," I said, waving a hand at the piled manuscripts on the table.

"Exactly. It was necessary to place everything. To define it in such a way that nobody again could lose track of it. It was one of these

Edenic impulses. . . ." I looked at him stupidly. "As in the garden of Eden, where Adam named all the animals and plants. Think what that must have been like. Adam woke into his life, from no life, a grown man, not a child, come to out of nothing, no dream or memory of life, no existence at all beyond the existence of the handful of dry clay God blew breath into. It must have been terrifying. Where on earth could we find such an experience now?"

"Vietnam?"

"Perhaps. Perhaps instead of firing wildly, if those boys flailing in the jungles had begun to name a world—leaf, stone, butterfly—they might have survived with more of their minds intact—though of course it's unforgivable that adults, the old men of that time, would send them so stupidly into such a world. Resourceless. Sent to a jungle prepared for an emergency in a shopping mall. No wonder they went mad."

He took a long sip of tea, his top lip quivering above the rim of the blue china cup. He lowered the cup carefully, like an old man, and touched his lips with his fingers. "This is another conundrum that we won't go far into now, but the fact is it touches directly on the center of existence, which is something, you must remember, that is, in its conception as well as its expression, entirely miraculous."

"What do you mean?"

He held his hand up to silence me, looked away toward the curtains, along the closed edge of which a single thin blade of white light hung straight down. The light made a wider yellow bar on the table and on the stacks of papers. "The essential miracle is simply that instead of turning toward madness Adam turned to naming. He got up off that ground, the claybank of his birth, and began not only to ask himself what all this was, these colored flying bits, these bright patches that smelled so sweet, this cold ungraspable substance tumbling over his hands—began not just to ask himself what all this was, but, which is more, which is the miracle, began to say to himself, I will call this a bird, this a flower, this a river. Now, of course, the more particular and important question is why would he do this, but perhaps this is a question that can only be answered within the circle of faith, perhaps it is the mystery we are required to accept, the one that makes life and its continuance possible, but whatever it is, it is the essential and fundamental—the necessary—move we all must make to survive on this planet." He coughed delicately into his fist. "What came to me was that for some reason I had been jerked back into some raw application of it. Those tufts of grass riding in the surf, those yellow, crusted starfish washed up under the holly bushes were not alien, they were original. This is what I realized. Smacked first by the strangeness of these articles wrenched from their usual configuration, confused and thinking them out of place; driven, I guess I have to admit, slightly off my rocker by this, I came to the only conclusion possible if I wanted to survive— there's another mystery: why we would want to survive"—"I've wondered about that myself . . ."—"sure; but listen, I discovered that I must, and this is curious, *must* try to name them, to define them, give them a place in the order of the world, to make an order."

"The new Adam."

"Not new, the same. As you are; as everyone is."

I was silent a moment. The house was quiet. I could hear the small metal tick of the clock in the hall. Then a faint voice calling from the kitchen: "John Bay, John Bay, bring me those buckets." And an even fainter voice responding: "I can't find no buckets—they're lost." R.B. sipped his tea and looked around him, slowly lifting his gaze from books to table, to lamps, to the butterfly shawl thrown over the back of a worn armchair—still, despite what he said—so it seemed to me— baffled by the ungovernable creations of this world. I sipped my tea, drawing in the woody, honey-sweetened bitterness of it. "But what if," I said, "it's only your own sweet spirit that makes you respond like this? What if instead of discovering your connection, you've confirmed your apartness?" And why was it now that the face of my child, Rachel, would come to me, and the face of my wife, a picture of the two of them as we sat together under our favorite buckeye overlooking the lake in Central Park? The last time we were there—it was spring—the buckeye flowers stood like small white candelabras among the new leaves—and as we lay on a blanket nestled near the radio which played the Bach concerto for violin and oboe, a band of young boys, no older than scouts, flown down from the fortresses of Harlem or the Bronx, began to throw stones at the couples rowing on the lake. As we watched, before any of us could raise a voice against it, a stone struck a young

woman in the face. From the hillside I could see the blood spurt, see
her collapse forward with a cry. Her companion, a young man in white
shirtsleeves, bent over her, ministering to her and protecting her from
the stones that continued to fly. From the other boats came shouts and
threats; a young Asian man in a black suit rose holding his oar over his
head, revolving it as he screamed in Japanese as if he were stirring the
air. The boys shouted back, laughing, cursing the impotent bourgeoisie,
taunting them with gestures. My wife, born amid this, leapt to her feet
shaking her fist, red-faced, the cords in her neck stiff with anger, crying,
"Leave them alone, you bastards." As I stood up, prepared, ambiva-
lently, to protect her and to protect my daughter, who yelled, too, in
mimicry of her mother, I felt a surge of pride that I was connected so
intimately to one so bold, so fearless, and to another—my daughter,
Rachel, who, perhaps intuitively, rose to defend the abused; but, as we
watched the boys, still yelling their taunts, begin to move off, why did
it seem such a sad and common story, a story without angels, without
miracle, without even a competent demon, one in which the scurrying
participants, the wounded, the taunters, the gallants, were only bit
players, actors in a script whose resolution, whose prior action even,
they were not privy to; why did it seem there in the midst of the
common responses of love and attention that there was no more meaning to our shouts, to the taunts and threats of boys, than if we were
dogs barking at each other through a fence?

I think I am a silly man. And it is no state secret why I rush so
headlong through this world. But it is not a crime to flee, if by fleeing
you save your life. When I wake in the night choking, I tell myself
this, repeating it out loud in the small voice of a child whose parents
have left him in the big house alone.

Now R.B. lifted his head and looked at me. He had the wet, runny
eyes of an old man. Not the eyes of sorrow but the eyes of fatigue.
Under his jaw the soft, slack skin was flushed. Spreading his fingers, he
brushed downward the thin hairs on his wrists. "It's only through
repetition that we discover a new way," he said. "Out of the heartbeat
a new music comes. It's not change we're after, but fulfillment. And
fulfillment is a completion, not a launching off into new direction. This
primitive process I am in the midst of, this maniac naming of the

obvious world, couldn't—it's impossible—place me at a distance from my fellows. Our separation is a lie we tell ourselves, concocted out of pride and the fear of our own powerlessness. We are awkward, we are often stupid, we fail continuously, but we are not apart. There is no such thing as distance."

Like a man shaking off amnesia—it seemed like this to me—I looked around the darkened room. Motes drifted through the pale bar of light falling between the curtains. In the eaves a wasp buzzed, stopped, and then began again, fizzing harshly. "Let me tell you about a man I know," I said.

"All right. Certainly."

For three hours, for four hours, as the light in the window changed from white to yellow, to orange, to the fatal blues of dusk, I told him the story of D'Nel, told him the gross lie, the truth, of the story that had been told to me—that had been lived out in front of me?—told him of the murderous career of this native man who moved across the landscape in a solitude so impenetrable that he was nearly invisible. I told him about the smells D'Nel, this X, described to me, the smells and the other categories of the senses—there was no way to tell the whole story; I gave him an outline and selected incidents—told him about the year D'Nel spent living as a fisherman on a small island off the coast of Venezuela, about how he would go out in the middle of the day, when the sun was so bright on the water that the water was white and on fire with sunlight, to fish with dynamite caps. He would bomb the fish out of the sea. *Like an air force,* D'Nel said, *like a destiny and a fate.* He said he was in mourning for a woman who had loved him. He said he made the explosions big—the white water leaping in the white sunlight—so that he would forget his lover's body lying in her grave. He told me that at night she called him to fuck her bones and how at night he would dream of leaving his flesh and joining her in the dark earth, bone to bone, two skeletons fucking in the loneliness of the grave. He bombed fish, he said, he tried to destroy whole species of fish in those pale blue shiny Caribbean waters, to escape his lust. *That's what it was about,* he said, *my lust; this capacity, this pull toward her rotting bones. You can't imagine,* he said, *what it was like to stand in that boat in the white sunlight with a hard-on, bombing the silvery fish out of the sea, every cell of my body wanting to die so I could live in a grave and fuck a skeleton.*

When I stopped talking it was almost dark. R.B. looked at me steadily from deep in his armchair.

"Where did you get this story?" he said.

"It's true, it was told to me; and I make it up."

He was silent awhile. A whippoorwill called from the woods. "It's what you are afraid of, isn't it?" he said finally.

"Yes."

We sat in the quiet, which was dense and tangible, like water, until Mattie rang the bell for dinner.

2. Dear Van,

Are there moments in your life when everything seems personal? On the way down here I stopped off in Granite City to see the presidential library. I thought I might learn something about the way we handle ourselves when we have ultimate power and money at our disposal. The library is a long low connected series of gray stone buildings set on a hill amid a sea of kudzu. When you look at the diagram of it on the map they keep under glass in the foyer you realize that it is constructed in the shape of the President's first initial. Do you think that was intentional? It is July but already a few of the tulip poplars are yellowing. The crepe myrtles were in full second bloom, and there was the scent of honeysuckle in the air and the scent of some other rich flower I couldn't name. The grounds were sketchily landscaped, descending in back past a fabricated stream and Japanese garden—expressing, I suppose, the ex-President's love and affinity for all things Asian—to a scummy pond beyond the dam of which you could see, maybe a mile away, the city raised like a silver-and-gray partition at the foot of the West. At the edges of the lawns long runners of kudzu had crept out onto the grass, like thin camouflaged snakes, and some of the trees that stood among the growth were shrouded, nearly shapeless under the thick vines, like furniture sheeted up in an abandoned house. The purple flowers smelled like grape soda. I saw a squirrel with a striped tail; he looked like a rat.

In the foyer—marble floor, tall granite walls—I passed several older southern women who were speaking about the President among themselves as if he were their handsome child. Rays of passageways opened into velvety darknesses off the foyer; inside I could see small lighted displays that reminded me of desks in some old library, vaults of darkness rising up beyond, a silence everywhere, or a hush. They wanted money before they'd allow visits into the interior chambers, just as mercantile as the pharaohs. I didn't want to pay, so I wandered out again, up across the lawn through a small grove of crab-apple trees toward a roundish wing under some oaks. The whole place had the clarity and stillness of a graveyard. I was thinking about D'Nel, about what he would make of all this, trudging along, you know, selecting sites in my mind—I hope you got the new script pages—picturing the way he would raise his arms like a creaky bird and caw at the Gulf, daring the sea and the night, God himself, to strike him. I believe that the idea that anybody might want to embrace the whole world is mostly a figment; mostly, we want to close the door and escape the world, even its smallest manifestation. Often it's this way. But D'Nel was (is) convinced that the world can't kill him. He fed (feeds) on the blood of the world, on its sap. It's like I saw once on a documentary about wine, how you could make wine out of any vegetable substance, out of cotton string or grass if you had to. That's like D'Nel, like X: he can draw the life off anything living.

I was walking along thinking about him—did I say he's tall, broad-shouldered, thin-hipped, with large outward-turning hands, rough-knuckled but oddly delicate?—when, as I came slowly up through a scattered hedge of nandina bushes, I saw through a half-shuttered window someone moving around. I moved closer—I was in a sheltered area inside a fence that ended against the hedgerow, on the shady side of the building—and saw that it was the President, the ex-President, standing in I guess his bedroom. He had on jeans and a T-shirt; he was gray, slightly paunchy, and needed a shave. He looked a little like one of the gray guys you see in run-down city hotels, some guy stumping along the hallway carrying a little bag of groceries and wine. He was leaning over the bed, drawing on a lapboard that lay on the covers. He would make a couple of strokes, straighten up and look, and then bend down and make a couple more. I stood there for several minutes watching him. The glass on the window must have been bulletproof, because there were no bars; there I was, an anonymous tourist, peering in at the ex-head-gunslinger as he practiced his sketching technique. It was thrilling; not just because it was the President, ex-President, but because it was somebody human who didn't know another was watching and so was vulnerable, this unprotected spirit. I had been thinking of D'Nel, of X, and maybe that was why the notion came on me: I wanted suddenly to do something violent and irrevocable; it was as if I understood (and became) one of these assassins who compulsively hurl themselves into the center of power—it's what we all want, whether it's sex or a corporation or the life of our child— it came to me that no matter what I tried to tell myself, no matter my protectionism, what I wanted was *more life*—any life, as much as I could get. They think madness— schizophrenia, alcoholism, movies—is a retreat, but it's not; it's a veer all right, but only away from harm, not life; it's just another way of getting more. *Everybody's* that way.

I stepped back—I don't know if you can believe this—to find a rock I could pitch through the glass—I was coming in after it—just as two men came barreling around the corner. Secret Service they were, wearing suit coats and, oddly, madras shorts. Each had a small white earpiece like a plug of wax in his ear, and one of them had his hand inside his coat pocket. As I turned toward them I caught a glimpse of the ex-President; he looked up at the window—he saw me; there was a look of rage on his face, not anger only or irritation, but rage, a fury like something in him was and always had been wholly dedicated to tearing what threatened him apart. It's maybe not fair of me to say this, to report on a gentleman who can't defend himself, but it was so remarkable to me—and so unexpected—that my knees went watery—I can't help but pass it on—and I'm sure that the face I presented to the bodyguards was a shocked one. They came straight at me, these clean-shaven, smooth-featured guys—everything about them was buffed and

trimmed, even their eyebrows—looking like well-to-do insurance salesmen gone suddenly berserk. The lead guy—a dark-headed fellow with
a sharp chin—dropped into a key block—just like the football coaches
taught us at Mark Twain High School in St. Louis—and took me right
out, bowling me off my feet head over ass into the nandinas. I don't
think he could have done it if I hadn't been so shocked to see the
President looking at me with such outrage, but he did. Some stob or
stick caught me in the back of the head and there was the smell of rot,
as if something had died under there, and pine straw stuck through my
shirt. I rolled off to the right, back onto the grass, and pushed to my
feet, as the other guy, who was slightly larger and had a smooth red
jaw and blue eyes like a cheerleader's, came at me with his arms out,
crabbing sideways as if I were a pigeon he was hemming in. They didn't
pull their guns. I was scared, but mostly shocked and pissed—rushing
the window had only been *in my mind,* after all (maybe they can *read*
minds)—and I shouted at them in alarm, like the befuddled tourist I
instantly became. "What are you guys doing?" I cried. "What are you
guys doing?"

The other one, the one who had knocked me over, walked past the
beater, the one who was hemming me up—they were sharp, these guys;
he knew I was harmless, or thought he knew—and took my arm. The
blue-eyed one caught my other arm and they frog-marched me around
the side of the house through a low steel door and into a concrete
bunkerlike chamber. There was blue carpet on the floor but the walls
were raw concrete block; there was a glassed-in den on one side and
a long corridor led toward a lighted area where I could see banks of
monitors and a couple of other guys sitting at desks drinking coffee and
talking. On one of the walls inside the glassed-in space someone had
pinned cutouts of cartoon characters: ducks and pigs and one large
reproduction of Yosemite Sam firing off his guns. I kind of liked that.

There were closed metal doors off to the side and while the narrow
fellow held my arms, the other unlocked one of the doors with a key
he took off a metal chain he hauled out of his pocket—like a working
man, like my father used to do unlocking the big door to the main
warehouse on the docks in St. Louis—and shoved me through into an
interrogation room that was so typical and depressing that it nearly

brought tears to my eyes. They sat me down. There was a green metal table, metal chairs, an empty cork bulletin board, a dismantled coffee maker on a red plastic table in the corner; no windows. There, sitting across from me like personnel officers, they questioned me. They were snappish at first, ornery, like anyone would be who had had his party invaded, and very serious, like graduate students interviewing some ridiculous freshman. I thought about the guns resting like black widow spiders under their arms and I thought about—you remember this—the scene in *Roundabout Revenge* where Tork McCardle stands up in the alley and begins to take off his clothes as the Mussey gang is firing all their hardware at him. I thought I could do that too, but then I thought I wouldn't—it wasn't a demonstration I was after but a breakthrough— and so I answered their questions, politely and with as much detail as I could come up with—after all, I was only a tourist who had wandered off the path; I didn't know the President actually *lived* at his library (like a deli owner living over the store, captain on his beached freighter)— explaining to them that I meant no harm, that I was a movie director on his way to Florida to scout background sites for a movie he was planning. They liked that, and got interested, especially the flushed fellow who as it turned out had seen three of our movies—though, like everyone else, he hadn't liked the last one ("I think you kind of fell off a little there," he said warmly. "There was too much talking, just too much . . ."—"Too many words," his buddy tossed in—"Yeah, too many words, and the story got so complicated I couldn't follow it . . .")—and they quickly became civilized and interested, perking up in that way that is wonderful to see, the way all us members of the human species will when we have the switch kicked that releases us from our fear and we begin to give in to the puppyness we are all heir to. They wanted to know if we were going to shoot a movie about the President, or if we wanted to use the library as a site. No, I told them, thinking about D'Nel, and how if he were here he would find a way to kill the President, doing it in such a way that he would escape not only with his life but without having been identified—I'm not romancing him; this is true—and then, in the middle of the conversation, for a moment, my hands, lying there in front of me folded on the table, seemed his hands, pebbly and long-fingered as his hands are, the delicacy showing through the coarseness, the moons on the broad fingernails nearly filling the surfaces, the tips tapered and roughened from work on his sculpture, and from the bony, bloody work he did rending the corpses of the old country aristocrats he'd just finished killing. For a moment the freckles on the backs of my hands looked like flecks of dried blood, and for just one second I could smell the sweet sumpish odor of blood and the stench of internal organs exposed to the air. Sweat broke out on my face and I felt a cold drop of it run down my side. The blue-eyed man had a small scar on his chin and it took everything in me not to reach across the table and touch it. For a moment, and you must believe this, I wanted to turn myself over to them for protective custody. I wanted to throw myself at their feet and beg them to take care of me. The hands seemed other hands, not mine; and the voice that spoke, issuing accentless from a mouth distant from me, carried the clear tones of speech I have become familiar with. I looked away as one will to change the thought, as one will look away toward a window out of which he might see the day blowing familiarly along, but there was no window, only the gray concrete wall, and in that room were no buddies and no women I loved, no one to turn to for clarification. I am lucky I suppose that this transformation—if that's what it was— came only after the boys had become glad to see me, because I know my face must have turned white, and I could feel the sweat on my skin. *Who do you see?* I wanted to ask them; *what kind of man is sitting before you? Have I changed?* But I didn't say anything because who would have been asking? The blue-eyed man went to get sodas and across his blue-suited disappearing back I saw the story of his life revealed, I saw the hidden muscle under the clothes and the pale skin sprinkled with wiry blond hairs, and I saw the place where his wife touched him as she held him in the dark, and I saw the dark like the dark inside a mouth, and then I saw Celest kneeling over my body the first night of our marriage, saw the razor blade nick the head of my penis and saw the blade sink in her hand between her legs and saw her part the lips of her vagina and cut there a small wound from which the black blood seeped; and I saw the blood, on our bodies and on our hands, saw her raise the fingers to my mouth and I tasted her blood that was sweet and bitter at the same time and saw her bend down to take my cock in her mouth, just the head of it, sipping blood; and I saw us then, in exhaustion and exuberance, couple together, fucking in the well of our blood like murderers. And—you will probably say I am lying again, but I'm not—it seemed to me that I was the man, which is something—idiot, you will say—I had never admitted to myself, I was the man who was there, who had married Celest and loved her and made a child with her; I was the man who was loved and held tenderly in the night and scolded and fretted over and praised and shoulder-to-shouldered, etc.—all that—not someone else. But that man was not here. Can you understand what I am saying? Those were D'Nel's hands, Mr. X's hands, lying rank as fishes on the table in front of me. It was his voice I heard. His smile in my mouth, his teeth, his greasy breakfast in my belly. When I shit it would be D'Nel's turd. But—and here is the question—whose blood was it? Whose blood?

There was a commotion in the hall, a stir of voices, and then the door opened and the President, the ex-President, came in. He is a small man, and something has faded out of him. He was smiling, well as usual, and his skin, though seamed, was very clear. In his eyes, like leftover glittery dust on a waxed floor, shone the residue of his rage. I caught it in the face and grinned at him. We shook hands firmly and chatted for a few minutes. I told him about my journey, about the dolphins I was on my way to see, and about Bess—it turns out he knows her; she was one of his supporters—and I told him I appreciated his work and was gratified to meet him. He said he was happy to meet me. Like everybody else, he loved the movies.

3. INTERIOR. NIGHT. Bess and I, in the long ago, were a spanky couple. I was in New York learning the movies, laying the tracks for my first feature, and she was a music student at the Manhattan Conservatory. She was a singer and a pianist, a specialist in baroque music; it was through music that I met her.

One night, tired of thinking about the disaster of the project I was working on, I went to a concert at the church down the street from my apartment. I was living in a pinched room in the Village, in an ornately grimed building that hung like a tedious cliff over the narrow leafy meander of Waverly Place. The front of the building, rising in low maroon tiers above the crowns of locusts and ailanthus trees, had a solemn, brooding aspect, and seemed to project a hush over the cloistered street. From behind, it was another story; its bald, white-washed posterior jutted over Seventh Avenue with startling brazenness. This duality was pleasing to me, though since my apartment was in the back, five floors up, I caught more of the clamor of the avenue than I liked. Often, roused by some sad siren, I would get up from my bed, go out, and walk the streets. The truth was I was burning with energy in those days, mad to make movies, brooking nothing in my attempts to learn more about them, to take the stories that shouted in my brain and make of them lighted patterns that someone—I—could throw whirling across a screen.

It was on such an evening, when, kicked out of restless reverie by the harsh declaratives of a passing fire truck, I had once again charged out onto the street, that I discovered Bess. It was fall; October; the locust leaves were yellowing. The streetlights, caught like solitary glowing fish in the locust crowns, turned the leaves pale, white-faintly-green and ghostly. The sidewalk was powdered with white dust from a renovation going on next door, and from a window thrown open across the street came the sound of a trumpet repeating the opening bars of an old jazz tune called "Summer Coquette." I stopped near the corner to speak to Annie Battson, the homeless woman who lived on a blanket against a boarded-up doorway. She was there in all weathers, tented under two dirty umbrellas in rain, bareheaded in sun, oblivious to elements nearly, like me someone vivified and obsessed with the projects in her life, which for her were what she called The Strangenesses. She meant the dizzying happenings of the street, the shout, the lunge toward a throat, the brisk uncalled-for dance. She saw herself as arbiter and critic of these affairs, sometimes as director—though she was only a frail woman rarely on her feet—and her conversation tended to harp pretty steadily on the relative merits of whatever late performance had occurred near her solitary station. That night she was bemused by having watched an elegant man dressed in tuxedo and white scarf turn from his conversation on the corner with an equally glittering woman companion to vomit suddenly and violently a stream of what looked like blood onto the hood of a parked limousine. Like me, she loved contrasts, and was excited by paradox, by anything that seemed proof of some greater, or at least different, reality, poking its hard thumb into the soft meat of agreed-upon life. I listened while she minutely told the tale, watching a small patch of light that gleamed like clear varnish on the top of her head. Her skull was small, doused with thin pale hair, and her face had caved in slightly around the nose, giving her an expression of asperity and obscure grief which vanished completely the moment she smiled. "I hold nothing against them," she said that night. "It was an electrifying performance, but I promise you surely that I would have enjoyed it more if the gentleman had actually hit the turf." She offered a snaggled grin. "If you build up something you ought to go through with it, and that particular sport had *pitch forward* written all over him. You know what I mean?" I told her I did. "Do you ever think of helping them along?" I asked. She was sometimes a shouter, but her shouts were directed at those she decided were hesitating, unable to begin, and rarely came after the confusion had gotten under way. "I think of it," she said, "and I often want to—you can see some of them groping—but I consider it part of my religion—I guess you could say that—to let those as are called to make demonstration work it out according to their own and God's way. You know what I mean?"

"Yes. But that seems difficult to me. I get nervous."

"All you people who shop in stores get nervous. You're afraid they might shut the store down and then what would you do?" She laughed her brief mucosal laugh. "Then what would you do?"

I looked away from her down the street where out on the avenue the goaded life of the city rushed along. At the Dragon Mouth, a jazz and supper place, couples sat at tables out on the sidewalk, eating delicate foods as they breathed in the sour airs of Manhattan, a practice I was never quite at ease with; it seemed to me a little like eating supper at the dump. An ambulance, lights blazing, but without its siren, streaked by, weaving through traffic. On the corner a child standing with a well-dressed woman who might have been her mother reached up to stroke the glittering bracelet on the woman's arm. Far away, down beyond the end of the street, on the other side of the river, I could see the small orangy gathering of what I knew were the lights of Jersey, though from here they seemed only the continuation of the street, bright blazing; the thick sky standing upright was neither backdrop nor storeroom of heaven, but only a black smudge not wiped away yet.

"Where did you come from, Annie?" I said. I had known her for over a year but I had never asked a question about her past.

"I forgot that," she said, touching the sparse hairs on her chin.

"Forgot?"

"It's been too long a tumble to here. What went on back then has slipped my mind."

With a home of my own, a calling, it was easy to romanticize her. I pictured her standing alone in a kitchen in the Midwest, just come from her factory job where she stamped out pieces of metal on a machine, snapping the top off a Budweiser and drinking it down in heavy unbroken gulps. I saw her wipe her mouth with the back of her hand, saw her place the can on the fluted drainboard and lean slightly forward, a woman who could still recall the young girl living inside her, pressing her stout waist against the lip of the sink as she looked bleakly out at the cluttered yard where maybe a couple of children played, dancing out a brisk game among a collection of old tires. I could see her thoughts move slowly across her face, troubling and changing her, but I couldn't hear the thoughts, couldn't hear the one that her mind pushed through like a grain of wheat pushed through a keyhole, the one that fell eerily and lodged in her gut and changed into the few small words she would say to herself in proclamation or testament, or maybe not words, into a silence that was stronger than words, more demanding, that she must act on.

But how could I know? In those days everything was a movie—as I suppose it still is—but then I hadn't learned the difference between movie story and life. I thought it was simply a matter—if it was a matter at all—of getting the angle right, of camera setup and lighting; that anything—anyone or any event—could be plucked whole from its perch and brought breathing and radiant onto the screen. I would shoot a movie with Annie in it. I would keep her as she was, a kind of Greek chorus chanting wisdom at passersby. But that was already fabrication; she wasn't wise, she was only worn.

"Do you need anything?" I said bending down.

"No darling, not tonight." She pulled a tissue from the box beside her, neatly blew her nose, and waved me away.

I started down the street but she called me back. "Here," she said, "take this."

She reached behind her and drew a dark bundle of cloth that I saw was a coat, a tuxedo jacket.

"Ah, the spoils."

"Get it away from me," she said. "I don't want the thing near me."

I took the bundle and moved off, heading south. As I walked I checked the jacket which was new and unstained. It was silk and crackled like a new bill. I put it on. It was a little large, but I liked the silky feel of it across my back and shoulders. I wondered about the guy it belonged to, about how Annie got it. The cloth smelled faintly of cologne, some musky brand with a steady deep-woods undertone. I wondered if the guy it belonged to felt good as he got dressed, some-where in a rich apartment Uptown, if he was whistling or running in his mind the promise of the night, and if the woman watched him as he fixed the studs and tied his tie, if she touched him on the shoulder and pressed for a moment the front of her body against his back, lightly and lovingly, careful not to let her colored lips or any part of her face touch the immaculate cloth of his dress shirt, and if he, for a moment not caring about getting mussed, leaned back into her, and felt for one second her heart beating against his spine.

It was easy to make up a life, but the truth was I was lonely. I didn't know it yet, but the pattern of my life was already set, my way of working and living, love so tender, all the components already clicked into place; I still thought of myself as a fresh article, surly but generous bright-faced knight of the West—though I was already twenty-five, married once and divorced, son of an already failing father, without— so I thought—any real ties—arrived at the center of empire, ready to ramble. I did not know then that it is not places or lovers that drive us down but our own hot hearts. I thought a change of venue, the new song, the new labor, the fresh bright lover doing her exercises in morning windowlight, were sufficient to change the heart's direction, that the old ways and life could, like a junkie's blood, be replaced, and we would walk forth invigorated and transformed. But like the junkie who discovers that it is not the blood that drives him but his own clamoring spirit—whatever that spark is—I was to learn that no bright bauble I stretched my hand out to touch could prevent me, could prevent arrival—right on schedule—of the outcome that had been sunk like a pacemaker long ago into my flesh, that ticked on mercilessly, impersonally, through all the changes and restarts, no matter what energy and good will I might bring to bear. It would take more than I knew yet in this world to spring new direction loose.

But as I walked down the street, observing here and there the conniptions of my fellow travelers, I did not think of these things. I was tired from the day's labor, my eyes ached from staring into a moviola, I was nearly happy, though thirsting for human company, and I noticed with pleasure the leaves going to color in the sycamores and oaks of Sheridan Square, the long sleeve of tarnishing wisteria trailing from the cornice of a brownstone on Christopher; and I listened with satisfaction—here I was, in my righteous place—to the snatches of dialogue passing between couples—the immigrant voices—to the execrations offered by a stooped man as he blistered the hide of a newsseller on the corner, to the cracked off-key song of a street musician torturing guitar strings on the stoop before—so a brass sign said—the headquarters of the Andalusian Benevolency Association.

The leather boys, the glittering fowl, were out on Christopher, and they nodded to me as I passed, winking at me, selecting or rejecting me, ravaging me and letting me go, jackpot or cipher, and I nodded back, lordly. There had been a time, not so long ago, when I had supped at that spring, but the time had passed. Even so the street still had for me the aspect of a familiar river, one whose snags and deeps were common to me, and as I paddled my way past the bars and the tight little shops where the paraphernalia of extremis was sold, I felt buoyed up, as if my brothers were passing me lightly from hand to hand.

Debouched shortly on Hudson I almost stopped to brush the glittery dust of passage off my clothes, laughing to myself; the shining lane behind me was another night street—if intensified and only slightly more addled—I would like to shoot a scene along, a long traveling shot maybe, the camera picking up, in a gentle and festive way, the silky harmony and flayed energies of the midnight boys. But tonight I had other plans; there was a garden down the way that I thought I might slip into and sit awhile in, a walled cloister behind St. Andrew's Church, where I figured the first flowers of fall—the asters and the goldenrods— were just tipped toward full. It was a place I retreated to, one of my havens—as the rivers were, anywhere along them—where, it seemed, I could open the pores a bit—where I could *identify* things—and let regenerative life infiltrate me.

I was groping for the gate—no streetlight there—when up ahead I noticed a fall of light on the sidewalk and heard singing. At the church, beyond a tall brick rose-hung wall, a choir was holding forth. The music music for voices—was familiar and unfamiliar both—modern, but not modern—and it poured with a rosy grandness from the open doors of the church. I tacked down that way, feeling a small and unexpected uplift in my spirit, thinking I would spend a minute on the steps listening before going on into the garden. There were a couple of others on the steps, and inside a scattering of listeners sat in varnished pews under tinselly metal chandeliers shaped like crowns around which hung nimbi of misty light. In the chancel a mixed choir, dressed in street clothes, sang. The air smelled of fresh laundry and, faintly, of a candied disinfectant. Forgetting my plan, I slid down a side aisle and took a seat near an old woman in a rainbow shawl, about halfway down. She snapped a glance at me—harsh, then pawing—and turned her creased face back to the music. It swelled, the intricate mass, in gusts and frills toward us, the fine high chorus of surrender and freedom, launched from fifty throats. The director, a tall man in summery clothes, threw up his hand and the music stopped. "We're a little stiff in there," he said. "Let's try that again." His voice was as clear as pebbles dropped on a marble floor. Later I would tell Bess that I had seen her from the first, but that was not true; in the beginning I noticed only the choir as a whole, my mind lifting with the music and my own thoughts.

Down the aisle, off to my right, a man pushed a heavy mop over the stone floor. He had a large bucket on wheels behind him that he plunged the mop into and dragged forward every few strokes. The noise was distracting and I wished he would quit. I leaned on my elbows on the pew in front as the choir started up again and listened as their voices glided rosily through a slow passage, the basses coming up under the clear ring of sopranos until the whole choir merged in a rising phrase that seemed to shimmer and shine before us. I let the music blow against me like a sea breeze. The guy with the mop, a gray-haired man in a suit coat and floppy trousers, moved steadily toward me, slapping the mop against the cold stone, ringing a few changes against the pews. The swipe of his stroke made oily-looking, gleaming patches on the floor.

My attention returned to the choir. They surged and wavered, surged again. The director restarted them, cautioned them, pressing both hands against the air to hold them back, then he let them go. The music seemed to falter, as if the choir had stepped back through a doorway and were singing, descending to whispers, in a shadowy room. The basses tried to hold the group together, but the sopranos, in trembling fear, fluttered and hesitated, speaking breathy faithless questions to the Great Being whom they served. It seemed fear would win, when suddenly, out of the silence that seemed about to override the silvery terrors, the clear voices of the tenors called out, accusing—o ye of little faith—striking like birch switches across the backs of the equivocating sopranos. Instantly the basses, who only a moment before had surrendered to an exhausted muttering, raised their great shoulders to support the others; the broad underfirmament appeared again—we are not lost after all—and the voices of the sopranos—miraculously restored—began to trill and coo, racing, like gay young girls running to catch a beribboned carriage, to join the others, to join and embroider the song which swelled with an irresistible urgency and zeal toward the light, the true source, the ground, which the tenors plowed easily now, of being. Together, in proclamation, affirming joyously, the choir—recovered fully from its terror—expanded and built on its newly discovered union, climbing the broad steps of a golden pavilion, belting out the notes like a workers' chorus, tossing flower petals and silver coins; only the basses, as they heaved the heavy bales upward, remembering—and here only as a kind of primitive rhythm, as a baby's heart remembers the rhythm of the sea—the dark lies that had nearly overridden them, the sullied odors and the heat they were now free of.

The singers, shoulder to shoulder under the misty chandeliers, seemed to rise on their toes toward the final transformation; the director, his head bobbing like a pigeon's, seemed about to launch off his platform with delight; from the side I could see the grin mashed onto his face like the grin of a child entering the circus for the first time—terror and joy intermingled—sweat shone on his hollow temples, he breathed hard, his thin arms hacked, torso bending like a fishing pole to haul out the great leviathan of the soul's denouement—it was at this moment that the custodian reached my pew. Swinging the mop he struck the side of the pew a firm blow, oblivious to the music which rolled over him in a tide. Bending down, he grasped the bucket and dragged it a few grating feet closer, plunged the mop in and drew out a stream of sloppy water, which he heaved before him across the floor. None of it hit me, but the sprung pool of it slid toward my feet which, I guess, he expected me to raise. Instead I crabbed over to the end of the pew and motioned him close. "Do you think you could leave off that business for a minute?" I graveled.

He stared at me with frank disdain.

"I mean let up on the mopping until they're through?"

"I got work to do, pal," he said grinding his teeth. His eyes were gray, very light, like clouds in winter.

"It'd pay you to listen."

"They pay me to mop the floor."

"Come on, brother."

"Fuck off, Jack."

I stopped thinking then, stopped listening. He hadn't missed a stroke. Slap . . . slap . . . slap. I leaned to my right, stretched my hand out, and grasped his arm. It was sinewy under the suit jacket. "Fuu . . ." he cried, jerked his arm loose, swiveled, and bopped me on the head with the end of the mop. The breath cuffed out of me. For an instant it felt as if he'd slammed a block into my head. I looked at him and he was grinning. "Get the message, pal?" he said. "Yeah," I said, "I guess I do." I let my left hand fall open on top of the pew in front of me, as if to accept collection or rain. He looked at it, just a glance. As he did so I snapped my right fist into his face. He went down like I'd tripped him. And came up yelling.

I leapt to my feet. "Jesus, buddy, shut up."

"Fucking asshole," he screamed. "Get off me."

He pointed the mop at me like a gun.

I took a step toward him and he swung at me, slop-end first. Splashes of greasy water hit my chest and sheened across the pews behind. I heard the old woman cry out and someone else barked *Hey*.

"You get away from me," the janitor cried, drawing the mop back like a baseball bat. There was a small crease of blood at the corner of his mouth. I wanted to hit him again, and, as always—why had this twist trailed me across the country, from Missouri to California and back to New York?—something else stirred, the strange notion that now that we had struck each other it was time for an embrace. I dropped my hands. "It's all right, mister," I said. "I'm not going to hurt you."

All this time the choir had sung on, rolling toward the high hill of destiny, but now they stopped, whether—I hadn't paid attention—from shock or mass's end I couldn't tell. A sadness came to life in me, as if I were fighting not this old man but my father, and defeating him. "It's all right," I said again. "It's okay."

Just then I was grabbed from behind. I jerked; two had me, a couple of men I hadn't noticed. A third stood off a ways looking at me fiercely. "Wait a minute," I said, "it's over."

They didn't let me go. I swiveled my head and caught a glimpse of a beefy face. I twisted, but they held me. "Come on, bub," one of them said. Then the janitor poked me in the stomach with the end of the mop. I kicked him as hard as I could—ha! fuck embrace—I wanted to snap the little bastard in two. As I kicked they pulled me backward and slammed me onto the floor. My head hit and I saw colored lights. The lights rushed like motorcycles across my eyes. I almost went out but something in me struggled to stay awake. I heard myself groan.

Then they lifted me and hustled me up the aisle and out the front door. They jig-walked me down the steps and pushed me away from them, like guards letting a swimmer go into deep water. The river would take care of me. The air smelled of dry leaves, of diesel smoke. There was a taste like salt in my mouth. "Don't come back in here," someone said, and they let me go.

I staggered to the side—the street was a stream of light—saw a dog trotting along up ahead; a couple swerved around me and passed on, I smelled pizza baking. I fell against the fence, caught myself, and dropped to my knees. Whoo, I thought, I'm gone. I looked up and saw the leaves of an elm above my head swaying and trembling in breeze. For an instant I thought I was in the country. I saw the Mississippi, the way it looked in early morning from my grandmother's porch, conjuring itself out of mist, the vague oaks on the Illinois shore shining with dew. I could hear the wind selecting trees, the drone of tugs. Ah, I thought, I'm wounded, but here comes the healing.

There was a low corner of stone near me: the steps. I edged back that way and sat down. It felt as if my head ended at my ears and some gross throbbing fish body took over from there. I touched; nothing broken, no blood. That was some music.

In Vietnam, American high school graduates were burning the homes of strangers, but here, in New York City, where you could buy anything you wanted, where you could do anything you wanted and no shocked-destroyed boy would show up to kill your family, to call out of the sky a burning liquid that no prayer or solvent could erase from your body, I sat on the steps of a church tending my wounds. I thought of the detainee, the V.C. suspect trembling on a Saigon street, whom the police commissioner, in the midst of conversation, turned suddenly to shoot, and I saw the suspect's head kick and his body slump the way a steer on my grandmother's farm slumped when my father pumped the .22 bullet between its eyes, and leaning forward toward the street where slick cars nosed by seeking the rich lights of Uptown I felt as if I were pushing my face into blood, into poisonous gas. It was then, slicked by music and combat, that my first movie began to form in my mind; I saw the raid, the family gone mad in the cornlands, I saw how I could push the action—simply without flinching, without stopping—until everyone was dead. I saw the questions and the good intentions and the not so good intentions of the family folk, and I saw the human fears of the attackers and heard their talk that was banal and wild, and I felt, as if in my bones the sensations moved, the sure power of mastery as they locked the chambers of their piecemeal weapons, saw the line it was easy to step over that was not some razor-wired wall or ditch filled with crocodiles but only a line no more menacing than a line drawn

with blue chalk on the sidewalk, that existed—if in fact the boys who
crossed that line were human—in all of us—it was the only way to
redeem them: for the rest of us to admit their actions as a possibility
in ourselves—so that, in all of us, as my movie would bring to light,
there existed a violence, a fury so profound, so casual and vestigial, that
no human power, no matter how attentive or capacitating, could eliminate it. Christ, I saw the movie so clearly it gave me a hard-on. I saw
the hand break suddenly through the windowpane to grasp the face as
if the face were a peach for biting. I saw the table upended, the
Chihuahua stomped, the baby flung into the oven. I saw blood dripping
from a woman's hair, and I saw her suck it off the ends of the curls gone
lank with gore. I saw the paralytic nailed through his shoulders to the
bedroom wall, saw the tent spike driven up the woman's ass, saw the
snakes writhing in the bed, the child's face slapped and slapped and
slapped. Ah, sweet moviegoer, I thought, you want a glimpse of the
dark world—I will give you a glimpse. But for it you must pay the
price. You must learn, *dear heart,* that this country you gawk at is no
distant place savaged and abandoned; it's your home, and you live there.
Then I saw the yellow leaves falling, heard the sweet chuckle of waters
dancing, I heard the loving voices calling children home. And I saw the
city street, just at twilight, the street perhaps where I was raised, and
I smelled the river and heard the clang of barges, and I heard the low
voices of men talking, and their laughter, as they trudged up Tremaine
on their way home from a long day on the docks. I smelled the mustardy
stink of the creosote plant, and I saw the shabby brick fronts of the row
houses where Virginia creeper climbed. I saw Johnny Blake chalking
Jeri Kreutzer's name for the one-thousandth time on the blank concrete
patch that shored up the crack in Mr. Harvey Lefwitz's side wall. I heard
Mrs. Joyce yell again at her retarded son ("Why can't you ever do what
I tell you to do—just one time") and I heard the mumbled soupy
pleading of his answer. I saw the flock of blackbirds wheeling over
Nancy Wash Park, their whirling soaring unison flight like an approxi-
mation of music, or of the sooty strokes of a language printed out
randomly through the holes in some other world. I heard my mother,
who never admitted anything, scolding the biscuits, explaining to the
furniture that life was difficult but thanks to her it was in hand. And

then I saw, as my head began to throb as if a hot indestructible light bulb were being banged against the back of it, a man rise up, as if a piece of the cobbled pavement had come suddenly to life, rise and begin to walk toward me—this is you, D'Nel, my Mr. X come so soon into my life—and I saw—by the way he moved, a darkness moving through a gathering darkness, one shoulder held slightly higher than the other, the hands large and opened, outlined by the clear river light behind him—that he was no ordinary man, he was no one I knew from this St. Louis neighborhood, but one come from a far place. And I knew as I watched him make his slow way toward me that he had come for me, he had come to teach me and to take me, to draw me with him into a world that was unlike any world I had ever dreamed. I was only a child in scuffed clothes, standing in the middle of a shabby street in St. Louis, Missouri, holding in my hand a baseball from which the gray cover had been ripped half away, a child dreaming in twilight, in the dream of childhood and its endless fertile days, its comedy and its terror, but I was a child about to meet someone who would change him forever, who, as if with mud scooped from the riverbank, would shape from him a life that no child—perhaps only a child—could imagine. *There is a mystery,* he would say. *There is a mystery. I will show it to you.*

I rose then, I staggered up, half snapped back into the real time of New York City, where a stranger might coldcock you with a mop, and the fever that was in me was the fever of my fate—that is the only word I know to use—and the energy was the energy of direction—of conversion, of surrender. There are godlike moments and that moment was godlike; it rang clearly, unsullied, perfectly in my mind, this story, this next step, this life. I can tell you that I knew myself, as anyone does when given wholly to work or love—to those two approximations of God's kingdom come on earth—and, serene and hot as a star—as I was—I can tell you that the hand that touched my shoulder then, which was a woman's hand, which was Bess Appel's hand, was no diversion and no delay, and when that night I bought a place in her temple with the irresistible currency of my passion, it was no lie, but only proof to me of investiture, of the shedding of my provisional, awkward past— anyone's past—so that when, after that night, after conversation, speech, wild claims, caresses, I thrust my bare face into the hot, coppery well of her sex, her plummy cunt, it seemed to me that I was pushing my face, my mouth, all my being, into creation itself, that her body, her hands stuck like gaffs into my hair, her face smeared with the spittle of lust, was gift and conveyance both, the fine starship of my launching as well as provision for the voyage. She seemed to me—if I might stay off my rocker one more minute here—some cleansed, fortuitous city Athena, stepped out of Olympus to lead me through the combat zone of my calling. She was fuel, proclamation, home-for-the-weary, sweet-singing bird, companion. When, rising from the blanket we had carried to the roof of her East Village walk-up, after talking all night, after making love, after fucking, she leaned over the complicated tin cornice, extending her hand to the sun rising over the dark city of Brooklyn, and said, of the sun, that sometimes it looked to her like someone trying to rise out of a grave, I could only congratulate myself—I wanted to turn back flips—I could only kneel down in awe and worship at the bounty of God, at the mysterious occasional complicity of hope and arrival—this woman with the skin of a girl, the coppery tusseled hair, the wide, long-fingered muscular hands of a pianist, the stout waist, the eyes in which flecks of pure gold ignited the brown—this woman come to me now on the night of my appointment, the night in which the door of my life flung wide. . . .

As I sat there on the church steps, rocking in the arms of my dream, Bess, a singer, a young woman from the saltwater farm country of West Florida, who had no business in New York City doing such a thing, touched me. Slim, cool fingers brushed my arm. I didn't shy. The hand withdrew. There was a silence in which I heard the breeze rustling faintly in the elm. Someone passing down the steps said "See you tomorrow, Bess." "I'll meet you at the Circle," she answered in a soft country voice. I glanced quickly and caught a glimpse of a fawn skirt, thick disheveled coppery hair. A light went off behind us, and then all the lights went off at once, drawing the gray street-tinged shadow of the city over us. She was silent another moment, then she said, "Oh, maybe I'm sitting in the dark with a madman." She gave a low chuckle, bright bits of breath in it.

"I'm not mad," I said.

"You're a pretty good fighter though."

"Not that good."

I hadn't looked at her any more than sideways, but out of the corner of my eye I could see her shift slightly, brush her skirt over her legs. "The Questal Mass doesn't usually attract fighters, though it *will* draw the occasional madman."

"I'm not quite sure what happened in there."

"You lost. But grandly."

"The music got the better of me. I stepped beyond myself."

"You were funny."

"I prefer grand."

"That too."

We lapsed into silence. Breeze whispered in the elm above us, fingering the dry leaves. On the sidewalk the leaves were curled like small burned bodies. I looked her way, but past her, downtown where the tall towers of finance anchored the world. They seemed the lit gates of darkness. Then my gaze drew back and I looked straight at her. She had been looking at me all the time. Her hooded eyes, night-steeped, stared at me. Her face, which was wide and high-boned, held an expression of naive and penetrating reasonableness. I almost laughed. "You were one of the singers," I said.

"I was in the front row."

"Yes you were."

"Does your head hurt?"

"It feels like someone's back there hammering. Are we alone?"

"Except for everybody else in New York City we are."

"Good," I said, "I don't think I could defend my position any further."

"Make amends," she said, abruptly it seemed to me.

"What?"

"Make amends. Look." She pointed past me. Out of the gate under the trees the janitor exited onto the sidewalk.

"What are you talking about?"

"Go make up to him."

"What are you—my fairy godmother?"

"It'll do you good. Finish it."

"I'd rather punch his head in."

"No. Go speak to him."

"Damn."

The man wore a shabby overcoat and I could see—oddly better in the shadows—that he was old. Ah, Buddy, I thought, you want to be so tough. I got to my feet. My head felt like broken crockery with nerves in it.

"Go on."

I looked down at her. Her face, upturned, held a pure ghostly brightness. Her long lashes looked like ink on her cheeks. "All right."

The man was twenty feet away, a shabbiness under the dying tree. "Fellow," I said, "guy—excuse me."

He shot a glance at me and began to move off, stepping with an arthritic quickness, one knee flaring out as he went. I caught up with him. "Hey," I said, "I want to tell you . . ."

"Get away from me, asshole," he said.

"No, listen—wait."

He swung his arm, not to hit me, but dismissively, nodding his head away, flinching.

"I just want to tell you that I'm sorry for my part in the ruckus in there. I know you were just taking care of your business."

"They pay me to clean up the place," he said. "I do a good job for 'em too."

"I know you do. That was one clean floor."

"I can't let you punks stand in the way of what I got to do."

"I know exactly how you feel."

I skipped along beside him, rocky in my brain. I wanted to get this over quickly, get back to my movie, which rocketed along inside me. Dead people everywhere. Murder. Back to this woman.

The man stopped, turned, and faced me. He was old. Beat, some guy just hanging on. He looked at me. I saw the wear in his face, the slightly in-sunk cheeks, the brow with three lines gouged deeply. He looked at me and then he shook his head. "You need a sense of proportion, pal," he said. "Entertainment's fine, but you got to let a man do his work."

"Okay," I said. "I'm sorry." In a minute, I knew, I wasn't going to be sorry any longer. Across the street the lights from a deli threw a rainbow on the pavement. From among the row houses up Grove someone shouted and fell silent. The sycamores ahead of us led toward a construction site where plywood and scaffolding made a tunnel over the sidewalk. The tunnel curved so that the entrance was dark, like the entrance to a cave. I touched my hands to my coat and realized I was still wearing the tuxedo jacket Annie B. had retrieved from the disintegrated sport. You are alone, I thought. *We all are.* I turned again to see the old man, the custodian, shambling away down the street. "See you later," I cried, but he didn't answer or turn around. The breeze shook the leaves above my head and let them go. Tires sizzled by in the street. *We all are.*

(And why did she choose me, for that's what she did? No sweet talk on earth could, without collusion, conjure such a one so smoothly into unknown arms; why did she decide—on the steps of St. Andrew's Church? at the bistro? in the garden? on the walk down St. Marks Place? under the clattery oaks of Tompkins Square Park? in her bedroom where the bed unfolded like complicated camping equipment? on the gravelly roof? in another life?   why did she decide to open herself to me? And why did she choose me at that moment? Why, when I turned again, away from my solitude, was she still standing on the church steps, waiting for me?)

As I say, we were a spanky couple. I saw the knowledge of this in friends' eyes, in my father's desperate face when he and my mother came to the wedding, on the street in her Florida hometown, in the galleries where we laughed out loud, among my fellow filmsters when she would come into the living room shaking snow from her shawl on nights when we worked until daylight sounding the depths of the movie that raved in me like a trapped maniac. I loved to walk out onto the avenue with her, to plunge into the streets of the Village and SoHo, to enter, as into a special fraternity, the company of glittery couples sashaying down West Broadway. She was a woman who, on a whim, wearing a mock-raccoon coat, played her recorder all afternoon in the Times Square subway station, earning fifty dollars that she used to take me for a grand steak dinner at the Old Homestead on Ninth Avenue. Coming out late, we walked the cobbled streets of the West Side under an icy moon, tossing words of cheer to derelicts trapped in doorways, to passersby, to men arguing with troubled women on the avenue. Charmed, exhilarated, I cavorted in the street, barking encouragement to taxis and festive folk, delighted at her attention and her sympathy. I explained my movie to her—already oblivious to her hopes, to any future beyond my own—acting it out in our living room before the fire that she stoked with oak and hickory wood, groaning and pleading as my townspeople faced their deaths—you have to understand, I told her, that it is more interesting, in the lives of these folk, *how* they go to meet their deaths than *what* it is drives them under—strutting as my killers strutted, mimicking, as they mimicked, the tortures of the blood kin, arguing, loosening in themselves the demons that would override everything human in that town. She followed me, trailing me around the house as I skipped through the scenes, clapping at the few noble moments, feigning horror at the horror, building, like someone weaving a basket, a framework through her own response, for the weight of the story I wanted to tell. She was committed, in those early days of our time together, to the fizzing alchemy of my enterprise, to the rush and clamor of its making; happy, I thought, to run along beside, to travel with me.

There was grant money, a little of it, but most of the money was hers, her inheritance, put aside by father and grandfather for her use, released to her in the first year of our marriage and handed over to me—$237,000—to make the movie that I couldn't live without making. Though I could invigorate her with the earnestness of my commitment, I knew—this is the truth—that she didn't really care if I succeeded or not, and I think I must have hated her for that; the money was a gift of love, not of faith. I wanted her to depend on this enterprise, I wanted her to feel, as I did, that the world would come to an end if it didn't succeed. "Don't you understand," I cried, "things only work out right when you've got your back to the wall. We're made for this world," I shouted, "but only at full pitch; we're like those toys where centrifugal force keeps a ball spinning sideways: you've got to get up the speed first to make it work." She'd laugh and look at me. "Yessir,

Speedo," she'd say and go back to her music, which in the first years of our marriage she continued with, graduating from Manhattan C., going on a few gigs even, small recitals in church basements and rented halls, and once as one of a collection of artists in concert at Carnegie Hall. She didn't seem to want much though, she didn't demand that the world bend itself to her will. She missed opportunities, forgot sometimes to practice, took the A train to Far Rockaway where she walked on the beach instead of pursuing the chances that increasingly failed to appear. She said she wanted a child, but I said no to that and then lay awake shaming myself for my cowardice and self-absorption.

She went on location with us, out to Missouri—executive producer was her title, though there was no job attached—and it was there that I began to see the natural ease with which she moved through the world. The crew was small; twenty of us including actors, all working for scale, putting up like a church group in the homes of my relatives and other local friends, eating communal dinners on the back porch of my grandmother's house overlooking the river; kids, really, all of us, excited by making a movie, by being out of the city, off on our own in America. She had no assigned role, and I didn't think to give her any; I didn't consider, as maybe someone else might, that it was her money and so at least for that I should make sure she felt a part of what we were doing. Or that because she was my wife and I loved her I should. If anything I ignored her—no, I didn't ignore her, I put her away from me; I even told her, sitting on the back steps of Miss Carmel's (my grandmother's) house, switching a sprig of heal-all against my leg as we watched a few of the crew members climbing on the jungle gym my uncle had welded together out of barge scrap, that I needed a life for a while without interruption. "I can't tend to anything between us now," I said, "so don't bother me with it."

She rubbed the flat of her hand on my knee, bent down and kissed the spot, and looked at me sideways, like a bird. "Don't joke, Bessie," I said, "I'm serious."

Her smile turned down. "I know you are, pal," she said. "You're the most serious boy I know."

She began to hum softly, some air from the ancient musical past. On the back of the flatbed truck in the yard, the rods of scaffolding for the camera platforms shone in the late summer sunlight—shooting would begin tomorrow—the last ripened rays drawing long yellow lines along their surfaces, touching the cobble pieces with soft splashes of red. The rhythmic creak of the swings, the shouts of the crew, the clattering of pots being washed in the kitchen behind us, all the noises of the evening Missouri world were soothing to me; like small prayers, I thought, offered to the gods of film.

Tomorrow we would begin to destroy the town; brother would strike brother; children would scurry away to safety that soon would not be safety, as one by one, the men and their violent women dismantled the protections of civilization and destroyed all those who hid behind them. Confusion, dismay, an inadequate heroism, collaboration, useless humility, dumb flight, were the means by which I would tell my story. The moral was simple: nothing can save you. Civilization, as I saw it, the raiments of culture—society, church, family—all we had created on earth to hold off the darkness, were as nothing before the simplicity of death. I wanted to bang through to the ruin at the bottom of things, the pool of rotten blood that we all must finally drink from. I wanted to see the banker—the good man, the deacon—kneel at the feet of his captors and lick his own piss off the floor; I wanted to see the young mother, her broken arms hanging from her sides, scream helplessly as her child was dismembered before her eyes, the high school football star pushed into the furnace. Ah, it would be a story written in blood and ashes, and nobody, neither murderer nor victim, would escape.

Vietnam raged, at home young boys in uniform, frightened out of their wits, were firing at students, young men barely out of childhood were slipping through the tamarack woods into Canada. I was about to make my statement. What I didn't know then, what was obvious but hidden to me, was that she was the sturdy oak I leaned against. No, not that, not a tree, not some bulwark different from me I could shelter against—she was companion and partner, the necessary other who made—in connection—the move forth possible. What I didn't understand was that it is in partnership that we survive, not alone. I pushed her away from me so, I thought, I could work in peace.

She didn't fight back, not then. She took over the catering, cooking with my grandmother and my aunts the meals we ate on the set, hauling them in the back of Uncle Ray's pickup truck to the site and presiding over the distribution. The meals were extraordinary, fabulous country delights, baked hams and smothered venison, fried chicken, greens, sweet potatoes, butter beans swimming in pork, yellow squash, black-eyed peas, hopping John, apple pies and blackberry cobblers, banana pudding and yellow cake, gallons of fresh-brewed iced tea. Everyone welcomed her, everyone was delighted to see her; she moved easily among the crew and among the townspeople hired as extras, charming the mayor and the priest, swapping country tales with housewives and farmers, bantering with river men. It didn't matter to me. I didn't care if she could cook or not—I had never asked her to—I sought no anachronistic relationship with her; I paid no attention. What mattered was the picture appearing on film before me. Every moment was crisis. Every moment was disaster.

At night the A.D., the line producer, the cinematographer, and I pored over the rushes, holding on like men in a hurricane to the line of our vision, to its interweaving. There was confusion, dismay, and a fistfight when Harry Stern, the cinematographer, announced that he couldn't make a traveling shot work with all the crapola, as he put it, I wanted in it—shouts first, then fists, and Jerry Glick, the line producer, pleading with us to act our age, to come on now, boys, nothing has to be taken that seriously. She was there then, in the back of the room—an old tobacco barn we'd converted—not saying anything, not commanding me to let up, to stop, not begging. I would look up and see her smiling at me, see her wink and nod her head as if there was a secret we shared that none of these other boys knew about. Late, as the summer moon rose over the river, laying down trails of pearl that seemed to lead like fancy avenues into the darkness of Illinois, I would slip into bed beside her, arrived like one exhausted by a long journey into the comfort of her articulate presence. The fruity, fragrant, per-fumed and washed odors of her body would meet me as I pulled back the sheet, the smooth white haunch—she slept naked—the nest of her silky hair, her cheek touched maybe by a silvery line of spittle, her hand flung out in a last stroke across darkness, thrilled and appeased me. I felt like an old furred beast crawling into his companionable cave, and I would snug against her like some marsupial child groping my way into her arms that even in sleep she opened to me, sliding my hand downward into the warm cave of her sex, touching her into life, experiencing again the transforming power of sex, the frail, indestructible spark embedded like a tiny diamond between her thighs that I would stroke into a fire whose burning brought me to life—or set me free of life—that would galvanize us, all the way up from the core of her sleep, from my exhaustion, into the hilarity and fever of lovemaking. It seemed in those times, moving in a trembling slow motion so as not to wake my grandmother, who snored out her thin sleep on the other side of the wall, that like out-of-control race cars we would skid over each other's bodies, leaving tread marks, gouges, rubbery smoke. There were times when I wanted to thrust my hands right through her body, into the well of her sopping cunt to grab out her guts; like swamp boots I wanted to put her on and stomp around the room reeking of her stink, screaming out her name. We made love like raging animals, offering each other everything, snapping on the light so one or the other of us could spring to the floor to lie there like a torture victim wholly exposed and undefended before the ravaging gaze of the other. I ate her ass as if the fruit of knowledge were hidden inside it; she sucked me, swallowing me into her liquidy mouth so that my cock seemed sunk in a cup of hot resin. We thrust up each other's ass, opening every place that would open to scrutiny, to exploration, to plundering. In those moments there seemed no line between hatred and love, and it seemed, as we hurtled down the greased passageways, that we were accompanied by outriders both angelic and demonic, that in my ears I could hear not only the soothing music of heaven but the brutal yapping of hell dogs. It was in those moments, when thrown out over an abyss that seemed bottomless, that I lost any sense of the common world, that something in me seemed to pitch past her, past us both, as if my body and its accompanying spirit were suddenly launched off the deck of her being into a flight toward some other region, one where there was no such thing as union or complicity, no such thing as anything, a place in which questions of place and knowledge did not exist, in which I was dissolved back into the fine single grain of solitude—as if the purpose, the outcome of fucking was not to join, but to decompose, to disintegrate, to reduce until that last granule of human light was smeared out into nothing. I fell back from this place into loneliness. The room seemed large, depopulated, without human breath. I would look at her trembling body and it was the body of one unrecognizable to me. When a man dies, they say, you can see his soul ride out of his mouth on the last breath. For a while we sustained our fidelities. They were true, but separate.

4.   Morning of bright sun, croak of herons, sweet scent of orange blossoms. I was alive again, on my feet at the window where beyond porch and green immaculate lawn the Gulf rode under snapping white-topped waves. The sky was completely clear and the air was still. The waves were an anomaly, created as they were by wind, but there was no wind. Maybe they were only a memory, the history of wind, a tale they told about what wind was like. They flopped harshly on the level strand, skittering up to lather the nearest cypress stumps. There was a knock on the door. It was George Boudreau, the downstairs servant, a yellowy, smooth-skinned black man who had a habit of wringing his hands and talking to himself as he went about his chores. I was thinking about Greece, about the pebbly November shore at Skypia where Celest and I had flown to after the film festival, going off alone to a small hotel recommended by Archie Duquesne, an independent producer over there to scare up a distribution deal, who three years before had retreated to the same hotel for the same reason. I was thinking of the evening I walked down to the beach, just after sunset, alone, to look out at the Aegean. The whitecaps brimming the cobalt swells looked like millions of eyes blinking. Turning to look back I saw the mountains which were white and eroded, stippled with bushes and here and there in the gaps a few olive trees, and the hotel, its faded red facade sharply upreared like the front of a movie building, and then, on the balcony of our room, Celest, laying the bathing suits out to dry on the rail. And what I was thinking now, as I stepped away from the window where here the Gulf whipped its concoctions as if it were the inventor of itself and its doings, was that as I watched my wife—with so much humility, so much attention, so much composure—drape the limp suits over the iron rail, that come this far, halfway around the world straight through the grand promises and cognacs of the film festival, to this abandoned beach on the ancient Greek shore not one hundred miles from the spot where Agamemnon sacrificed Iphigenia, his beautiful daughter, to the gods who required it of him simply to make a little wind to blow his ships to Troy—what a deal!—I could find no solution, no way through, no explanation or practice that would promise continuity for us, that would keep us together. And what amazed me was that here in this foreign place, within earshot of the ancient Delphic oracles, where we leaned toward each other one more time—better vacation than divorce—she continued her round of simple chores, arranging clothes on a balcony, offering, it seemed to me—without her even knowing it I'm sure—the same collection of gifts—the yellow robe flapping about her legs, the body rosy from the shower, the quick inventions of a good mind, the stories about childhood jaunts up Lexington Avenue—that once I had desired as I had desired breath, but which were now only ashes to me. I could not understand this. Restlessness, fear, the torn world all played a part. But they did not explain.

I came to at the knock. "Yes," I said, "who is it?" thinking it must be Bess come to drive me out to the fields. They were taking the tobacco out of the barns this week and I had asked her to let me watch. But it was George, delivering a telegram.

"This come for you," he said. "I hadn't opened it."

I took the yellow envelope from him. "I wouldn't mind if you did. It can't be anything but bad news."

"I know that," he answered, looking off down the hall. He had a tallowy burn on his neck where, he'd told me, his mother had tossed a pan of boiling water at him when he was four. What did you think of that? I'd asked him. Nothing, he'd answered. I just bided my time till I could get a chance at scalding *her*. Except for the occasions when, in one of his fits, R.B. had run him off, he'd worked for the Appels for thirty years.

"Thank you, George," I said closing the door.

He raised his hand. "Miss Bess said to tell you she's already gone off."

"I figured that. Did she say whether she was coming back for me?"

"I don't know. I didn't ask her."

Maybe hostility was just a disease some people caught. D'Nel said that no matter what was wrong with a person it was what was supposed to be wrong. *Everything fits,* he said, *don't kid yourself about it.* In other words, the question was not *why me?* or *why this?* but *what now?*

"Okay," I said and closed the door.

The telegram was from Van. It was six sentences long. *No money anywhere. No chance I can see. One too many disasters they all say. Sorry Buddy. I have to go with Metro no other way out. Sorry Buddy.*

I sat down on the bed. *I knew he was gone,* I said, *but I didn't believe it until he told me.*

On the Greek shore, in the faded red hotel, I had sat across the bed from Celest. I'm not one of those, I said, who demands that he be told the truth. *Just don't say anything* is my policy. Maybe, before I find out, I will have become a different person. One who doesn't love you so much.

5.

"I just saw an opossum hanging from a pine branch."

"They're native to this area."

"I know that, but it was still strange. He was hanging head down with his tail wrapped around the limb."

"Possum yoga."

"Is that what it was?"

"Sure."

We were in the barn, a long, dark plank affair with narrow open windows running the length of it and the tobacco hung in cheesecloth on racks in the rafters. She leaned back to look up into the gold-and-white array of it. "Careful there, Willie," she called, "you don't want to tear it." It was wrapper leaf—the high class of tobacco—the leaf they use to wrap cigars in. She said it sold on the market for more than two dollars a pound. The barn floor was gray sand, fine, soft as dust, dimpled with ant-lion holes. Beyond the windows, planted in rows that ran unbroken to the distant pinewoods, were camellia bushes; all the varieties, she said, in the world. She wore a yellow shirt spotted with small white horses, and jeans.

I leaned against her, brushed my fingers against the back of her neck.

"Don't do that, Buddy," she said laughing. "Not here, not at work. And not anyway."

I dropped my voice. I made an accent. "Oh, sweet girl, oh, romping beauty, oh, lovely market flower."

"Shoo, boy."

Some morning, a while back, I had walked out of my garage into the street. I had stepped out into bristly spring sunshine. I had entered the Korean deli on Spring to buy a sack of red plums and saw there a man, a young man in a white T-shirt, a Korean man, screaming into the telephone. His rage barked and clattered into the phone, he squeezed the receiver as if it were the neck of a hated being, he screeched. The boy behind the counter winked at me and rolled his eyes. Some Manhattan craziness. Nothing unusual. But the voice, the yelling, the sound of it in the early morning—it was like a cold wave breaking over me. I winced, and turned away, chastened. The bright panel of the doorway, through which the clumsy beginnings of Manhattan day reared, was strange, unrecognizable. The flowers stacked in tiers, the iced piles of fruit, were alien. I was strange to myself. I did not recognize me, or my place. I did not know who I was, or where I was headed with this bag of plums in my hand. What now, I thought, what now, little guy?

I said, "Bess, why do you cough so much?"

She tapped her chest with two fingers. "A virus, I guess; I've had it for months."

"Disease?"

"The doctor thought it was a virus. Now he doesn't know."

"Maybe it's anxiety."

"We don't have that in rural Florida."

"What do you have?"

"Fear. Aggravation. Freaks by the dozen."

"What are you afraid of?"

"Not being able to provide food and shelter for all you hangers-on."

"Me?"

"I can see it in your face, Buddy. You still think you can get me to give you some money."

"Not some—a specific amount."

"Forget it, Pancho."

My eyes must have blazed because her eyes got hard and a thin smile unreeled across her mouth. "Life's tough, isn't it?" she said and grinned.

"Fuck you, Bess." Oh, Van, oh, my good never-to-betray-me friend.

"Go for a walk, Buddy. The gardenias are blooming. Go look at the gardenias."

"Fuck you," I said like some numskull.

She waved me away, she turned back to the tobacco. "Hey, Willie," she called to the black man sprawled in the rafters, "this isn't flying practice. We want the tobacco on the ground, not you."

At the door, the foreman, Bill Tilton, caught me by the arm. "Go easy on her," he said, wiping sweat off his bumpy forehead with the back of his wrist, "she's not feeling good."

I pulled my arm away. "What the hell do I care?"

"Yeah, well, she hasn't been feeling good for some time. You ought to be gentle with her."

"Shit on that," I said pushing past him, "I don't care how she's feeling."

I clanked off into the camellia bushes. I pulled leaves off, crushed them in my hands, smelled their waxy bitterness. Just another little boy throwing a fit. What did I care how she felt. Wasn't that what life did to us: beat us and mocked us and marched us until we were just too worn out to give a shit? Until there was nothing left to do but lay our weary bones down beside the road, and die?

6. One day Molly takes Banty into the bedroom and shows him the guns they keep in a cardboard box in the closet. They are tossed haphazardly in the box like old shoes: revolvers, automatics, a shotgun as short as his forearm, a rusted machine pistol with a broken plastic grip.

"You must be expecting trouble," he says, fascinated and terrified.

"This is the new fun."

"A box of guns?"

"What do you want? Oh, I know, you want to walk down to the pasture and look at the peach trees."

"They're coming along nicely."

"I don't doubt it. Here, pick one up."

He reaches into the box that smells faintly of oil and of the worn slattern smell of ground metal—what was it?—and plucks out a revolver, balances it in his palm. It is a .38, he guesses, with a longish barrel, black.

"Close your fingers around it."

It is heavy, it would wear him out; he grips it, slides his forefinger inside the trigger guard, presses against the slight curved tongue.

"Point it at me."

"Is it loaded?"

"Point it at me."

He raises the gun slowly, the weight dragging in his hand, until beyond the small brow of the sight he sees her face.

"Doesn't that feel good?"

He doesn't answer.

"It's your hand, grown longer and deadly," she says. "You can make anything happen."

"Not anything."

"Try it."

"Okay." He aims at her chest. "Pack your bag and come with me."

"Oh," she says, "I forgot." She raises her hand in which a small black snail of metal gleams. "I have one too."

She holds the gun on him. In his own sight he can see the squinted slant of her face, the black hair glossy from the bath, hanging like a mass of sprigged ribbons off her head, the pale eyes the color of green blackberries. And she sees him, clearly now, more clearly than she has seen him for years; she beholds him—that is the word that forms in her mind—the high smooth forehead greasy with sweat under the close-cropped carroty hair, the arch of the cheekbones, the slight boyish fullness under the jaw, the narrow wings of the collarbones, the slender flare of his torso. "Ah, you're beautiful," she says. "Just beautiful."

They are six feet apart. Shadows hang like tapestries between the windows; she can hear the light grinding of wasps in the porch eaves; and, as always, there is a brightness at the edge of her mind—at the edge of her body—a brightness as of the rims of the sunny sea cresting slowly toward her, and she whispers, *I am insane, I am a damned and lost person and I don't care, I want to see what will happen. Let it be irrevocable.* She hears the clap of a shot, and then there is another shot, and then a third, and she hears D'Nel's voice crying out angrily from the kitchen—"Jesus Christ," he yells, "you've killed the damn refrigerator"—and there are two black holes in the lime-green wall above Banty's head and blue acrid smoke swirling in the room. There is another shot, and another, and she crouches as she sees him lean toward the window, watching the gun rise again, knowing without thinking that he is not trying to hit her; she sees the red flash leap from the muzzle and hears the whack of the shot and feels it like a rocket bee whiz by her face, and it is crazier than she ever knew it before as she seems to come awake to the two of them kneeling across the bed from each other—*How did he get over there?*—firing not at each other but parallel to each other's body, as if each were being attacked from the rear and it is each other's job to provide covering fire: BLAM BLAM BLAM until the revolvers are empty and they are abandoned by bullets, deaf and abandoned in the violent domesticity of their intimacy amid the blue impenetrable smoke and the soundless shouts of D'Nel, who stands now in the doorway, a black automatic raised in his right hand, covering first the man then the woman, the muscles in his long white forearm twitching, the scorched proficient eyes above the black barrel passionless and rapt.

"Gentle Jesus," he says, "I have signed on a crazy country pair."

Then, without crouching, munificently, as a man might deal cards into a game he can't lose, he sprays the nine-shot clip into the room. The shots make a sizzling sound, small thuds; each hits something: china lamp, the small purple elephant she won at the county fair, her silver hairbrush, the pale blue captain's hat that she wears to weed the garden, hanging from the back of a chair. Articles explode. They cover their heads, they sink to the floor. Her body seems to expand, to fray; she sees herself sliding out like a steam liner on long greased rollers, the ocean taking her in a great splash like applause.

Then it is over, she can see he isn't firing anymore, see he is only standing there in the doorway licking his lips, his eyes shining, smoke trembling and billowing slowly around him. There is a ringing in her ears.

"Everybody all right here?" D'Nel says.

"Yes, sir," she says meekly.

Through the smoke she sees Banty crouching on his knees. There is a childlike fright in his face; his eyes blink rapidly. He raises the revolver, touches the barrel with two fingers, and throws the gun on the bed.

"How's it going, partner?" D'Nel says, grinning at him.

"Not too bad."

"Good. We want you to have a good time." To Molly he says, "You ready to go yet?"

"Yes sir. We were just cleaning up the room. You ready, Banty?"

Bantling sniffs his hands that smell of cordite. "A little cologne for the road," he says. They both giggle. Then they begin to laugh in the abandoned way of children.

"I'll be in the car," D'Nel says.

"We're coming," Molly says.

She whispers, *It's possible to entrap anyone, even the ones you love; sometimes you can't help doing it.* There is a flare of soot on his forehead; his shirt is streaked with sweat. She can see he is shaky and impressed. Through the open window she sees the tatters on the windmill arms

blowing in the breeze and hears the rusty creak as the blades turn, and
she hears the screaking of gulls mingling with the paler cries of mead-
owlarks rising from the tall grass at the edge of the woods. There is a
faintness about them—the cries—that seems through her dimmed hearing to isolate and particularize each sound so that they are like pebbles
dropped one by one into a well—an effect of distance and waiting—an
effect also that appears in the movement of this boy—who is a boy only
and always to her—who, just now, strips his shirt and pauses for a
moment—in the same slow motion—so she can regard the planes and
swells of his chest and stomach. A single spiral of smoke drifts toward
the window and is drawn slowly out as he turns from her, passing in
front of her so she can see his back now and the heap of muscle under
his neck, the round scar low down where he had a mole removed when
he was ten, the knobby backbone that she'd played scales on as they lay
beside the bay eating pineapple sandwiches and telling fantastical stories
about their adventures in wild lands they'd never visited. Sometimes—
this came to her now—she could see the whole scheme of her life as
something separate and apart from her, like a string of tin cans tied to
the bumper of a car, clattering and shining as it was pulled down a
cobbed street, and then it is as if who she is and everything she knows
is being drawn away from her until, for a moment, she doesn't know
anymore who she is, or even *what* she is—the way it was when she woke
from the spells; as it had been this last time when she woke in the bed
to the familiar body of this boy sleeping beside her; the way it was just
now as the shots crashed around them—and she loves this, she is not
frightened by it, she wants to wake again and again into a world that
is a mystery to her, the way, once—the only time this happened in her
life—after drinking too much she had blacked out and come to—hours?
days? later—to discover herself coming up the front walk of her house
in Occasion carrying a peck basket filled with peach blossoms. "Whoo,
Banty," she says, her voice filled with tenderness, and touches him on
the shoulder. He casts a glance at her, smiling. "This is some rigama-
role," he says.

"Isn't it though."

"Your high-speed life."

"Yes."

And then, as if he can't shake even for a minute his solemn purpose, he says, "Since I'm yours forever I have to keep on doing this, trailing you, bugging you—whatever it is—but I want you to know I'm not scared; I won't run."

"Do you think that's important?"

"It is to me."

"But there is no need for you to be here at all. I'm going on with something that doesn't include you."

"Whatever you do includes me."

"You mean because you're my brother of the heart."

"No. I thought it was that, but it isn't."

"What is it, Romeo?"

"It's a lot simpler. It has to do with the fact that you're here, with the fact that our paths have crossed."

"You tracked me down. You hired a detective to do it."

"It would have been possible *not* to find you."

"Not as hard as you look for something."

"Sure it would. It's like the dolphins, like something you come on that you have to carry back home with you no matter how it disturbs your life. I love what we do together. I've always loved it. It makes a peacefulness and an energy in my life, but I don't think I really have any say-so about it."

"Bigger than the both of us, huh? That's stupid. That's ridiculous. You're an idiot to think people are just fated for things. Life is not a magic mystery. It is very clear. Things add up, but they're real things. You think it's some kind of fate because you can't see the connections, that's all. Those dolphins aren't angels. Neither am I."

"I'm not calling you an angel. But I do know there are some things we are born into. They are challenges, the ones we are given."

"Challenges? Jesus, tell it to the Marines. Sometimes I hate talking to you, you're such a self-righteous solemn little fuck. You want to see my titties? Is that why you're here? Or did your detective guru tell you this was your celestial fate? You know why you're here? Because your life is so goddamn dull. Because there's nothing in it but those dolphins and the books you read and a glass of lemonade on the porch. You're thirty years old and you are afraid—having, whoo boy, come suddenly awake—that nothing is ever going to happen to you unless I make it happen. You're here trailing after me because you don't have anything better to do. I ought to punch you. I ought to beat the living shit out of you. Hell, I should have shot you just now. I should have put you out of your mewling misery."

"Why don't you try it?"

"You don't think I will?"

"I don't think you can."

The car horn sounds. They hear the bip, bip, bip of it, D'Nel's impatience. "Come on," she says, "we've got to go."

"Come on, we've got to go," he mimics.

She throws her pistol at him. He dodges and it bangs against the wall.

He picks up the revolver from the bed and aims it at her. "Now," he says, "you come with me."

She laughs. "No," she says and walks out of the room.

He follows her out and gets in the backseat behind her. D'Nel glances at the gun. "Better leave that here, partner. Don't want anybody to get the wrong idea."

Bantling gets out and puts the gun on the porch and gets back in the car. A milky scattering of light lies in the top branches of the live oaks near the water. The day is overcast, the clouds like gray cups of milk lifted from the south. He feels like a dog, his dog's teeth exposed, his gut gummy, his back whipped until his spirit cringes with love. In accommodation of this he curls down in the backseat, draws himself into a ball, and covers his face with his hands.

"What are you doing, partner?" D'Nel says.

"Worship," Banty answers, his voice small, helpless.

"That's fine. It's good to do a little of that every day."

"He's an idiot," Molly says and swats Banty's shoulder.

He begins to make a sound like moaning, but then it isn't moaning, it is words. She can't make them out. "Stop it," she cries. "Quit babbling."

But Banty doesn't stop, he raises himself and licks the hand that lies across the seat. She jerks it away and screams at him. He licks at it again, his long whitish tongue seeking her flesh; he moans.

This goes on as D'Nel smoothly backs the car around and heads out of the driveway. This continues, this moaning speech, these attempts at licking, this sorry display, as they speed down the coastal highway under the shaggy bodies of the live oaks, past the windswept fields of marsh grass, by the black streams upon which float branches and the bits and flecks of the broken-up natural world, above which soar ospreys and gulls and terns and skittering flocks of purple martins. Bantling hears the jangle cry of doves as they rise from the shoulder grass, the cry like small metallic wheels engaging, and he hears the cries of crows that sound exhausted and receding, recalling as he hears them what it had been like as a boy when he rode crunched up like this with his parents, nested in the backseat, sunk low, while the world rushed on above him, indecipherable and grand.

7. From the porch I watched the headlights lumber up the drive. Lining the white crushed-shell roadway, Bess had set out first tulip poplars, then sycamores, then magnolias. Each planting in its turn had withered and died. It was a humiliation to her, but the failure didn't stop her. The soil was acidic, diseased, but in the world there had to be some tree that would grow in such soil, if she could just find it. She planted pears, black willows, even three or four box elders, a northern tree. Each died, yellow rot climbing the leaves, scales white as leprosy appearing on the bark. Her customers remarked on it, this drive lined with dead trees. Finally she gave in and planted cabbage palms, the weed of West Florida. The palms prospered from the first day. "There's a moral to this," she told me when I asked about it. "What?" "I long for exotica, but my cut is local."

The headlights flashed in the trees, the light glistening on the dry fronds like rainwater. The car, a dark boxy affair, creaked and groaned to a stop below the front steps. I watched the guy check his hairdo in the rearview mirror, pat his pockets. He flipped the latch and got out, a tall man in a dark blue suit. The breeze trickling over the yard carried the scent of the Gulf, its mystery, salt distances. I leaned forward in the rocker, peering down at the guy. "Whoo," I said, "you are well turned out."

He looked up at me in surprise. His face was sun-reddened, the features sharp, a little overcarved. "Hi," he said, patting the top of his head.

"And I believe you're right on time."

"I think so." He long-legged it up the steps. "Is Bess ready?"

"No," I said. I waved my hand at a rocker nearby. "Have a seat."

He hesitated, shot a glance at the house—the front rooms were dark—and sat down. He got right up again. "I probably better let her know I'm here."

"She knows you're here. A rabbit comes up that drive and she knows about it. She wouldn't miss a sport like you."

"I guess not."

He fumbled a cigarette out of his shirt pocket and sat back down. "Smoke?"

"No, thanks."

I watched him draw the lighter out, flick it, and bend his face into cupped hands. The trembling flame lengthened his nose, struck shadows into his dark, wetted hair.

"What's your name, partner?"

"Robert Wise."

"You from around here?"

"Not hardly. I'm from down at Clearwater."

"What do you do, Robert Wise?"

"I'm an oculist."

"Occultist?"

"Oculist. Eye doctor."

"Oh. Good. Better than a witch."

"What?"

"Nothing."

I gave silence a chance, the West Florida version of it: click of tree frogs, breeze ticking the dry palm leaves, sob of an owl. The dark flesh of the earth, breathing.

He exhaled a sheath of smoke that the breeze caught and spiraled slowly away.

"It's interesting," I said, looking at the smoke, "how you can see the magnitude of your breath that way. What we breathe out is a shape as large as our bodies."

"I should quit."

"Oh no. Don't do that. Pleasures are hard enough to come by, especially continuing pleasures. Suck up all you can get."

He swiveled his head and looked at the darkened living-room window. From upstairs came the faint tinkle of piano music. R.B. tapping out his messages. *Save me. Let me go. Save me and let me go.*

"She'll be along in a minute," I said.

"I guess." He pulled sharply at his chin. "We don't want to be late for the movie."

"What are you going to do *after* the movie?"

"Probably go out to the springs and see the moon rise. Bess likes that."

"I'll bet. You going to fuck her there?"

"Hey." He bounced up from the chair as if someone had turned on the juice. "Listen, I'm going in to see if she's ready."

"No, no—I'm sorry. I've been under a strain." I put out my hand. "Buddy Drake. I used to be married to Bessie. It was a long time ago. I'm sorry."

"Oh. Jeez. You scared me." He took my hand, offered out of a crouch. His palm was soft as silk.

"Yeah," I said as he sat down again. "I've been a little frazzled. Business troubles, ha ha, all that."

"Ah, I understand." He took a quick drag on his cigarette, flashed me a look. "It's terrible what they've done to this country. It's like a beautiful car that they've just driven without oil until it's burned up."

"That's pretty poetic."

"It's the truth. I wouldn't have thought this two years ago but I believe we are headed into another depression. And I'll tell you, this one will make the last one look like a trip to Disney World."

"It already looks like a trip to Disney World."

"Ha. You're right. A circus out of control. Jesus." He placed his palms flat on his knees, spread his legs and pressed them back together. He snorted. "The whole country's drunk—that's what it is—the country's drunk and it needs to sober up. We're on a spree."

"Out of our heads."

"You bet. And there is going to be one hell of a price to pay on the day the liquor runs out."

"Hoo-wee."

I leaned back in my rocker, pushed, then caught myself. Movement made me dizzy. Something white, lost night gull, flickered above the pines. There was a strong smell of the sea.

"You ever think about shadows?" I said.

"Shadows? No. What about them?" His voice was still rough and quick with his enthusiasm.

"How sometimes they look so black and solid you think you could just reach your hands down and scoop them up."

"Yeah, I know what you mean. It gets awfully dark on this coast. Last night, before the moonrise, my wife was out on the porch and I went out there and I couldn't even see her. We were five feet apart and I couldn't see her at all."

"You're married?"

"Well, yeah. We don't get along. My wife's nothing compared to Bess. She doesn't stand up to her."

"Who does she stand up to?"

He looked at me sharply. "Oh, I see." He flicked his cigarette over the rail, a red arc trailing sparks, and stood up. "These mosquitoes are pretty fierce," he said waving in front of his face. "I don't see how you can stand it."

"They don't bother me."

"Well, I'm going in to get away from them. You coming in?"

"No."

He crossed in front of me and almost made the door before I stopped him. "Wait a minute."

"What is it?"

The look he gave me was scared, but he stopped, held his ground. I noticed how small his chin was.

"I think you better go home."

"I don't think it's any of your business where I go."

"Don't make a mistake like that."

"What mistake?"

"The one where you back-talk an outraged ex-husband."

"You haven't got any say-so over what Bess Appel does."

"Some say I have none over what *I* do, but I'm afraid that's not the problem."

"What's the damn problem?"

"How you're going to get off this porch without me beating the shit out of you."

"What did you say?"

"What you heard."

"Now listen."

"Huh. Fuck you, man."

I came up out of the chair.

He stepped back awkwardly. "Now wait a minute, Mr. Drake. What I'm doing is all right with Bess. She knows all about my wife."

"We'll tend to Bess later. Right now I want to see you put your ass in gear."

"Damn. *Fuck.*"

He moved away from the door, his hands out. He was trembling. I thought: man, I like this.

"Damn," he said again, hesitating.

He looked back at the door; its rubbled glass was dark. He looked as if he was about to call out, and he looked, I couldn't help but noticing, like a little boy denied his sweet. Even when we're wrong, losing hurts.

"Move on, my friend," I said taking a step toward him.

His shoulders slumped, he turned away—so close!—and headed down the steps.

Despite it all, I claim a tender heart. In Missouri they thought I was a quiet boy, studious, respectful of his elders. And I was. What I did next was only what tenderness sometimes comes to. With him turned fully away from me, headed tensely down the steps, I stepped forward and kicked him squarely between the shoulder blades. The kick sent him sprawling. Face down into the white shell dust. He came up covered with it, a sudden ghost, raving.

"You asshole," he cried. "What in the hell are you doing?" He flicked down his front. "Look at what you did to my suit. Do you see what you did?"

I came to the edge of the steps. "You're a dumb guy," I said.

"The hell with you."

"I mean, you give when you ought to stand; and vice versa. Up here was the time to stand. Down there's the time to give."

"The hell with you, Jack."

"Get out of here, pal."

"I'll get out of here. You watch."

He flung the car door open, reached under the seat, and came out with a pistol. I couldn't believe it. A doctor.

He laughed, a croaking, phlegmy sound. His head bobbed, straightened. He poked the pistol at me. "What do you think of this?" he said.

"I already know about it."

"You just move down the porch. I've got business here and it's all right with everybody else."

"I keep telling you, partner, this blossom's not for you."

"You haven't got any say-so about it, asshole."

He thought our positions were reversed.

I grinned. "Do you know how ridiculous you look?"

"I don't want to hear about it. Move down the porch."

" 'Fraid not, squirt."

I took a step toward him. He took a step, not toward me or back, but to the side. It was what D'Nel called the step of confusion. Even so, I wondered for a second if I was going to get hurt this time. If this was the time I'd be beaten down so hard I wouldn't get up. If you can stop me, friend, stop me. Let's see.

"If you shoot me," I said, "you'll never see Bess again."

"That sounds like a plea. It's too late for pleas."

"What is it with you crackers? Are you all crazy?"

I took another step toward him. The gun leveled at my chest. It was as if it were a vacuum, drawing my breath out. There was nothing on earth as large, or as powerful, as the gun.

"That's it," he said. "That's it. You're done."

I raised my hands. "All right. You win."

I walked down the steps, but at a slight angle, my hands out from my body. He moved aside, thinking, I suppose, that I was about to walk out of the scene. In a movie I could whirl, knock the gun from his hand, and then pummel the shit out of him. I couldn't see how to do it in real life. Then lights went on, the front of the house blazed, the front door opened, and Bess came out. She had on a yellow shirt and a dark blue loose skirt stamped with red and yellow flowers. Her hair was pulled back and held with a narrow blue band. There were scratches on her hands—from work in the barns, I guessed—and her face was sunburned.

She looked at us, and smiled.

"Doing all right, boys?"

"I'm sorry, Bessie," the goon said, "this fellow was threatening me."

He put the gun back in his pocket, took a step toward her. That was the break I needed. I caught him with my right hand, flush in the ear. He staggered against the car and almost fell to his knees. He pushed with one hand back upright. I came around with a left, my knuckles striking teeth through his cheek. He groaned, fell back against the car door, and looked at me, stupefied.

"Do something," I said. "Go for the gun."

I was tense with violence. With murder.

He shot a look at Bess, and it was a look of appeal.

"Buddy," she said softly, sadly. "Oh, Buddy."

I reached around the guy, into his pocket, took the gun out and stuck it in my belt. Then I folded him and pushed him into the car. "Start your engine, pal," I said.

The man, Robert Wise, started his car, leaning against the wheel. There was spittle in the corner of his mouth; he looked dumbly ahead of him. The headlights came on, flashing against the pines across the yard. Birds—waxwings—startled by the light, rose from among the branches. They flowed, rising and falling, against the light, the curve of their flight making a curve like the long edge of a blanket snapped in the wind, baffled suddenly and homeless. Day birds, they wouldn't find their perch again when the lights went out. The sight touched me, struck me with a sadness that made me want to console the fellow gripping the steering wheel, another bird marooned in the air. Who do I serve, I thought—who?

I leaned into the car and kissed Robert Wise on the cheek. He didn't flinch; he was too bamboozled for that. I wanted to choke him; I wanted to hug him. Robert Wise looked straight ahead, like a man who had just seen his fortune. I pushed the gear lever into drive. The car lurched forward, Wise came to life, and I stood back as the vehicle trundled slowly up the drive. Wise leaned out, spit, and pulled the door closed. The headlights checked off the palms one by one, steadily. All around us—I hadn't noticed—the air was filled with the yellow blinking of fireflies.

I turned to Bess, who stood in her romance clothes, patient on the steps. Now we would speak in the present tense, now who we were would rise out of the vat of the past where it had been set steeping, and we would strike at each other, flush with the briny sap of our failure and knowledge, all in present time. How many nights had she, like me, lain in a worried bed conjuring her life back into shape, touching the marriage, pressing her fingers into it, caressing it, pounding it, crying out to it, ordering it to give her a drop of love, to go away. Memory is so slight, so cheap. What lives on in us lives sunk so deeply that what we call memory never touches it. Not for an instant. We forget, we forget—everybody forgets, forgets the kiss, the license number, the light on the pond, the pet name he spoke into the darkness. But there is something deeper than memory, deeper than understanding. And it tells us that we are not here to remember; we are not here to understand. What lives in us, its bones and blood streaked with the stains of love, knows nothing of faces, of walks in the summery woods, of the accusations. It is a finer child, lone sailor, voyager carrying its treasure over the endless seas of time. What stirs its speech is not the latest figure of our mad dancing, the plea, a morning on our knees in sunlight trenching the garden; these are only the doors it speaks through. Movement is all, it says; breath is all. Everything else is dust on the water.

Ah, Bess. Speak to me.

I climbed the steps and took her in my arms. She struggled, she cried out, but I held her. I pulled her silky head close and spoke into her ear.

I will kill you, I said. *I will fuck you and then I will kill you. Nothing has changed.*

I knew I was out of my head, but there wasn't a thing I could do about it.

8.   I tied her to a chair. It was easy. She knew me, and knew I would kill her if she didn't submit. She even told me where the rope was. I pulled her arms back, tied her wrists with double half hitches, tied her ankles separately to the legs, looped the rope around her waist and shoulders, shanked it down behind her, turning the knot in under the chair. It was a good job. We did it in silence, we did it in her bedroom where the silver and golden fishes bounded over the walls, cavorting in a blue glistening sea. The windows were open onto the porch; she could have called out, but she didn't. There was the smell of tea olive, the smell of the salt sea, the low crackle of the surf.

I left the light on by the bed. Its simple radiance made the pillows look like stones, the rumpled covers look like frozen marble carved in the shape of bedclothes, caught in the articles on her table, polishing the spines of books, the crystal bowl in which a single damascene rose floated, the curious small packages she set around the room tied up like Christmas presents. (If I opened her closet I would find gifts for all of us—boots, books, a pair of binoculars—presents that she had bought years ahead in anticipation of birthdays, Christmas. I could see my life in them if I wanted, stretching through the years in a wealth of gifts: the sleeping bag she would give me at fifty, the collection of Japanese river rocks she would give me for our wedding anniversary—which she still celebrated, year after descending year—the book on islands, the stuffed monkey, the Nepalese sweater for my old age.) She watched me all the time, her eyes following me as I tied her, following me as I moved about the room touching the private objects of her life. I lay down on the bed, propped myself on pillows, and looked at her. Her face was sad, strangely worn; there were tears in her flecked eyes, but she didn't ask me to release her.

We followed my father's coffin to the grave like dogs. It was raining, November, we had come by train from St. Louis to the hilly burial ground above the town where he had been born. Through oaks you could see the Mississippi in the distance, a crescent in a bend, gray as smoke. The rain beat on the coffin, beat the yellow lilies and the chrysanthemums and beat on the heads of my relatives, clotted in my mother's veil. They carried the coffin under the tent and set it on the ground. My uncle Ray sang a song, some ballad that long ago had been carried down the Ohio, carried tucked away, like the seeds they carried in leather bags to build their lives with in Missouri. As he sang, the old high words flowing unaccompanied among us, through the trees I saw boys passing. They carried shotguns—on their way to hunt squirrels in the falling November dusk. I watched as they moved silently and carefully through the oaks and the brambly underbrush until they were out of sight. Then the song ended and the preacher turned to my mother; he stood aside for her to approach the grave. She leaned over the open coffin, a heavy woman who had loved my father every moment of her adult life, who had no recourse now, and touched the smooth gray face. As she did so two leaves, coppery and wet, fell from the oak above her head onto my father's chest. The preacher reached in to pluck them off, but my mother stopped his hand. "Let them go," she said, "he wouldn't mind."

Afterward, after my mother had shut up the house and moved in with her sister on Mercedes Street, I thought of those leaves, of those bits of the world carried into the dark earth with my father. They seemed a designation of some sort, a proof or badge of existence, like the household articles buried with Egyptian kings, and all that was necessary. He had lived, only partially long, only partially well, and failed, and been loved closely by a few, and died and was buried here on a hill in Missouri overlooking the river with two small red oak leaves on his chest, and life was nothing but a wet wind blowing through a sack of bones, and it didn't matter. . . .

I told her this, told this story to Bess as we stayed our vigil through the long summer night. Toward dawn the breeze shifted to the south and freshened, bringing the sweet smell of the islands. The dawn was D'Nel's time, and Molly's time, and the time of Banty Jakes who loved Molly and who followed her as she followed D'Nel, followed her down the long piny passages of West Florida to the next house of murder and the next. I asked Bess how one could come to murder, but she couldn't tell me. I need to know, I told her, because I have to understand how not only Molly Picard but Banty Jakes, the fool who loves her, can come to a place in which they are willing to kill another human being. Molly is most important because she is the one who leads Banty into it; at least she is the one who kills first. What is it that D'Nel tells her that would propel her into such an act? Or is it anything that he tells her; is it only who he is, what she sees in him?

I said you have to be able to picture it, picture them driving along a stretch of beach, past the little settlements of convenience stores and churches and hot-dog stands; you have to imagine that it is early in the morning, before even the garbagemen are up, and on their right the ocean is gray, still soaked with the night, and on the left the houses are separate and lonely in their little yards among the hibiscus bushes and the yuccas and the pines. Maybe they are hungry, maybe they are tired, maybe they are half drunk from the beer, maybe it is only a twitch that presses into the blood like a jabbing thorn, but whatever it is they stop at the top of a driveway leading down a low slope toward a house set among some woods. You can see them there, the three of them, the car idling; sitting there, D'Nel and Molly in the front seat, Banty in back, looking at the house which is painted light blue and has a flat roof covered in white gravel. It has screen doors and a porch off to the side where bathing suits are pinned to a line. Maybe there's a stroller in the yard, a string of plastic beads tied to one handle. The grass hasn't been cut recently, the pines behind the house are dying from beetles.

D'Nel slips the car out of gear and they glide down the short slope and park behind a grapefruit tree. There is a small clatter as they arrange the guns, the bucket, the rope.

They step out of the car, stretching, taking deep breaths of the salty air, filling their lungs. Banty looks away toward the Gulf, which is out of sight beyond the rise of the dunes. Sea oats blowing in a slight breeze that doesn't reach them seem to be beckoning, commenting among themselves. The world in that moment seems to him a world of voices and intelligence, a world in which every small object has a say and a place and a soul. The thought strikes him as strange but he welcomes it. *Life,* he whispers, *starts over every second.* D'Nel, smiling, presses a finger to his lips. Molly kisses him softly on the cheek.

I looked at Bess; she was tired, she slumped in her bonds; her heavy shoulders seemed to be erupting from the ropes, her feet below her thick ankles were reddened slightly. I could see the pulse beating slowly in her soft throat. At table she would often reach across and cut my meat up for me. As if I were a goddamn child. The house was quiet.

Let me tell you, I said.

There is a certain insouciance that comes when we loose the last restraint. What is it that binds us one to another? Is it a common agreement, or is it something built into us that gently scolds us— sometimes not so gently—toward consideration of our fellows? Or is it only a lie, thought up long ago by those who would enslave us, to convince us of our weakness, so we might dumbly live out our lives without causing trouble to the ones who run the world? I won't let anybody touch me anymore. Flesh against flesh—it erodes my mind. But listen, girl. They approach the house, all is still, you can hear water dripping from the spigot near the wall—*pick . . . pick . . . pick* on the grass. They circle the house once—it is small, curtained—and return to the front door. The door is unlocked, they enter through a screened-off space—it was a garage once—and try the main door. Beside it are two buckets containing cochinas. The clams stink terribly. Molly archly holds her nose. D'Nel tries the door: it too is unlocked. It creaks on salty hinges, but D'Nel is careful; he opens it slowly, lifting it slightly so the thin board won't make noise. It opens into a kitchen through which they can see a living room and beyond it a corridor leading toward the back of the house. They go in; the linoleum crackles lightly under their

bare feet. On a table in an alcove off the kitchen are the remains of
supper: hamburger trash, cold french fries, gouts of ketchup in a small
diminishing trail across the white Formica. D'Nel takes a french fry,
sniffs it, bites, spits it back. This scares Banty; he thinks, Maybe they
can analyze spit, use it to catch us. D'Nel, who seems to be able to read
his mind, looks at him and grins. He draws from the waistband of his
jeans a short black pistol, hands it to Banty. He bows as he does this,
a theatrical bow, sweeping his arm against his waist. The anointment,
sure, Banty thinks, taking the gun which feels as slippery as a slug in
his hand. Molly leans into him a second, kisses the top of his head.

They pass through the living room, which is sad in its declarations
of ordinariness; the flat plastic cushions on the sofa, the scrap of fishnet
tacked to the wall, the scuffed straw rugs, the wire basket filled with
plastic balls have each a wan delicacy, a forlornness like children left
out of the game. For a second Bantling wants to stop and touch each
item, to brush it with life, and for a moment longer the thought comes
to him and sticks in his mind that each object in the world, not just
lovers and dogs and children, is waiting for loving touch, is standing
like an orphan in a field patiently waiting for the touch of someone
loving to free the energy and life in it. He thinks that maybe someday
he would like to do this: travel around the world touching those objects
that are never touched, the discarded furniture in attics, stair railings in
abandoned houses, old women reading their Bibles in bed at night,
derelicts on the street. . . . He thinks of the dolphins, of walking out
onto the dock late at night to whistle them in, how they come to him
gaily like dogs, diving through the phosphorescent waves, so genuinely
glad—it can't be anything else—to see him, poking their snouts out of
the water to bang against his outstretched hand, nuzzling him, chirping
and barking; how he rises before them—do they think he is a king, or
ridiculous?—strips his clothes—what do they think of his body, its
paleness, its long collapsible fins, its hanging sex?—and dives in, plunging deep so that he rises through the sparkling night water with the
dolphins above him, coming up between them, feeling their slick skin
in his hands, the soft portions of belly and womb, the sex slit, the hard
sides, the almost prehensile fins. They are like dogs, he thinks—dogs,
not people, though their emotions are more clarified. Their genius is in

their strangeness, their faithfulness to water; like anything living they are, when looked at a long time, complex, intricate, revealing an endless array of possibilities and connections. . . .

He thinks this but says nothing because they are moving without a hitch down the hall now toward the bedrooms, down the pale green hall in which the webs of night still cling to ceiling and corner, where someone has hung an aloha shirt on a doorknob that D'Nel plucks off and puts on over his gray sweatshirt—dressing for the day, not the dawn—and models for them, pulling the tails out, mincing—before he turns the doorknob briskly, steps into the darkened room, and fires three shots.

There is a cry from a bedroom farther on—Who there dreams of monsters appearing in the night? Who there was afraid all along death would arrive like this?—as D'Nel slams the first door shut, crouches, grinning like a wolf, and aims at the next door. Molly stands behind him, a pistol raised now in her hand. She chucks Bantling with her elbow; there is sweat in the down on her lip; her hand trembles; he sees his own hand rise like something freshly magnetized, and the gun sight quavers and steadies. The door flies open, a man in yellow boxers pulling on a pale robe appears, and in the second before D'Nel shoots him Bantling thinks he has never seen such a look of horror or surprise on a human face before, a look that is like the look on a face in the middle of orgasm, it is that distilled, and he thinks—this is so strange to him—that for once in this man's life he has rushed past every inhibition, rushed naked into the courtroom of his truth—not to say his fate—though he could not, just whacked from sleep, could not possibly realize—even if death crossed his mind—that he was about to die so quickly; which he does, as D'Nel pulls the trigger of his small automatic twice, creating magically two black coins in the center of the man's chest.

Ah Jesus save me! Bantling cries as D'Nel leaps to catch the man in his arms. He himself fires a shot wildly—unacknowledged by his resinous mind—hears the whine-whang of it (D'Nel brushes the sound away as if it were a fly)—and watches as D'Nel pulls a mirror from his pocket and holds it over the man's face—to catch the soul on it, yes—no— which is rapidly going white, though there is no blood at all, holding the mirror six inches above the man's face—a moony face with small straight nose, small fleshy mouth, dark round eyes—holding the man's head in the palm of his right hand, propping him—so he can see. The man's eyes dart wildly and settle, like black birds settling, on the nightscape, the death's-head of his own reflected face. There is shock, awareness, bamboozlement, terrible fear, and then something else, something like tenderness—*tendresse,* darling—something that would appear on the face of one looking into the face of his favorite child; but Banty knows—and he doesn't know how he knows—it is not into his own face the man looks—and he knows that D'Nel must see this too—it is into another face he is peering, or not into a face at all but into another dimension. . . .

Abruptly D'Nel flings the mirror down and thrusts the man from him. "I can't get it," he cries. "Fuck, I can't see it!"

He heaves to his feet, leans sharply down, presses the muzzle of the automatic against the man's temple, and fires. The shot makes a flat, rubbery sound like an inner tube hit with a rock and the man's head kicks on his neck and falls back.

Even in the dawn light, even in the dinginess of the hall, they can see the blue smoke drifting. There is silence in the house. Then the refrigerator creaks and shudders into life. A calendar detaches itself from the wall and falls fluttering to the floor. It lands with the scene of a covered bridge in New England, vivid fall leaves, uppermost.

Through a door at his right, beyond a room that appears to be empty, Banty can see the dune line across the road, the pines heavy in their crowns with dew, the sea oats whipping. Beyond the heaped sand the world stops and starts over as something new. It makes up a whole new version of itself and fills itself with life that bears no resemblance to us, that does not have any interest in us. God is not God, he is just one more crazed entrepreneur. Isn't it clear to everyone that there is nothing in this world larger than us that cares for us?

A low sobbing, cracked and muffled, comes from behind the closed bedroom door. It is the door the man came out of, that he shut behind him in a last, Banty thinks, act of kindness. Who could be there but his wife, whom he maybe only reflexively but still actively tried to protect. The man lies on the floor crunched in the corner, his chin pressed into his chest that is fatty, sown with a few dirty hairs, white as a potato, a chest probably no one outside his family has seen for years. The sobbing stops, is caught in the midst of itself. D'Nel leans his forehead against the door, pokes out his lips. *Darling,* he whispers to the one inside, then louder: *Darling. You are,* he says, *the most magnificent of women. I couldn't survive without you. Wife lover mother daughter friend—you are all women to me. I see you lean into the light brushing your hair and my heart stops. My life is a devotion offered to you. Sweet peach, cool drink offered in the deserts of hell—I would die but for you.*

He pulls away from the door, like one detaching himself from an embrace. He thrusts a moony, wild-eyed look at them, a caricature of adolescent love, shades of dementia and power passing over his strong features. His eyebrows are as black as printer's ink. His lips are dark and moist, as if he is wearing lipstick. He turns the knob, pushes the door open with one finger. A shot cracks, splinters a hole in the door just above his head. Banty falls to the floor, Molly weaves, but D'Nel doesn't duck, doesn't even flinch. He flicks his face at them, grinning. *Steady, children,* he says. He leans back, out of the line of sight, and pushes the door open. Two more shots are fired from the bedroom; they make black holes in the hall ceiling. *Oh,* D'Nel whines, grinning, *a hot breakfast.*

Here, in another Florida, a single long finger of rose lay along the horizon, reaching toward us from the east. The sky and the Gulf were the same mossy gray. The low, tousled islands were black as wrecks. The sea was oily in the troughs, thin, almost breaking on the low crests; a long-legged sea was what Bess always called it. I knelt beside her and pushed my face against her waist. My life—not the next move of it, or where it was going, but its definition—was unmoored. I said, "How far do you think we've gone by now—is this new ground?"

"New enough, Buddy." Her voice was faint, breathless.

"Do you think I can get out of this?"

"No."

You cut loose from everything and you walk out of the house—you're still breathing—and then as you're making your way down the street you notice morning glories blossoming in a fence. You see the bees tumbling in the flowers and you notice the shreds of a red kite caught in the branches of a sycamore. You pass a diner and inside you see a couple arguing and you see the counterman pouring himself a cup of coffee and you see one guy off by himself, a guy in a brown suit sitting with his back to you. You're just passing, everything in your life has come loose, but for a second there, as you glance at the back of a man bent over a cheap counter, you know the deepest secrets of all those lives, and the deepest secret of life itself—it is on the tip of your tongue, the words are as real as gum in your mouth—and for one son-of-a-bitch moment you can almost, you can almost say the words.

—Let me tell you, Bessie, let me tell you that those three people in Florida, those killers, go into that room—bullets don't stop D'Nel; he knows he won't be hit—they go into that room and they take from that woman, that now ex-wife, that widow sobbing in the bed, they take everything from her in this world that she loves. They—or D'Nel—have killed all her family, murdered, as the newscasts will tell us later, three sleeping children and the proprietor of a plumbing business from Opp, Alabama. The widow woman knows this; there is an absence all around her, the chalky air is vivid with it, the holes D'Nel Boyd has punched out. Does anything pour through these holes? Can she see through them as if they are windows? Do you think the universe can crack? Or is there only blessed numbness? I will tell you what it is, darling. It is as if your body is filled with cold lead. It is the weight that trees bear in winter, the weight the ocean bears of itself, the weight of stones. Who cares what death means, it's life we have to figure. And this cold weight exists. It is not only a weight in the heart, it is a weight in the ankle and in the collarbone and in the eyelashes. It is not the explosion in your brain of a stroke, not the blade in your breast from a heart attack, not the anguish of guilt, or the terror of lost wages; it is the weight, it is the settling massive body, ancient and indestructible, pressing upon every cell in your body until it becomes a weight not separate from you but you, it becomes you so that you are the weight, you are the dense, impenetrable volumic presence itself—nothing less. Oh, what can we say to this woman who is about to die? Is there comfort on this earth? Can there be comfort at all if there exists any

region where its warmth cannot reach? How can we comfort the one
for whom the expression *drawn and quartered* would be a reprieve? And
do you know that there is much worse? Physical torture is only vivid,
it is not necessarily profound. What is profound is suffering over time,
is the father working for his measly wage, is the householder staggering
home each day carrying his life like a sack of scrap metal on his back,
is the woman with six kids and nobody to help her, is the woman for
whom life is not a reductive argument, not a proposition, but a sentence,
one in which there are no exaltations beyond the four minutes writhing
on a pallet with some whipped creature like herself who can hardly tell
the difference between her and the floor; and let me tell you that even
if you come from Opp, Alabama, where, rotted and stuck so far down
into the throat of the world it can't be coughed out, life is nearly as
meaningless as life gets, but where you can still, on a Saturday morning
rinsed by rain, buy a dress or a chocolate malt or a gun or a jar of 'shine,
even if you have been raised up to the heavenly exaltation of a good
job in Opp, Alabama, which to two-thirds of the djinns on earth would
seem like paradise, you have been waked now at dawn on the eroded
coast of the Florida Panhandle to the sound of your children being shot,
to the sound of your husband slipping his last breath onto the hallway
tile, and now not in your dreams but in this particular moment of your
life the last door you will ever see through has been thrown open and
coming toward you is a tall man with black hair slicked back like a
gambler's, and the gun is buttery in your hand, is slipping out of reach
just like you knew it would, it is falling to the floor as your life lunges
backward in your body until it becomes a small round pebble at the
center of your being, a pebble in which all the precious matter of
memory and hope and passion and humility is collected but which you
realize, with a clarity that is stronger than anything you ever knew
before, can't—won't—be protected or evaded, which this man leaning
over you, his breath smelling of wintergreen, will reach into you for,
will probe more horribly than any greased finger rummaging your ass,
until he finds it and draws it out of you, not a heart or even the womb
where your babies rocked in the dark, but your soul. Is there protection
then? Why doesn't God speak? And why do we all go dumbly to our
deaths? The last words of the pilot whose jet overshot the runway were

not *Jesus save me* or *Mother* but *Oh shit,* which seems to me about as eloquent as it gets in this world—but this woman, this widow, this thirty-seven-year-old ex-mother of three will not cry eloquently into the darkness that enfolds her. Death is not like you think it is—D'Nel would point this out—it is not, as they say, a colorful swarm of memory, not the afternoon you swam in the pond with your sisters and later drank beer on the dock, not First Communion, not the smell of oatmeal—what it might be is simple persistence, the woman who calls her neighbor to her deathbed charging her to retrieve the packet of forty-year-old love letters from a box in the closet and destroy them; it might be, as it was in St. Louis two years ago, my father, for one moment on the bed where he died, recognizing me—but it is not a white corridor opening into heaven, it is not a song, it is not wisdom, it is not consolation.

D'Nel approaches the woman. She cowers on the bed, flashes a look at the window where outside a mockingbird splashes in the metal pan set on a post for a birdbath, and in the sky some feeble constellation that has stood with its back to the wall all night falters finally—but there is no escape there (the bed is pushed against the wall and D'Nel is advancing powerfully and her bones have turned to syrup); she tugs at the sheet, but ineffectually (it is caught under her hip), cocking her head, wiping her chin on her shoulder (which if she could see herself she would stop doing); then she sees the others, Banty and Molly, and something that she didn't know was tottering falls and plummets ten miles through her gut—it is as bad as possible and then it gets worse—so that now, without her knowing it, she is moaning, emitting a cry that is the distillation of the heart's plea against darkness, is the precipitate of a life boiled down to one last adventure of terror and destruction; so that when D'Nel kneels on the bed and offers his hand to her, like a father offering his hand for his four-year-old daughter to spit her gum into, she chokes, the moan catching like fur in her throat, and begins to hack and retch, each burst of coughing like a fiery tear in her head so that he is touching her before she realizes she is being touched, so that as he takes her head in his hands she is aware of a gentleness—it is nothing less!—a tenderness even, in the way his palms cup her skull with its thinning pale hair—so that, in the midst of this moment of concentration, of effort even, she misses the instant, is not prepared for him to, as he does, crack her skull sharply against the wall. Rings of red fire rush upward, the life in front of her eyes turns to blue powder, to dust dancing, as huge metal doors fall on her and fall on her and fall on her; something spits, gives, tears away from her, she hears a voice crying *atteroar, atteroar . . . cross . . . ah . . . cross . . . the moth*—there is a sudden distension, like a fault in a rubber tube swelling, and a fire, and a fire, an assault, like ice in the face; and then nothing.

It was dawn red as roses, and I saw my bitten, intemperate life. My ex-wife slept in her ropes. Countrywoman, queen of hardship, she took her rest regardless. I got up, went into her bathroom, drew a glass of water, and drank it down standing at the sink. My face was craven, lined down both cheeks with the grooved furrows of fear, age, and bafflement. In the clear glass I touched chin, forehead, eyes, I wiped a finger across the wide, self-defending mouth. In the other room, trapped in a singlet of dawn light, her buckeye hair shone. Wake up, Bessie. Listen to me again. Please listen. Already the first stirrings had begun in the kitchen downstairs; in a moment the woody thump would sound as Mattie began to beat out her breakfast biscuits. And then Uncle Porto's hollow coughing would sound from the downstairs porch, his exclamations and curses at another fine day. The tame heron would croak and flap. A child would cry out, refusing direction. From seaward would come the low throb of outboard motors as the mullet fishermen put into the bay. The sun would touch and tangle the grass hair of the islands. And far away from here Celest was waking. Across her Upper East Side courtyard the sun crept like a cat through the wisteria. From the table beside the bed, off an embossed china plate, she would pick up with two fingers the scrap of pastry she fetched from last night's party and eat it, nibbling it crumb by crumb. The light lancing a corner would fascinate her a moment, she would cock her head, studying the paler color against the darker, thinking of an arrangement of household articles on a mahogany desk top, of the smooth surface of her lover's hair, of a curl of French meringue. Nearby, in a room with walls the color of sunlight upon which were strung rainbow stones from the

Indonesian archipelago, my daughter slept, a blue sheet wound about her waist, her face driven, like a face fallen from heaven, into the pillow. *She sleeps as hard as you used to,* my father had said as we stood in the doorway looking in on her one night when she was still a baby. In her face then I could see the faintly sketched lines of my father's face, a small abbreviation of his own bone and flesh, one among the many faces that made her.

The night he died, as he breathed out his last moments in the stony body of his human passage, I carried her in my arms into the room. She looked on his graved face, on the still body from which, as if from stone, small breaths were milled, and her eyes lit up with awe. She reached her hand out to him, a plastic Cracker Jack ring shining on her finger, and I brought her close and bent down with her and let her touch his face. "A kiss, Daddy," she said, and I bent lower, my face next to hers, and with my father's dying breaths on my mouth, she kissed his lips. For three seconds—a lifetime—I breathed him in, but she was the only one who kissed him. Then I lifted her, hardly listening to her new theory of death—which she knew she was visiting—to her enthusiastic explanation that people were stars that God chose for mortal passage, and took back, when they died, as stars again in the heavens. But when with her small fingers she wiped the tears from my cheeks, I did not flinch. I pressed her body to me. *You stand for me, darling,* I said, *and thus I am shamed.* And then I let my girl forgive me.

And yes, far downtown, farther away from that brownstone in the Seventies than this breezy Florida house was from Manhattan, the sun got slowly to its feet in the windows of my garage. In the long upstairs room, above the soundstage and the cutting room, where the silence lay like gray ship's paint on scaffolding and prop and moviola, it slid sock-footed across the dark blue floor. The dirty white leather sofa, the cracked glass table, the Chinese screens, the burlap tapestry like a giant's shot-up jacket Celest had found in a client's attic in Brooklyn, the Frigidaire, the wine-stained kitchen table, the clutter in the sink were rubbed with immanence, like works of art. And the wide bed, the bed I bought for Bess, the bed I brought Celest to, was, in its shaded nook, a bed floating in a sea. Upon that bed I had tossed through wild flights with the women I was called to love. There, grinding to orgasm, her slight breasts like two doves in my hands, Bess had looked into my eyes and told me she was leaving. There, where on my knees, with a white sheet wrapped like a cowl around my head, worshiping in the fruity sumps of Celest's body I recognized for the first time the chill of betrayal, realized in the skin which, though it glowed with a predatory heat, seemed to recede from me, the caresses that seemed curses flicked at a stranger, the mirror of my own distance, and the consequences of my own refusal to love another. On her skin, on the fresh, pale skin of my wife, I had tasted the sour sweat of another man's body, and with my tongue I licked his residue off her, and swallowed it, like gall. But now, in the tender light of Manhattan morning, where outside a push-cart clacked down the cobbled street, and the sparrow hawks, the city's highest tenants, soared above the light-splashed streets and towers, the bed was empty, the congealed sheets stony as if who struggled there had been drawn up, like Elijah, suddenly from the earth. I could see the dust, I could see the ocher stain, I could see the light lying like a yellow cat on the floor. What I could not see was the one who lived there.

"Bess," I said, holding my hand in front of my mouth as I spoke, "do you remember the bed, do you remember the morning you woke up and we were making love and you told me you were leaving?"

She didn't say anything.

I ran water in the basin and plunged my face in. The water smelled sulfurous; there was a black stain around the drain. Raised, held before the mirror, my dripping face, red from sun, pinched here and there, swollen from lack of sleep, looked as if something was working its way out, as if bits of my soul were about to break through onto the surface.

"Do you remember that?" I said. "Isn't it curious how sex has a power of its own? Who knew that so many powers on earth would simply be tools for us to use? That we would have to become directors in our own lives? Is it a tragedy that I want to think more than I am able to think? That I want my mind to run smoothly down a road that leads to a glorious city built out of light? You never knew what it was like, you never believed me when I told you you could travel down that beam of light into a world in which all joys became one joy. You never believed me when I told you that every dream you ever dream could become real. All you need is a little technical knowledge, cameras are not impossible to master, there are men, men who will help you, who know how to set lights, pull a shadow across a face, there are actors who have given their lives to bringing forth separate lives out of their bodies, who will give their voices and their limbs to the created action of your vision, who will bring it into a reality you can experience."

I pressed my face into one of her clean yellow towels. It was as soft as lamb's wool; it smelled of life and order. From it, as from a strand of DNA, you could re-create everything here: house, farm, sighing Gulf sea, every human life. It took almost nothing, just a grain, to make the whole world possible.

"Do you remember the time I let you beat me up?" It was after my third picture; she was tired—worn to death—of my going off, excluding her. All right, I said, hit me, and she did. She hit me in the face with her open fist, she struck my body, she kicked me, she beat me until I fell to my knees. With her fist she pounded the back of my head like someone pounding a nail, yelling the whole time *you asshole; betrayer, betrayer.* Toward the end the heel of her hand caught my temple and I was knocked silly. I went out for a second and came to on my side with her straddling me, looking down at me with an expression of disgust and glee on her face. I could see up her dress. She had on bright pink panties. Small ringlets of coppery hair protruded from the leg-bands. I reached up, as if out of a dream, and touched her sex through the satiny cloth. It was soaked, hot as an oven.

"Do you remember that time?" I said, but she didn't answer. "I've put that in a movie three times now, the woman recklessly beating the man, her lover, until he is beaten to his knees. The last time we did it for laughs; she beats him with a leg of lamb. At the end his face is covered with grease. He looks like a hog just raised up from the trough. There are actors—did you know this?—who love to be beaten. Who knows why somebody would like that? No, I don't mean that—of course I know. Christ, though, don't you just sometimes, I mean some-times just love it all? I mean even the meanness and the terror? Some-times don't you just want to plunge your hand into a wound? Christ, I sound like you. This Florida cracker country has gotten to me. That guy, what was his name—Robert, old Robert—I couldn't believe that guy. What were you going to do with him? Drive him crazy? Man, he looked like he had found the honey tree. He couldn't wait to get off and show you the stars. A doctor with a gun—Jesus, what is this world coming to? God, Bess, sometimes, I tell you, I just want to set fire to the ocean. You know? Don't you feel that way, like you want to make love to the devil? God, it's in me, I feel it. I can't help it. Am I supposed to want to? What do you think?"

Wrapping the towel around my neck I looked out at her. She slept on, oblivious to my ranting. Damn, Bess, I am getting close here. "Bess. Girl. Bess."

Stepping through into the future, stepping through the hole down which my life would plummet in free-fall forever, I crossed the room and knelt beside her. The dawn had painted the windows pearl. I leaned my face close to hers. Her head hung down, her long black lashes soiled her cheeks. A thin red streak ran beside her nose, her mouth was slightly open. I raised my fingers slowly and brushed, so lightly, the cold skin of her lips. She wasn't breathing.

I reeled back as if she had struck me. No, I said, not this. I cocked my head, pushed my face up to hers, my nose under her nose, like a foolish kisser. No breath blew on me. "Murderer," I cried leaping to my feet. *Maudite.* You've tricked me. "What the fuck are you doing?" I whirled in a circle, arms out, flying. I kicked her chair over. Tied to it, her body roped and red, red blotches on her neck and face like the paw prints of small animals, she fell cohesively—that's the word that came to me—in a clump—her shoulder hit the plank floor, her head bounced. "Fuck you!" I cried. What is it you think you're doing? I dropped to my hands and knees, crawled a circle around her, growling, spitting, gnawing air. I pushed my face against her face, I banged her face with my own. "Bess," I whispered, "cut it out."

I shook her, I pleaded with her, I cursed her. Bess you idiot Bess. I thumped her. I nudged her. I licked her eye: nothing nothing nothing.

The room rang with its silence, with all the horrible, demented overbearing silence of natural life, of rustling breeze in the curtains, like rats scurrying, of faint sea sounds and birdcall, of breath, my breath. An acid rage began to peel my veins from the inside, all my veins at once, all over my body. I leapt to my feet, flailing, lunging as if goons were jumping me. Life roared on, every bit of it, every particle and thought and shimmy of light, every smell, every goddamn molecule in its self-centered little dervish dance—all but this one here on the floor, so stupidly, clownishly fallen. This one wouldn't play. I dropped to my knees, I scrabbled at the ropes, I pulled her free, I lifted her, I hurled her onto the bed. Her arm, falling, described an arc through the air—she was alive again!—and came to rest on the pillow, palm up. Through half-open lids she looked at me, something in there looked out at me. I flung myself up beside her, knelt over her, straightened her out as if I were about to nail her to a board, pulled her head back, and began to breathe into her mouth. I didn't know how to make it work—her lungs resisted, it was like blowing into a heavy rubber balloon. *Ah, girl, you're not used to this. You didn't plan for this. Wake up, pearl.* I pressed my hand to her chest; a whistly groan of air belched out—it smelled of the acidy blueberries and cream we'd had for dessert—I caught the breath in my mouth and tried to blow it back into her lungs. Wake up, oh, wake up. I pressed my hand on her chest, pressed until I felt the bones start to give. Her breasts, her ribs, the underskirts of her body—the bones, the squash of lung fiber, the tough lump of her heart—all lay under my fingers, resisting me. I banged on the door of her flesh; I pummeled her, I beat her, I struck her blow after blow.

Out the window the dew shone like a fresh coat of varnish on the floor of the porch. A catbird, off among the pine, began its sorry meowing. Years ago, on my last visit before the divorce, we had driven through the night to a beach south of here. At a small hotel on an island, Plum Key, I had waked the proprietor who, in his underwear, snorting and puffing, gave us a room overlooking Willis Bay. Frazzled, totally bamboozled, at the end of what that night seemed everything that mattered in our lives, exhausted, we had stepped out onto the narrow balcony to catch breath before trying to sleep. Out in the bay, under a hunter's moon, the white fishing skiffs bobbed like celestial toys. I took her hand, and I held it, there among a few of the last moments of familiarity and fealty, and as I held her hand, she turned her body toward me, she leaned her rosy flesh against me and kissed me once, lightly, as a sister would, on the cheek. In that moment, for the first time in my life it seemed to me, I knew what it meant to lose something

I couldn't do without, that I couldn't get back, ever. You know what I mean? Gone for good.

I drifted down beside her, I snugged in close. She was still warm, still dead. I said a few things to her, evoked a few memories. It was like the end of a war. Or a battle, only that maybe, when you're lying in the elephant grass and the bright rustle and thwack of the shooting stops and you can barely hear the sound of the choppers coming and it's nearly as quiet in the rice paddies as it ever gets. From a little ville over there beyond the banyan trees, you can hear a woman calling to her child, maybe that's it, a mother's voice it must be, calling to her child. Someone blows his breath out and swears. You can smell your skin suddenly, and it's not just a stink of sweat and grime, but of all the years you've worn it, all the accumulation of days and miles and time. It's like you are coming back from amnesia, into the familiar, troubled world. Someone begins to whistle a tune, and it's something you remember from years ago, from some party on the river when you danced late into the night and held another sweet body in your arms. You start to say the name of the song—you want to say it out loud—but then you can't remember it and then, for just a second, you can't remember anything, and you want to say something about this, about how remarkable it is, but then the choppers begin to sweep up over the tree line and the men around you begin to scramble to their feet; life scurries into action again, and the moment slips away as your life catches hold, fires, as you rise and rush to take your place, as you hurry, among all the others, to begin again.

I kissed her hard, sunburned face, I kissed her lips, I pressed my tongue into her mouth. I slid my hands over her body, touching her throat, her frail breasts, her thighs, her belly, her pubis. I touched her everywhere, for the last time, up and down the length of her, and as I touched her my cock began to stiffen. I pressed it against her ass and I slid my hands under her shirt and undid her bra and touched her breasts and held them gently in my hands. I pulled her skirt up her thighs, leaning over her to kiss the purple work bruises. She wore underpants fashioned of white lace woven along the edges with thin red ribbon—*party pants,* my daughter would call them—and I remembered the guy

I had run off and then I pictured the two of them, pictured Bess taking the poor guy's cock in her hands and stroking it, pictured her as she looked out the car window at the Gulf where the phosphorus winked like lights going off and coming on again in the surf, pictured her wondering, as I knew she would, if there would ever be anything out there for her, wondering if maybe something fabulous and irrefutable was ever going to rise up out of those waves to take her in its arms—as I would wonder, as we all might—and so, the thought like a silk ribbon falling through her mind, leaning down over the flecked trousers of a man she couldn't possibly love and taking his cock in her mouth, making what she could of what she found in the world, fashioning for a minute a way to give herself and someone else a little happiness, a little peace.

I bent down and kissed the heaped hair under the satiny cloth, and then I slid the pants down her thighs and took them off, and I dropped my trousers and I spread her stiffening legs, and there, in the bed that had belonged to her ancestors, in homage, penitentially, humbly, bitterly, I fucked her.

What I remember is this: coming around the corner with Van to see Bess standing near one of the dark green mail-collection boxes on Spring, looking radiantly up at the buildings across the street. She had just come from her second abortion, and I had missed it, off with Van negotiating the contracts for the next movie, and I was hurrying back to the house to be with her. We came around the corner, the two of us half bundled—Van large and bald in his green loden coat, me smaller in a dirty cowpoke slicker—against the cold fall rain that misted in her hair like soft polish and shone on her face as she watched some starlings wheeling above the cornices of the low buildings. Van gave a small transparent cough, said, I'll see you, and slid away across the street, reflexively, as was his way, understanding that there was nothing he could do here, and not wanting to intrude. She was all alone in the street among the few passersby hurrying through the gray rain, standing there collecting herself and doing what she must to make her life possible. I came up to her from behind and took her in my arms and held her silently for a minute, and then we went upstairs. She ran water for a bath and got in the tub and after a while I came in the bathroom and sat down on the toilet lid and looked at her and tried to say something. She wasn't angry at me and she didn't seem upset, but the radiancy of her grief shone in her face and in her eyes. I asked her if she was sore and she said yes, she was sore as if someone had dragged a rake through her guts and punched her—she laughed at this—in the cunt. After the first abortion she had cried herself to sleep, thrashing in the bed under the pine-tree quilt as if the act continued to assault her, crying out even in her dreams, explaining something in words that though I lay wide awake beside her I couldn't catch. But this time there were no tears; she carefully washed her body, touching tenderly with a washcloth her thick nipples, kneading her thighs that were sore and slightly bruised near the groin. There was a moment, and this is what I remember most vividly, when, her hair thick with green shampoo, she turned on her side and thrust her head under the water; for a second, half curled, knees drawn up, arms crooked, her hands sunk in her thick dark soap-gauzy hair, she seemed to me a child herself, fetal waif crouched in the oily waters of the womb, helpless and human. As I looked at her then, small sleek fish submerged, the thought came to me that all suffering is innocent. The thought came to me that it isn't guilt that kills us. It is grief.

1. There is a man now, forty-two years old, not tall, not small, who crosses a room in which daylight is rising among the articles of memory and affection, who slips through the door onto a white balcony. Beyond a yard planted in yuccas and azaleas, beyond the tussocky grass and the red mallow flowers bent with dew, the Gulf of Mexico is level and calm. The yellow sky in the east prepares for the sun. In the distance three orange-and-white helicopters chop along in single file just above the horizon. Already the day is hot. Already the cicadas pitch their song from the bushes. Inside him there is a desolate rain, or there is nothing; inside nothing, or a desolate rain, or nothing. A tingling fills his hands, moves in his arms, pours slowly down his body.

Romance, tenderness, sex, the splendid momentum of work, the few friends to say yes and no to, the blustering city, the memory of time's passage, a daughter—these make a life. I am not old, he thinks, but I am tired. I can smell the dew on the grass, I can smell the sea, smell the small sweet and distinct odor of tea olive. There is a shining world; there is this world, that shines. The way she butters toast, as if she is sharpening the knife on the bread. The way she licks butter off the knife until the knife is clean. Stop this, please. Please stop this. The way once, when I was leaving and turned back on the stairs to look at her, she kissed the doorpost and smiled at me. Stop please. The briny sea smell under her arms, the smell of her sex like overripe plums. Stop. Her small strong hands breaking bread. The small noise of her sipping tea, her fey cackling laugh. Stop. The way—stop. Ah. Stop stop stop. Stop.

2. We were thirty miles out in the Gulf when the visions began. Out of laughter they came, out of the sunlight like electricity pounding off the water, out of the blue, the indigo, the ultramarine Gulf, out of the small chipped tops of waves, the slant sea running toward Mexico, they came to me. They came slowly, partially, then vividly and suddenly, fully: a human glint in the water among a pod of dolphins running ahead, white flesh or something, that I turned away from to listen to a man named Archie Brooks telling a story about running aground on Emerald Bank—Oscar Demopolos leaning against the gunwale looking him straight in the face the whole time calling him a liar and grinning—and then turning again to squint through the sharp white sunlight to see it was not a scrap but someone, a person diving along through the breaking sea, someone naked and sleek, traveling with us toward the sponge grounds.

We were headed west and south, running across a rippling sea, the slight white boat yawing a little in the low troughs, smacking crests, as Archie held her at twelve knots. I bit my lip to keep from crying out, and I nearly pointed, but R.B., sitting up on the bow, was watching the dolphins too and he didn't say anything. I crawled up along the cabin and sat down beside him. He was dressed in white, and the breeze had whipped his shirttail out of his trousers and blew the red scarf he wore around his neck like a thin banner backward. There were bits of spray gleaming on his narrow face and he was grinning, happy as a boy on a roller coaster. He shook my hand as if I had just arrived.

"Look at them," he said, pointing. "Sometimes they'll run the whole way with you, night and day without any letup. They're stronger than horses, and sometimes they're more loyal than dogs. Aren't they beautiful?"

I allowed that they were, squinting into the glare. That shape, white, no, the long pink back—it was gone.

I had come for him directly after leaving Bess, barging into his dawny room to discover him in his bush helmet pulling on a pair of blue-striped drawers and singing what he told me was a Nigerian harvest song. "I learn them off records," he said, smiling like a child. "They're useful to my investigations and add piquancy to the entries in my dictionary." He looked at me. He said, "Your face looks like a face painted on porcelain." I laughed—a hollow, gross sound; or so it seemed to me. He patted me on the arm. "All this will work out just fine," he said. "Life can't help itself; it just keeps offering itself to us until we accept." I could hear the blood rushing in my ears. It was the blood of intention, not accomplishment. Come to tell him—maybe I am lying, maybe I had not come for anything of the sort—I stalled and veered.

He had no objection to leaving that minute on a fishing trip ("It's the one Bess suggested," I told him. "She said we could go out on the sponge boats." "Of course," he said.) and stopped only to collect suntan lotion and a couple of notebooks and a small packet of fresh biscuits—as my head screamed—from Mattie, who, risen this morning to forgiveness and a slightly pompous benevolence, patted him on the head and shooed him along. We passed Uncle Porto crouched in a rocker on the front porch scraping mud off a pair of rubber boots and cursing his wife's small pinto Chihuahua that barked and snapped at his hands, but he only hailed us and passed us on into the clear, lifting day, charging us to catch aplenty and not fall overboard.

The sun was getting to its knees in the yard, casting handfuls of pale yellow onto the grass and up the trunks of the cabbage palms and into the frothy tops of the willows and the mimosas. Out in the fields dew gleamed on the crests of a thousand azalea bushes and shone like rainwater on the green roofs of the outbuildings. The white dirty sand heaped around the base of the garage we backed my car out of looked like snow and made me think of the season in the Dakotas when I met my D'Nel and we rode to the set in my station wagon talking about dreams and the mystery of the world. He was kindly then, or seemed so, eloquent and courteous in his formal dark suit, bobbing his head slightly as he spoke of boating on the Delaware River, of how the love of a woman was a misery and a promise.

It did no good to think there was another now who would not step out onto this kempt drenched lawn, that the army of souls marching witless and exhausted down the dead roads had added another, because I could not believe that she was missing. Stiffly, refusing, touching the plastic dashboard to feel the presence of the world, turning in my fingers a withered banana skin, smelling the aroma of fresh biscuits, carrying on a skimpy conversation with R.B.—for a moment I went blank, unable to recall her name or what she looked like, unable to remember a single detail of our lives together. Did she tell me, larking, that I would come to no good end; did she once describe to me how, after a tornado, the world smelled of turned-up earth and the floor of the woods was covered with leaves and pine needles as if fall had come all in one night? Had that been her standing clad only in a pair of pale blue panties in a rowboat on Wildeman's Slough? And did she—was it she—really sob into the pillow on our wedding night, one year to the day after the night we met; did she tell me that if the truth were known she would rather live in Jerusalem than any other place on earth? What happened seemed no different from what I could make up, and I couldn't tell which was which. All my life I dreamed stories, lighted tales that flashed on the screen of my mind and then, through work and will, onto the screens of theaters in the American towns, but I could not say now which were the true stories and which were the figments I had brought shining into life. There was no difference between fact and dream.

As we drove my heart beat in my chest and sweat broke out like hives on my body. I looked at R.B., who in his shining helmet looked happily out at the fields and woods of his family empire. Over there was a gray cistern from which at night came the croaking of a thousand frogs; beyond the pines were clearings where in moonlight deer came out to crop the tender leaves of wild carrot and mustard; beyond that curve of headland the land drew away, giving in to marshes and a shallowy surf where blue crabs skittered like roaches over the submerged sands. I could see the details of the world, but they were like pearls fallen off a string, and the string was a rotted rope in my hands, pulling apart as I tried to grasp it. I glanced back as we bounced up the drive; the house, set against the rising blue of day, against the emptiness of Gulf and sky, looked to me like some fake carpentered temple, white and immaculate, raised for actors to posture awhile in front of, that would be taken down soon in slabs and carted away.

Inshore the water was green as emerald, fading to lime and then clear as tap water as it soughed onto the floury beaches, but beyond the banks it was deep blue, dark enough, it seemed, to leave a stain on you, and today a robust, heavily muscled sea ran east under a freshening breeze, the small tousled wave crests streaked along their backs with white. A few gulls bobbed on the water, lifting into the air as we passed, circling us for a few minutes before flying off toward the other boats. We were part of a scuffed armada, and it seemed both odd and pleasant to me how as we progressed into the open sea the boats, which had seemed large and capable when tied to the dock, became frailer, little slips suffering the whims of the sea, and now, dispersing on the vastness of the Gulf, lost their cohesion, so that after a while, as the sun glittered and the diesel throbbed its song of journeying, we moved toward and into a solitude augmented by the diminishing, vanishing passage of the other boats, until we were alone.

I toured the boat, which was a simple affair maybe ten feet wide, thirty feet long, containing a large well shaded by a green canvas awning which was attached to the roof of the open wheelhouse. A narrow doorway beside the wheel led down into a large cabin in which there were a table, stove, and sink, and, hung against the hull by chains, four bunks, which were folded up and latched. The equipment was simple: a J. C. Penney air generator and hoses attached to regulators, wet suits, short-handled rakes and net sacks to put the sponges in, a couple of rubber-spring spear guns. They had no radio, but there was an elaborate depth finder set on a rack above the wheel.

"Not much to it," Archie Brooks said as he watched me poking about, and I agreed that there wasn't. "There's a little action out on the fishing grounds but this here is just time passing, which often ain't too spectacular." He reached into a cooler at his feet, plucked out a beer, cracked it, and handed it to me. "Mostly Ody and me drink ourselves silly for a while and sleep it off and then go to work, so whatever you want is fine with us as long as you don't get crazy and set fire to the boat."

Ody snickered and spit over the side and stared out toward a few puffs of white cloud that rode in the western sky, nodding as if he were picking up something that was important and private. Their bodies could have been the bodies of twins—narrow and muscled, sun-torn on the shoulders and across the bridge of the nose—but Ody, the Greek, was the fair one with blond kinked bushed-out hair and a straight, ascetic nose, while Archie was dark under his burn, his skin containing a muddy underlayer, like a streak of tannin; his features were clayey half-formed attachments stuck onto his round face like raw ornaments on an amateurish jug. They asked me what I did for a living and I told them I worked in the movies, but they were not interested in movies.

"I don't get to many of 'em," Ody said. "Don't have much time to go."

"Yeah," Archie said as he rolled the cold beer across his bare chest, "me neither. Life's richer than movies anyway. Movies don't stand up to what goes on out here."

I didn't disagree.

"I'm glad you could take me along," I said. "I've wanted to see all this."

"Anything for R.B.," Archie said, grinning.

I was thinking that maybe kindness was about to take me over; for a moment a cordial meekness filled me amid the briny stinks of diesel and old dead sea life, and for a moment as I looked at the fishermen going about their tasks, settling into the routines that would carry them for miles across the brimming Gulf, I thought—terrified—that now soon I would join the circle of other men, I would sit down with them in Manhattan or St. Louis or Occasion, Florida, and in a sweet voice I would ask someone to pass me the bread, please, pass me the butter and the jam, and I would smile my new obedient smile and say My Lord my lords and I would speak in a detached way about how life is a genial mystery and about how God is good and how there is always hope and a new day etc.; and then I thought—it came to me like a splash of seawater over the grimy gunwale—that now Bess had me, that now finally, fifteen years too late, she had me where she always wanted me—fixed on her, beholden to her—and then a fire, the hot poison snake in my guts, began to bite at me, and sweat broke out in bumps on my forehead and my hands went cold and I looked at the fishermen, this Ody, this Archie, looked at the two of them yammering, and I realized that soon I would pick up a bar or a gun—the doctor's gun was in my pocket—or a knife, and I would kill them; I saw that an hour ago—two hours ago—I had crossed over, not like a man crosses over into the love of sweet Jesus but like a man crosses the trench line into the domain of his enemy, and that there in that country, on that ravaged terrain, I would slay my enemy—with my gun or with my hands or with my teeth I would slay him—that my breath, all of my life, was built for this, that I was willing to die for the victory.

It was then that I saw the dolphins running ahead, seven or eight bottlenoses frisky and gray-backed, shooting toward the bow and retreating, and then that I saw the slip of white, saw the streak of flesh that was not flesh but my angel outriding with me. I stuck my hands in my pockets and gripped my thighs hard and stared at the line of sunlight swaying on the foredeck, and I looked at the pile of net sacks stacked by the generator, and I looked at the generator, which was green and the size of a small natural-gas tank and had a flywheel and a neat little gas motor on top, and at the coils of hose and at the plywood decking which had once been blue but which was now streaked gray where the paint had been worn and salted through, and I forced myself to think of my child, who would be perched at the kitchen table now arguing with the maid about the shapes of the animals floating in her cereal bowl, and it seemed that I was being pulled into the heart of something enormous and devastating, but empty, and I had no say-so about it and never had, no matter what I—and the bonny, ridiculous world—had claimed about such things, no matter who I thought I was and where I told myself I was going. Sometimes, even amongst your enemies, you must throw yourself to your knees and beg for mercy, and I thought—just as suddenly as I knew I would kill them—I wanted to put my arms around the necks of these Florida sons of the sea and kiss their blistered skin and promise to love and serve them for the rest of my life; and though I wanted with all my heart to do this for someone, wanted simply to walk off with a hoe into some grubby field and begin to work, I didn't do that, not yet; I lurched away from the cabin— Christ, where to go? (they called to me hilariously, asking if I was seasick—no)—and climbed onto the salt-speckled roof and crawled hand over hand to R.B. and swung myself down beside him and looked out with him into the brilliant sea booming with light and began to talk to him about small things that had nothing to do with death and its consequences or a life stripped to its veins.

I lay down on the deck, on my stomach, and felt the boat rise and fall under me. It was easy to believe that the rise and fall was the pulse of something great, but it was only the sea. The water hissed and crackled under us. You don't have to stay out in the wild world too long to realize that everything makes a human noise if you listen long enough. It's no big deal how we are related to everything living. I don't think the guys who trekked across the Bering Strait and down through the ice valleys all the way to the Amazonian jungles thought about it much, I don't think they lost much sleep worrying about what God's purpose might be, I don't think they whimpered over their failures to communicate or demanded that God reveal himself to them. I believe if they thought about anything they hated being alive, and hated their stupid magic and the endless crying of children and the cold and the vicious beasts they chunked their puny spears at. I don't think this is some kind of kingdom of light we've got going here, and I don't think we're going to get out of it alive, no matter what the preachers say. A sunset is beautiful but no sunset will save your life. Listen, I said, and I was talking to R.B. now, there is nothing on this planet that can prevent you from ruining your whole life. There is nothing that will stop you. What are we? Just a bunch of ex-cavemen, ex-peasants, working for the gang lords, who keep trying to tell ourselves all this means something more than the obvious vicious joke it is.

Here I was, out at sea. The Gulf looked like a blue shellacked trampled floor. The boat pushed through it—this thirty feet of boat—waded, it didn't soar. Terns wheeled above us, their black markings shining. R.B. beside me wrote furiously in his notebook, trying to save his life by getting an accurate picture of it down on paper. Nobody would do something like that who hadn't come to the end of things. In the west scattered clouds were armaments piled on the foreign gates. I had come to an end, I wouldn't recover, the movie drifted in my mind like a dead cat washing with the tide, and I had begun to hear voices, to hear D'Nel speaking, hear Molly as she cut lemons for a pie speaking to Bantling Jakes whose terror had withered him to a nub, to Bantling who crouched on a stool in the kitchen of the sun-washed Gulf house that we would make look as if it were the house of pleasure, the house lovers would come to to play out their beautiful and doomed game of love, sunny, pastel, sweet-smelling house. . . .

.   .   .

When I turned her over her right arm fell away from her side exposing the scar. It was a wicked, vicious thing, grooved deeply into the flesh. The muscle around the scar had a sucked-out look, as if bone and tissue had been drawn though the cut. The cords in her wrists protruded, permanently stretched. I bent down and licked the tallowy flesh. I was human, I breathed, had guts and a cock and a bicameral brain, but once, on a rainy night in New York City, I had tried to kill the woman I was married to, I had lunged at her with a spike that with all my being I wanted to drive into her heart.

Without looking at her, my mouth on the scar, my right hand sunk into the groove of her pubis, my left hand spread open on her breathless face, I whispered, *Bess, I meant to do it; I meant to kill you.*

Ah, D'Nel, tell me your story. Speak it to me in your liquid eloquent language. Explain to me how a man can come to murder. I want you to tell me it is good and acceptable and human. I have walked a long way from that rubbishy TriBeCa loft, I have married again and fathered a sweet blond child, and I have made movies that tear at the hearts of those who watch them. I moved, in my predatory lope, across the landscape of my country, I carried men with me and women, and I learned a trade and a style and I became a man among men, one who could treat the afflicted with kindness, who understood the uses of mercy, who brought light and entertainment into the creaky lives of his fellow travelers. I am no cipher, no low-rent quarreler, no whining failed intruder. I come to you as a man, one who has accepted the means and requirements of his time on earth and used them to make his bounty. I did not stand aside mimicking the accents of my betters, I did not blame others for my shortcomings, I did not seek from the world any more than the world has to offer. So what is this, my friend, this trembling like palsy in my hands, this salt in my eyes, this love in my heart that can find no place to light? I want a simple explanation, my camarado, I want you to speak to me as you would speak to a friend driven a long way across rough terrain, who will believe what you tell him and use it for the good in himself and others. Ah, D'Nel, why must you kill me to make me understand?

Ah, but what was it but lies? I had asked a killer for comfort? On a movie set in North Dakota I had sat up nights listening to the story and wisdom of a murderer? Was I simply another naive American fool, plunging forth optimistically into a world that darkened as he went until it blanked out everything familiar? Was it my direction—my choice—or simply me? Or was it the world? Had I only made a mistake; could I carry my little broken wagon of a life to God and ask him to fix it, please? Or had I romped dumbly into a wilderness that was itself the world, the only world? Had I, in my self-absorbed, blinkered way, marched as one among a long line of idiots—all of us: idiots—down a road that anyone with eyes could tell me was the road to destruction, and the only road? Was there not a point, was there not a moment, perhaps once on the street in New York when the sun bounced like an acrobat off the windows on lower Broadway; or that time coming out of a restaurant on Seventh, when Bess, her face shining with happiness, told me her five favorite smells; or the night when Rachel was born, when Van and I raced up the hospital stairs to the roof where we shouted across the tarry, polished river *Wake up, Brooklyn—the queen has come*? Or, the reverse of this—was there not a moment such as the one when I shouted at Morton Glick, Van's line producer, that if he didn't get the equipment I needed I was going to kill him, and meant it; the time I lied to save my picture; the young actress I lied to to gain her sullen favors; my wife, my daughter abandoned—was there not a point when I could have called to the driver of my juggernaut to stop the vehicle, could I not, if he refused, have grabbed him by the throat— whose throat?—could I not have wrenched the wheel from his hands, applied the brakes until the heavy tires ground to a halt, and then stepped down at last and walked away singing into another life? Oh, Beelzebub, I think not. Look at it this way, Padrone—if it is true that God created us with the ability to choose between good and evil, and we choose—wrongly; no argument about that—and the world is simply a fucked-up place, nonetheless there is pain, relentless, specific, eliminating pain, torture undeserved, unsought, undefeatable—if this is so, in a world that recalls a paradise some grave error long ago excluded it from, then how could it be a world that is anything more than the conjured whim of a demon? Ah, D'Nel, ah, my Mr. X, I see you standing in your white clothes at the rim of the sea, blood dripping from your hands, and I am afraid. I am afraid.

I looked at R.B., at his lotion-speckled face, his narrowed pale eyes, his brow creased with labor, looked at him scribbling in his notebook as he drew forth from the world an order that would save him. I looked over his shoulder at what he was writing. He didn't shy. "Sometimes the light is peach," he had written, "sometimes it is lavender like the perfumed handkerchiefs the Spanish captains drew from their sleeves to the amazement of the Indians. We have forgotten this, but along with disease and enslavement, the conquistadores brought colors never seen before in the New World, and scents unlike any smelled before on this continent. They brought art, which is always the handmaiden of warfare; they brought the comfort of religion, which is always the companion of misery—thus brought the truth of the world into the New World—that with darkness comes light, that with death comes life. . . ."

I started to say something to him, when he glanced up and said, "Look up there—on the edge of the windshield."

I looked—the louvered windows were cranked open, the glass angled out—and saw nothing. "What? Where?"

"There at the upper corner. The butterfly. You see it?"

"Ah."

There was a small white butterfly, partially wedged into the crack where the metal window rims joined. Its wings were folded; the breeze flicked at it.

"An hour ago it wouldn't have seemed strange—and wonderful and sad—a butterfly fluttering around the docks—it's funny how you see them all the time on the beach—but now, thirty miles out in the Gulf, it is mysterious and, if you're that kind of person, heartbreaking."

"Yes." I looked back. Our wake was a bridal gown trailing us across the sea. Where the land had been was only piled white cumulus, stacked like the aerial equivalent of earthly construction, high-tiered and leaning, that the fresh sun spanked with light.

"No way to get him back," I said. "He's done for."

"Beautiful and sad. Once when I was a child my mother told me they were angels."

"Yes, angels. I'll save it."

"No, don't."

"Yeah. I'll put it in something."

I sprang up, the boat yawed, and I fell against the windows. I went to my knees—unhurt, the windows intact—and when I looked the butterfly was gone.

"Ah shit."

"Yes," R.B. drawled, rubbing his narrow chin, "sometimes you'd think it was hopeless."

He cocked his head and looked at me, and for a moment it was as if he saw right through me, as if he knew everything about me. His look however was not one of judgment; it was a look that was sad and full of compassion. He laughed his small, grainy laugh. "It's a clumsy life isn't it?"

Off to starboard I saw her walking along, my angel, in a yellow blowing rain slicker, her hair tied back with a green ribbon. I raised my hand to her, as one would salute an act of genius, and something moved from my body and stepped out into the crested sea toward her. We were in the woods then, it was cold November and raining, she knelt before a small fire feeding beech twigs into it. There was the smell of moss and the deeper smells of bread frying. Nearby a stream clattered faintly. She lifted her face to me slashed by firelight; she opened her mouth to speak. Her mouth was filled with blood.

"Isn't it curious," a voice said—it was R.B. reeling me back in— "that we live in a world where it's like that—isn't it curious to you?"

I said that it was.

From the bridge came the sound of the two boatmen arguing. I looked that way to see Archie Brooks swinging his arm to make a violent point at Ody. Ody shouted back at him, words I couldn't hear for the wind and the noise of the engine. Archie pointed at the wheel and then he whirled and disappeared down the companionway only to reappear almost instantly with a quarter wheel of orange cheese in his hand. He shook the cheese at Ody Demopolos. "My money . . ." The wind blew the words away. Ody threw up his hands and rushed down the companionway himself. He reappeared shortly with a paper bag filled with something bulky that he held up to Archie, taunting him, before he tossed it overboard. "Asshole!" Archie cried, skipping back to the stern. He peered out at the splash mark where the bag had gone

under. The look on Ody's face was one of grand satisfaction. "You
bast—" Archie cried, shaking his fist.

"Are we in danger?" I asked R.B., indicating the fracas.

"Oh no," he said, smiling. "They've been like this since they were
children." He adjusted the chin strap on his helmet. "Though sometimes
they don't come off it until just about everything portable's overboard.
But they usually stop at the food. Archie wakes up and realizes there
won't be anything to eat for supper but fish, which he hates. They're
loyal as geese."

"I'm very confused."

"That's often a sign of spiritual progress."

"Is that what it's about—the spirit?"

"Maybe for you."

"Every conclusion I'm drawn to is a damning one."

"Maybe it only seems that way."

"You don't know me."

He squeezed his nose, closed the notebook. His ascetic, nearly emp-
tied face looked out at the sea. "Let me tell you something," he said.

"What is it?"

"A story. Sit down. It's interesting."

I sank down beside him. He began to talk.

"Once I arrived in Chicago, Illinois," he said, "with no idea what
I was doing there. It was snowing and the wind blew the smell of dead
soil off the plains. I knew I was in Chicago—a street sign told me—but
I couldn't figure out for the life of me why I had come. I decided to
take a taxi to the Loop and look around, thinking maybe the reason
for my being there would come to me among the people and the big
buildings. So I did that, but when I got out of the taxi and began to
walk around I became even more confused than before. Was this really
Chicago? The buildings had a strange slant, it seemed to me, and the
light glinted in an alien manner off the windows and seemed to fall in
the street with a palpable shape that was unfamiliar. The wind tasted
of salt, not of the pale winy sweetness of the lake. I stopped a man to
ask him if this was in fact Chicago, Illinois, and he answered me in a
foreign language. I thought then that I was going crazy, that I had gone
crazy."

"What did you do?"

"I stood in the middle of the sidewalk, trying to ponder. People whirled about me, the wind blew against me as if it were trying to tear my clothes off. It came to me that I could make a scene of some sort, go into conniptions on the sidewalk, and someone would come to my rescue, someone who would eventually tell me where I was. But I didn't do that. My fear was too great. I lurched into the street, almost blind, and hailed a cab. The driver stopped, I got in, and he asked me where I wanted to go. 'North,' I said, 'take me north.' "

"Why north?"

"I'm from Florida. Anyplace north would be something new to me."

"You decided to go adventuring."

"Yes. We drove through the city. Gradually the buildings began to diminish in size, the landscape became a weary one of warehouses and sooty tenements, old women sitting on front porches looking meanly out. It was all new to me, all strange. Then on a corner near a grocery I saw an old man talking to a boy who held a small dog on a rope leash. We were stopped at the light. The man spoke to the boy and the boy, as if in turn, bent down and spoke to the dog. The dog said nothing. I asked the cabdriver to let me out there."

"In the middle of nowhere?"

"One of its seamier districts. I went up to the man and the boy and asked them where I might find a room. They directed me to a boarding-house down the street. It was an old three-story frame house that had once been painted yellow. I got a room there for fifty dollars a week, complete with meals. An old woman in her eighties ran the place. Her whole family, three generations of it, lived there with her. The boarders and her two daughters had rooms of their own but the rest of the family—a wastrel nephew, three or four grandchildren—slept on pallets in the halls. If you got up in the night to go to the bathroom you'd have to step over them."

"Is this true?"

"Yes. I moved in and lived there, took my meals with the family—northern food: potatoes, steamed cabbage, and pickled meats—and began to explore the neighborhood. It was one of those burrows that the world has stepped on and abandoned. The men worked in the steel-fabricating plant, in garages, they peddled trinkets in the city or did nothing, sat miserably in chairs leaned against the front of the corner grocery cursing the country and each other and themselves. The city had planted locust trees along the sidewalk but the trees were shriveled and ragged, the leaves covered with soot, and there were gouges in the trunks, splits where the bark had shriveled, or where children had slashed their names. The streets were full of potholes where rain collected and stood so long that the water turned black and shone with rainbows under the streetlights. There were cries in the night, wild arguments that began abruptly, raged a moment, and were snuffed out just as quickly, running footsteps in the street, faint poundings far off as if someone were madly and randomly hammering boards.

I looked out at the chipped sea, listening to him. His voice was soft, but penetrating.

"Across the street from the boardinghouse was a building that had collapsed. The owners had fenced it off, but at night children came and gathered pieces of lumber and bricks that they hauled away in sacks. They would sneak in through a hole in the wire and pull the ruined materials out and carry them away. One night I saw a small boy—he couldn't have been more than ten—running down the street under a sheet of plywood that must have been eight feet long and four feet across; I don't know how he got it over the fence. He looked like a boy trying to fly, and I called to him, something, making a joke, 'Boy, you need finer wings than that.' My shout must have broken his concentration because he stumbled and fell in the street. There was nobody about, it was late, I had been sitting on the porch steps practicing a little song in my mind—I jumped up and ran out to see if he was okay. He was lying there under the plywood sheet, trying to get up. I pulled the wood off him and helped him to his feet. He had a cut on his forehead and a bruised lip but other than that he was all right. There was something sweet and ruined in his narrow little face—you could see who he was: just a neighborhood boy with already the thunderclouds of his future shadowing him, blotting out the meager beauty that was nothing more anyway than youth and dumbness—and it touched me. I shouldered the sheet of plywood and said, 'Come on, I'll carry it for you.' He didn't mind.

"I followed along behind him for a few blocks and then we turned down an alley and came to a shabby fence behind a row house which he said was where he lived. I remember the gate was made of slats and there was a withered-up pyracantha beside it still full of berries. He opened the gate and we entered a grubby yard that was made of dirt and had a coarse brick patio extending back from the house. There were no lights on in the house except on the back porch which was screened. The single bulb inside the three walls of wire made the porch look like something floating against the dark side of the house. He asked me to take the plywood over to the corner, where the back and side walls met, and I did. He had a little gray duck over there, tied by one leg to a stake in the ground. What he wanted the plywood for was to build a hutch for his duck. His father told him that if he didn't pen the duck up he was going to kill it. I didn't see how he could build a cage out of such a big sheet of board but he had the thing all figured out in his mind. I knelt down and stroked the duck's back. It was soft. The duck swiveled his head around and gently bit my finger. His name, the duck's name, was Frankie, the boy said. Frankie the duck.

"After that I visited him often. Together we built a hutch of panel and wire and the little duck prospered. He was a fine little boy, snared, probably for the last moment in his life, in fineness, no bestial anger or resentment or loss taking over his life yet, just a boy. I was happy to be with him, and sad for him, so sad that it came to me that I should take him with me when I left, carry him to Florida and raise him, give him advantages. I clumsily asked his mother about this, but she would have none of it; in fact, it made her angry and she barred me from the house. Shortly after that Bess's detective found me, and then Bess herself called me on the phone and told me what I was doing, and gave me directions, and so I was brought back to myself and my life and returned home."

He opened the notebook and closed it again, marking it with his finger, and looked out to sea. A small flight of birds dipped and soared in the distance, nipping down over the tops of the low wave crests. The clouds in the west had become streaky; they lay like loose strips of gauze along the horizon. For a moment my life was a simple passage through a southern sea, the white, red-trimmed boat pushing steadily outward toward distant fishing grounds. R.B. touched my wrist. Normally I would have withdrawn my hand, but I didn't.

"What do you think of that?" he said.

"It's a beautiful story."

"It is, isn't it. But what does it call to mind?"

"I was struck when you said you didn't raise a fit. I saw myself then: I would have caused a commotion, I would have kicked around me until I got the world's attention."

"Yes, I think you would. Probably, if I weren't an afflicted person, I would have, too."

"I wouldn't have had the patience for that life. I wouldn't have been willing to let things just happen."

"One thing led to another. Each next thing showed itself, like a guide come to fetch me. I was like a horse grazing in a field who at the end of the day looks up to find himself miles away from where he started. It was curious and strange; I realized it would be possible to live my whole life that way, just going quietly on to the next thing, whatever it was, trusting in motion."

The notebook was bound in red leather. It was stuffed with loose pages, and pages in different colors that he had folded and placed there. The rims of the papers and the binding itself were worn as if from long rubbing. He stroked the red surface absently and fondly, the way one would stroke a cat. From his pocket he took a thick rubber band and carefully stretched it around the book. He slipped the pen under the band. Then he pulled a small olive canvas satchel toward him and zipped the notebook into it. "You came so hurriedly into my room this morning," he said, smiling, "that I almost forgot this."

"I was in a hurry all right."

"As if the devil was after you."

"——"

"I know you want money to make your movie, I know that's why you're down here. I don't mind. If I had control of it I would give you some. I like your movies and I think that a man should be allowed, as much as it's possible in this world, to continue down the road that's his

to go down. It helps us to help out. But Bess I don't think sees it that
way exactly. She thinks a person ought to learn to live with whatever
he's done. Sleep in the bed you've made, is the way she puts it."

"She just wants me to grow up."

"She wants you to cut the ties, stop using her."

"I think about that. It's a dilemma. The movie has to come first; I
have to do whatever is necessary to get it made, eat any shit between
me and it. I know it's like that, I know it won't get made if I'm not
willing to take on anything, push through anything, but sometimes I
wonder."

"I don't think you do much."

I laughed. "You're right. I don't care what's in the way, what I have
to do. That's part of the fun."

I didn't know anymore what I thought. My head sang with memory,
with disease.

"It's funny," he said, "she's going to leave all her money to you
anyway. You're the last person in the world she'd want to leave with
nothing. I don't know if you have any idea how much she loves you."

Just so, the world makes a joke of our lives. No, not the world. I
sat stunned in my blankness, blankly looking out. The scattered white
wave tops looked not like waves but like splashes, as if invisible objects
were being tossed from the sky. It was always invisible. It was always
what we didn't expect. For some the dangers of life make them love
more deeply, for some the dangers make them hate—for some there is
only the daze of continuing breath. I wiped my finger on the deck and
pressed salt into my tongue. Soon now—in a minute—I would confess
everything to him, in a minute I would place my hand on his and tell
him that I had killed his sister; I would tell him that in that instant when
I dragged her into my arms and felt for the first time in my life the
dull weight of my dead wife pressed against my body, I knew there was
nothing in this world that could stop me from doing what I was going
to do. There was no good advice, no noble interlocutor who could bid
me stand down from the war I had organized for myself, no devised
mesh of kindness and mercy that could keep me from what I longed
for. I was about to tell him, I was about to get to my feet on that yawing
boat in the middle of the shining salt sea and admit everything to

him—I didn't care—but then I didn't. There are moments sometimes when as I am speaking to someone—leaning across a velvet table, or in the back room of an abandoned house, or in bed, or in the lobby of a theater, surrounded by red plush—it seems, for a second, maybe for a few moments longer than a second, that we are part of each other, that we don't end where the other begins but keep . . . beginning, not continuing exactly but beginning, in the shape and voice of each other, so that—if this were actually true—it seems, in that second or just more than a second, that our whole life could be this steady—at least possible—beginning again in the minds and the lives of others, that it would be possible to move endlessly through the world becoming again and again more than we were before, simply by the touch of our affection, of our identification, with whoever it was standing before us, whether priest or laborer, murderer or saint, that, even, our happiness—conceivably—exists in this, this continuous fresh beginning, as awkward and desultory as it often is, in the life of another. I saw for an instant, as through a clean window slamming shut, what R.B. was trying to tell me—if he was trying to tell me anything at all—which was simply that, as far as he was concerned, there was always a little way, an opening in the fence, a shabby path to follow, that maybe the problem wasn't in finding the path but in allowing ourselves to go down it.

Yes. Of course. That is what he was saying to me. But I wasn't a man put on earth to learn anything. The truth is we shouldn't expect to return alive from what we have given our hearts to. We shouldn't expect that.

3. Late in the afternoon the fishing grounds appeared. There was first a dark emerald smear on the blue, like a floating patch of dye, then a lighter green like a light rising slowly from the depths, then a sandy whitish green where the ribs of the reef began to show through, and then shoals, the surf breaking lazily over rock between a couple of bell buoys like old-fashioned oil derricks clanging away in sea time. We were seventy-five miles out, escaped, like space pilots, from the pull of the land; it was eerie to me, and troubling, to see shining up ahead the rumpled shoals of reef way out here, the apron of shallow water.

Ody tossed the concrete chunk they used for an anchor overboard; we let the sea-pull turn us toward the buoy and settled in. The water was forty feet deep back from the reef, or fifty, dead clear when you looked straight down, though this afternoon, under the running swell, it was a little silty, as if wispy clouds were moving through it. The bottom was covered with a series of parallel sand ridges, white-toned or slightly yellowish in spots furrowing steadily into the murk. The reef was gray and mostly dead; it had the look of a desert, with clumps of red and blue coral in crevices and out on the sand plain among heaped stones; and there were patches of ornate dark gold turtle grass, rainy-looking under the water, bent with the push of the current, among which were islands of sand and clusters of ferny coral like broken trellises and obscure junk piled up.

I saw this as we came over it, and watched the bottom taking shape as we swung at anchor, lying on my stomach over the sea rail in the bow, as Ody and Archie Brooks broke out the galley.

You would think I would be beside myself, but I wasn't. Not only did life shuffle steadily on, but my life shuffled on, the next thing rising and the next, Ody handing me a loaf of hard bread to slice, R.B. clearing the small table, wiping it with a rag, while Archie opened cans with a knife. The two fishermen bustled about preparing dinner, which was beef stew spiced with basil and thyme, laced with tomatoes and okra from Ody's mother's garden. The sea calmed with evening, stretching away glassy and sun-shattered like a stretched tarp beyond the portholes, and the plywood walls and decking from which the blue paint had nearly worn away and the hissing lantern light made the small cabin seem like a house constructed for a child, a playhouse in which four children bustled about in mimicry of family life preparing the small fastidious meal. The visions had subsided, which made doing my part easier, but I was not frightened of them; in fact, I almost welcomed them—like an agonized drunk might welcome blackouts—because they seemed to me to contain a kind of continuity, as if what had gone before and what continued now stretched unbroken, like a filament groped forward into the world; nothing I could conceive could alter or change the way my life worked itself out.

I was crazy now, I know, I met the requirements for insanity, but still my life continued, still these boys moved around me begging pardon with an awkward, almost formal courtesy, still the cabin filled with the smells of frying beef and stew and the bright scent of lemons. The light dipped yellow fingers into the glasses of beer and gleamed on the polished coils of rope and on the pearl buttons of Ody's blue cowboy shirt hanging from a hook on the bulkhead. R..B., sitting in his undershirt at the table, sang a song, and Archie danced a couple of saucy steps and Ody balanced the plates on the tips of his fingers like an elegant waiter. From my perch on the steps I watched them and I thought that it was probably true that no matter what happened there was a way to find a moment's peace in simple human community, that it was a shelter from the storm, that if they were about anything movies were about this. It had always fascinated me that movies, unlike books, were enjoyed in company with others, that it was there in the darkness shoulder to shoulder with other strange but human individuals that we allowed into ourselves the frets and contortions of the giant painted characters whirling across a screen. If the screen was God and the picture was God's imagination, then we were, as R.B. perceived us, Edenic figures crouched in the darkness as the new world unfolded. And the sights, the memories that the sights began to coil in our brains, the prospects that the confusion of sound and light projected forth, were features impressed in the same manner into all the minds crouched there—recollection, fantasy, hope, faith, plunder, and the promise of peace—we were all united for those few hours, washed clean of our daily despairs and contortions, even our happiness, and so sewn up together in the silver bag of light, in which there is no such thing as a false move, no danger that will not end.

Gladly, expressing thanks, I took my portion of stew, my hunk of meaty bread, my beer; I pulled myself in a sagging canvas chair up to the table, and I took sustenance with these men. We talked, I listened mostly, it wasn't my place or situation, I had too much on my mind, I had almost everything by now on my mind. As night pulled itself up out of the seabed and took over the presidency of heaven and as its minions the stars and its first lady the moon shuffled out of the wings to take their places, tamping and spitting into their instruments of light—all that business—as each yaw of the boat, in my condition, seemed the moment when the whole shebang was about to tip violently over and like a breaching whale streak for the bottom, as the hands and faces that leaned in and out of the wispy lantern light became crisped and contorted by a thousand unacknowledged pressures and secrets—so that I thought of the expression *nail it down,* thought of it literally as if I might take out a hammer and nails and pound hands, feet, expressions, scraps of speech, and the moment itself to the bulkheads that also seemed to sway and nearly give—as the cabin like a vat we steeped in took on the odors and rich fecundities of stew and male bodies and the gauzy salt-stirred frankness of the sea, as the talk hummed and squirmed, I felt my being—my consciousness, my will, my sanity (whatever it was)—begin to kink and clatter in my head (and not just in my head: in my arms and legs, in my joints; as if murder, as if death, were a carrier of a stinging arthritis), so that the faces and my own mind seemed to be winking at me, leering possibly, taunting me, so that I began to believe that any moment I was about to leap up cursing and wailing. The thought was so strong, so imperatively true, that the muscles in my thighs and forearms tensed, and the muscles in the arches of my feet began to draw on themselves, cramping, and I knew that soon I would leap to my feet and begin my sorry speech, my peroration on the nature of destiny and character, as Bossy Conrad, that remarkable movie figment, conqueror of worlds, hero of my fifth picture, as the burning pavilion crashed about his head, began to scream out the story of his childhood visit to New Orleans—I knew that soon, helplessly, my life would become utterance, a voice only, rapid, ridiculous speech.

Archie and Ody argued about the monetary value of various sea creatures, creating vast fortunes out of ghost whelks and tiger spirals and black coral, piling up treasure in warehouses. Then Ody began to tell a story about a wreck he had come on while diving, and I forced myself to listen. I took my mind by the shoulders and I wedged it in the door of this place and time, and stood over it with a gun saying *pay attention.* It was one of the old paddle-wheeler steamships, he said, from late in the last century. A storm had washed off some of the sand that had buried it, exposing a part of the hull and the naked spokes of the drive wheel, which he said was one of the eeriest sights he had seen in his life: the huge compass of the paddle wheel, like a giant fan resting on the bottom of the sea. The ship had apparently been carrying molasses, he said, because he found nothing but a few gunked barrel staves and the rusted hoops that bound them. The sand out from the wreck, he told us, was strewn with broken crockery, some of it as clean as the day it was last used, but all of it broken as if some wild madness had overtaken the party and caused them to ruin everything.

"Tell them about the skeleton," Archie said. "That's the best part."

"Well, you're right," Ody said, "that's a good part, the skeleton."

"He always forgets that," Archie said, raising his eyebrows. "It's the only interesting part of the story and he always forgets it. He's just about the most stupid person I've ever seen."

"Now, Archie," Ody corrected him, "I'm not stupid, I'm just not as interested"—he said, *inter-rested*—"in certain things as you are. You're the one likes all the twisted details, not me. I like what's pretty."

"Tell about the skeleton," Archie said.

The three of them—with R.B.—were sitting around the small table; I had pushed back from the table with my bowl of stew on my knees. The Gulf rocked us in its arms.

"Tell me again where this happened," R.B. said. He had his notebook out, and he was writing in it.

"Leave off your scribbling, R.B.," Archie said. "You're always scribbling. I don't want to be in no book."

"It's all right," Ody said. "Besides, you don't even know what he's writing. It's probably not even about you." He turned to me, confiding openly. "Archie thinks everything that happens is about him. But it's not."

"Some of it is. Your mama told my wife last week I was down to Tampa when I wasn't anywhere near Tampa."

"Leave my mama alone, Archie."

"I'm not saying anything against your mama, I'm just saying you have to watch out for what people say about you. Some of 'em's cruel

sometimes without meaning to be." He took a large, shaggy swallow
of beer. "There's too much talking in this world anyway, entirely too
much of it."

"Tell us about the skeleton," R.B. said. "I'd like to hear that part
of the story again."

"Well," Ody said, passing his large hand over his face, "the wreck
was down south of here, just off Corson's Reef—you know that place,
R.B.?"

"No, I don't think I do."

"Well, it's about seventy miles southwest of Tampa—where Archie
claims he didn't go last week . . ."—"Now watch out, Ody . . ."—"just
this little cut of reef shaped like a horseshoe. There's a twist in the
current and it piles against the eastward side, so the water is usually too
silty to work in, which is why nobody goes sponging out there much,
it's only sport fishermen, and they don't usually go out that far, not for
long anyway. The shrimpers stay clear of it. The wreck's been lost and
found a bunch of times. Hurricane'll wash it clear and then the next
storm'll cover it up again. It's like a ghost coming in and out of life.
There never was no treasure on it, and it's a steel-hull boat so nobody's
that concerned about it, not for history or anything, I mean."

"What about the skeleton, Ody?" This was Archie again. He leaned
back in his chair and scrabbled four beers out of the cooler, passed them
around. He had asked my name half a dozen times before he remembered it.

"Let me set the scene here, Arch."

"It's set."

"Okay; well, that's where it is, out to Corson's Reef, where the bait
fish swarm and the water's dirty and a ship full of molasses went to the
bottom of the sea."

"Thank you," R.B. said. He smiled at them both.

"I'd been down on her before," Ody said, "just looking around, but
like I say, usually she wasn't nothing but a big bulge in the sand—if
that—and the bulge wasn't nothing but cant of gunwale and bridge; the
ship was buried, sunk deep. This time the current had cleared some of
the sand away. It was like a floor covered with sawdust, how spots of

linoleum will show through, just a patch here and there. But like I say, the paddle wheel was exposed and part of the bridge which had come loose. I went down on the hose; Maury Stanos was with me"—"His cousin," Archie put in—"and I remember how curious it felt, falling in on that ship like a parachuter, descending on her. I dropped down below the paddle wheel and moved around looking at it. The wood had rotted off the spokes leaving just the steel, which was thin and rusted out; it looked like a windmill with the sails torn off, all naked. The bridge was easy to get to, but I didn't go over there at first, I don't know why. I had a light and I pushed through a hole on the foredeck and poked around, but there wasn't nothing down there but a few pieces of barrel and one old speckled moray who thought he owned the place. I conked him on the head with the gun and backed on out—there wasn't much to look at. I still didn't want to go onto the bridge, into the wheelhouse, which was leaned up against the paddle wheel; I had this feeling, it was like I dreaded it—I've had that feeling before"—"He's bad on them feelings," Archie said—"and they're always trying to tell me something that is the truth—so I made off toward the scatter, toward all the crockery I told you about which had spilled out of the ship, I guess, as she settled. I stirred around among the scavage, but there wasn't nothing to keep, though it was strange all that crockery being there, even teapots and a few old black spoons, turning my back, you know, on the ship. The water was murky, snaky the way it gets, these white, silty clouds blowing along and turning the distances into silt fog, shimmering like, but just as closed off from you as a curtain. When sharks come sometimes they'll swim just at the edge of that curtain, like they know its providing cover for them"—"They know about it," Archie said, "ugly bastards . . ."—"which has always seemed very strange to me, 'cause to do it right they'd have to know how far a human being can see through that silt, which they seem to know; it's curiously gruesome and strange . . ."—"What about the skeleton, Ody?"—"Well, I'm getting to that, I'm leading up to it."

He dropped his hands in his lap so that his face hung over the table. It was a skinny, fair-skinned face under his sunburn, but strong-featured; his mouth was full and bowed like a child's, the runnel under his nose deeply grooved, a small horizontal crease drawn straight under his bottom lip, his nose narrow and reddened, eyes narrow and large and oily blue. His flat chin hung two inches above the table.

"There weren't any sharks," he said, "and despite what Arch says, they're not usually any trouble anyway, not to spongers."—"They're biding their time," Archie said, "they're waiting for the right moment"—"Twenty-five years?"—"What?" I said—"Twenty-five years," Ody said, "that's how long we've been coming out here . . ."—"They're picking their moment, setting it up right . . ."—"The ones after Archie are anyway, yeah. . . . Well, I stopped and looked up at that wheelhouse; it was leaning down on one side, knocked crooked in its frame; it had windows all around it, like a sun porch, a few left intact but they were clouded over, barnacled, and the others the current sighing in and out of, the whole thing half buried in white sand. All of a sudden it came to me that I didn't want to go in there. My face got hot and the mask misted up; I had to take it off and clean it out. I had this feeling, this what do you call it"—"Premonition," R.B. said—"yeah, this premonition, like sometimes you get when you swim into a cave"—"or go to a visit over at Ody's house," Archie chuckled—"Shut up, Arch . . . yeah, but then I thought, hell, I'm not going to let this stop me; it was just a wreck and I've seen a hundred of 'em, so I pushed on; I climbed up the plate and over the gunwale and I got to the side of the house. There were little wisps of white sand mist curling out of the windows, and it was murky inside, gloomy. I slid around to the door, which was still there, but off its hinges, lying across the entrance like something you'd set up to keep a baby inside the house. There was a spiny sea urchin right next to the door, like a little black sea shrub somebody had set there; half its spines were broken off. I could see in the cabin a little bit, there was a jumble in there, crusted coils of wire, old metal facings heaped on top of each other, cans or something, round objects that the coral has whited over. It had that wintry, snowy look that things on a reef get, all that lime secreted over everything, so at first I didn't see anything unusual. I pushed in, nodding away from the bubble stream, thinking, still uneasy, that I would maybe find some little piece, a medallion or something or a sextant, that I could take home and sell, when I noticed the wheel. It was placed to the side, a little off

the center line, and still on its post. The crust looked like it had been
chipped off, it showed the black brass underneath—I was surprised
somebody hadn't salvaged it—and then I saw something connected to
the bottom of the wheel . . ."—"Whoo, wet Jesus," Archie shuddered,
"it scares me even now to hear you tell about it"—"Yeah, it was
spooky, but I didn't see at first what it was. I slid over that way, and
even when I got close to it, some pile of coraled sticks, I couldn't make
it out. I bent down to get a better look, and as I did that I saw the skull
wedged up behind the post and I saw the rib cage and, my God, it was
a human skeleton, or what was left of it. Jesus Christ, it scared the shit
out of me. If I'd been out in the air I would have fallen over backward.
As it was, I shoved off the wheel, streaking for the door. I didn't look
back. I swam off until that wreck was out of sight. Jesus, it felt like that
thing in there was going to rise up and come after me, and I couldn't
go straight up, not as fast as I wanted to, so I swam along the bottom,
running, you know, and swimming—damn, it was the only time I've
ever hated being in the water—until I was exhausted and had to stop,
and I hung there just trembling till my breath started coming back a
little, and then I turned toward the surface and followed my bubbles
to the top."

Archie patted Ody on the shoulder and grinned at us. "That's not
all either," he said. "Tell 'em, Ody."

"Yeah," Ody said, "that's not all. It wasn't just seeing the bones that
made me panic."

He pushed back in his chair and looked around. A small clock fixed
into the cupboard face ticked loudly. My mind drizzled, and a sad, stiff
wind blew on through my body. I stared at the edge of the table, at
Archie's thick fingers tapping out a rapid, silent music.

"What was it, Ody?" R.B. said, touching him lightly on the wrist.

Ody grinned at him, a countryman, a country fisherman, holding his
trophy behind his back.

"Yeah, Ody—what was it?" Archie said and yucked. He poked out
his large bottom lip, and grinned.

Ody cocked his head. "Yeah," he said.

"What?" R.B. said.

"Well, what got me wasn't just seeing the bones, it was seeing this little shank of arm bone that was still handcuffed to the bottom of the wheel. . . ."

"My God," R.B. said.

"Yeah," Ody said drawing his mouth into a thin line, "and what was most curious and scarifying was that the handcuffs were new."

"Oh no," R.B. said, "you don't mean it."

"I do mean it."

"How could you tell they were new?"

"They didn't shine, but they weren't corroded yet either, not bad. If they'd been down there any time at all you wouldn't have been able to tell they were handcuffs."

There were tears in R.B.'s eyes. "How sad," he said, "how sad."

Archie pressed his long arms out along the table. "What do you think happened down there?" he asked R.B.

"Lord, I don't know. Do you think the person was alive when they put him there?"

"Why else would they handcuff him?" Ody said.

"And you never went back?"

"Not me. I didn't know what might be lurking around there; it was a hurt place, it was one of those phantom zones where you can be sucked down and disappear. One of those Hell Doors you run on."

"What is that?" I said.

Archie laughed. "That's one of Ody's figmentations."

"Naw, it's true. I've seen 'em."

"What—doors?"

"Yeah, you know, these little dark holes, you see 'em sometimes in the woods and even out here, these places where you know if you go through you'll never get back into the living world. My mama told me about them."

"His mama is a witch," Archie said.

"She's no witch, Archie. She just knows some of the old stories."

"Let's go there," I said.

"—What?" Archie said. "Go where?"

"Out to the wreck."

"We're not going to any spook wreck."

"I want to see one of those doors—are they doors?"

"Yeah, sure," Ody said.

Archie slapped the table. His mouth twisted as if he had bitten something sour. "You crackers are crazy," he said. "You know what that wreck was, that wreck wahn't no Hell Door, or if it was, it was the kind of Hell Door that's real—that was some gangster dumping ground, that was the place where those fucking Cuban hoods from Tampa take the sons of bitches they want to get rid of. It's no goddamn demon den. The people who did that are real. And those people'll hurt you. No sir, not this Christian boy from Occasion, Florida, not any of this boy's going back to that place."

I said, "I don't see why the guy was necessarily alive when they put him there."

"Why the handcuffs, then?" Archie said.

"So the body wouldn't float off."

"That might be true," Ody said. "I couldn't tell, but whether he'd been alive or not he was down there, and somebody had meant him to stay."

"Let's go look at it—find out what happened." I felt a tremendous desire to go to that place. It was time for a pilgrimage, another pilgrimage. To move close and honor the dead. "R.B., don't you want to go see that place?"

"It's all right with me," he said sweetly. "I'll tag along whatever we do."

"It was two years ago," Ody said. "There wouldn't be anything left by now."

"And it's fifty miles from here," Archie said. "Who's going to pay for the gas?"

"I'll pay for the gas," I said, "and for whatever time you lose."

"Whoo, I don't know," Ody said. "What do you think Arch, you want to sneak off down there?"

"Shit," he said, "what do we want to go off down there for? We're spongers, we're not the damn rescue squad."

"No rescue—just look," I said, desperately, happily. "Hell, I'll never get another chance in my life to do something like this. I live in New

York City, where they haven't got anything but streets and buildings."

Archie laughed. His teeth were greasy and large in the hissy lantern light. "You want to see you a wild thing, don't you?"

"Yes, I do."

"You go down on a hose to the bottom of this Gulf and you'll see plenty of wild things. You don't need to go to Corson's Reef to do that."

"But there's something about this that's special. It's eerie."

"It's that, yeah."

"Why don't we go?" R.B. said.

And that was that. If R.B. wanted to go, Archie Brooks and Ody Demopolos were willing to take him. They stopped grumbling and began to explain the reasons for going to each other. Like all of us, once decided, they began to pave the way for themselves.

I went up on deck, around to the bow, and lay down on my back. The stars were spilled sugar, glittering on the black. Small, shattered points of light danced on the sea. The breeze licked itself softly and lay down. Soon, I thought, what wants me will come. It will fly over this ocean to get me. I wanted to hold my child in my arms. I wanted to tell her a story about where she came from and where she was going. I wanted to make the world up for her, invent it and build it and set bright objects and loving folks in the midst of it for her. The night she was born Bess called me. It was late, she was drunk, she talked to me for an hour. She never accused me of anything, she never said it was my fault. I want to come up there and see that baby, she said, I want to hold that baby in my arms. She was crying so hard when she said it I thought her tears might short the line out, drown us both.

After a while R.B. came up and we sat together looking out at the night. There was a huge pressure in me, but I kept feeding it to the waves and to the night and didn't say anything. Here, you take it, darkness, you take it, black, indestructible Gulf, let me save it from this cordial man beside me. I had become something I didn't dream possible. I was like a character in one of my own movies, not the hero-killer or white-heart, but the third lead, the disposable guy who falters in the clutch, who sweats too much, who doesn't come up with enough courage or integrity to get the job done, who chooses the momentary glitter over substance, who learns nothing, who is either rejected or someway ruefully parted from by the heroes who, though they get shot or raped or lose their children—or do this to someone—come through in the end, brandishing their humanness like a wedding bouquet.

R.B. shaded his eyes as if from glare. "The dolphins are gone."

"Did I tell you I stopped off in St. Augustine to find out about dolphins?"

"No—I can't remember. Did you?"

"They told me over there that they're terribly sexual. Sensuality is the big deal with them."

"I can believe that."

"It was a surprise to me."

"They've got no hands. I expect that if we were like that—having to rub bodies to touch at all—the sensual would take us over too."

"If we were like them the air would be something we swam through and floated in. Our needs would change."

"If we had cities," he said, "they would be cities of silk."

"We would sleep in the tops of trees, or up near the stars."

D'Nel talked all the time about the stars shining in daylight. He talked about taking a plane so high you could see them shining up above the soft blue of the atmosphere, like eyes watching all the time. In North Dakota he told me—once he began to visit regularly—that there is a very thin line between civilization and chaos. I said I already know that; that's obvious. He said, you only think you know it, but what you don't know is that the line's being tested every day, right here in this town, right down the street, right here. What do you mean, I said, what are you trying to tell me? Don't get scared, he said, I'm not going to jump you. I just want you to know what's going on. I already know, I told him, I make movies for a living; there's nothing I know of that will teach you more quickly how close chaos is. That's not what I'm talking about, he said, that doesn't come near it. What is it then? I said. It's right there, he said, and tapped me on the breastbone—you're it. It what? I said. The line; your body is the line. No, I said, not me. Yes, he said, yessirreebob. You, boy.

. . .

The night looked ageless, elegant, and posing among its stars and endless space, lying on its stomach above us. But the sea was a changeling, taking on the color of whatever sky appeared above it. Under clouds it was gray, under blue sky it turned blue and green, at night it was black. The sea didn't care; heaven couldn't teach it a thing. It slipped against boats and against the naked knees of the world and it didn't say a word. You could ride on it and swim in it, you could sink down five miles into it, you could take it into your mouth so your membranes burned with salt, you could throw your lover into it and hold her under until she drowned, but the sea didn't care, it went on cresting and falling, giving itself up to the sky and the clouds, taking itself back in rain, throwing up dead sharks on the beach and throwing up yellow barnacled grass and the timbers of boats and bones, taking them back. Fish might be built for it, and we might have come from it, our vestigial gills and fins infolding, the womb a dipped gourd containing it, and birds might ride on it, and maybe, if the explainers were telling the truth, every place was once covered by it so that in the cut of a stream high in the Himalayas you might find the stony bones of a saltwater eel, and our blood might be made of it, but the sea didn't care. You can go in the woods and think the trees are talking to you, you can hear your mother chuckle in the voice of the creek, and the breeze sinking through birches is sometimes the touch of a lover, and the grass in a field where the Queen Anne's lace is just coming to bloom may shine like the bed of your dreams, but the sea knows none of this and doesn't care. Its voice is not human or loving, it will not hold you up, or teach you of love, it will not give in or give in, it will not play or fight; it has nothing to teach you and nothing to promise and holds out no hope; it is cold and clear and breaks indifferently on the rocks of the world. We can love it if we like, but the sea doesn't care.

And now, R.B., now, instead of speaking, I will take your face in my hands and press my fingers into your skull until I feel the slop of your brains running through them, and I will press deeper, into the center of you, past blood and tissue and bone, deeper until I come to a place where there is something called a soul, and I will take it between my fingers and squeeze it until like bones into coal it will transform itself into fuel for my body. I will take you into my mouth, my friend, and eat you, swallow you down like a plum, take all of your good and your bad, all your niggardly self-frightening ways, all your love and your griefs, your miseries, your cold mornings on the dew-struck porch of your Florida house, and all you love and have lived beside, your parents and friends and your sister dead and rotting under a yellow sheet, and all that has gone before and will come after and all that has ever been and ever will be—I will take it in my mouth and swallow it whole and digest it in the belly of my body and become you and become all that you are and all that you know—become your blood and your shit and the fire that jumps between the nerve sprouts in your brain. And your race memory and your inbred knowledge of good and evil I will become—my friend my brother; and your faith in God and your fear of the Devil and your sweet solitary prayers and your blasphemies I will become; and your journey to Chicago and your dictionary and your strange suppers with a house full of relatives I will become; and your disconsolate mutterings as you bend over a piano parceling out a few notes that might change your mood, and your walks on the beach after midnight, when the cows, broken out of your neighbor's fields, wander ghostly and mooing in the sand, and your days fishing for flounder off the dock in Occasion, and your high school memories of agony and wishing, and your celibacy I will become; and your boat rides and the taste of salt in your mouth, and your fights with your sister and the failure of your life I will become—I will strip off your skin and wear it, I will snatch your brain from your skull and fix it in my head, and your heart I will take and plunge it into my own chest so I might hear your blood beating there; and I will love you and I will kiss you and I will drink your piss and your come, and I will taste all you have tasted and smell all you have smelled and touch all you have touched; and I will speak in your voice, I will cry out not for forgiveness but in praise; I will stand up, one foot sunk in the earth, one foot sunk in the sea, and I will raise my hands to heaven and I will pluck the stars like apples from the sky, and pluck the moon and the sun and the planets from Space, and gather the worlds into my arms.

Something in me leapt up, and my body followed it. I tore off my shirt, stumbled out of my shoes, stripped my pants, and dived into the sea. I heard R.B. gasp as I went under, but I didn't pay any attention. I fell downward through the black that enclosed me like belief, pulling myself down into the sea that only a few hours before had been clear as sink water, pulling as I fell, stroking with my arms and kicking my legs, driving my body downward through the tons of water, my ears cracking, my open eyes burning, downward into the bloodsea, falling. I swam straight down to the edge of my breath and then swam on. There was a bottom down there—I had seen it—a white and ribbed floor, but I didn't find it. It seemed to me that the sea opened like the mouth of a lover and took me into itself so that I swam not toward the simple sand plain of the Gulf but into the heart of the world, and with that thought came another, that somehow, despite my energy, despite my lunge toward what I thought was the new fresh object of my desiring, I was being thrown back into the dense center of what I had tried all my life to get out of—idiot, I thought, you are sinking, not rising, you are falling, sweet flower, you are falling—and it was as if then the truth of me swam with me as my ears began to ring and my chest kindled a fire that burned my body like the body of a man on fire; and still I swam, downward and downward, until the black around me was the black inside me, Bess, and I died.

4.   I was born in 1945, in the Soulenes District of old St. Louis, raised there, two blocks from the river, among the dockworkers and the river men, and the truth is, except for the river, I hated my life there and I left that place as soon as I was able, on a tug pushing a grain barge south to Memphis, when I was fifteen years old. For ten years I traveled, making my money mostly as a laborer in the migrant camps, though I worked too as a stevedore in New Orleans and as a museum guard in Philadelphia, and, briefly, as an obit writer for a weekly paper in Cleveland, Ohio. I had loved the movies from the beginning, but I did not think at first of making them my vocation. In those wandering years what fascinated me was the stories people would tell, which I listened to and pondered on and used, along with the books I read, to teach myself about life. I wanted to know how people saw it—life, that is—what it had done to them and what they thought they had done to it. From their stories I made my own, tales of a childhood in the swamps of South Florida, or of a childhood in Hell's Kitchen or a childhood raising avocados in the San Jacinto Valley, of parents who had immigrated from Ireland or the Ukraine, of bus trips across the Great Plains snowy and endless, of a schoolyard in Kansas where the spring winds blew the blossoms off the cherry trees, of balsam firs shaggy with snow in New Hampshire, of the Quetico, the Red River, the Gulf of California, the Willamette, the Platte. I walked out of a dream on a street near the bus station in Milwaukee with fourteen cents in my pocket and a smashed watch strapped to my wrist; I sold peaches from a barrow off the interstate in Virginia; I took instruction in the techniques of holistic medicine and tea service from an old lady in Rhode Island; I punched a boy in the face, a boy who had worn me to pieces with his talk about his crippled sister, in some woods off the B&O tracks outside Bondurant, Maryland; I lost four thousand dollars on a horse named Service the Queen at the Arkansas Derby; I was baptized into the Church of Christ Indivisible in the shallow green waters of Albemarle Sound; I shared a venison ham with a man who claimed his father had been hanged on the King Ranch in Texas; I walked the Appalachian Trail; I drank sweet crystal water from the Thunder River in the Colorado Gorge; I gave an Indian in Nevada a false name; I stole a set of snow tires from a car trunk outside Topeka; I learned songs in eight different languages; I read the great Russians and the British Victorians; I was jailed in Utah for assault, and joined the Army to escape prison and was sent home from Vietnam with a medical discharge; and I returned at twenty not to St. Louis but to Bar Etienne, Missouri, and met a girl there who was the cousin of my uncle's wife, and made love to her in a skiff under some willows in a backwater of the Mississippi River, and we fell so in love she married me three weeks later, and I abandoned her six months after that, and divorced her in Puerto Rico. Martine loved me, I think, and for a while I loved her, but by then movies had come into my life and I was soon haunted and fascinated by those huge silvery lives lived out on the giant screens, and I realized that the stories told there and the lives the characters lived were not so different from the stories and the life I lived, that I too yearned for the big score and was willing to sell my birthright to get it, and I too wanted to love a beautiful woman forever, and rob a bank, and sail a ship into the teeth of a storm, and that with only a little twist of the facts, that was what I had done, and was doing; and so I went to Hollywood, abandoning my wife of six months—I left a letter and all my money (I could make more) on the kitchen table—crossing the country for the fortieth time, and took what jobs I could get at the studios, running errands, climbing in the grids, building props; pushing myself forward in a way both general and specific, willing to do anything. I took a room in a small yellow apartment court built into the side of a hill overlooking a small tangle of streets drifting down the side of Belvedere Canyon, and at night I would work on screenplays that were foggy with inexpertise and mayhem, attempting to lay down a coherent line that would lead through a series of plausible actions to a denouement both thrilling and surprising. I took what courses I could, studying with actors and defunct old directors, running the same silly scene through the typewriter four hundred times, playing it out with an imaginary camera—like a boy playing army with imaginary weapons—until it crumbled to dust and dismay. On Sundays I would drive with friends into the hills north of Pasadena to film with a rented camera outrageous escapades devised not particularly for our amusement but for our education: fights, a naked woman walking in and out of the light under an avocado tree, a man searching a stream on his hands and knees, a child tossed in the air, wasps buzzing around the netted form of a girl.

I worked at what I could, always on the sweaty periphery, and nothing happened. There were hundreds, thousands, like me, young men and women, often from the Midwest, who worked as extras, as caterers' helpers at the big parties, as gofers, as scene pullers; they were driven, they were loafers, they were venal or kind, they persevered or gave up like slapped children, they invented lives and histories, they had attended the Actors Studio or prison, they had special skills or no skills at all beyond a look in the eyes like Captain Courageous, they held small jobs in social services or at the market, they memorized scripts, they attended the screenings of famous, transforming films, they studied animals at the zoo and old women gossiping in the sun, and children embellishing lies; they talked incessantly, building lives out of talk, nurturing hopes, encouraging each other, making a little progress occasionally, or giving up, heading home to Kansas City or Cincinnati, moving on to New York.

Time passed—it seemed years—I had a life but not the drama I yearned for, not the vocation. The bitter Santa Anas blew down from the hills, shaking the leaves of the peppertrees, peering into alleys, stirring the grit on the walks. The women wore summer dresses in winter; as they crossed the street you could see the sunlight shining through the flimsy cloth; on the beaches their bodies glistened. It was there I learned to dress up in strange clothes, to make identities for myself that had nothing to do with my past. Life was possibility, but only in terms of change. I began to believe that age was simply the realization that your time is only your time: it has no meaning beyond the fact of your living through it. Quietly, I began to steal; quietly, I began to cause pain.

One day I passed a helicopter crashed in the street. It had just happened, a solitary policeman was just beginning to push people back, there was no fire but there was debris everywhere—bits of metal and glass, the front window of a department store shattered where a rotor went through—and there was a man, lying on a thin strip of grass between the sidewalk and the street—the pilot—his headphones still around his neck, his dark blue windbreaker ripped down one sleeve, the knees ripped out of his khakis, his eyes closed, a red scum of blood between his lips. He was barefoot; someone had set his shoes beside him. All day the choppers passed over saying *What, What, What;* at night their searchlights swept the yards, climbed like white monkeys into the eucalyptus, dived into canyons. Through our car radios the pilots spoke to us, telling of traffic and weather, events just over the horizon. I thought of them as beings from another world, not some off-earth world but some world like Vietnam, where men covered in red clay dust climbed single file up a small forested mountain, where butterflies with wings as large as cabbage leaves hung in the trees, and at night rock apes screamed like trapped human babies, and the choppers lifted from the LZs in a whirl of dust and leaves like small furious changes of season, hoisting the wounded, returning with the beer and the rations, the slings of ammo, the blank-faced boys from Harlem and Grand Moraine, as the pilots shouted to us over their radios, repeating the coordinates, joking like gods, whom we loved.

The helicopter lay on its side, its rotors snapped, its glass bubble burst. There was fuel in the street but no fire; the cop shouted and waved people back. A man—maybe a doctor—in a green linen jacket knelt over the pilot. I slid through the crowd that was meager yet and knelt beside him.

"It's all right, sweetie," the man in the jacket said to the pilot, "you're going to be okay; just hold on." I thought he must be one of us, one of the soldiers; they were soldier words.

The pilot was young, crew-cut, he had a tan, his nostrils were naturally flared. There was a deep bloodless groove in his head, running from the hairline back, like a groove in dough. As the comforter spoke to the pilot, bending down so their faces were close, the fingers of his left hand worked gently beneath the fallen man's shoulder and drew out a gold chain and medallion and slipped it into his pocket. It must have been the pilot's jewelry. I said nothing, no look passed between us. Then, as we knelt there, the pilot died. He had been breathing in the light harsh way of a child about to snore, but then the breathing stopped. I looked at the jacketed man to see if he would start resuscitation, but he didn't. With both arms extended he pushed himself up and got to his feet. He cast a single look down at us, at the small death scene, and it was a look of such bitter resentment, of such hatred, that I was stunned. Then he was gone, reabsorbed by the crowd.

A paramedic pushed me aside and began his work. I got to my feet, my face, my mind stinging with the murderous reproach in the jacketed man's eyes. It seemed worse than the death. I tried to find him in the crowd, but he was gone.

Later, in my disheveled room, where a breeze smelling of lemons and dust ticked at the papers strewn on my desk, and the fuzzed sourceless light of California crept like a yellow tide across the floor, I lay on my bed pondering the look the man had given me. I had seen fury in a man's face before, I had seen determination, and the wild, rootless madness that can come into a man's face when he fights for his life, but I had seen nothing like that. When he looked at me, for a moment, I had forgotten who I was, forgotten what I was doing there. In some way, at that moment, the features of the life around me, the radio playing in a window up the street, the smell of the crowd, the young policeman waving his arms, the pinched face of the dying pilot, the breeze stuttering in the pine trees, had become undifferentiated, like faceless, equivalent cards shuffled and strewn from a deck—no way to tell one from another, no way to see a pattern or draw a conclusion. And in that space of confusion had appeared, dense and particular as a stone mask, the face of the man stealing a gold chain from around the neck of a dying helicopter pilot, a face that was a kind of claim and proof, but proof of something so apart, so alien to the rhythm and commonality of the life around us, that it was unendurable. Unendurable—unless one turned away entirely from the agreed-upon world. And as I lay there pondering on the narrow disorderly bed, I saw that this was possible, that it was possible to step through the arrangement of furniture and breath we had convinced ourselves of in this world, into another dimension wholly apart, in which another chieftain ruled and another constitution applied, and that here among us, in Los Angeles, in the dry canyons of California and out in the desert and on the plains and in the woods and in the cities, there were those who had done this. Whether by choice or birthright, they had done this. As I thought this, it was as if the air in the room took on added weight; it began to press on me, to push down on my body like the weight of the sea, and I smelled the dry dead smell of unopened rooms, and I heard the crackle of a flame running through grass and then a whispering just at the edge of my mind like many voices talking at once, and there were several shades of blue stacked like bolts of cloth against the wall and I couldn't breathe properly and I couldn't remember the history of my life; and I seemed to see, as if from a great height, men dressed in the skins of animals moving slowly across a rocky landscape, and then from that height, as if lifted from the rocky valleys the straggling men crossed, I seemed to hear thin cries, so bleak and hopeless that my heart began to hurt in my chest, and I turned my face against the pillow and wept.

Later I called a friend and tried to explain to him what had happened, but he didn't seem to understand, so I called another, with the same result. It was by then late in the day; the sunset threw a decrepit orange light against the hills, and I called a woman I knew who told me to come over, which I did, and we made love in the unfurnished adobe mansion she rented in the Hollywood hills; and for a moment as we lay in each other's arms on her cotton pallet, I thought I could love her and I thought maybe I did love her, but then I knew I couldn't and didn't and a dumb, animal sadness came over me, and I was sorry I had called her up, though not because of anything she was or had done; and then I tried to tell her what I had seen and thought of during the day, describing carefully the pilot's body and the helicopter in the street and the face, the look of the man who had glanced at me, and then what happened later, but though she was sympathetic and offered me comfort, it wasn't exactly right, I could tell she didn't get what I was talking about; and what had happened began to become confused in my mind so that it might have been a story I had heard instead of experienced, and I laughed in that way a person does when he wants you to know he realizes he's making a fool of himself; and I turned my face against her skin and breathed in the scent of her—it was the scent of oranges and something resiny like spruce—and then we made love again, very carefully and slowly, the way, I thought, old people might, as if speed or roughness could break bone; and later, as I was driving away from the house, I glanced back and saw her standing in the window holding a candle and saw the wind surge suddenly in the citrus trees just outside the window and I remembered how when we first met she told me a story about her father's hands, about how large and corded they were and about how sometimes when she was a child watching him shave the hands seemed for just a second to want to turn on the face and rip its skin off.

It seems strange to say a man looked at me and I left, but that is what happened. A man looked at me, and he startled me so that I gave up my life. The truth is, I wasn't making it anyway. I didn't have the skills I needed to penetrate Hollywood. By then I knew that I wanted to make movies, not act in them, or run a camera, or sell them to people, but devise them, come up with the collection of images and story that could be thrown onto a screen to ricochet into the lives of an audience. But

I couldn't get close enough to the levers to begin to pull them. And then the man looked at me. He pulled a curtain back and showed me something I didn't know existed. I had seen death in the villes of Nam, but it was death in the faces of enemies, in the faces of friends, and that is different. The horror there was in the suddenness, in the sudden reach beyond reason that a torn body could pull you into, and, perhaps, the discovery that, despite what you had been taught, you could be pulled so effortlessly into the carnage too, into the constructing of it. But the truth is, those of us over there, the boys who fought, were not evil, we were just soldiers. We didn't invent what we did. And maybe I am only another faux naïf to claim such a turnabout, and to claim even that what I saw that day in the street was unusual, but I do make these claims.

I left my apartment in the sun-washed court and I bought a bus ticket and I began once again to travel around the country. My earlier journeys had, always, in my mind, some sort of purpose; I wanted to see the sand hills of Kansas, or the brick streets of Philadelphia, or I wanted to live a while in the deserts of the Southwest among the scrubby live oaks and the cactus, or I was following the harvest, cutting wheat in Nebraska or grapes in the San Joaquin or picking apples in Oregon; but now I moved randomly, not seeking a new home or adventure in the places we stopped, but trying to make for myself, if I made anything, a home on the bus. In those days you could pay a single price and travel for six months on one ticket, anywhere you wanted in the continental U.S. I was observed by the old men sitting on benches in the courthouse square of Murrayville, Kentucky; a couple in matching turquoise T-shirts watched me get off the bus in Baton Rouge; a young mother with two snaggle-toothed children noticed me eating a hamburger at a lunch counter in Dubuque; a beggar with his phantom leg pinned up against his thigh asked me for change in Evanston; in Richmond three boys in black leather jackets shouldered me out of the way. What I was looking for was not a place or a venue, but a person: I wanted to see that face again, I wanted to meet the man who had shown me on a street in L.A. the death of us all. I was like some guy who needed just one more score to make his fortune. I put it to myself that way. Let me see this, let me see that face again, and I will be okay. Then I can go about my business. But I couldn't find the man, or his brother, or his tribe, and I grew tired of the search, it began to seem ridiculous to me, so that when the bus reached New York, the bus I was on, I got off.

I took a room and began to think of the movies again, and I started up my life, the old engine of it, and it began to run well. I made progress this time. In New York they were making movies in the streets, and anybody could do it. In New York you didn't have to have anything but desire and the audacity to make a claim. It is the center of great art, New York is, but more important, to most anyway, it is the center of bad art. You can throw your pocket of pukey change onto the counter of art's temple, in New York, and there are those who will gawk. It is a city in which there is nothing to prove, and that is its glory.

I bought a camera, and I began to make movies. I took a few courses, I wrote screenplays, I met other independent operators, I made films with them that we showed in lofts and church basements, in a burnt-out garage called The Ransom—where some of the best new films were shown, where Bobby D'Ace and Jill Constantine got their starts—I launched a few ventures that fell flat, I kept going, I met Bess Appel, we got married, she gave me her money, I made a movie called *Blood Tie,* I met Van, I was on my way.

So I prospered. Van was my friend, mentor some, brilliant driver, producer by nature, director by design and will, keen for the main money chance, for the scene that would stick in the mind, for what catches the eye. I wrote screenplays, directed some—the first picture was almost wholly mine; it was only during postproduction that I met him—stuck my nose into everything, let Van handle the money, the distribution deals, let him tell me how a scene should go, plan the angles, cut my scripts into shapes that would take the light of a camera; but they were my stories, my tales of light challenged by darkness, my little puddles of rainwater I peered into to see the endeviled face peering back. I loved the instruments of death and all death's ways, the preposterous carnage you could muster on a screen, the quirky, irresolute characters that life swept relentlessly away, the murderer trying to explain to the woman he loves just how he has come to murder, the cold man, the unforgiving, chillingly beautiful woman, the hollow-gutted friend, the soldier whose future explodes in front of his eyes, the child twisting from beauty to misery to anarchy to murder. Van, tall and balding, with

his moist, dark eyes, his hands that chopped off pieces of the air as he
spoke, his quivering, the way his shoulders shook as he tried to explain
what excited him so, was my friend and my support and my guide. Six
years older, scion of a New England mercantile family, famous already
in his way among the streets of SoHo and the Village, and in the
Uptown culture emporiums, the living rooms and the ballrooms and
the boardrooms, he shaped and teased me, prodding me back onto
whatever necessary path I might have strayed from, joined me in my
flights of fancy and high spirits. We were collaborators, successful for
a while, bringing to the screen remarkable visions of mayhem and loss,
of the impossibility of getting out of this life alive; for a few years these
stories of stabbers and shooters, these tales in which a naked man hung
his mother by a wire from a railroad bridge behind his house, in which
a farmer sent his children out into the wheat field and then set the field
on fire behind them, in which a mother taught her baby son to swim
by drowning him in a number-two washtub, caught the fancy of city
intellectuals and of the small-town drive-in set—our bread and butter—a fact which seemed to Van and me hilarious proof of the dictum
he operated by—"The way to the front is the same as the way to the
rear"—propelling us onward in a clamor of creation that, so it seemed,
would last for all of our natural lives.

But it didn't last. We faltered, lost the thread somewhere; the pictures
became diffuse, fashion moved on, our audience had seen enough, the
smarmy suburban-souled epics of the film-school cuties took our place.
The hurt boys, the miserados, the dark web-slingers fell out of favor,
and we began to have to scramble.

It was a scramble I wasn't prepared for. Though I was frightened of
change, with Van's help I could get through it, but retreat was another
matter. I didn't want to soften anything. I wanted to press on, into
wilder country. "Your movies have stopped making sense," Bess said,
"they're not portable enough," and instead of listening, I turned my face
away from her and pushed on. It was very American, I thought, to do
this. And I couldn't stop. I would explain this to friends, ranting in their
midst as they leaned away from me, as they *walked* away toward the
buffet table, toward the spinning surf off beaches in the Hamptons,
toward the arched glances of their wives or husbands; and I could hear

my voice becoming petulant and hollow, I could feel the skippy pulse of fear dancing in my chest, until, one day, I began to see, finally, in Van's mordant eyes, the first flickerings of *his* desire for flight. This turn brought Bess's quietly nurtured desire to return home into full flower. My failure fed that weed. As it turned out, she told me, she had always hated the city; Florida, her father's saltwater farm, was the place for her, the place for me too if I would come. I thought she had gone crazy. Me go to Florida, I said—are you nuts? What I didn't realize—what I didn't want to see—was that it was the only thing left. The only thing left for our marriage. I had denied her everything, excluded every possibility, dragged her behind me like a chuck wagon to feed me solace and attention, and she was tired of it, she was ready for something else. I could not take the heat. I raged against her, argued, threatened her. The peace I had made with what stabbed in me gave way, and I was afraid again.

I don't know where the turn is, I don't know where the place is that a man comes to when he decides—when he is propelled—into destruction. Maybe you don't pick up a gun first, maybe you pick up a word, maybe you tell a small lie, maybe you cheat just a little, maybe you don't even notice, or maybe you do and think it doesn't matter, or maybe you know it does matter and for a second you don't care, maybe the wind of your passage is blowing too briskly, maybe you will take care of it tomorrow, maybe the day of reckoning is too far away to bother with now—I don't know. I did things in that time that were dark and unexplainable, that were gouges in my spirit that time may not heal, if that is what time does. I lived in a miserable selfishness, worshiping a lost order in which my dream sang like a drunken sailor, calling forth from me wilder and wilder episodes. Ah, Bess, I hated you then, I wanted you to die.

It was in the Dakotas—and this was later—that I met my man, that I found him again. He came to me quietly, walking up a frosty driveway early on a fall morning, and he said he wanted to help me. We were eleven weeks in that place, that small grain town on the rim of the ancient badlands; from the edge of town, beyond the yellow stubbled fields you could see the gray shapes of the Ghost Range, rising like the reconstituted remnants of giant stone palaces, against the western sky. They look like breath, the man said, standing beside me, they look like all the ages of Sioux breathing trapped at the edge of the world and turned to stone. He said, the world is a mystery, it can't be deciphered, and that's why we hate it so much.

I told him I didn't think we hated the world. I told him I thought our problem was that we loved it too much. We're like rejected lovers, I said; that's why we're so angry.

Not rejected, he said—ignored.

He was tall, slim-hipped; his body was angular, muscled but bony; it seemed to me not like something grown up but something cut out, a shape torn from a larger shape, leaving ragged edges and sharp angles. His movements had a strange awkward grace, a slinking angularity, like the movements of wading birds, but there was flow to them too, a sliding quality that you see in cats and small otterlike animals, and there was a silence about him that was like the silence of certain animals, the night hunters, the day lazers, tree climbers. He was the kind of man who seemed at times to blend with the landscape—you might not notice him at all—but then, stepped forth, moved away from the sheltering maple or the fruit display, seemed so apart from the things around him, so separate and different, that you wondered how he could ever belong anywhere.

I was traveling one night across the high plains, he told me, and I came to a town on fire. It was strange and troubling, he said, something glorious about it, this jaggedy launch of flame, this speck of the world that for these townspeople was not a speck but the world itself, being destroyed, the piled grain smoldering and spitting, corn kernels cracking, paint peeling off the museum train and the collection of plow handles in Mrs. Holenfield's garage smoking, the roof of the Congregational church smoldering, then bursting into flame, the water in the municipal pool steaming, children crying out. I parked the car and walked about the town, he said. Everywhere people fled, carrying their belongings into the fields, running for their lives. The fire was so bright it put out the stars. As I looked into the faces of the people I passed I saw some who had been damaged beyond repair. Some that from here on out would live unreconciled. These are the ones, he said, who interest me; these folks who won't get over it. The world is a mystery; it is not here for our pleasure, it is not here for our puny salvation, it is not a means to or an emblem of glory. I was interested in the ones—you could see it in their smoky faces—who knew this now. They were the ones who had been given a secret, a secret they never suspected, a secret that would separate them—no matter what they did next and from now on—from their fellows. One day the fire catches and your world burns up. The killers come and they take from you everything you love.

Ah, boy, he said, and touched me then on the shoulder, there is no home in this world. You look around you and you think you can see a pattern, a design in the movements of nature, in the rise and fall of the seasons, in the coming of the snows and the spring that follows and in the sweet summer light on the pond, but you don't have to walk deeply into the woods to hear the bear groan, to see the owl fail again and again, to see that she-demon nature toss up one more sack of dead thrushes, rubble of torn fish on the seashore. Where do you think this is happening, boy—at the center of the universe? This is only one world among many worlds, pal, and soon the old people fleeing before a fire into the hills will begin to strike their brothers across the back to keep them away from the last chunk of bread. Fathers will sell their sons into slavery, mothers will choke their babies—you know this; look at your life's work—sons will turn their backs on everyone who loves them.

Look, he said and opened his hands. His palms were yellow as brass. I offer you not the world—you don't care about riches; you don't care about fame—I offer you knowledge; I offer you the irresistible secret; I offer you complicity. We hate civilization, we hate love, we hate order, we hate God and all his sticky works. All these, all this arrangement—natural or devised—are the monster we have been trying to escape. That's the secret, my friend, that's the rune written on the heart of the world. We don't believe in any of it, and we don't want to believe. *Fuck it*—that's the heart's cry. Fuck it all and shovel it into hell.

He said this to me as we walked in a field planted in birches. It was Sunday afternoon, the day, no matter the project, I always took off. The young trees were filled with leaves the color of lemons. On the ground the leaves made yellow wreaths around the trunks. His voice was soft and comradely, like the buddy-to-the-world voice of a man selling me insurance. He had been there and he knew and it was all right because he knew I knew too and he had come to tell me I wasn't alone. And it was true—I knew what he was talking about. He said, brother, it's a hard world, and it's not going to get any easier. As he spoke he touched his lips gingerly with the tip of his finger, as if they hurt him.

I don't mind it being a hard world, I told him. I don't expect an easier situation.

Of course you don't, he said. I know that even in hell you'd still be trying to complete the job you set for yourself.

Yeah, I said—make movies; I do that.

No matter the cost.

Right, I said, no matter the fucking cost.

It's noble, he said. Very noble.

I'm not doing it for that.

Yes, he said, nobility doesn't even enter into it.

I can't help myself, I said. It's gone past the point where I could help myself.

Right, I understand. It's momentum, inertia, movement. The car's rolling.

Yes. At high speed.

Sometimes it's scary.

Sometimes. Yes.

But this is what you wanted, he said. This is what you signed on for.

I called the dance. As they say in Missouri.

They say that everywhere.

I begged for this. I wanted it more than anything.

And now you've got it.

But it seems to be coming apart.

Yes.

We came to the edge of the field. Beyond a wire fence stubbled wheat fields stretched away toward a river in the distance. The river shone faintly, like a sword in the grass. In the troughs of the wheat rows, among the gleanings, a thin snowfall had collected. The brief snow made white stripes in the field. I thought how the natural world was a place where sometimes you thought you could just go walking off into it, make a home, like a bear or a bird, in the middle of it. Cities weren't like that. Cities were feats that you had to perform feats to live in. At least that was the way I put it to myself. Van, who like me was born in a city, didn't agree. It's that jungle out there, he would say, tossing his hand at some benign landscape, some park, that's dangerous. No telling what might creep up on you.

I leaned on a fence post, bent down and sniffed the creosote it was saturated with. The dark, funked, sappy smell of the preservative took me back to St. Louis, to the wood-treatment plant on St. Charles. We played games of hide-and-seek among the gunky barrels, dreaming in a world of smell and shape.

Yes, he said, pressing his hands down on the top strand of fence wire, memory. How do we press out that wrinkled cloth?

I've been a long time away from Missouri.

You should see your father's face now. You should see what life has done to him.

I don't blame anything on my father. I don't want to be like him, but I don't blame him.

Of course not. But he's a man, and we have to learn from other men. How is it the saying goes: Through our brother God speaks to us? Your father's your brother too. He's your reflection. Everybody is.

I didn't know you would talk like this.

You thought I would—just kill you?

I thought you might.

He looked at me. His eyes were blue, but dark. The light pierced them deeply, but stopped, deep in, and disappeared. Sorry, he said, but I can't let you off that easy.

What are you for?

I have a certain tonal quality. A reference.

I meant what was his purpose, and maybe that's what his answer meant, but maybe it meant something else. Whichever, he was a liar.

I have to make this movie, I said.

And then what?

The next movie.

What if they won't let you?

I'll find a way.

Let me help you, he said. I'll tell you a story.

I have plenty of stories.

You don't have this one.

What is it?

He sighed, hitched up his pants with his wrists. A long, thin stroke of orange light pierced the sky in the west. The dark, snow-streaked ground seemed to reach up toward it. It's a good story, he said. It begins in Florida.

He said to himself that he didn't believe he'd do it, but inside himself he believed all the time that he'd do it. They have driven along the coastal plain, in and out of the pinewoods, all the necessary miles, to the farmhouse in the cove. Randy Strunk, his helper, meets them at the gate.

"I knew youins was coming," he says. "I had a sight of it, and I knew this'd be the day."

"Randy," Banty says, "you remember Molly. And this is D'Nel Boyd." Boyd lies in the back seat, negligent as a king, eating figs, wiping his hands on the paper sack they came in. "Hi, Randy," he says. "Want a fig?"

"I never could stand 'em," Randy says.

Randy won't get in the car. He trots alongside as they bump over the cattle guard and trundle down the two-track drive toward the house. It is a tall gingerbread house, unpainted. The eaves are warped and there are loose boards on the porch. Salvage trash, old nets, pieces of farm equipment are strewn everywhere in the yard and piled on the porch. The azaleas his mother set out long ago hunker near the porch like blasted refugees. Some of them have been dead for years. Little collections of naked branches among the living bushes, like ruined articles at a thrift sale.

"This where you live, Banty?" D'Nel says. "It's quite a place."

"My great-granddaddy built it."

"Looks like yall've preserved his memory." D'Nel speaks in a cracker accent, all the words heavily subsidized by mockery. The way he talks makes Banty wince. In the field beyond the house cows crowd against the fence, lowing. "Every time they see somebody," Randy says, "they think they gon' get fed." He picks up a rock and flings it at the cattle.

The rock hits a red heifer in the flank. The cow shies, in a slow motion, lowing, that makes them laugh.

D'Nel hangs his head out the window. "Them things," he says to Randy, "makes a man wonder how come God gave us dominion." He draws his head back in, cackling.

From the floor he lifts a bottle and takes a long pull. "Hey, Randy," he says, "want some?"

"Nah, sir," Randy says. "I never touch that element. It would rot me down."

"Smart fellow, Randy," D'Nel says.

Banty stops the car below the steps. There is a circle of grass before the house, in which are planted half a dozen queen palms. The tops have been blown out of three of the palms. The others are ragged, the fronds yellowed and coarsely flacking in the breeze. Everything all about them has an air of decrepitude; there is nothing new, or even carefully preserved, anywhere. Vines, Virginia creeper hang from the eaves. The cedar shingles are warped and strewed, knocked away entirely in places, as if small explosions have taken place on the roof.

Banty gets out of the car. He moves awkwardly, his body cranky and slow, like the bodies of old people. D'Nel climbs over the front seat and swings his legs out onto the sandy drive. "Senility," he says, looking at Banty. "It's a fatal condition."

Molly presses her face for a moment against his back. "You smell like plums," she says.

"I don't know why I've brought yall here," Banty says. "I can't believe I've done it."

D'Nel smirks, coughs a laugh that he catches in his hand and rubs out, as if it is a greasy bug, onto the seat beside him. "You can't resist us," he says. "You can't resist anything about us. Such is true love."

"True love?" Banty says. "Pure madness. That's all it is." He looks up at the house, craning his neck. "This old place," he says. "This miserable old place."

"It looks like the snake museum," Molly says. "That's what I've always said." She unpries D'Nel's fingers from the bottle and takes a series of short sips. A thin wisp of smoke curls up from the back seat. The smoke catches Randy's attention. "Got a fire?" he says.

"That's Banty," Molly says, her eyes twinkling. "He tried to burn us up."

"You want some water?" Randy asks nobody in particular.

"Get that fire extinguisher from the kitchen," Banty says. Randy ambles off around the side of the house, following a narrow path in the grass.

"Sweet fellow," D'Nel says. He pitches out of the car onto his hands and knees. "Jesus God," he says swinging his head, "I remember the time the Federales got me. One of them opened the door, it was down below Obrégon, and I fell out like a sack of potatoes onto the road." He cocks his head, looks back along his body at Molly. "You remember the time we shot the shark?"

"Yes."

She gets out of the car, stretches, looks up at the house. "We ought to spray-paint this place, Bantling."

"I like it like it is."

"Some pastel color. Bahamian pink or evening purple."

D'Nel lurches upright, falls against the car seat. He finds the bottle, takes a long pull. "That was some shark, some whale of a murderous shark."

"You killed it before it could eat me," Molly says. She throws her arms out, spins around.

"I shot him in the head. You should have seen that thing thrash."

"I did see it."

"I mean Banty. I mean Banty should have seen that shark. You ever kill a shark, Banty?"

"I've caught one on a line."

"That's not the same thing. Shooting a shark is different. Especially when it's after you. Mano a sharko—that's the only way."

The front door rattles, there is a pounding, fist against wood, and Randy staggers out onto the porch. He carries a large red fire extinguisher in his arms. "Door's stuck again," he says smiling sweetly. He's unshaven, red-haired, his beard is carroty, his skin so densely covered with freckles it appears brown. "Where you want this?"

"Down here," Banty says.

The smoke, gray, thickening, seeps from the open back window. It has collected on the seat like one of the slippery liquids, tetracycline, mineral spirits.

Banty takes the extinguisher from Randy, opens the door, and aims the heavy black nozzle at the smoke. There is a throaty, rasping gush; a glittering white cloud shoots into the car and spins over the roof. Everyone flinches, everyone except D'Nel, who leans against the front doorjamb, sipping from the bottle. The dust obscures him. Banty presses the lever again, and again the cloud spurts over the car. It leaves a rime over everything. Even over D'Nel, who as the cloud clears they see is covered in white. Molly begins to laugh. She doubles over laughing. The others follow until they are all laughing wildly. D'Nel sips from the bottle, which is a white bottle in a white hand, pressed against white lips, unconcerned. Then Banty hits the lever again, and again the white dust blizzards over everything, hiding it all. Molly peers from around the side of the cloud. She looks at Banty. "I think it's out, boy," she says, but Banty doesn't stop. Flitting the lever he sprays dust over everything. He keeps it up until the extinguisher hisses and dies. In places along the backseat the dust is four inches deep. It is caked on D'Nel's head, dripping from his left ear. Banty sets the extinguisher down beside him. He's trembling. He and D'Nel look at each other. D'Nel smiles a broad whiteface smile; he grins. "Don't you wish it was poison," he says, "don't you wish I was dead now and you had finally done it."

He gets up, cackling to himself. There is a crying of birds, of crows, among the pines across the yard. They can hear gulls screaking over the water which it is possible to see beyond the house. D'Nel cackles to himself; he mutters. "Banty," Molly says, "sometimes you are a complete idiot."

D'Nel presses a hand against the side of the car, doubles over, and suddenly and violently vomits. The vomiting goes on for several minutes. It is outrageous, explosive, accompanied by huge groans and coughs, shouts of pain. Molly leans over D'Nel holding him around the shoulders. The others look on in awe. "What's he got in that bottle," Randy says, "gasoline?"

D'Nel pushes himself upright, he staggers a few steps and falls to his knees. The vomiting begins again and goes on for a long time. D'Nel falls to his side in the grass, pushes himself up, falls back, and pushes himself up again, on one elbow. "Goddamn," he says, "I've puked so hard it's given me visions." He wipes a yellow string of spittle from his mouth, flicks it into the grass. "That, my lovely folks, is what the body's for—to give us visions. The body's a diving board. We spring off it into the acrobatics of our visions." He falls over on his back, looks straight up at the sky, which is clear and bright summer blue. Everywhere there is the flacking of leaves and palm fronds, the crying of birds. "Ah, God," he says, "that puke was anchored in my fucking nuts."

"You look tired," Molly says. She looks tired. Her face is pale, grooved with fatigue. There are small patches of color in her cheeks and purplish dents under her eyes, like the first signs of angina. She's on the wild edge of things, the cliff walk that comes before her fall into a spell. Banty sees this; he looks at her, studying her face. There is white goo on his forearms as if he's stuck them into snow, a few curlicues of white on his face. He says, spitting, "I think it's possible to be bold in ways you people haven't even imagined. Here," he says, and hands the fire extinguisher to Randy who takes it and sets it against the porch.

"Yes, yes," D'Nel says, laughing, hacking, spitting. "There are bolder ways than we imagine—though there are many bold acts you haven't thought of yourself—but the difficulty is not in the imagining. It is in committing the acts you *can* imagine. That's the problem, bro. Everybody sits around thinking of the conquistadorial acts they might perform. We all want to save the dying lady. But the problem is, none of us do. We shuffle on along and hope somebody else'll take care of it." He coughs, wretches, presses his hands against his chest. "Oh, heart, beat on, beat on awhile yet. I take advantage of that. I reap the outfall of that."

He pushes to his knees and looks around. For a moment there is a childlike bafflement in his face. His skin is white as an onion. Molly, looking at him, says, "You can do anything. I am amazed at you. You can make yourself into any kind of creature in the world. Rabbit or tiger, it could be you."

D'Nel grins. His teeth are mossy with vomit. "I'm a marvel, aren't I?"

He surges to his feet, reeling; he whirls, arms outstretched; he spins and falls against the side of the car. "Let's look at the presents. Hey, fellow," he says to Randy who has sat down on the steps, "is it anywhere near your birthday?"

"My birthday's in April."

"Then it must be a miserable time for you now. Everybody born in April has a miserable time in the summer. It's a well-known fact. Some deny it, but all know it's true."

"I don't know it. I like the summertime. 'Cept for the heat. Occasionally the heat's a ridicule to me."

"A ridicule—yes, that's right. Heat like this here makes us all ridiculous. But come here a moment, my man." He moves around the car, supporting himself on its dusty flank, like an old man groping a banister. He staggers around to the trunk, waits there for Randy who gets up and comes slowly toward him. "Are you crippled, my boy? Is that why you move so carefully?"

"Nah, it's not crippling. I don't know you."

"I'm here with Banty Jakes. He's brought me here to show me his ancestral home. This Florida fortress on the bay. Where, I understand, he keeps wild dolphins and such. You know about the dolphins?"

"I feed them things. I know about them pretty well."

"Okay, then look at this."

D'Nel pops the trunk lid. It springs open revealing a welter of clothes, guns, jewelry, money in crumpled strewn bills, stock certificates, oddities including a pair of white patent-leather shoes with red buckles, a stuffed parrot, a souvenir plate from the 1939 New York World's Fair showing the faces of the Dionne quints, a pair of dirty rubber waders, a baseball bat.

Randy peers inside. "That ain't much. 'Cept for the money, I've seen it all before."

"Oh shoot. I didn't know we had a sophisticated person here."

"It don't take much to know clothes when you see 'em."

"Ah, maybe you're right. Maybe I'm a silly person, thinking I could amaze a farmer. Here, you want some of this?" He scoops a fistful of money and offers it to Randy.

"I don't need no money. I'm doing just fine."

"A principled man. Jesus."

D'Nel begins to sniffle. Tears appear in his eyes. He cries outright. "Ah, gosh, I try to do something nice, and nobody appreciates it. I ought to shoot myself."

"I want to go to sleep," Molly says. "Can I sleep in your bed, Banty?"

"No."

Banty is looking out across the yard, toward the cattle gathered at the fence. "I don't want to be here," he says. "I don't even want to be in the same country as you people." He doesn't turn his head as he speaks.

"What's going on, Mr. Banty?" Randy says.

The pines near the cattle pasture whip their shadows over the grass. Banty can hear the restless chucking of the sea. He takes a step away, obviously random, and another, in a slightly different direction, almost like a comedian feigning indecision; he takes another step, skips. His face is hard, oily, but there is a small, flickering gaiety in his eyes. It's the look of someone worn past reason. A marathoner, or a soldier. He says, without turning his head, "Have you seen that detective?"

"That Tubby Wells? That old man?"

"Yeah, him."

"He's been around here. He sits in his car up there at the front of the driveway. I thought he was some kind of government man. I went up to talk to him and he said he was looking for you, said you were in trouble." Randy spits, wipes his lips fastidiously with two fingers. "I didn't know what he was talking about till now."

D'Nel has pulled a gold sequin-flecked dress from the car and is struggling to pull it on over his clothes. "You think we're in trouble, Randy?" he says. "You've come to that conclusion on this smattering of evidence?"

"Yall are not hard to get a fix on."

"How you do this?" D'Nel exclaims, wrenching the dress. It is sideways, half on.

"Step into it," Molly says. "You have to *step* into it."

"I thought you were supposed to pull it over your head."

"No, darling."

He wrestles it on. The dress is long, a ball gown, stacked with ridges of yellow sequins that make a pattern of diagonal bands across the bodice and raised horizontal lines across the skirt. The cloth tears, but D'Nel is able to get it around him. He shoves his arms through the narrow straps. "How do I look?"

"Crazy," Randy says.

The sequins make rainbow patches that appear and disappear on the bright yellow cloth. As he moves, shimmying, bobbing, and weaving as if the cloth is gripping and turning him, the light bounces and leaps along his body; it is as if the light is embodied, playing a game, showing itself and disappearing, participating. "I love dresses," D'Nel says. "I love to wear them. I want to feel what a woman feels. I want to know everything that goes on when she puts on some slinky number and sashays around."

Molly says, "I tell you all the time."

"Yes you do, and I appreciate it, but I want to know what it's like in your most private moments. Everybody's turned a little by eyes on them—everybody is. I want to know what you do when you're alone. What part of yourself you touch first, and what part second, and where you linger, what you think."

He rolls up his pants. His legs are remarkably hairless. He kicks his shoes off, prances a step. Then he reaches into the trunk again and pulls out a large red wig.

"I can't stand this," Randy says. "This is over my head."

"Pick a prize," D'Nel says, "any one you want."

"I don't need prizes."

D'Nel looks at him a moment, taking him in. The look he gives him, eyes narrowed slightly—but they seem to be wide open too—his mouth very still, the full lips straight, head erect, stops Randy Strunk entirely. It is a look with the power of conjury that freezes. For just a second he is transformed into stone. Then Randy shudders, steps back. He bites his lip, shakes his head. "What you think, Randy?" D'Nel says.

"I got to go look at these cows."

Banty says, "Take the extinguisher and put it in the truck."

"I'll do that."

D'Nel fits the wig on his head, straightens it, pulls it around his ears. It is like a hand passed over the actor's face, splintering the expression, remaking it in quick conjury into something else. The whiteness of his skin, the full lips—dark, almost liverish against the paled skin—the precise black eyebrows, a softening under the chin, a flush there—he looks like a woman. He says, watching Randy hurry off toward the garage, "Does he make biscuits for you, in the morning, biscuits and syrup?"

"Sometimes."

"I would like that. I would like that very much. I've always wanted a housekeeper, someone I'm not *attached* to who takes care of daily business for me." He leans his head back, looks up at the sky. Only his Adam's apple is male, protruding from his throat. "Don't you sometimes hate all this democracy business? Don't you just sometimes think it's completely anti-life?"

"No."

"I do. But then I don't know; maybe all those guys—Jefferson, Madison, Franklin, all those guys—maybe they were on to something. Maybe they figured a man would work for you even harder if he thought it was going to lead to something. What a joke. Hey, Randy. Hey, sport."

Randy half turns, but he keeps walking.

"Hey, Randy, you know we're all headed to the grave, don't you? You got that straight, don't you?"

"Watch out you don't make him too mad," Banty says. He shakes the white dust off his arms, looks at Molly, who is watching the scene, watching D'Nel with her predatory, amazed eyes. Expressions move across her mobile face, the expressions of one sheering toward collapse. Anger, joy, grief, delight, sadness, a child's defeat—they are all there, moving slowly, like cloud pattern over her face. She says, an odd smile—she's wearing bright red lipstick—flexing on her face. "Everything we touch in this world touches us back. Did you know that? Fingers, guns, persimmons, your great-aunt's lace underwear, the pared toenails of a crippled child—they all touch you back. Did you know that?"

Banty says, "I don't want you ever to leave me. I love you so much I taste it in my mouth, I feel it on the backs of my hands like grass itch. . . ."

D'Nel: "Mr. Romance . . ."

"It grinds me like the ocean grinds, it never lets up. I'm throwing away my life for you. . . ."

"I can't bear the touch," she says, stretching. "Sometimes the air's too much. It's like shocks of electricity all over my body. I want to be a fish in the sea with a hard, glittery, sea-slick skin, sliding through the water. I want to be that."

"Come here," D'Nel says. He is transformed. Even the movements, the slight purl of his hips as he moves, the elbows canted slightly outward, knees brushing—he's a woman. The wig bunches around his face like red fur, like the unruly hair of a wakening animal. He pats the wig with the tips of his fingers, smoothing it; he presses the back of his hand lightly to his lips. "Come here."

She leans, she slides, she tacks toward him. He takes her in his arms. It is a woman taking another woman in her arms. "You remember that woman in Port Jack, that woman in the blue nightgown?"

"The gown had gold lace at the throat. I never saw that before."

"Do you remember kissing her pussy?"

"Yes. It tasted like olives. It tasted just like a cock."

"You remember afterward, the next day, riding in the car along the bay?"

"I remember that."

"You leaned out of the car with your mouth open. I was driving eighty miles an hour. You said the sun was shining into your mouth."

"I could taste it. I could taste the sunlight."

"That's what you want, isn't it?"

"Yes. I want to taste the sun, I want to taste rocks, the ocean, blood."

"Riding in a car at eighty miles an hour."

"In the sunlight. Along the seashore."

"Kiss me again."

"I want to taste you."

"Kiss me."

She thrusts herself against him, her mouth open wide, her wet teeth glistening; there is only a two-foot space between them, but she hurls herself across it, as if he is an abyss she is throwing herself into—this man who has transformed himself into a woman in a gold ball gown—

pouncing onto his body, crouching it seems into the mound of his flesh; she kisses him, she gnaws at him, gnaws at the woman in the gold dress, tearing with only her lips at the flesh of his face so wildly that it looks as if she must draw blood; her legs snake around his legs, her weight sags against his waist; he leans down to her face, he sinks to his knees holding her, her legs splay wide, she presses him back, her right hand rises, strikes downward at his groin, into the rustly stiffened center of the gold dress, her hand seems to sink into the sequins, she grasps him there; he cries out growling, snarling, snorting, he shouts, he screams a thin, tearing scream; he arches into her grasp, she has him, she holds him fully like a hard fruit in her hand, pressing all the time her flushed, sweating face into his, eating at his lips, thrusting her open mouth against his nose, his eyes, his mouth, as if she would jam herself onto his face, attach her body violently to his—now he begins to rise, begins to gather his legs under him, and he staggers up, one arm shoots out to brace himself against the rear bumper, he cranks his feet under him, pushes up, rises with her snarled in his body, rises to his full height, releases her so that she is clinging to him without support—legs, arms wound about him—he staggers, stumbles, his legs catch in the hem of the dress, he nearly falls but catches himself, whirls sideways, leans, staggers a few steps, reels, whirling, spinning slowly, his arm flails, he cries out again in a voice like rocks breaking, breath thudding loudly, he sings out, some snatch of nearly coherent song, some credo, some foreign words, some American words—as if he is dispersing languages—cries out loudly, starts forward carrying her, staggers, leans down, scoops up the bottle, raises it, pours it over them, shakes the drops out, throws it away—it sails glittering, catching the sunlight, lands in the grass—he says, "Banty, the truth is, lying is easy, it is easy to perform the foul acts, it is easy to betray your lover, shoot someone, put your head higher at the expense of someone else. You can ruin everything in a minute—it's not difficult, it's a snap, you can drive the knife in to the hilt, you can gouge out the heart and eat it, you can stomp the brains into porridge; oh, Banty, you know now, don't you, you know how easy it is. . . ." He reels, he staggers under her weight, he lurches forward, reaches the steps. . . .

"Tell me, Bantling Jakes—is there a limit, is there a place beyond which we cannot go—as the preachers say—is there anything we cannot do?"

He lifts her, leaning backward, as a man reeling a fish-bent rod would lean against the drag of the line, lifts and turns her in his arms, settles her over his shoulder so that her head hangs down behind him. She is limp in his arms, accessible, without resistance.

All the hardness is gone from Banty's face; he watches intently and it is possible to see—in the loosened mouth, the widened eyes, the empty disks in his cheeks—that he is seeing acted before him his dream; that she, this woman—someone he loves—would become, for him, this surrendered, this vulnerable; that for a time—seconds? days? the rest of his natural life?—she would give in completely—that someone would (that something on this earth would); that she would sprawl in his life, like someone beaten by illness, broken by a fall, by love, helplessly accessible to him, someone to whom he could do anything, before whom mistakes are not unforgivable, errors not grounds for punishment. But then, as we realize this greed, this blandishment in his face, we can see, sliding in behind it, overtaking it, the repulsion, the fear, the hatred—the refusal—that pushes up out of him.

"Not me," he cries, "not this, not me, not now, not any time."

D'Nel stops as if he has been struck. He turns. His scorched blue eyes glitter. "Do you wonder how I can do this?" he says. "Do you ever wonder how I can create these little tableaux that illustrate your deepest desires?" He swings her in his arms, slowly, in the rocking one-two-three motion of someone about to toss a body. Her eyes are closed; she rides in the sea. D'Nel's lip lifts off his teeth, like a muddy chain lifting off the seabed. "We all offer you the chance to lay your burden down," he says. "We all know the burden; we all wish you didn't have to carry it."

"You want to kill me."

"Either way you go, that's the price."

"I can refuse."

"Sorry—no."

"I can walk away."

"To where? This is not Newton's universe, my friend. There's no place to walk off to."

"I love her."

"You think that is an answer."

"It doesn't matter if it is or not—I can't help it."

"Your father died cursing you. Your mother died just as inflexively dumb on the last day of her life as on the first. You can't save anyone."

"Maybe I'm not supposed to, maybe I'm only supposed to try."

"And what kind of fucked-up world is that? One in which we rehearse our deepest desires over and over, launch off on missions that fritter apart in the woods, until we are driven so crazy by our *total uselessness* that we wind up smashing our own faces against rocks? Come, come—you want to live."

"Not violently."

"The world *is* violent. Love, to be love, can't discriminate."

"Let me hold her."

"In your turn."

"You're going to kill her."

"No."

"Yes, you will."

"The world is a decoration, old scout—that's all. Don't expect too much from it."

"When you go to sleep I will take her away."

"It's not that simple."

"I will simply do that."

"You don't understand."

"I understand what I need to understand."

"No, friend, you don't."

He hitches her up, lifts her. Her arms slip free and fall down the gold sequined back; it is as if she is dead, or asleep. D'Nel starts up the steps, which are worn, splintery with human passage. He lowers his head, raises it; his face shines. "You're the one who's going to kill her," he says. "Not me—you."

It is night. He sits in the bedroom window, feet outside, placed carefully on the loose cedar shingles. The wind whistles in the pines. He hears the flat chinking of the surf, the hiss as the spume runs up into grass.

There is movement in the yard. The grass is tangled, uncut for weeks; the starlight shines grayly on it. From time to time he can hear the bark of a dolphin, a splash, then another quick, peremptory cry. The movement in the yard, over there a hundred feet away among the fig bushes, where the scrub oaks encroach onto the grass, is a man. It's Tubby Wells. Banty watches him, watches his shadow, his slender form, move like part of the night that draws itself into itself: move, fly across the grass from one pool of darkness to another, and stop. His mouth twists to call out, but he says nothing. The oblong, bent shadow leans out from behind a loquat bush. The shadow is like a feather sticking from an Indian headband. The surf whispers, hisses, sighs; there is the bark of the dolphin Estelle—then a trilling series of clicks, a sharp, high whistle. The shadow leans, leaps forward followed by the dark crouched form; it vanishes beyond a small ligustrum bush, the branches of which are slung so low the bush seems to be squatting on the ground. The bush shadow is a black hole in the grass, the size of a closet. Banty leans out the window. The breeze lifts his thin hair; with his fingers, fastidiously, he pats it down. Behind him the room is dark. He waits to see the shape move again. For a long time nothing happens. The camera holds steadily on the gray tiers of massed leaves, the angle of grassy yard, the flicker in the left mid-ground of lighter beach, until it is as if the scene is a still picture, a photograph; as if time, the movie which is its vehicle, has stopped. Then the shadow moves, it dips slowly out of its dark hiding place, poises like a thumb on the fist of the bush's shadow, like an upraised thumb signaling Excelsior! There is the crack of a rifle shot. The body falls into its shadow, disappears. The dolphins cry out, barking, clicking, chirping; the surf hisses faintly, fading.

5.   Then I returned to New York carrying on the whispery jet my wound-up film, my collection of 207 camera positions, my 183 scenes— some shot from two different angles—my producer, my A.D., some of the crew, my assistant, an actor or two, flying over the rolling black earth of Minnesota and Iowa, crossing the river that even so high we could see smoking, stretching the silver anaconda length of itself against the high vaults of Illinois; we changed planes in smelly Chicago, leapt over Indiana and Ohio, over Pennsylvania, where the mountains lay like green westward-reaching battlements, over New York State and down the Hudson valley where we had once planned, Bess and I, to buy an old stone house in Wynadot Ferry, at the end of a windy road lined with yellow birches, where we would put in a garden, raise beets and celery and asparagus and red-jacketed potatoes, and sit out in the yard on spring evenings with a few friends, drinking wine and listening to the birds, where we would wake early in the blue-exuberant light of a river dawn and walk out naked into the dewy grass, where we would—but no, we never did any of this, we never did anything more than rent a car one Saturday and drive up the river, arguing the whole way, exchanging accusations until we were exhausted and despairing; and so descending, so pressing downward, the great wheels down-locking, the flaps lifting, the huge plane settling back into a long jolt clumsily onto earth; and then the dispersal, and the ride in the cab to the empty yellow garage with its great arched stone door through which, a hundred years ago, cavalrymen led mules to their stalls, and then the climb up the blue stairs to the empty apartment, where by the dust I could see the places she had revisited, and what she ignored, saw the bed with its covers neatly pulled up but containing still the outline of her body where she had lain down and thought her thoughts about marriage and her life and the new life she would live without me. And then the anger, the rage which I couldn't explain or justify, rose in me, like dark, crying birds lifting from the winter-ruined trees; and I dialed the number of a friend's house where she lived now and got her on the phone, and I spoke to her in a quiet voice so that for the last time in our marriage she believed me, agreed—not reluctantly, but wistfully—to meet me at a house in TriBeCa where I wanted to show her something—as if it was a house we might live in—yes, she would do that, she would come and did, an hour later, making her way carefully through the murky, sulky junk in the loft Van had bought for renovation and resale, into the tall room where I lurked waiting for her; where, in a moment of absolute clarity, I lunged from the ensnarling shadows, and stabbed her.

V

1.

There is a shyness in the eyes of the drowned. A sweetness, as of a child lifted gently out of a fever sleep, or as one arrived in a land without names—a humility and a tenderness so that as the dead hand rises to touch the face of the rescuer, in wonder and sadness, a torrent of love passes through the helpless body—that the living, in their panic, cannot imagine.

With their fists they pounded me back into life. I woke coughing, vomiting, my throat torn, my lungs burning. In my flesh, in my bones, in the coils of my brain I could feel the weight of the water, its acceptance and its refusal. R.B. held my head in his hands; with his fingers he wiped the salt from my face, smoothed my hair. Archie Brooks beat on my chest, with his fingers he reached into my throat and cleared the vomit. They fired the pump and forced oxygen into my lungs. The chilled, brassy air burned in my throat. I heard them laughing with relief, the skittering, hysterical laughter, the gruff jokes. I sucked on the respirator, tasting the bitter rubber in my mouth, looking up past their hovering faces into the stars that were random and opulent and disarrayed. Wisps of white cloud hung among the gales of light that after a while I saw weren't clouds but mist, some residue in my eyes of the sea. I had heard voices shouting down long, empty corridors; I had heard questions, imperatives, a quiet, impoverished pleading. I lifted my hand and touched R.B.'s sleeve; I loved the feel of the white cloth, the softness of it, the pliability, the realness of it. I turned my head and kissed his wrist, I licked the sour flesh.

"He's crazy, right?" I heard Archie say.

"Not really," R.B. answered.

"What was he doing—a little midnight bottom-walking, huh?" Archie spoke harshly, but his hands were gentle, for just one moment they lingered on my wet, bared chest, the heavy fingers hesitating among the sprigs of matted hair between my nipples, forgotten maybe as he looked R.B. in the face, but tenderly, nonetheless, touching me, so that I saw, looking up into his face, a specific human gentleness, something that shone under the hard planes and grooves of the weathering, something sunk there and alive.

"Maybe he just fell in," Ody Demopolos said, bending down to free the line I sucked on. "It's happened to me."

"You hadn't ever tried to drown yourself."

I pressed my hand over Archie's. "No," I croaked, "—no." It hurt to use words.

"What you say?" He bent down close.

"Not drown—see."

"He was looking for that skeleton maybe," Ody said. He hawked and spit over the side.

Archie straightened up. "R.B., I don't mind you coming along, I don't mind doing you a favor—I never have minded doing that—but I didn't come out here to baby-sit. You got to tell this boy that the boat is the thing we try to stay on. We live on the boat, not in the water."

Ody said, "What's the matter with you, Archie? There ain't no reason for you to be so touchy."

"Well, it scares me when somebody shoots overboard in the middle of the night. I'm not prepared for it. R.B. said he just jumped. And he wasn't swimming."

"Jesus, I swear."

And then I listened while their talk frittered away into accusation and defense and then on into laughter and comradery, and my mind slipped away, not far, to a picture of my daughter, to a picture of her riding in my arms in one of the Central Park carriages, and I thought maybe that is something of what children are for: to get you to do things you would never do on your own, things like clopping around the park pulled by an aged horse while your daughter tells a rushed, tedious story about the little boy at day school who pulls the ribbon from her hair, and then asks, "Daddy, what is sportswear?" Like all the returned dead I was quietly happy and sad at the same time, a little ashamed, baffled, and exhausted (as if death really was a journey you took, that wore you out, like a car trip to Milwaukee), and I wanted to be left alone to ponder on what had happened to me and where I had gone. Like a man who has lived a long time in a cave, I was unsure of the social exigencies, out of step with what went on around me, a little amused and slightly frightened; it didn't occur to me there might be someone to talk to, only that I would probably be interrogated, and I didn't know what to say. But R.B., my ex-brother-in-law, was a gentle man who understood these things—or, if he didn't, was at least natively kind—and he began in his sloppy, bustling way to ease a passage for me back into the life of these boatmen, who more than anything else were frightened by the presence of a man who had, for no reason they knew, stripped his clothes and dived straight down into the night-dark Gulf. It was that I'd stayed down that frightened them. Staying down gave me away.

"Let's get a little sleep, boys," R.B. said, and he indicated for Ody to help him as he began to raise me to my feet. "Can you stand?" Yes, I could, in a wobbly way. They helped me up and walked me aft. The grand V of Taurus, the Pleiades—all the late-summer constellations—were bright in the sky. In the east there was a pale glow along the horizon, like the lights of a distant city—moonrise. Ody switched the air pump off and the boat drifted back into its silence. The chipping of waves against the hull, the rusty clang of the buoy off the starboard bow, the creak of the hull as it settled and resettled into the bed of the sea were the noises now. What I'd done was somehow shameful and it put me at a disadvantage with these men. My action had reduced me—a grown man doing a childish thing—and I could feel as we made our way below deck the absence of what they withdrew from me; they didn't want to see any of this in themselves and so had to think of it as less than what they were, the action of someone not quite as capable or as brave. Oddly, I didn't mind. I was, after all, already a man apart.

I lay down in one of the forward bunks. R.B. pulled a thin blanket over me. I looked into his pale narrow face. "Did I bob up on my own, or did somebody go down and get me?"

"Archie did. He dived in after you."

"Caught you by the foot, goddamn it," Archie said as he cracked a beer. "It was total luck. I just ran into you. I went down and stretched out my hand and there your foot was, like a white mouse. You're a lucky man—or God's favorite, I don't know which."

I began to cry. It had nothing to do with being saved. Human love—we believe in it because it's sweet and there isn't anything else to believe in. But no matter what, it always ends badly. Fuck you, Bess, for giving up. Just fuck you. You can't ask me to please you anymore. You can't try to please me. One thousand miles—the distance between my Manhattan garage and your green nursery land—was not enough, but now, darling, I am finally out of range. Why did you not have me arrested? Why did you tell them at St. Vincent's that a mugger did this to you? Why, when I followed you to the hospital and lurked in the corridor with my hand covering the bruise you laced against the side of my head, why did you not point me out to them, why did you not cry *J'accuse,* there he is—arrest that man? They took you into the trauma room, took you behind a saffron curtain and worked on you. I could see your bare feet under the curtain; I could hear the doctor speaking to you, I could hear his laughter. *Isn't life strange, isn't it wild*—is that what he said to you? And what did you say to him? *Why* did you say to him—I could see your face (no matter the curtain), I could see your pale face lifted, see your gray eyes shining in your head—why did you say that you forgave me; why did you say to the doctor, *I forgave him a long time before he did this to me?* And why, deep in the night, am I pounding in my dream on my own door, why am I pounding on the door and calling my name *Buddy, Buddy;* and why do I never answer?

I raised myself on my elbow, and with my free, sea-wet hand I reached up and pulled R.B.'s face down to me and I kissed him on the lips. He pressed the back of his hand, his knuckles, against my shoulder, not quite to push me away, but not quite to let me in either. It didn't matter. There was nothing I could do to free myself from what I had set loose, I didn't expect forgiveness from him, or even understanding. I was liable for my actions, and I would pay. For just a second though, despite everything, I wanted to give something, something that mattered.

"This is already an unusual trip," Ody said.

"It's too crazy for me," Archie said. In the hazy, sulphurous light— the air seemed soaked in the sea—I watched him tip the can and drink hugely, and I thought, looking at his thick throat shudder, yes, that's it, that spark that pummels and kicks and enrages us—that's what we love, no matter what it's up to; just the fact of it, the presence of it, delights us; we can't help it. Then a blankness crawled over my body and took my head in its hands, and pressed me back into the night of sleep.

2. In the morning I had to talk them into staying out. Maybe I didn't have to, but when Archie said he thought it was best for us to head back in, I disagreed. I claimed everything was fine with me—I wasn't going to do anything foolish again—and it was silly to turn around now. They seemed relieved. It was, after all, their livelihood. Ody fried eggs and bacon, which he and Archie ate out of the pan, and then they went about their business rigging the dive. Nobody said anything about heading south to the reef. They didn't want to hear any more foolish tourist ideas about hunting for skeletons. The sun was molten glass on the water, shimmering and sparkling. There was a pile of white cumulus in the west, tall chimneys of stacked cloud reaching up to tremendous heights, not a speck of gray in them. The diving routine was simple: fire the pump, put on wet suits, take up the regulators attached to the long coils of black hose, find your rake and a couple of net sacks, adjust your mask, step over the side, and descend. Nobody mentioned my drowning.

Archie manned the pump and the line and Ody made the first dive by himself. The water was clear for the first twenty feet and then it clouded, became pearly from silt stirred by the current; I watched Ody descend slowly into it, watched him slide down like a man sliding down a rope; he never disappeared entirely, but after a while I could only make out the vague shape of him, a patch of darker gray in the milky silt. The sponging was like picking apples. He came up regularly carrying the filled sacks that Archie heaved over the side and spilled out on the afterdeck and the fantail. The sponges were large, dark brown and gold, a couple as yellow as goldenrod. As large, some of them, as basketballs—alive, animal—they were full of guts; Archie set us to work stomping and washing them, breaking the guts loose from the insides so they would drain out. It was a long, tedious procedure that had to be repeated several times. The sponges were firm, like flesh, and bits of shell were glued to them and there was a pliable but tough inner core. We stomped them in tennis shoes, treading the grayish guts out onto the deck, rinsing them with seawater forced through a hose.

R.B. hummed to himself, happy in the world of his mind. It pleased him, he said, to do a little manual labor. He worked in his white clothes with the trousers rolled up; the hair on his legs was as thick as animal pelt, and rusty, lighter than the hair on his head.

We spoke occasionally, but mostly we worked. The sun climbed high, turned white, seemed to stall. Wind skipped across the water. The sea built slowly. The wave crests were green, almost clear, breaking at their tops nearly into light, but the troughs were deep blue, bruised in the bottoms. The world was empty. Our talk was lazy, offhand, celebratory. For moments I was almost free, for moments there was almost no other world than this one, sea and sky, the white, tilting boat. R.B. offered small gifts from his world.

"Argentine," he said, handing me a small blond sponge.

"The country?"

"No. The adjective. Silvery. It's a word I love. I've put it in my dictionary."

I leaned back against the rail. The generator throbbed its breath song. Archie, sitting in the wheel chair, squinted out over the sea. He wore a long-visored cap pulled down over his eyes. His dark hair curled out from under the brim.

"Argentine sea?" I said.

"Probably not."

I said, "I've had this idea lately, tell me what you think."

"What is it?"

"I keep wondering about God. Do you think the only way to connect with God is through someone else?" Like all the drowned, I had become spirit-minded.

He looked at me and a small pale smile appeared on his face. "What do you think about that?"

"I've lost someone dear to me. I think she might have been my connection."

"Sentimental or spiritual?"

I laughed a quick, hollow laugh. "I can never tell."

"The desert fathers—St. Basil, St. Jerome, and those fellows—might disagree with you about needing someone else."

I lifted my foot off a grainy yellow sponge. It slowly reassumed its shape. "Maybe," I said, "it was the intensity, the degree, I mean, of their identification that drove them to the desert. Maybe they went out there to tone things down. Maybe the hermit life is only something that can come after."

"The proof that God exists is that we can imagine that he exists. I'm not sure the buddy system is necessary."

"You mean we make God up?"

"No. We can't imagine what isn't there."

"But can we imagine God?"

"Someone did. We talk about him, pray to him."

"But maybe that's just a figment."

"By figment you mean something that doesn't exist." He gazed off toward the bell buoy tottering in the slow swell. "That's an impossibility. If we can conceive it, in whatever form, it exists. The imagination can't draw off a vacuum."

I dashed water over the sponge. "Well, here's another one. If God takes no action in the world, then how can his existence matter?"

His white cuffs were stained with guts and grit. The sponges in his fine, narrow hands became objects of delicacy and importance, he turned them gently; even, pressing the guts out, his small foot seemed to be pressing out a soreness, like a parent massaging the stiff flesh of a sick child. He cocked his head and said, "I think it's possible to argue that God *does* take action, but even if he doesn't, that doesn't mean we aren't affected and are without obligation."

"How so?"

"Maybe it is similar to the way planets are affected by each other: by magnetism, by gravity. Maybe our names for the forces in the universe—those two, and the strong force and the weak force—are only our somewhat awkward designations of the characteristics of God. By studying the orbit of Uranus we discovered another planet beyond it. Maybe only in the shadow play, the respondent motion, can we know—physically—the motion and influence of a greater being."

"But isn't that saying we need someone else to notice it through?"

"Maybe anything will do, not just a person. Maybe a rock or a drop of water. Maybe that's why the world, which is so familiar to us, and which we use so carelessly, can sometimes, when it catches us unawares, just knock us out."

"At a given moment, anything will do."

He laughed his grainy, swallowed laugh. "At a given moment, it's all too much. Maybe *that's* the problem."

"Action," I said. "That'll save us."

"What?"

"Oh, you know—my old approach. *Get moving.*"

"But, unfortunately, we wear down. And what's looking for us can move too."

"What's going on on this planet?"

"I think it's one of God's small shops. A factory outlet."

"Thrift store maybe."

But the sun was just a ball of fire, white, out here in late July on the Gulf. Ody's head poked up among the small, flashy waves. He looked like a seal. Swimming sidestroke to the boat he trailed a green net bag of sponges. Archie shouted at him, making fun. In work the day became good. The men felt their strength, a sense of purpose. The muscles in Archie's stomach, as he bent down to hook the bag, looked like knife cuts in brown dough. Ody clung to the gunwale, resting, "That's it," he said, "I've cleaned the place out."

I raised my right hand to shake off grit and my hand was in Mexico; I saw beyond it not the Gulf but Bess buying an earthenware jug from an old man in a faded blue poncho. In her hand silver coins blinked. Lost to myself, I admired the draw of cloth against her thigh, the hard curve of her buttocks that were hard only in the looking, soft to the touch.

R.B. said, from another zone, "What we have to defend we don't believe in."

I didn't understand; I let it pass. Then I watched her climb a flight of white stone steps that raised narrowly against the side of a white building. Once we stood at the bedroom window watching our neighbor raise his tricolor over Manhattan. She said, leaning her shoulder against me, "It takes only that little bit—that flag—to make me love the world." I said, "My life is a fit I can't shake off." The flag snapped in the breeze, imitating gunshots.

I said, "Bess was the most creative sexual partner I've ever had."

He held a sponge to his nose, breathed in the inky, burned-metal smell of it. "I think she would be game for anything along those lines. She's a festive woman."

But no, I didn't remember her as festive. But then my memory couldn't be depended on. You make a movie, a story which in the factual world is clearly a lie. Mr. President, why did you build such a grand house for yourself? Are your dreams different from mine? Could I have a pardon?

We used to walk in Chinatown. Long walks that took all day. She was slow on her feet, she dawdled, she stopped in the middle of the sidewalk and looked up at the sky, gathering her thoughts; the crowd swept around her. I would look back and she would be standing there looking at me, still talking, waiting for me to turn around and listen to her. She would pick up things from the street-side vendor bins and walk off with them, not noticing that she had a papaya or a string of juju beads in her hand until the tense salesman woke her with his shouting. "Pay attention, girl," I would say, and she would smile in her hazy way, like someone who had just taken off her glasses, and apologize. "Look at this," she would say touching the yellow speckled back of a fish, "I've never seen anything like this in Florida," or she would bend down to peer into the small canvas-roofed sidewalk shop of a shoemaker who squatted among piles of brick-red soles and cloth uppers, sewing. Once she bought a turtle and brought it home, but its hissing frightened her, so she took a train out to Long Island and let it go in a field. "You can't make friends with everyone," she said in explanation, "but you *can* get out of their way." Her dark hair was so fine that strands of it would cling to her face, as if they were wet.

I said, "There was nothing she wouldn't do. It amazed me. I never expected it."

"Good to have surprise."

The words were in my mouth, but I didn't say them.

The day passed slowly over us, the workingman's day that ended at sunset. We had moved about the reef, traveling from ridge to ridge, sinking the anchor, Ody descending, occasionally Archie taking a turn, R.B. and I tromping sponges. In the late afternoon R.B. went up to the bow again and wrote in his notebook. I continued to work. The sponges piled up on the transom, on the deck. The boat wallowed in the sea. There's no such thing, D'Nel had said, as redemption. There's only pursuit. My life screamed in me.

3.   I lay in my bunk pressing the knuckles of my scarred right hand against the bulkhead. Everything was fleeing me. The boat rocked on the easy swells; it was dark, everyone was asleep. R.B. in the bunk below me snored fastidiously. I had filmed a scene once in which a man, trying to stay awake, poured scalding coffee on his hand. I could do that, but it was my mind that was going, not my body. D'Nel said it was possible to step right back through the whole evolved structure of the brain into a reptilian primitiveness. We haven't lost it, he said, it's still there, and not hard to find. My mind, my knowledge, my attempt—my agreement—to see the world in orderly, acceptable structures, lay in pieces around me. The gray starlight falling through the open companionway whispered of disaster. The raspy tick of a clock in the cabinet door was the chuck of tooth against bone. I saw the palm trees burning at Duc To, the rotor wash whipping a torn yellow shirt across the courtyard. Some people make it in this world. Some people don't—like my father who didn't make it; now it looked as if I wasn't going to either. I don't want to complain, but how did this come about exactly? D'Nel may be from another zone, but I'm human, I'm just a guy. I could make my life into a dark passage but it was still just a life. I liked Shredded Wheat for breakfast, raspberries with cream, a good porterhouse seared just right. As a child I'd helped string Christmas lights in the big holly tree in Nancy Wash Park, I'd sung carols with my friends. My mother baked Tollhouse cookies; she drew a picture of a sailing ship on my Cub Scout scrapbook. On her dresser she kept two magnolia leaves that had been sprayed with silver paint.

I was forty-two years old and I knew nothing. God, how many men had said that? Life goes on. *There is no way to stop it.* Could I be forty-two thinking this? R.B., wake up and give me a definition. What does this mean, R.B., *time's passage,* our names scratched on a rock? I can't be the only one who's dying, I can't be the only one who knows he's soon going to vanish forever. Oh, but the old don't mind, they're tired and ready. Still, some resist. My father hated his life. Stroke took him down, but it was as if the stroke was his payoff for a pact he'd made: *I trade you my addled life for this short death.* Sell out—that was the message he spoke to me. It was the only thing he could think to do. But it didn't work. It's just breath we want, one more breath. Nothing is beyond us in our attempt to get that. I will kneel before you and drink your piss if you will just let me live a little longer. But if life is the god, what of death? And then I saw my father in the narrow hospital bed, saw his face in the last days when the anguish and defeat had left it. Let me go, he said, I'm ready. It's good there, he said, everything will be all right. I hated him; it seemed one more surrender, one more giving up and going along with the big boys. Daddy, fight this thing. Resist. Bess, Bess, don't give in.

She wouldn't press charges. I was so twisted with hatred and anger that I thought her refusal to prosecute was just another ploy to humiliate me. Charge me with something, I screamed—fight me. But she wouldn't. I'll take the money, she said, I'll take the money and I'll go on with my life without you, and that will be that. You didn't love me, she said. I raised my hand against her (we were on a street corner; she was on her lawyer's arm; her hair was wet with rain) and she stepped back, fright in her eyes. That's why I tried to kill you, I shouted, because you accuse me of that. But it's true, she said, you know it's true. I lunged at her, but her lawyer, a beefy fellow in a chesterfield coat, caught me by the arm. He spun me around and pinned me against a railing. Walk away down the street, Bessie, he said; I'll meet you at the place. What place? I cried. Where will you meet her, asshole? Take it easy, Buddy, he said, holding me tight, it'll cost you if you come apart. The slanting gray rain fell on us. The dark buildings rose in tiers; it was like in a black-and-white movie. What will it cost me? I cried. What can you charge me for this? He said, You'll have to spend the rest of your life working for her. Near us, at the curb, a glossy woman in a sealskin coat urged her Pomeranian to take a shit. "Do your business," she said, "do it for Mama." I gave up. Okay, I said, you win. You sure? Yes. He let me go; he shook my hand; he hurried away down the street. It was the only time in my life I've been in that position that I didn't hit the guy.

I saw Celest's reflection before I saw Celest. I was standing in a doorway in SoHo, arguing with Van about the changes in the new movie—fresh disaster—when I saw her. Saw the wet cap of blond hair, the archaic profile, saw the small, sharp-knuckled hand touch the point of the jaw. I guess it was the hesitation, the slight shy momentary indecision I saw there in the fair rinsed beauty of her, shining on the dark plate glass of the Raisonne Gallery—it was a movie beauty of gesture and enlargement—and so, without explanation to Van—*Hold on a second*—I darted out of the doorway and approached her. I said, My name is Buddy Drake and I live around here and I can tell you that everything in that store is overpriced. Is it, now? she said.

Well, the truth is, there is no such thing as a casual encounter, and it's also true that we often don't want a new thing as much as we want assurance that the new thing is the same as the old. Much of our joy in the world comes through its helplessly repeating itself. She raised her hand to her ear and tugged at the small red lobe, and though I only half recognized it then, it was a gesture of my mother's, and thus dear to me, and familiar. I said, I live down here, and I can tell you are a stranger; perhaps you will allow me to direct you.

She said, I have lived in New York all my life.

Ah, I said, just as I suspected: a master of camouflage.

I'm not looking to be picked up.

It would be my pleasure to buy you a drink.

Why do you talk like a beggar?

I'm directing a movie. It's about beggars.

I don't think you are telling me the truth.

You see that man over there? The burly, bald fellow in the doorway?
He can vouch for me.

He's your parole officer?

My keeper perhaps, but I haven't done jail time; not yet.

I wouldn't mind.

Ah.

Yes.

Yes?

Yes.

What it was, what was to come, was talk. For a long time we didn't
make love. And it was Van who saved me, benign in his bearish coat,
fond with his droopy eyelids and his sorrowful mouth and his deference.
She told me later that when she saw him she thought that I couldn't
be dangerous to have such a sweet man in tow. She redesigned houses,
she told me, took something old and used and transformed it into
something new. It's that people love it when they can experience
something new in the same old circumstances, she said. They pay me
a lot of money to do that for them. I loved for her to take me through
the houses in talk, to walk me room by room through the palaces of
Manhattan where tables gleamed like violins and the sugary light was
heaped around the ornate golden feet of a decoupage sideboard, and
through a half-open door you could see a pitcher of orange juice on
a glass table, red silk sheets wadded in a corner. I loved for her to let
me spy. Something in me was so wounded now, so hurt, that I only
wanted to look. We never lived together. Even after we married—in
the flowery living room of the house her father left her—I continued
to live in my garage, commuting as it were to her house, arriving hoarse
and demented for the weekend, when she would throw open the upstairs
windows to let the light and the rain in, let the sneaky smells of
Manhattan and the shouts of joy and pain in. I was riding an old success,
about to spin off the rim of it, but for a time it looked as if I knew
what I was doing. I would continue making movies, she would renovate
houses, we would grow old together.

At night behind a yellow paper screen, her shadow undressed. In an
amber light she moved in flowing yellow to my side. She bent down
and kissed me on the lips. Her hair drifted over my face. If beyond her

supple, slender body I saw other shapes move in the shadows, for a time they did not frighten me, for a time I could look calmly into the dim recesses and not be terrified.

Her breasts were small and stiff, unblemished, the thin nipples only one shade darker than the skin. She took my penis shyly into her mouth. It is through another's love that we come to love our bodies. I have seen it, the awed grave regard, the tenderness. I sank, as one might sink through his own reflection into a ferny pool. I licked the bitter sweat from under her arms. She nicked me with the blade and drank my blood. Our faces glistened.

Now, she said, let's do what the adults do. No one can stop us. Put yourself inside me.

There was blood on the sheets. The white of her eye was red. Tell me a story, I said. All right, she said—listen. *He pulled me by my legs under the water. I could see the surface, I could see the oak branch like a long crooked arm hanging over the surface. He pulled me down into the darkness. He pinned me in the mud. He drowned me in his body.*

In the shadows of the upstairs room, shapes moved; I heard a voice speaking quietly to itself; a small, knowing laugh. D'Nel, I whispered, come in.

Then, like a distant rumor in a time of war, the child entered our lives. My movie work steadily failed. I made a picture the critics hated, no one went to see it. I made another and the same thing happened. I mortgaged the garage, I cashed my securities, and made another picture, this time attempting to reproduce not only the story line, but the violent call and response of my first movies, the shadowy undefeatable figure that moved across the landscape of small towns and back roads charming and destroying the citizens, the clash of wills, the dance of good and evil, the antic nihilism (a summary, I guess, a series of quotations), that the distributor (a studio I had once competed with that itself was only a broker) refused for a year to release and then only agreed to distribute as part of a horror double bill for the drive-ins. It was embarrassing the way people avoided me, it was embarrassing when they ran into me how solicitous they were, as if I had a major illness—you don't have any idea!—the way some earnestly offered suggestions, the way, even, they were glad the few times I got drunk and spilled my guts, moaned and raged in somebody's living room—glad once, not twice—embarrassing the way some began to suggest that I change my focus—*change my focus?*—try teaching maybe, go to work for someone else, even sell the studio (which was only me, sometimes Van, and the name, Thief Productions), that I write a play, act, go into business, take a vacation, try therapy, exercise, eat vegetables, go to bed early, move to Europe, find a hobby. I said, I have discovered that the story the world is telling me will go on even when I am not there, and this alarms me. I don't know yet how to put this on the screen, but it is what I am working on. We don't understand, my friends said, and smiled and made suggestions. I dreamed of bears pulling apples from a tree in a mountain orchard, I dreamed of a tree swarming with bears like flies on meat and in the dream I could smell the sweet burst fruit and the blowing green grass under the tree and the sweet stink of bear shit, but I could not find myself in the dream and could not understand myself as tree or bear or fruit or high-flown eye simply looking. I walked the floor at night, alone in SoHo or in the sitting room next to our bedroom on the Upper East Side; I sat at a small Louis Quatorze table and wrote long lists of what I loved in the world, listing them by senses: all the smells, the sights, the sounds I loved; I wrote down the names of friends, wrote the names of towns I had lived in or passed through, I wrote vernacular scenes and scenes of exposition and memory; I wrote a short history of my life and then a history, in the form of a list, of my family, following the journey backward down the Mississippi and up the Ohio and on eastward through the wild woods to Philadelphia and Manhattan, across the Atlantic to the crofts of Scotland and the ruddy, bleak Isle of Skye where my people first came to themselves on earth, unimperial Celts without wealth or power, tree worshipers, rock worshipers, sea worshipers; stooped, sooty folk who moved in weariness and ignorance across a stark landscape. And as I wrote I saw the simple, incidental lives of my forebears, I saw how the days stretched forth in their unchangeableness, I saw how a man could come to praise a tree, marvel at a fish disturbing the surface of a stream, a season, saw that it was in the permanence of things, their apparent ability to endure forever, that we discovered the miracle of the world, that is to say the moment when there is a small flash of light in the trees that is only the light of the sun streaking the back of a maple, and how this bit of light, this small red stone polished by running water, this dragonfly wing hanging in a spider's web, could take on an immanence, an elasticity, a kinesis, that if it was not in fact God was from God, was *of* God, and how this knowledge, that was not knowledge any more than the surge of blood in the body is knowledge but was something more akin to sensation, to movement itself, could cause a man to place the actions of his life above themselves, to give them greater meaning. I saw this possibility, this response, as a natural consequence of routine, of the roll of seasons and tide, and saw how it is only the *will* of man, his ability to choose and pursue choice, that brought change or the illusion of change, that what we had done since, that what we had piled up in heaps that became buildings and ships and stockpiles of weapons, was simply an expression of an original—an inherent—tendency, the edge, the single hair that separated us from the world around us—that was, after all, still living in Eden, if Eden was, first of all, an arrangement of *unhindered* communication—so that what we had created, or had assisted in the creation of, was not something apart from us or in any way against the grain of our natural movement, but was in fact inevitable and necessary, and so beyond any designation as good or evil; simply was. I saw how we lived by invocation, by a conjury (that was not conjury, was not magic, but was in fact a calling forth, as one would call a dog) based on a purposeful forgetting that nonetheless drew forth as one drawing up an anchor chain inevitably draws forth the original, fenestrated, single-cell advocate, the moment just before the explosion of consciousness, the infinite though unchangeable, particular though unmeasurable point or incident of our creation—so that, it seemed to me as I bent over the polished, lemon-smelling table, I could turn my hand any way I pleased, I could do, I mean, anything I could conceive of doing, without it for a single instant departing from the channel of our original being and meaning; so that everything that was was good, was necessary, was inevitable, was, in that sense—as an action of continuity based on an action of continuity based on a continuity—everlasting.

And for a while it seemed that the passage was all. The lockstep march up the eons from mossy Scotland to this place, this well-upholstered room in Manhattan, U.S.A., the continuance, no matter how battered or wrong-headed, was all.

My mind grazed on the night. I saw my father sitting in his rocking chair under the pear trees in our backyard, father who could be tricked out of anything, who was lied to and stolen from by his employees, by the barge men and the river captains; a man who, even as a young man, would rather lean back among his fellows and tell tales of his childhood on the grassy banks of the big river than make something for himself in the world. I saw the warehouses filled with junk that he would rather dream about than sell, that in his mind became repositories for a strange and beautiful ransom that could light the heart of a king but which was, in fact, only stacks of bunk beds and washbasins torn from junked ships and boxes of battleship paint rotting in their cans. He would make a deal, he said, he would make a deal like no deal anyone had seen before; he would—and he did—trade ten thousand number-two washtubs to the Mexican National Militia for a hundred tons of hemp which he would sell to a mill in Ohio for credit to purchase the mineral rights on nine hundred acres of desert scrub in southern Arizona which he could then trade for the crawfish harvest on Singletary Island, Louisiana, which would finance a half-share purchase of a nightclub in New Orleans, which was two weeks away from being burned down by the other half-owner, a Mafia underling with a mistress he was trying to pay for, who, wisely and unbeknownst to my father, had arranged the insurance in the mistress's name only. So the baroque deals converted from gold to lead. My father was always surprised. What now, Scotty, his friends would laugh, what have you got going this time? It was always something spectacular, some tottering circus giant of a deal that any moment would lose its footing and come crashing through the roof. He never learned, my father, he never learned a thing. Having read Shakespeare and the Bible, the *Decameron,* Chaucer and the fables of La Fontaine, he believed the world an arena of will and portentous meaning, one in which emotion and outlandish acts could reveal the true heart of things. Sometimes he saw himself as a pirate, an adventurer, free trader on the ancient banks of the Great River, passing goods to travelers who would use them to open up the dark wilds of the world.

I believe he saw each pile of junk as a treasure from the dragon's lair that he had somehow made off with, that he would sow like Jack's beans to make a new world grow. He lived in dreams, and as I grew older—the child turning away—the dreams began to take the place of acts, so that his deals more and more often became deals of the mind, grand enterprises that he made stories out of to tell his friends, but which never, in the real world of grit and money, materialized.

I loved him crazily, and so I hated him. Even as a kid, lost, it seemed to me, on the city-tangled banks of the Mississippi, a child, it seemed to me, without any real home, I had assessed my father and found him wanting. I was frightened by his detachment, by his failure to *engage* the world and draw out something enduring from it. Even as a child I raged against him, even as a child I argued with him, accusing him of foolishness, of laziness, of stupidity. To me, born on the banks of the Mississippi, life *went somewhere,* it turned the bend carrying its cargo of supplies and perishables, it rolled on *toward something,* toward a place where men could make use of what was offered to them, where real exchanges were made, where you gave something and got something back and were richer for it.

I left at fifteen, but even then it had already been years since I began my journeying, since I had begun my short and longer trips upriver and down, my walks away from the family hearth, my bus rides to Willawette and Big Crossing, to the old family compound in Bar Etienne, where my grandmother and my aunts told me stories of the times when we were travelers, when we lit out down the Ohio for the territories following the tide of the river westward.

I had just returned from Bar Etienne one evening in my fifteenth year, having ridden the train all afternoon, I had just walked into the front hall when the phone rang and my father's foreman, a small Black Irishman from Donegal, asked to speak to my mother. From the fear in his voice I knew that something was wrong. As my mother spoke to him her face turned white and she clutched her plush, brocaded chest. She dropped the phone; I picked it up and rigidly, not wanting to hear, asked Pricey McCann what the matter was. "It's your father," he said. "He's on the Marquette Bridge." I didn't get it. His car had stalled? I had a wild picture of him running through rush-hour traffic. "No," Pricey said, choking, "yer papa's bound to jump."

I looked at my mother. She had slumped into the chair beside the phone table. She leaned over her knees kneading her hands. "Tell yer mama she better come quick," Pricey said.

"All right," I numbly answered.

The late-afternoon light pierced the slender hall windows in splintery beams that illuminated dark red patches on the old rug and climbed halfway up the wall, almost to the portrait of my grandfather stiff in his mercantile clothes. Beside a jade plant on the table opposite, one of my father's pipes, black as an object chipped out of tar, lay on top of a library copy of one of Forester's sea stories, a boy's book that my father who should have been home by now, who should have already come through the door whistling one of the arias that enchanted him, would read with marveling relish tucked into his bedroom wing chair, hardly bothering with dinner or my mother or me, launching directly, with an almost elegant lack of hesitation, into the next dream world he preferred to life on the planet.

"We're on our way, Priccy," I said into the phone and hung up.

I touched my mother on the shoulder. "Come on, Mama," I said, "we've got to go."

She looked up at me with furious, pale eyes. "Go and do what?"

"We've got to go and get Daddy."

"I don't want to," she said, a sudden pleading in her voice. "I've got business to take care of."

"Come on, Mama. Get your hat."

I ran outside, down to the corner taxi stand, and got a cab. Through piled clouds the color of doves the slender orange rays of sunset streamed. The air smelled of creosote and burning leaves.

When I got back my mother was standing in the hall with her hat on, a baffled look in her face. "Come on, Mama," I said.

"What is going on?" she said. "I am so busy."

"Come on."

We rode in the back of the cab through clamoring traffic. My mother looked out the window, her smooth face sad and bewildered, her small mouth gathered in a childish petulance, as if we were all doing something to her against her will that she couldn't stop. I took her hand. It was dry and cold. My mind raced, something from deep in the center of my chest dragging me, pulling me, like someone attached to a rope. The evening light falling on buildings and stoops and on the uncovered heads of passersby had a tangibility like snow or rain; the broad yellowed patch of it on the side of the Armistead Insurance building had a permanence like paint or like the color of the brick itself, so that for a second it seemed as if we were racing through a landscape that through will or exhaustion had fixed itself in permanency, like a museum reconstruction. I didn't think of my father; my mind soared above and past him, like one of the river gulls, rising in the currents of air, so that in my mind I looked far downriver, in the direction of ancestral Bar Etienne where the barley and the oat fields were crowded with light, and other lives went on quietly in ignorance. Then rage began to employ itself inside me, growing until it stood like a burning stick of metal in the center of my body. The cabdriver's neck was stippled with purple boil scars. His black hair was ruffled above the scars like the short feathers around a chicken's ass.

I reached forward and grabbed the seat beside his shoulder. He flinched. "Let's go," I said, "let's go, goddamn it."

The cabbie, who was a man I knew, a local fellow, leaned his chest against the wheel, as if to get away from me. "There's a lot of traffic," he said.

"I don't care," I cried. "Make the fucking car move."

"Buddy!" my mother whispered.

I reached over his shoulder and beat the horn with my fist.

"Easy, Buddy," he said, "we'll get there." He began to wave at the other cars, as if he were saluting them.

"Come on."

There was a small crowd on the bridge; policemen in the street moved the traffic along, preventing anyone from stopping. One lane was closed. In it were parked several police cars and an ambulance. The cabbie let us off down the slope behind the last police car and we walked through the crowd. My mother clutched herself in her arms, whispering a prayer, the words of which seemed to fly over the railing. The spidery, rusted struts and spars of the bridge hung crankily in the air above us, and it seemed to me that the roadway swayed, slowly in a large and almost peaceful rhythm, under our feet. The rage began briefly to freeze into a chill so that I became aware of my body under my clothes, of the denseness of my flesh and its awkwardness. I couldn't see my father.

Below the bridge two small white police boats held their place against the current. Men in dark jackets stood on the decks looking up. The rage, the anger, snarled and stalled; behind it a sadness, a grief, a desire to make this stop came on. I wanted to call out, not to my father, but to the crowd, to reassure them. My mother hurried along beside me, her head down, breathing harshly, as one called beyond her capacity to face inquisitors. We reached the back tier of onlookers and for just a moment we hesitated there, for just one moment neither of us willing to push through, and for one moment I saw the small human inadequacy of us, the timid, shy faltering that had always been at the center of my family, that enraged me, that shamed me and drove me to break free. I thrust my shoulder hard at the nearest back, and clutching my mother by the arm, pushed through. "We're the family," I said to a young policeman who stepped forward to stop us.

"Could you wait here a minute?" the policeman said and hurried off to find a guide for us. My mother clutched my arm. "Oh, Buddy," she said, "what is this to us?"

I didn't answer her because beyond the burly khaki back of the policeman in front of me I could see my father. He sat on the rail facing the water, his feet bent under resting on the rail below, his hands clasped in his lap. He leaned slightly forward, almost teetering. Near him, apart from the crowd, a few men stood by; two men, one with a hemp rope tied around his waist, wearing a gray fedora, the other a policeman in shirtsleeves, stood closer. The roped man was talking to my father. His voice was quiet, and soft; I couldn't hear the words, but I could see his mouth move and I could see the concentration in his face, in the burred, gathered brows, in his eyes that never left my father's face.

A man came up to us, took us by the arm, and moved us up near the coatless policeman. The policeman shook my hand quickly and strongly and nodded to my mother. "William," I heard the roped man say gently to my father, "your family is here."

My father turned his head slightly but he didn't look at us. "I'm sorry," he said. "I'm so very sorry."

Small and thin, he looked like a boy perched on a ballpark rail. Beneath him and beyond him, the brown, featureless river pressed southward, quietly, steadily urging boats and barges, debris, scum, a large slick patch of oil the size of a school yard, away from this place. Breeze murmured in the bridge struts, whistling in the wires. Behind us traffic honked as workers rolled steadily toward home. "William," the roped man said, "they are here because they love you. They don't want you to leave them."

The policeman, a tall man with a prominent jaw, touched my mother lightly on the arm. "He's been there for two hours. Someone passing by recognized him, so we called his place of business. It might help if you spoke to him."

My mother ignored him. She pulled her beaded gray sweater around her and looked away down the bridge span. Policemen moved about, keeping people back—the few there were—moving quietly, almost reverently, like men in a hospital. The policeman leaned closer to my mother. He was thick-shouldered, dark-skinned, hatless. As he leaned between us I could smell his after-shave and the frank, bitter odor of his body. My mother leaned away from him. The man said, "He needs to know there's still something here for him. People forget that sometimes, they get lost a little bit and forget that they have a family and friends and a life here that's worth something to the people around them."

My mother stamped her foot. "I don't know anything about this," she said. The man gave her a long look, at first quizzical, then somber, then slightly sad. He sighed. In the east the sky had darkened, the clouds merging with the coming night; westward a fading orange glow shimmered along the seams of the grape-colored cumulus; the city hung between the bridge and the extinctions of night like a dark, toothed facade, an erection of sticks and paper above which smoke swirled; the air around us was bright. "William," the roped man said, "it's a beautiful evening, fair and free. I know you can remember other beautiful evenings in your life. There's nothing like the midwestern sky."

The policeman rubbed his arms. "I'll speak to him," I said.

"Thank you," the policeman said. He scratched his forehead. The roped man shot him a glance, looked at me. "William," he said softly, "your son is here."

The shirtsleeved policeman guided me closer. I was only a few feet away from my father, just to the side and a little behind the roped man. None of us were quite close enough to touch him. I looked down at the water. It was far away; it looked like a dark brown floor. Half a dozen gulls soared in the middle distance, rising and falling through their own harsh cries. "Daddy," I said, "Daddy, it's Buddy."

My father stared straight ahead, upriver. The wind ruffled his thin, brindly hair. He looked lost, frail, tired, someone without a clue. I felt the quick spur of my rage, but it dissolved. There was a tightness in my chest, for a second I couldn't catch my breath. The roped man touched my shoulder. "It's all right," he said, "we're just up here talking. We're all here; everything's going to be all right. William," he said, "your son's come all this way. He loves you."

No matter what in my adolescent bed I had dreamed of gallantry, it was gone now. This small, beaked man perched on the rail of St. Louis's highest river bridge was my father and I didn't know how to save him. "Daddy," I said, "Mama's making corn chowder for dinner. Won't you come home with us?"

The roped man leaned near my ear. "That's good," he said, "let him know you need him. He needs to know he's needed."

The crowd seemed close but totally apart. I saw a man pat the top of his head, lean down to speak to a woman next to him. The woman smiled, stretched up on her toes, and kissed the man on the cheek. My mother had stepped back, only a step or two, but enough; I could see how frightened she was, see that she wanted only to be outside all of this, a stranger to it, called here by mistake. She clutched the sweater to her chin, stretched her neck as if she wanted to separate her head from the rest of her. How I hated her. From above us came the hard, indifferent cries of the gulls. "Daddy," I said, "we've driven all the way across town here, I mean you had the car, we had to take a cab because Pricey called us and said you were out here on the bridge about to jump. Please don't jump, Daddy; I don't know what to say, but please don't do this. You got Mama and me scared to death." I stretched my hand out and took a step forward, I stepped past the roped man to touch my father. As I did so, without looking at me, my father bent slightly forward, as if he were about to spit between his legs, and pushed off the rail. "Ah, God," the roped man cried, springing after him. He caught my father around the waist as he fell, as they both fell. There was a surge toward us. The rope held. The short-sleeved policeman knocked me aside as he grabbed it. "You got him, Stoney," he cried. "You got him, hold on."

I watched them draw my father up. Slowly, hand over hand, they hauled him back into the world. The roped man—Stoney—clung to him; he had his arms around my father's chest; his legs were scissored around my father's legs. They drew him up; hands reached out, and they eased the two men over the rail. They propped my father against a stanchion and two men held him by the arms. For a moment I thought they were going to hit him, the men's faces were so red and grave. A man in a blue suit, a doctor, gave my father a shot and then they unfolded a canvas stretcher and lay my father on it. Someone put a cigarette between his lips. The roped man, free now, knelt beside my father and spoke to him. He took the cigarette, shook ashes off, and put it again in my father's mouth. He patted my father on the shoulder. Then four men picked the stretcher up and they loaded it into the back of the ambulance. The sky had darkened; in the west a band of deep red tilted toward the darkness of clouds and the darkness of night. The ambulance door swung shut. The roped man patted the door, as someone would pat the side of a good horse. He turned and looked across the crowd at me. It seemed his eyes were asking who I was, who we were, what had brought us to this place.

The Passage: life eternal simply because life is ongoing. Movement, in other words—our eternity.

The dark shapes moved about me. Flickers of light on the sea, a recombinant genesis, the world reinventing itself as it went, reliving its original creation. Sound: whisk, small slap of waves, chuckle, drain of sea, creak of boat, the soft helpless snores of my fellow travelers. Sight: darkness compromised by moonlight falling through the open doorway, falling onto the open hands of Bess Appel. *Come with me, Buddy.* Lifting her hands she shows me the stars, the diamonds in the crossed lines of her palms. *These are angels,* she whispers. I believe her. I would rise, I would throw off the thin sheet, rise, and follow her—Bess, I will go with you this time—but she fades, the white body fades. *Bess.*

My mind grazes on the night. . . .

Celest said: Once during my first marriage a robber broke into the house and tied my family up. It was terrible, she said, you don't realize how terrified you can get until something like that happens. My husband had two small children from another marriage and the burglar took us all, my husband and me and the children, and he put us in the living room and he tied us up. He sat us on the sofa—it was orange silk—and he said he was going to rob us and then he was going to kill us. He was a thick, strong-looking man with knobby shoulders and a thin, grim mouth. He was very calm. I could see his reflection in the windows, bobbing in his dark clothes, and I thought how did he get in here? It was like grit, poison, cancer in the system. My mind didn't want to understand. He tied us up, and he pointed a small black gun at us and he began to rummage through the rooms, he began to put our belongings into two pillowcases, I remember, two pillowcases that were pink with small peach-colored flowers embroidered on the hems. I wanted to hold the children but my hands were tied, I leaned down and kissed Jason on the temple, I told Isabella to sit close. They had begun to cry.

My husband, who was a strong man himself, was very angry. I could see it in his eyes. As soon as the man left the room, searching out valuables, he began to work at the knots that held his hands. He grunted, bared his teeth, bent forward across my knees as if his stomach hurt him, his hands jerking and twisting at the knots. We all understood what he was doing, but we were silent, we understood, we didn't say anything. I looked across the room, my eyes were still hazy with sleep; I thought, I have to get rid of that breakfront over there, I mean it was as if I saw the imperfection of things, the way they didn't quite fit together, and everything in me, like a bound heart beating, strained to rise and set things right. My husband fought in the ropes, he fought, he and all of us sitting there, any moment the robber about to appear again to shoot us; and then he was free, his hands were free. He whispered to us to stay quiet and then he leaned back on the sofa. Suddenly I was terrified for him, I wanted to throw myself down and beg the robber to spare us; I didn't want my husband to do anything. I would have jumped up, I would have jumped up, not to save us, but to stop the next thing, to stop the world moving in this direction—sometimes you can do that—to throw myself on the tracks, to cry *Look at me* so this man wouldn't look at the others, maybe he would forget the others, maybe they could get quietly up and go back to bed and pull the covers up over their heads and sleep and wake up in the morning to sunlight and toast in the kitchen—but I didn't do anything, it was only a thought after all, just a coil uncoiling for a moment and then coiling again, just nothing, so that when he did come back, when the robber slunk back into the living room with his pillowcase—my pillowcase—over his shoulder—I could hear silverware clanking, the rustle of jewelry—I didn't say anything; I pressed my shoulder against the boy and I looked a silence at both children, at the girl especially, who was a nervous child. And then we waited, I knew we were waiting, my husband was waiting for the moment when the robber moved close—his feet were still tied—when the robber moved close enough, and for a second I thought of us walking in the park, walking through a little grove of ginkgo trees near the Sheep Meadow, and how the buttery little hand-shaped leaves were all over the ground, so many of them that the ground was yellow with them, bright yellow but the trees still full, it was so odd, as if even as they denuded themselves the trees made new leaves, like something they were sneaking in on us, new yellow leaves, bright as paint in the trees and covering the ground at the same time, the children running through them up ahead—thinking this without thinking it, you know, the thought just coming into my mind; and then the robber came close, he reached his hand out to touch my hair, I could see in his eyes that he wanted me, that he demanded me, that as far as he was concerned I was foregone and gone. For one second his eyes locked on mine, they seemed to go click and locked on my eyes and I could see that in his mind he was stepping through me, stepping through my sex and through my body to the other side where for a few seconds he would be all right, where everything was peaceful, and I thought, *Isn't it odd, fidelity won't save me, isn't it odd . . .* thinking—but then my husband leapt, my husband exploded from the sofa and he grabbed the man and threw him down—the gun, the pillowcase went flying—and he held the man down with his knees and he beat him in the face, he beat him as the man cried out, as he screamed in terror—I will always remember, he cried *Don't hurt me, please don't hurt me*—but it was too late for the robber, my husband stopped him with his hands, he grabbed the man by the throat and he choked him, he choked him there on the floor in front of us, in front of the children who were screaming too and me, he choked the man until he was dead.

This is what I remember, the story she told me in the sitting room as she lay on the paisley chaise while I wrote it down in my notebook at the table across the room. She was naked and the soft amber light of the lamp on the table beside her seemed a warm liquid that she lay in. As she spoke she slowly kneaded her breast, massaging it like a knotted muscle she was easing. She was pregnant then and her large smooth belly with its distended navel seemed to me a bud about to open. She never seemed more a part of the natural world than at that moment, a beast or a flower, a river rising in spring against its banks, a tree blossoming. The movies spun away from me that spring, they receded from me, dwindling into a murky distance that I could not run fast enough to penetrate. I was exhausted by my losses, and oppressed by that general male uselessness that overtakes expectant fathers, the understanding that comes to them that they are bystanders, that the role they play in the stride forth of creation is a small one, almost silly. Her body—so it seemed to me—had become a world to her, a world in which she wallowed as a fish wallows in the sea. New purplish veins had risen in her legs like stinging seams, and her darkened nipples ached as they filled with blood and milk; sometimes she had headaches, and sometimes, she said, her mind seemed so far away, or so deeply inside her, that she would come to out of that interior wilderness to discover herself standing at the kitchen window, lost, as one only that moment initiated into the wobbling world where the sycamores budding in the garden were brisk with intellect and the streaked sparrow pecking at a bit of grime on the top of the wall seemed in some way a part of her, not grandly, but simply, as her fingernails were and the ends of her hair; she would stand there at the window, for hours it seemed to her, watching the bright tide of sunlight move slowly across the garden floor, waiting, as one might wait, so she said, for a passing migration of butterflies. . . .

She said: But here is what is strange. My husband killed the man, and the house, the peace of our home, was broken. Policemen, investigators, reporters invaded the house, they filled the rooms, measuring, photographing, asking questions, reassuring us, directing us. I said to my husband, Death isn't the mother of beauty, it's the mother of confusion, it's the mother of mess; I was trying to comfort him because I could see that he needed comfort. My heart went out to him, I saw that he had reached past some kind of boundary, he was troubled, something had happened to him that the investigators and the reporters couldn't help him with; he had saved his family, but he had killed a man in doing it, and that fact, that death at his hands, had changed him.

It was strange, so odd, she said. I don't think a woman would feel what my husband felt. I don't think a woman would worry that she had killed someone to save her family. I don't think a woman would think twice about it. Death is natural to us, and it is natural for us to resist it as best we can. We don't have that kind of morality, the morality that would drive a man into silence. The lives of my children were more important than any burglar's life, a burglar was nothing against the lives of my family, my family's continuing. But the fact that my husband had killed someone separated him. He began to see himself as a man different from others; he had experienced something other men hadn't, and this frightened him. It threatened the stability of his world which was based on identification with other men. Though men are aggressive and they are constructed—they talk all the time about how it is their way—to go forth and hunt, they are bound by their community much more than we are; and, I think, the erosion, the displacement of that community unhinges them. He had bad dreams; he tumbled crying out from nightmares in which once more he rolled on the floor choking the robber. He woke up sweating, whimpering, he clung to me like a whipped child. But this was only at night. During the day he was sullen and scornful, and anger grew in him that he cast off at us; it was dirty, like slop, and it stung us, it frightened us. The children were becoming like little dogs that got beaten too often; they cringed, they didn't want to come home; the boy said, *You aren't my daddy anymore,* and my husband slapped him and then broke into tears and sat down on the sofa and stared at his hands.

One day as I was walking up Lexington I saw him in a restaurant window, sitting alone as he watched the wind climb through some sycamores, and he looked as if even in the placid enclosure of glass and a restaurant's benign furniture, he sought some simpler, redemptive resolution, and I remembered how once, when we were first married, and I was the frightened one, afraid of my sudden family, afraid I was a woman of too limited capacity to be wife and mother, he brought home one day, like a wild, delighted little boy, a branch of plum blossoms, a blossoming branch, and gave it to me, not a bouquet or an arrangement of flowers but a whole branch torn from some tree that was the living expression of his love for me. . . .

I watched her across the room, her slow, white, pelagic body turning grandly in the lamplight, and I thought how light, how all light is theatrical, how it is proscriptive, containing the potential and the promise of drama, that it is light, not darkness, that haunts us, that it is the stepping out of, the stepping through, the coming to rest in light that isolates our moment in time, how the metaphor is *bringing forth,* is *birth,* is *apotheosis . . . ;* and as I thought this, my time in Dakota began to come back to me, I saw a movement, I saw a girl or a young woman leaning out a window as she fired a rifle at a running figure, and I saw that this game, this impossible, unbelievable game, this girl or woman firing a .22 rifle at the dark-clothed figure of a lithe, laughing man running from light to shadow to light, was the proof, was the embodiment of what I knew about the world. I saw her line up on the scuffed windowsill the brass shell casings, I heard her call out to the running man—gay, death-defying cries—and heard the man call back to her, laughing, and saw the background of brilliant slopping sea, and the grassy islands far out in the sea, shining like the tousled, sunken heads of giants—and this was not Dakota, but this man sprinting under the mimosas was the man I met there, this D'Nel Boyd, this arch-prophet. . . .

I said, What then? What happened then?

She said: I tried to comfort him, but I couldn't. He would wake up in the middle of the night and walk around the house—like you do sometimes—just hopelessly agitated, going from book, to television— I'd hear the channels switching, big smeared dollops of sound—to cooking—he'd bake brownies—to rummaging, to silence. The silences scared me most. I would lie in the bed listening for him and I wouldn't hear anything, and I would wonder what he was doing, and after a while I would begin to fear the worst so I'd get up and look for him. I'd find him in one of the third-floor rooms staring out the window. It was winter then, the trees against the back wall were bare, and he'd be standing at the window looking out at them. I would come and stand beside him, I'd touch his shoulder—it was like touching wood—and I'd look out with him. I wanted to feel what he felt, to take some of it on myself, to let him know in some way that he wasn't alone. He'd saved our lives, I loved him, we all loved him; no robber's life or death could matter against the truth of that. He would stand there, tall and skinny, leaning like something half broken, about to fall, looking out. I would press my body against him and feel the cold, lonely weight of him, and I would look out the window, too, trying to see what he saw. I wanted to share it with him, whatever it was—this loss, this solitude— but I couldn't. He would raise his hand slowly and press it open-fingered against the pane. "They are so exposed," he'd say, "they are so naked." He meant the trees, the bare sycamores against the back wall. "They're beautiful," I'd say, misunderstanding, or trying to direct him back to us. "No," he'd say, "they're so helpless. They can't get out of the way." "They're just trees, Danny," I would say. "Spring's coming and they'll fill with leaves again." Then he'd laugh. A small, cold, cracked laugh. "But I'll remember," he'd say. "Spring might come, but I won't forget the winter." And it was so strange, it was so odd; I thought of my father then, of the year my mother took us to Palm Beach to get away from him. It was the last year before he stopped drinking, the year he was wild and murderous, and she sneaked us away, hid out with us at my aunt's house on the beach. It was a big white stone house set among oleanders and bougainvillea vines. My mother thought we would be safe there, but we weren't. My father found us. What I remembered, what I thought of standing there at the back window with my husband, was the night I woke up to hear my father shouting and crying and I sneaked downstairs and saw my mother standing in the living room with all the lights off and a pistol in her hand, pointing it at my father who was outside in the rain beating on the french doors. I remember looking out—the lights were shining on him—and seeing him kneeling there on the terrace, soaked to the skin, beating on the door frame and crying for my mother to let him in. I was still asleep, I was walking in my sleep really, but walking, I was just a child, but I will always remember my father's face, how the rain ran down his face, how the grief and the sadness and the terror in his face blurred in the rain; how helpless and lost and crazy he looked. I don't know what happened really, but soon I was back in bed, with my aunt tucking me in, and soon it was day, and my father wasn't there, and my mother was in the kitchen crying in my aunt's arms, and I didn't see my father again for nearly a year, not until he was sober, when he came to visit us in a white suit bringing a piñata for me, and for a while we were a family again.

All this came into my mind as I stood there with Danny trying to console him, to be, at least, a part of what hurt him; and as I thought of it, as I thought of my father's fall and his rise, if that's what it was, I remembered that even after he came back to us it was different, in some way even though he was sober and changed, there was something, something for my mother, and something I guess for me, that was too broken to be mended. It wasn't a matter of forgiveness—I could forgive him—it was a matter of distance; somehow, because of where he'd been, and where we'd been, there was no way to make again what had been broken, and though what was new and rebuilt was fine, we were somehow building it, and living in it, with bones and bodies diminished by what had gone before, that ached now, and that lived and moved in a world that, though similar, was a different world, a world that included him less, that had, despite itself maybe—since we loved him— gone on without him. Oh, Buddy, I was so sad. I saw my husband, I saw what had happened—this was over time—and I began to let him go. He could not come back, and even if he could, he could not come back to what we had promised each other. It was terrible, and ruthless, and I couldn't help myself. My life went on despite him. I think it's true that we can't wait for anyone. I think we can travel together for a while—maybe, if we're lucky, for all of our lives—but if one stops the other can't, the other must keep going, the other is carried along and away, no matter what she might wish. . . .

She raised her knee and pressed it outward against the arm of the chaise. She ran her small hand over the crest of her belly and down into the crease where her thigh met her body. The nest of veins there burned, I knew, like a small, hot fire. Her pubis, dark and bristling with light, shone. I wanted her like crazy; for a moment I was mad for her body, mad to sink myself to the hilt. She said, "I don't understand what anything is about, or why we live the way we do."

I said, "And you make your living renovating old houses, reconstructing them so they are finer than they were before."

"Yes," she said, "I do. Isn't it odd."

I think the story was her way of preparing me.

But I was gone, D'Nel, and I was long gone before I was shown the door. My lists became a memoir, and the memoir became a story, and the story became my life. It was all a lie—you know that—but I told it anyway. Start anywhere—I remember you laughing as you said this to me—and you will wind up in the place you are meant to be. The thought thrilled and terrified me: that it didn't matter where I set out from, whether from a wheat field in Dakota, or from a bodega in Spanish Harlem, or from the gangplank of a ship returning from a voyage in the Seychelles, or from my mother's arms—it didn't matter; and it didn't matter—this by implication, inference—how I stumbled, or what detained me, or what gaudy paths I tried to choose; still, still, no matter, I would wind up, winded maybe, limping and brokenhearted maybe, crying in chains maybe, in the place I was bound to be. I believed you, and thus my life became my fate. It was my error, I know, my fatal error. The promise of certainty. So I was damned; so the doors of the execution chamber closed at my back. But maybe it isn't too late. Maybe there is still time.

4. I didn't have to talk R.B. into going down into the water, but R.B. had to talk Archie into letting us. The bright day tap-danced on the sea. We had moved south, following the sand ridges, onto a sea plain that was the deep green of emeralds. Patches of brassy weed floated on the water. The sky was clear, cloudless, so blue in the heights that it seemed one shade darker would bring out the stars. The waves looked like waves on a swimming pool, homey and random and small. R.B. thought it was a fine idea to go on a dive. "I haven't done much," he said, "with what lives under the ocean. It might be a good idea to bring those articles in too, before I close the book." He hadn't been under the water since he was a child. "I went down once," he said, laughing a little shyly at himself, "and wasn't able to pop my ears and had to swim up through a school of moon jellyfish. They didn't sting me badly but the experience frightened me to death."

I had been underwater last in the Aegean. In Greece, on the trip—flight—with Celest, when we admitted to each other that our marriage was over. She had taken a lover, I had not touched her in a year—only our crosstown lurid telephone conversations stringing a sexual life between us—she no longer visited my garage, but in the moment when we turned finally to face the crack that could not be mended, she was shaken with rage. Even at this distance, across the Atlantic and Europe, I could still smell the brassy stink of her lover's body on her skin, even as she screamed at me *How could you have let this happen?* Wholly defeated, with open hands, I could only stand, slumped before her, unable to look her in the face. Her rage rolled over me like a wave. *Tell me,* she screamed, *wake up and tell me.* The room's red walls were streaked and muddied, as if they had been painted by a flood tide. *You are no different from the rest of them,* she cried, *you say you can do it, but you can't.* In the courtyard wind shook the gray olive leaves, like a cat pouncing. The white road leading toward the village shone like snow in the sunlight. I said, *I love you in the center of myself. It's true and I can't help it. Fuck the center,* she said, spit bristling on her thin bottom lip, *you were supposed to love me out here in the world, where I live.*

There was nothing to say. Like a guy in a movie, I bowed to her, gathered the equipment I had rented, went outside, untethered the hotel rubber boat, drove it across the bay to a cove where the white-and-green cliffs rose like the tiers of an ancient dream, clad myself in artificial oxygen, pulled on the mask, and sank myself, like a child falling into his mother's arms, into the peacock-blue waters of the Aegean.

When I got back to the hotel she was gone, cleared out, no note or explanation, no message at the desk. Later we would talk on the phone, later she would let me again, at first simply, then elaborately, construct erotic scenarios over the wires for our pleasure, later we would laugh together as she recounted the daily adventures of our small blond daughter, and later she would begin to forgive me and a tenderness would come into her voice as she spoke of our marriage, but never, neither then nor later, would she let me see her again. I stood at the concierge's pale wooden desk with seawater dripping off my body, asking him to check messages one more time, and it was as if the droplets, the small pool at my feet, were not some alien liquid draining off me, but me dissolving, my body and the wayward spirit it so loosely contained draining away. What was left, or what slipped like an assassin into the empty space, was something different.

Archie thought we were crazy. "No way I'm going to let you guys go down on my line," he said. He sat in the high seat behind the wheel eating a banana sandwich. On the dash was a lined-up selection of speckled cowries, each smaller than my little fingernail. Tacked above the windshield was the dried skin of a sea snake. It looked like a strip of crumpled brown paper. "I might let you go down, R.B., if you want to, but there's no way I'm going to let him."

"It was not what you think it was, Archie," R.B. said, nodding solemnly.

"What was it?"

"Maybe you could think of him as a kind of explorer. He likes to go look at things that most of us don't think of looking at."

"Like what—his own asshole?"

R.B. cast a fond and sad glance at me waiting in the wings of the bow. "I expect so. I expect he's attempted to peer into that abyss too. But we can't shun folks just because they're driven in directions that are not ours."

"I sure as hell can if it's my equipment they're taking with them."

"You know I can stand good for the equipment."

"Damn, R.B., you don't have to say that—I know you can—but that's not the point. I can tell that when this guy heads off somewhere things start happening, things I don't like."

"He'll be with me."

"Who would have a hard time controlling a puppy."

"That's true, isn't it?"

Archie turned his head and spit discreetly over the side. Bubbles from Ody's hose broke faintly and lightly on the surface. The sea looked like a trampled mirror. He shook his head and smiled. "You're just like in school, Randall. You keep on smiling and telling the truth of things like somebody who's too dumb to know better. But you do."

"I would really like to go underwater with Buddy. It's too rare an experience to miss."

Archie sighed. "I don't know why you would think so, but okay. But not for long—twenty minutes, that's all I'll give you."

We had to wait until Ody came up dragging his bag of gray sponges. The boat stank of sponge gurry and the stern deck was slick with it. The first sponges had been washed with the pressure hose—uncoiled from the well in the deck—and they were racked—dark, dusty gold puffs—on the shelf along the starboard side. Dry, they were stiff as starch, but when you wet them they became coarsely soft. Even trampled and washed, they still smelled broadly of the flavors of the ocean.

Sea, sky—there was an emptiness. No visions, and even, for a moment, no memories. D'Nel had retreated into the shadows. I felt not a calmness but a stillness, a pause, the moment between, before what has wound down is wound up again. The sharp sunlight glancing off the waves could have been a message but it wasn't, and the scattering of horsetail cirrus high in the east could have been a slate upon which was written the story of all our lives, but it wasn't. The small white boat wobbled in the hand of the sea, but there was no intelligence, not at that moment, in its rhythm. I had spent a long time trying to shuffle the world, until—in light and motion—it became a recognizable story, but I couldn't say now, not in this life as I lived it, what would happen. I knew why I wanted to go to the bottom with R.B., but I didn't think what I planned to do would help; it was simply the next thing.

We tugged on the dead, slick skin of wet suits, selected masks, let Ody show us how to use the regulators—"slow and steady," he said, "there's no hurry underwater" (I could taste his mouth on the black rubber)—and we clambered over the side, sliding feetfirst into the warm, light-penetrated sea.

Descending, we nearly became entangled when R.B. shoved himself, in an attempt to find his balance, against me, but I swam off a ways and we fell steadily through the levels of shade. We seemed brothers, two descending, leading our streams of bubbles, and for a moment I had the impulse to take his hand, the way I might if we were children out for a walk. The pumped air was cold and brassy, raw against the back of my throat. Here and there thin yellow strings hung suspended, which I realized were sea worms when I touched them. The floor that we hung above as we popped our ears was furrowed, gray-white; mounds of gray boulder coral, like the remains of battlements, lay heaped about, stacked in places nearly to the surface. There were a few patches of rusty turtle grass between the outcroppings, and here and there near the base of the boulders there were collections of red and blue fan coral, like ornaments. R.B. swam close, pulled his respirator out, and grinned at me. He pointed down and off to one side where a small stand of lace coral nearly filled the narrow space between two walls of boulders. A small troop of zebras idled above the patch and a puffer drifted along just above the bottom, but the terrain was mostly empty of fishes. The distances were mist.

I followed him as he swam toward the lace. His feet were bare; I had never noticed how narrow they were, how deeply the arches sank into his insteps. He swam awkwardly, scooping slowly at the water as if the two sides of his body were slightly unhinged, kicking randomly. In my mind as I swam I began to find the end of my movie. I saw the morning light bristling in the dewy quince bushes off the porch. I saw the detective's body, clad in a rumpled gray suit, under the ligustrum bush;

I watched, as if I were there—as if I were the actor, standing at a second-floor bedroom window looking out at the flat and oily sea—watched D'Nel trundle a wheelbarrow across the lawn, lift the body into it, and push it off toward the woods. I—the actor, Bantling Jakes—did not stir, could not. He—I—watched as D'Nel negotiated the gate, pushed the barrow along the fence, and turned in among the pines. Hands in my—his—pockets, I gripped my thighs, squeezing until I made pain in the flesh. A woodpecker throbbed, stopped, throbbed again.

The mind is not energetic now, it is not quick. My mind. It is not as you think it would be, it is not as it is in a movie, when action is like a stream of bubbles rising from a seafloor: coherent, unbroken, bound for the surface. I am very tired, too tired even to know that I am tired. Sunk deep, the body starves for lack of oxygen, the mind starves.

I watch my man, my Bantling, turn from the window to look at the woman on the bed. In his face, worn by these last days, the clumsy features more awkward than ever, there is something new, a determination, an expression fixed like the worked face on a metal shield, and in his eyes there is a flat, opaque light. Molly's head is a darkness, her hair black, covering the white pillow. She came to me in the night. She lay with me in my arms. There has never been a moment when she wanted me to save her. There will never be a moment. I see her slender arms, the small crease above her belly, the slackened breasts. Why does what moves out from us toward another move so strongly, like another body, alive, yearning, trailing the cumber of our stupid, incompetent selves? In her tarry sexual hair gleams the paste of my life. Lost and bereft, I have eaten his spunk out of her cunt. Why are we helpless?

There is no moral ground in your work—someone, a critic or a friend, said that in print. I took it as a delicate and straightforward attempt to awaken me, but I didn't know how to answer, or change. Why would a woman go off with a deadly man? Why would a good man, following her, let himself be drawn into murder and flight? And what of all the other stories, the ones that came before, my murderous families with their scabby secrets they killed each other to protect? And my blue-eyed men walking off the desert to kill? And the women who opened their

arms to them, and their sordid deaths? R.B. said if we could think it
then it existed. And not only God, but hell's minions too. It is not just
the knife in the ribs, the son betraying a father, the mother betraying
a son, that are fantastic to me; it is the cup of gunpc ·der tea by an open
window on a spring afternoon, light on the water, the wind moving
like an invisible panther through the top of the sycamore, the broken
shoe next to the empty fireplace. My man, my man Bantling Jakes stands
at a window on the Florida coast and turns to watch another man, this
man, this killer D'Nel Boyd, as he pushes Tubby Wells in a wheelbarrow into the pinewoods. He is unable to cry out, he is unable to stop
what is happening. A clock ticks on the dresser, there is a dried bouquet
of purple water flowers tacked to the headboard of the bed, the woman
sleeps on her back, her arm thrown as if in surprise over her head,
snoring softly. Last night she had a fit; her body crooked like a stick.
There was an electrical throbbing that ran like a stupid cry along the
surface of her chilled skin; it seemed to me the pulse of space. *Have you
ever thought,* D'Nel said, *that you'd like to fuck her when she's like that?*
If you can imagine it, it exists.

We drifted over the field of lace. The coral fans were each wider than
a human chest, filigreed and woven like ornate fire screens, slick black.
Among them swam tiny silver fishes. We were tethered from above,
so couldn't go far, but just beyond the patch was a cleared space. I
tugged the line, felt it give, and moved that way. R.B. knelt by the
coral, touching it with his delicate white fingers. I broke a branch off
and motioned to him. He grinned around his mouthpiece and followed
me a couple of strokes. The bottom was hard white sand, it looked as
if it had been swept. He slipped my way, awkwardly stroking, as if
pushed by a strong, slow current. He hung beside me, slightly above
my right shoulder. I hovered head down over the sand and wrote
carefully with the coral stick the words: BESS IS DEAD. At that
moment, moment when my life loosed its tether, I could have turned
and swum away into the descending mist of the sea's underworld, I
could have kept on swimming, but I didn't. I looked him in the face.
I saw the grin fade, I saw the bafflement, I saw the disbelief and then

the pain fill his eyes. He shook his head. I nodded yes. He pushed back against the water, as if he were pushing against a wall, but I caught his wrist. It felt as if I were grasping cold bone. I raised my hand, one finger, leaned down and wrote: I KILLED BESS.

He struggled against me, thrashing in a slow desperate motion; he screamed, a throbbing, grained, humming sound, like speech before language. The sound pressed into my ears. Above us the surface was white and silver sky, terribly far away, like the sky of Manhattan on a cloudy spring morning when winter has stomped back into the world for a day, like a bully, to remind us who runs the world; a sky like a sky in a dream of sky, limited and tangible.

He pushed and struggled—it was as if we were in slow motion wildly shaking hands—and then he stopped. We drifted above the bottom as our breath forced heavy clouds of bubbles out. The small, insistent hand of the current pressed against our bodies. He looked me in the face, across the few feet of clear water, and I know that what he saw there said I wasn't lying. My face was a screen upon which was projected a terrible fact. I saw it reflected in his brown eyes, a message carried across water and returned to me, as over great distance, perfectly. And I saw the blow—like the sound of a shot reaching us from far away across the bay—saw it reach him and break through mask and flesh and bony skull and penetrate his brain. My father's last words to me, after my daughter kissed him, were a question. *Can you see it in my face?* he said, but I could not see it, and as I knelt beside him and asked him what it was—what?—he died. But now I saw. I saw the large eyes blink, and saw the life collapse and saw the pain that was not pain—that was beyond and could not be described by the word pain—that was recognition, that was the curtain torn aside before the gross, cackling mystery, before death itself and the hopelessness of death—I saw it in his eyes as I saw his hand rise, floating, and touch my face, as the cold fingers stroked downward across my face, as the hand, softly, in caress, touched my face and drifted down my body, in acknowledgment, in love, in farewell.

I let him go.

The soft bottom current lifted grains of sand off the letters scrawled below us, leisurely erasing the words.

He kicked loosely, staggering in the water, and drifted a few feet away. As he moved he unsnapped the line from his waist. With his left hand on the line, he tugged three times: the emergency signal for ascent. I swam toward him but he continued to kick away. He took the respirator out of his mouth as the line began to rise; it pulled the black fist of the mouthpiece with it. I cried out and lunged through the water, but I couldn't reach him. He tore his mask off. For a moment his face, water-flushed, was the face of a blind man, blindly polished by the sea. He was ten feet away from me, fifteen. The edges of his body began to dissolve in the mist. I saw his mouth open, he raised his face toward the surface; he breathed in. The rope held me back, slowed me: I unclipped it, spit the regulator from my mouth, and swam for him. Something, a streak slightly darker than the mist, skidded by beyond him. I had a moment, time; a minute: that. He flapped toward a rise of boulders, his body turning as he swam, as if, as before, he was carried by a strong and gentle current. Upside down, stroking overhand, he looked as if he were crawling on a ceiling.

I swam hard toward him; just as he reached the wall of boulders and veered—I guess to disappear behind them—I caught him by the foot. He didn't kick at me, he simply continued to swim. I held on, trying to drag him, but he grasped the coral, stuck his hand through a fret of spiny rock—I saw the rock tear his skin—and held on.

Then my breath was gone. I'd made a mistake letting go of the air line, but I thought I could get him up. For a second I saw his face as his body revolved; he was elsewhere.

I pulled but I couldn't dislodge him. There was fire in my lungs.

I let go, swam for the surface forty feet up, forcing the last of my breath out as I swam. Pause and swim. Pause. Swim. My head hit the air. It was like hitting a wall.

Archie, his face filled with rage, pulled the hose along the surface. Ody leaned over the side. He was about to come in.

"It's all right," I cried, gasping. I swam for the hose, grabbed it. "Let out the line." Archie shouted something. "It's just a game," I cried. I don't know if they could hear me. I don't know if I spoke at all. There was a rushing in my mind and something stiff and unbending in the middle of the rushing, like a leafless tree standing in wind. Like a windy day, when you shout out loud and no one can hear you.

"What the fuck are you guys . . . ?" Archie started to say, but I didn't want to hear. If I heard him, if I explained, then this would be happening. "Let out the damn line," I cried.

Ody jumped into the water. The other hose hadn't come up. He had no way to take breath down with him. He reached for the regulator, his wet hand flashing in the sunlight, but I wouldn't let him have it. This all in seconds of time. The sky was a rolling blue hoop, my life, D'Nel Boyd, wife, child, Bess, all of them, tumbling along. The white boat swayed in the sea. You could picture us, you could make us up, it was that simple, it was the world at the beginning, or a world a child might draw—blue sky, blue sea, white boat rocking on the breast of the sea, the small figures of men on the boat and in the water, and you wouldn't know—as a child doesn't know—that the simple scene, with its four and a half colors and its perfect demarcation between sky and sea and its brown stick figures waving, concealed another world.

I spun through the changes of light, descending through salt. The sun followed me down, growing fainter like a lover calling, receding behind me. You can't tear the water apart. I could only swim. There was water in my mask; it stung my eyes, half blinding me. My mind was a drizzle in my head, just a dark, endlessly rainy season. The bottom was there, the field of sand, the rocks like gray wrecks, the patches of coral: I soared over it like a man flying out of the sky, free-falling toward the bottom of the world. I didn't see him, but I remembered the stacked, addled rocks he had disappeared behind. Dragging the line, jerking it as if it were the line's fault, I skidded that way, riding over the black rictus of coral fans, over the violet and brown spikes of feather and candelabrum, over the empty sleeves of tube sponges, the scatterings of black coral grit like sweepings from last night's party, until I saw him, lying on his face in a small declivity filled with sand. He lay on his side with his knees drawn up, his hands clasped under his chin: a little boy self-hugged against the cold.

I lifted him in my arms, thrust off the bottom, and rose, kicking toward the surface. Ody, free-diving, a spear gun in his hand, met me a third of the way up. He pointed down and behind. I saw the gray streaks of two shark bodies slipping through the mist. I took R.B.'s cut hand in mine, covering it; kicked. Ody trailed behind, rising with his back to me, but the sharks came no closer. The surface was a membrane of light, crackling silently above my head. His body was cold, his long dark hair trailed over his face, the fingers I held in mine were wrinkled and cold and white. I lifted him as we rose, pushing him ahead of me. His head broke the surface; I wanted to throw him out of the sea like a father on a beach outing might toss his son high above his head—the old surf play of father and son, of the heels grasped in the father's hands as the boy squats on his father's knees and then the rising rush, the father lifting—such strength!—and the boy feeling the rush of water, and then the clean spank of air, his body rising and then let go, flying free, tumbling so high that it seems to him—for one second—that he has flown over the edge of the world, and then the sprawling fall and the smash of the surf that breaks him free of his body, and the joy—I raised him above me, for an instant lifting him wholly out of the water, but I stood on nothing; he was too heavy, and we sank back earthbound into the sea.

5.

I can tell you what happened then, but it won't do any good. I can tell you that first Archie, then Ody, believed I had killed R.B., I can tell you that Archie shouted at me in a voice so broken by rage that I heard his throat tear, that Ody looked at me out of his tea-colored eyes with a look that drove a blade into my heart, and I can tell you that according to them somewhere down in the limy depths of the Gulf of Mexico, I lost my humanness so that it became necessary—imperative—that they remove me from the order of things: they tied me up, hustled me by the arms into the cabin, and they tied me into one of the canvas bunks, a lower one, where I lay on my back trussed into the metal frame all afternoon while above me the anonymous weight of R.B.'s body sagged the cloth above my head, and the seawater from his body—from his ears and mouth, from his lungs and lights—dripped onto my chest.

They wouldn't speak to me. Once, Archie, as he made peanut butter-and-banana sandwiches over the small kitchen counter, stopped—I saw a shudder pass through his narrow shoulders—and picked up the speckled peel of a banana and looked at it as if it were a new strange discovery from the seabed, dropped it into the sink, turned, crossed the room, and hit me in the face. "Stop it, Arch," Ody said, but he didn't get up from the table to make him. I looked up into the foreshortened face that was burned white across the nose, stippled with silvery stubble. I could see the roof of his mouth. His face was alien and sad and I looked at him with sorrow that caught in his eyes a second—I could see it penetrate—but he only shook his head, once, quickly, as if to bring himself to himself again, and lunged away, fetching up back where he started at the counter.

They had tried to save R.B., but R.B. was a dead man. Archie had knelt over his back and pumped the water out of his lungs—there was a lot of it; it ran across the deck like water squeezed from a sponge—and then he turned him over and raised the pinched and pale face and blew his breath into the sodden lungs, he massaged the heart; he breathed into my former brother-in-law—for a moment the world's representative: the world: its breath—but it was no use. I sat on the deck, my back leaned against the wooden bulkhead, watching. Oh, I wish I could tell you that it was then—at last—I felt all the deep things. I wish I could say it was in that moment when this good skinny man lay in the embarrassment of his death that the truth of the world, its joy and pity, broke over me; I wish I could say in that moment I learned we are all equal here under God's blue eye, that suffering does not distinguish among us—that humility and tenderness transformed me—but that is not what happened. A coldness like cold fingers reached into my body and closed over my heart. I looked out at the sea on the back of which floated the abandoned orange gown of sunset and beyond the boundary of which the sun itself drowned, but there was nothing human there; there were no correspondences, no connections, no means whereby terror and grief might be transformed into love.

R.B.'s chin pointed at the sky. The knot of his Adam's apple shone like a polished buckeye. Archie'd zipped his wet suit down and his narrow, hairless chest looked like the cold breast of a chicken. Underneath his checked old man's bathing trunks he had a thin hard-on. His eyelids were pushed up slightly, as if he were squinting at the light. Archie sat back on his heels. He looked around wildly, started to get up and sank back. He looked at Ody, who leaned against the railing kneading his hands. The generator throbbed steadily, the boat tilted in the sea. "I can't believe this," Archie said. "I can't believe anything about this." With two fingers he closed R.B.'s eyes, he brushed the dark hair off his forehead, he rocked.

We were a hundred miles out, twelve hours or more from port. In daylight they could have run straight across the Gulf, but darkness caught us before we were beyond the reefs that run up from the south, and they had to turn the boat north. We ran between reefs and bars, like moving up a furrow (though they were so widely separated you couldn't see any sign of shallow water), making a roundabout headway toward land.

The moon came up and laid its white fan over the water. The boat stank of gurry.

They took turns watching me. Ody sat at the table holding the spear gun across his lap. He didn't look at me and he wouldn't answer when I tried to talk. I wanted to tell him about D'Nel. Lying there on my back with R.B. hung like sacked fruit above my head, the water dripping onto my chest, I began to think that it was all interchangeable, that the obvious was in fact—this time—true: they were all the same or they were interchangeable, all these loves and figments. I thought yes, what I am trying to do is sort them out. I already know, yes, I already know that we are all the same, that each is in the other, but which each is in which other, who goes with whom? I am Banty Jakes, yes, but I am also Molly Picard, and I am D'Nel. But Bess is Banty too, and Bess is Molly—is she?—as Celest is Molly, and my father is Banty, but are they D'Nel—are any of them? Maybe I had made a mistake. I thought I could show that what was in D'Nel Boyd is in all of us, that any of us, run through that funnel, could murder, could turn so violently against the world that the only solution was destruction, the only hope. But I was not a psychiatrist and I was no philosopher. My ex-wife and my ex-brother-in-law were dead, one on land, one at sea. Each breath I drew was beyond their reach. And then in my mind I could see her, Bess, standing at the water's edge in her awkward clothes looking out to sea. I saw her stoop and rise holding a small bronze starfish. She turned it in her hands, ticking each star point as if it were a daisy she could tell her love by. Then she held it toward me, smiling her rich smile of complicity and affection, but I was not there, I could not take the starfish from her. No, it wasn't to press the silly point that the possibility of D'Nel Boyd lives in all of us that I had thrown my life away for a movie, it was simply to make it possible, or to show it possible, that such a one could exist, that such a one—this frank murderer—does breathe, here on earth where men and women knot pieces of bright cloth around their necks and head forth into the world where they try to teach each other to love, and fail, and try, and where they break each other's hearts, and give their souls away for dust, and go to meet their enemy, death, dressed in finery, as if death were church, as if it were a wedding. But no, not even that sportive rig was reason. Reason was only illusion: there was no reason. Or if there was it didn't matter because I was helpless. It is possible to reach a place where you can no longer say no to what stalks you. Not because you are brave or wise or even indifferent to consequences but because whatever in you could say no has simply worn away. And like light after dark, after no there is always yes.

So I waited. I waited my turn. The canned peaches stacked on the counter said *Jesus Christ, help me,* but I ignored them, I ignored the saucy whistling from the bulkheads, and the whispers of my name that drifted through the hull out of the darkening sea. I lay in the bunk looking up at the blank sag of my brother-in-law's body and I waited.

After a while Archie relieved Ody. I watched Ody's humped back as he climbed the steps to the wheelhouse and I heard him sigh as he settled himself into the high chair, and after a while I heard him begin to cry.

Archie sat at the table tallying sponges in his waterproof notebook, drinking a slow beer, not looking at me, or at R.B. He cocked his head as if he were listening to calls from the night. From a yellow bowl of fruit on the table he picked out an apple and sniffed it. The sea slipped along the hull, whispering.

I spoke to Archie, but he didn't answer. I spoke to him, croaking; he glared at me, but I continued to speak. Maybe that was all it would be, just a yammering on into the darkness. I said, "Archie, I guess you don't understand how a thing like this could happen." He pressed the apple against his cheek, stared into his notebook, reading the tallies. "Let me tell you," I said. "I'd like to tell you a story that is so disastrous you will have to believe it."

I said, "Do you know I have a child—a little girl almost four years old? If there is anything I love in the world it is her, Rachel, my little girl. When she was two she thought she could touch the moon. I mean she thought she could reach out her hand and stroke it, and when she couldn't she wanted me to lift her on my shoulders so she could get closer." I sighed. Like a schoolchild, I thought, he pretended I wasn't there, that my voice was no voice, that my body didn't exist. It was another way of dealing with death. I said, "She taught me that we have to invent the world. All of it, every big and little part is strange to us, it's a chaos, and we assemble it and give it names. Every human being in the world goes through this. But what's amazing—please listen to me—is that it is only *under protection* that we are able to do this assembling. It's from our parents' arms that we reach for the moon, not from a barren ditch. You loved R.B., I can tell you did—ah, not did: do—and he understood this. He understood it as only an adult whose world has come to pieces can understand. Who knows what causes that, that crumbling and falling apart? What was so good about him was that he didn't ask those questions; he didn't sit around brooding about how bad things were for him—his schizophrenia, his terror, his inade-quacy—but he set about—as a child would, but a child with years of experience—to make up the world. Did he ever show you his dictio-nary? You should take a look at it. It's a beautiful book, crazed and true and heartbreaking. You think I wanted to kill him? You think I wanted to hurt him at all, ever?" My voice choked in my throat; I squeaked, I whispered. "Personal life," I said, "Jesus, it murders us every time. My life, my personal life, the way I am trying to go about setting myself free from what has captured me. I don't even know if I *am* trying to set myself free. After a while it begins to look like my thrashing is only a way of getting closer, not free. R.B. simply, hopelessly, set about to name the objects of his world, one, two, three, rocks, trees, salt endlessly banging sea. He was a noble . . ."

"Shut up."

He swung around, like a bobbin on a swivel. "Shut up," he said, "just shut the fuck up."

"I can't help myself," I said, "I have to tell you this."

"No, you don't. You have to be quiet else right there in that bunk I'm going to beat you to pieces."

"No," I said, "you won't do that. Listen: there is someone who lives in this world who wants to kill us all. He is not afraid, he is not confused, he is not lonely, he is not even crazy. He has been seen in California, in the Dakotas, in New York City, and in Occasion, Florida. You don't believe me. When we get back he will be standing on the dock of your hometown. He will kill you. He doesn't know pity, he doesn't know loyalty, he doesn't know love. He will kill you without reason." I giggled; I couldn't help it. "It's like life, Archie: he will step out of the bushes and strike you down and walk on."

All I wanted to do was scream and never stop. There was no other way but screaming to tear my spirit loose from my body. Oh, it isn't that *spirit* is bad—our soul—it's that it clings. What kills us is the grip it has on us, not the letting go. Or the grip we have on it, our measly fears that won't let *anything* go.

"Archie," I said, "getting free always includes the possibility of disaster. You understand that. Look, you leave the safety of the harbor to enter the wilderness of the sea—the last real wilderness there is on earth—you break free of the bonds of landlocked life sure enough, but as you travel outward you discover the possibilities of disaster, the raw sun and the reefs, and now this."

He threw the apple at me. "Fuck your mouth," he cried. "Shut up!" He leapt to his feet; I could see his hatred of me twitching like electricity in his cordy arms. He swept an orange out of the bowl and flung it at me. It burst against the bulkhead, bounced against my cheek. The sticky juice dripped down my face. From above, at the wheel, came Ody's voice: "Arch, what's going on?"

"You fuckhead!" Archie cried. "You damn bastard! That man up there"—pointing—"that son-of-a-bitch in the bunk above your head was my friend. I've known R. B. Appel all my life. Christ, you *fucker,* I went to *kindergarten* with R.B. He was the smartest man I ever knew, and the kindest, and the most generous. He didn't ever hurt a thing in his life—nothing. Sick as he was, as crazy as he got, he never complained, he never blamed anybody, he always tried to be good to you." He grasped another orange—it was all he could do, I saw, to keep from slugging me, from killing me—and banged it on the table. The pulp squirted in his palm. "I don't want to hear anything you got to tell me. I don't want to hear any explanation you got. I don't care if it was a accident, I don't care if you can prove to me four hundred ways how you didn't have a thing to do with it. You're a fucking liar; I saw it when you came on board. There isn't a thing you can tell me. The truth is if you hadn't made him go down in the water with you—if I hadn't sweet Jesus let him do it—he'd be alive right this very minute. Right this very fucking goddamn minute." He grasped the chair from behind him and flung it at me. There wasn't space for a good throw; it bounced against the bunk chain and ricocheted onto the floor.

"Archie," Ody cried, "what is going on?"

"Fuck you, Ody," Archie yelled. "Come down here."

Before the other man could appear he headed up the steps to the wheelhouse. The metal treads rang hollowly. "You watch him," he said to Ody. "I can't stand to be near him."

I waited.

Then it was fully dark, and late, and the only light in the cabin was a kerosene lantern turned down low. The ports were open and I could hear the sea smirking against the hull. All around me were my figments, my characters, my women and men made of light and color, but they were dim, like shapes of mist in the misty light. Ody sat at the table tying and untying knots in a length of grimy cord. He had asked me not to speak to him and I hadn't. I watched him work, watched the cord form and unform the mysteries of a sheepshank, clove hitch, and sailor's knot. His hands were long-fingered and lumpy, deft, and dark from the sun. His blond, razzled hair was thick as sheep's wool. The ropes contained me, but I had twisted so that the band across my chest had slackened. There wasn't much holding me. I waited until he glanced at me and then I said, "Ody, I have to go to the head."

He didn't say anything at first.

"Really I do," I said.

"Ah, shit, yeah, I guess you do." There was a weary sadness in his voice, a weakness like the exhaustion after heavy effort.

"I'm sorry about all this," I said. "I am so very sorry."

"It's about the worst thing that's ever happened on this boat."

He touched his neck, gently probed with two fingers the smooth skin under his jaw. Each evening, unlike Archie, he shaved, carefully scraping his dark beard into a blue enamel basin he set among the sponges on the fantail. He said, looking at R.B.'s blanketed form, "Here I was, telling yall a story about some mystery man handcuffed to a wreck sixty feet down and now right here on my own boat is the body of a good man I have known all my life." He looked out the port; the moon traveled along beside, outrider. "Now they're gonna tell a story about this boat and its crew, and it'll be a mystery and a strangeness that'll make the people that hear it shudder to themselves." He pulled gently at a curl of hair hanging over his wide forehead. "You don't know, I guess, when your life's going to become part of a mystery. You listen to those haunted stories all your life and they are just stories—even though they might make you shiver—but even when you believe them they are pretty far away. You don't expect to have one knock on your own door." He touched the back of his forefinger to his nose. "Poor R.B., he would have loved to hear it."

"Let me get up," I said. "I have to go."

There you are, my friends, moving in and out of shadow. Now Tubby Wells, the country detective, lies under pine needles in a forest by the sea. Now D'Nel Boyd, sweating slightly, the strange cold odor that he carries with him everywhere efflorescing off his slender body, stands under a large ragged maple watching a yellow-throated vireo—

rare in Florida this early in the season—proposing from an alder thicket the few husky notes of its low song. I was born in St. Louis, two blocks from the river, and raised there. My father, silhouetted by the hall light behind him, terrified of frailty, sang an old Scottish ballad he had learned as a boy. In darkness my mother stood under the willow tree fingering the tapering leaves, asking in a soft voice, almost a girl's voice, *Who are you? Why are you here? What have you brought me?* Later, in the coal-lit dark of their bedroom, as I listened through the wall, my father would tell my mother stories that were so sad, so hopeless, that she turned away and wept. It was then, in her weeping, that he would take her in his arms, then that the slow and heavy caresses would begin, would begin and continue in the constant dark until the moment came when he would heave his scrawny body onto hers, like a man rolling off a wall, and I would hear her voice begin to transform itself as the weeping became small cries like the soft cries of kittens, and then my father would fumble for the coupling and find it, would slide the rigid flesh—probe and offering—into her compliant body, and it was then that I would leave my bed—a child of four, of eight, of twelve?—and creep on bare feet to their unlockable door and crouch there until the soft, uncontrollable cries became the cries of abandonment and death— of life—and then that I would push the door open and slide my body in and kneel on the floor in the darkness, my face uncovered, my eyes uncovered, and watch as my father drove his skinny flesh forward and down, as my mother—her pale veiny breasts slicked with sweat, the oddly dark bottoms of her narrow feet cocked rigidly, as if she probed for footing in deep water—as my mother rose to meet him, as her cries, which were without mercy or hope, flew like pale birds, and her white, creased throat lifted so that for a moment it seemed her flesh might burst—it was then that the two rulers—the sovereigns who governed my life—entered my life: terror and fascination; and I knelt there on the night-ruddy carpet in shame and love and horror, come to their service, now and always, child and man, forever.

What are you thinking, D'Nel, my Mr. X, as you stand deep in pinewoods near the sea? Do you think of us, small and frail, do you wonder about us, who we are, what we believe, what keeps us? Do you miss what we have? Do you ever, in a moment of weakness, wish you were one of us? Do you ever? Or are you only a missionary from the darkness, sent to convert us, without thought or concern for our meager human glories, our fetes and escapades, our childish tears?

Now the camera moves silently along its double track, the boom swings, and the filtered lights pick out individual leaves from the water maple above his head. Through the trees he can see the Gulf blinking in sunlight like a million bright eyes. The camera tracks in, pulling in from behind and then behind him, rises so that we can see the wind-fondled maple leaves above his head and the clear sky beyond; his face begins to fill the lens, this narrow, wide-browed face with its cheekbones like closed knives under the pale skin, its scorched blue eyes. It is all in the face now, all in the movement of life and death across the elegant features; we see the skin from poise begin to shiver, see it return to poise as the life of the man collects in the eyes and fills them; we see the glitter, like salt, in the opaque eyes, we see the stations of menace and destruction as they are reached and passed—dog to wolf to demon—see the eyes narrow and then open wide, see, at last, a quiet composure, as movement—as expression—stops: it is mask and not-mask, filled and empty, ghost and flesh, nothing and all; and it is completely familiar.

I lay quietly as Ody untied the ropes from my body. My joints were cement. There was a huge fatigue in me, like sorrow, heavy as river water, but under that was something else, something strong and on fire. I swung my legs around—the dried salt whispered between them—and creaked onto the deck in a crouch. The small of my back hurt; for a second I could feel the ropes, as if they were still across my chest.

"You look done in," Ody said.

"Done in is about how I am, I think."

"You want some water?"

"Jesus, yes."

With the spear gun in his hand, watching me, he let me go to the sink and pump a glass full. I drank it down, the glass raised, hard, gulping; it was the water of heaven. I pumped another glass and drank it down more slowly, letting the fresh, clear, round flow of it stream down my throat. It tasted slightly rusty, but it was cool, and it stirred my insides as powerfully as a drink of whiskey. Just before sunset the sea had turned the same pale blue color as the sky. The surface was slightly ruffled, but only slightly, unbroken. The orange disk of the sun slid evenly down behind a thin band of blue-denim clouds—each day it's a shock that it doesn't pause there, at the edge of extinction, that it doesn't stop for just a moment, that for all its long journey swinging around our heads like a chasuble, it moves so steadily, without hesitation—the evening had opened like a hand. Everything was available to me now, as at the end of a picture when after the months of filming, the rewrites, the arguments with Van and the actors, when exhaustion is constant and sleep is a dream of pictures, the world, as if it has no choice, becomes a reservoir, a source, a returned explorer offering all its riches to me; then there is nothing I can't use; the bird cry, the rustle of rain in the curtains, the long forefinger drifting down the lifted flute of a woman's throat, the cough at the edge of the bed are all available, all able to take their places in the picture. It is as if the world were made only to become part of the picture, as if each tick and rub of creation had swung round into harmony for this single purpose. It is then that I can do anything, it is then that error is no longer possible, it is then—when the actors can no longer tell the difference between their own lives and the lives they are playing, when the sound man hears only the sounds of this *created* world, when the cameramen see through their lenses only the world of the set—it is then that all the mistakes of my life, all the moments of failure and anger and loss, become treasure; it is then that Celest, standing naked by the window in the dark cradling a crystal goblet, is leaving me only to enter this picture; it is then that Bess, stepping carefully through the musky dark of a TriBeCa loft toward her wound, moves fluently and gracefully into the scene; then that my father, in the midst of a tongue-lashing from another supplier he's failed, finds his place; then that my own clumsy life speaks its lines. And it is not as the simple would have it, that we—or the world, or the moment—are redeemed by this—it is not about redemption—it is that we—the world, the moment—are *attended* to, welcomed, allowed, seen, in shabbiness or disarray, or, like Aztec kings, in a glory of painted feathers—drunkard and priest, madman and saint, commoner and king—that *attention*—brief and passing perhaps but real—is offered. The love is in the looking—*regarde, mes frères*—as always.

So I drank my glass of water, as behind me, barefoot, carrying a spear gun, a man who had done me no harm waited. My anger was gone. She wrote me this, Bess, it was the first thing I received from her after the divorce was final, after she moved back to Florida: *Every horse we rode together is dead. The bay, the pinto with the white face. The fields have turned from grass to tulips. From the grove a new white house, yellow-trimmed, steps forward to greet me. Love, we are old, and my hands are broken.* I used it as a speech Myra Blake made to her husband in *Orchards of Fire,* as they walked, in Nebraska, along a fencerow that ran over the rise and fall of the sand hills for miles—forever maybe—into emptiness. She speaks to him in that final way we must come to at the end of movies. He tells her he doesn't know what she is talking about.

"I keep thinking," I said, swiveling slowly around, "about how long it takes to get over things."

"This is gonna take some time," Ody said.

"Do you think there are spaces between things, between events?"

"How do you mean?"

"Do you think when one thing stops, just before another begins, there is a space between them, a hole like?"

"I don't think about that at all."

"But do—would you? Do you think there is a gap?"

"You mean like after I go to the store do I sit down awhile, and then a little later my mother calls me to supper?"

"Yes, something like that, but I mean even more particular."

"I don't know, man, maybe there is a space, but my heart keeps on beating right through it, and what the shit, that kind of thinking's stupid; it's useless."

"I don't know," I said, "sometimes all I want is rest. I guess that's what makes me come up with it."

"You need to get out in the country more—out on the ocean."

"That's what Bess told me."

"R.B.'s sister?"

"Yeah. I used to be married to her."

"Oh. You're that guy."

"Yes. I'm that guy."

R.B. lay on his back under a blanket. Archie had placed R.B.'s red bandanna over his face. Oddly, for a moment desperately, I wanted to snatch it off, let him breathe. The cabin was filled with a thin kerosene haze. Above the lantern a faint rainbow shimmered. The boat creaked and throbbed; under my feet I could feel the life of the engine. "I'll just be a minute," I said.

"Take your time." He placed the spear gun on the table. "Archie's crazy sometimes. I don't think any of this was your fault. Archie'll realize that too, after a while."

"Then again, he might not," I said.

He sighed. "Maybe."

I went into the head—it was as small as a closet—and closed the door. The pistol was in my pants pocket, hanging with my shirt and drawers from a hook behind the toilet.

I said, not out loud, "What comes next, what is at the end?" thinking that the end was a painted wall, a road dwindling, an emptiness. But life goes on. This play will be played out, it will *occur*—its jumps and yips—and life will go on to the next thing. It wells up around our feet—life—it fills the room like a slow flood and either we must rise and swim with it or we must drown. It doesn't come to explain, it doesn't come to charm, it doesn't care about us, it only moves, it flows around and by us, and we must either go with it or die. But what if we are crippled, and what if we are frightened, and what if the waters are simply too cold? What of those who are too feeble, what of those who don't understand, what of those who are not paying attention? What do we do when we see it's hopeless? What do we do when we are not able to give up hope?

I took off my wet suit and trunks and put on my clothes. The closet stank of shit and the sharp chemical smell of disinfectant. I slipped the pistol out and weighed it in my hand. Where did this gun come from? Oh yes, from Bess's oculist boyfriend. I pictured a blind child sitting in a heavy doctor's chair, groping for the face above him. Though the room was filled with light it didn't matter; he couldn't see. What does he think as his fingers touch the soft planes and ridges of the face flesh leaning over him? What world does he make?

Then I saw them, I saw D'Nel Boyd and Banty Jakes, saw them standing at the end of the narrow wooden dockway that led like a crooked trail into the cove. It was dark; a silver sliver of moon lay toppled in the east. The cove was as smooth as a lake, reflective; stars bobbed in the oily water.

The camera tracks slowly toward them, we see that they are talking, the taller man leaning slightly away from the smaller, peering into the cove's middle distance. "Call them," he says.

There is a silence in which we hear only the sounds of the natural world: the breeze shaking out its hem in the maples, the wave whisper among the reeds along the shore, the creak of a board as Banty shifts his feet. "Call them," D'Nel says.

Banty lifts his face. The starlight shines on his rough, half-shaped features, twirls in his hair. A numb despair barely animates him. His lips contract, purse, as the lips of a child about to kiss someone, and he whistles, three short notes, then one long rising note, then three short notes again. It is a redbird call, the call the male makes alone among the pines. Out in the cove the surface breaks, there is a short snatch of running clicks, like a machine rapidly ticking a pawl, and then the four notes, three short and one long, are repeated, slightly higher. The surface breaks again, smoothly; they see the dark projectiles of two bodies rise and fall, and then the surface moves, like a hand running under cloth, releasing not a turbulence but a faint swelling only, and then near them, maybe ten feet away, the water breaks, a single dolphin rises into the air, its body held in that strange smoothly clenched way of dolphin flight, flips entirely over, and falls back onto the bow of its spine, splashing them. D'Nel steps quickly back. "Damn, they're jokers," he says.

"They like to tease."

"Spoiled children."

"They're smarter than that."

"How smart are they?"

"They can tell the difference between what's important and what isn't."

D'Nel laughs. The laugh is gravelly and unnatural in his throat. "Unlike you, eh."

"I suppose."

"Call them in, I want to touch them."

Banty looks at D'Nel. It doesn't matter anymore.

D'Nel feels his stare, turns and cocks an eyebrow at him. "I told you you would kill her," he says. "You wouldn't believe me."

"I believe you now."

"You think you did it to save her, but you only did it to kill her."

"I don't know why I did it."

"You do, but you're not ready to look at it yet." He drops to one knee. "Here, dolphins; here, sweetie pies."

The dolphins, both of them, lift their bodies out of the water and pose a moment, balanced on their tails, chattering. They make clicking, small ripping sounds.

"What are their names?"

"Eustace and Estelle."

"Those are ridiculous names."

"I know."

"You're the loneliest little man I've ever seen."

"Yes."

"Get them to come up here. I want to touch them."

Banty kneels, puts out his hand. The dolphins slide to him. The larger one, the female, who has a faint white blaze, a streak, on top of her head, pushes in front, nuzzles his hand. D'Nel, kneeling beside him, stretches his hand out and with closed fingers strokes the dolphin behind the jaw.

"Don't touch her eyes, and don't push. The skin is hard but it's very thin."

"Sweet creature," D'Nel says.

The smaller dolphin, Eustace, swings his snout lightly against the face of the other, dips and raises his head under D'Nel's palm. D'Nel shakes the snout as if it is a hand. "Jesus," he says, "they're like puppies."

Banty leans out toward the dolphins who rock back and forth on their tails before them, their constant smiles gleaming. He doesn't see D'Nel slide the gun from his pocket, notices too late the black toad of it in his hand, has only begun to raise his own hand when D'Nel snaps two quick shots into the faces of the dolphins. The shots flare redly in the dark.

There is no thought in him, no emotion, no understanding, there is only the cold, sharp tearing away of everything. He feels it go but it is as one feels the turning away of the body of a loved one in sleep. There is blood on the water, like oil; one of the dolphins sinks away, the other thrashes wildly, crying out, screaming, its tail jerking toward the head; it turns on its side, he sees the black, intelligent eye, he sees the terror in it that is simply the terror of death, the terror of pain, and then he sees the eye blink and die and sees the body slip smoothly beneath the surface.

Then there is silence, only the indifferent world.

Feebly, light with shock, Banty raises his hand, places it on the gun. Lightly, as a baffled, brokenhearted child would plead the hand of his father, he tugs the gun, tugs D'Nel's hand, lifts it, draws it to his face. He pulls the gun into his mouth. His eyes, fastened on D'Nel's pale face, are without distinction, and only beg. He tries to speak, tries to say two words, but he cannot. *Release me.* D'Nel shakes his head, slowly, his burnt eyes like black thumbs pressing into Banty's face. "No," he says, "sorry, boy."

He drags the gun from Banty's mouth. He rises, looks briefly out to sea. He lifts his hand, throws the gun; it makes no splash, only a small *shunk* sound. He turns, looks down at Bantling Jakes. He smiles, the smile slicing neatly through his cheeks like a razor blade. Bantling hungers in his gaze. There is nothing, there is less than nothing. There is only existence without existence, life without live.

The moon is a tossed fish, frozen in ice. D'Nel opens his hands, reaches, fingers a wisp of Banty's hair, lets it go. "Sorry, pal," he says. "I condemn you to life."

There is no other journey but this journey, there is no other life but this life. I came out of the head with the gun in my hand. "What the hell?" Ody said. He half rose, dropped back.

"Shh," I said, "we're not going back to Occasion."

He looked at me and his face fell, as if I had slapped him.

"Archie!" he cried. "He's got a goddamn gun."

"Ah, shit," I said.

I moved toward the table, sliding out of Archie's line of fire, but there was no way out. He rushed down the stairs, heavy as an apc, furious, the spear gun green and silvery rising in his hands. In the vivid moment as he came I saw the rage in his human face, nothing in his face but rage, saw the scuffs on his knuckles, the tear in his gray trousers just above the knee, saw the smear of banana paste on his stubbled chin, remembering, for one second, crazily, the time outside Duc To when Bandy Wells, my little buddy from Biloxi, driven mad by a .50 cal firing from a patch of bushes—that later, when it was over, I was amazed to discover were sheffaleria; thicker, larger, but the same dumb houseplant my mother kept in pots under the back parlor windows— leapt to his feet and rushed out into the red stream of fire, wading for three seconds into the beautiful, bitter impenetrability of it, before it caught him, like love finding its object, and tore his left arm and his head off his body.

I fired, diving to my right, falling to my right. My arm struck a chair, but I held on, firing the clip as terror stood huge and immobile in me, transfixed for a moment. I fired every bullet in the gun, hearing each as if they were shouts, as if they were the cries of my girl child, hearing the flat crack of bullet striking wood, the pulpy thunk of bullet striking flesh. I fired, alive in the firing, alive and suspended both, life beyond life, fired as the two men heaved before me, swelling and shrinking, their bodies flaring, seeming to appear and disappear, odd bits projecting like offerings: a hand—was it waving?—a face, the edge of a mouth where two small beads of spit were gathered like pearls, a cry. I heard the sizzle of a spear fly, I heard the breathing like blows on a drum, smoke rolled in the room, the boat seemed to toss, to rise and fall.

Then I was down on my face, I was lying under the table with my head on my arm, the gun waving in my hand above me, clicking, snapping like the empty mouth of a snake.

One was dead, the other was nearly dead. Archie lay head down at the bottom of the steps, his arms out in front of him, still clutching the spear gun. Ody, barely alive, lay on his back, with his shoulders pressed into the ell of the counter, half sitting, his head hanging off his neck as if his neck was broken. The room stank of cordite, of kerosene, of shit, and oddly, for a passing moment, of creosote.

I crawled between the two of them, checking their bodies. I had hit Archie just below the hairline and once high in the chest. The hole in his forehead was round and formal, slightly black, nearly bloodless; his chest was soaked with blood. Ody, eyes closed, his right hand lying open on his thigh, breathed shallowly, a sound like a small breeze moving distantly through grass.

I lay down next to him, on my side. One bullet, that I saw, had hit him, just below the center of his chest. I didn't say anything for a while,

I just lay there. His breathing went on and on, small, thin as a feather.

The lantern made a small orange circle of light on the table; the shot spear hung from the bathroom door. On the bunk, shadows were heaped on R.B.'s body so that it seemed there was more than one body under the gray blanket, a stack of bodies, or a stack of stages, flesh dimensions, that R.B. moved through, on his way out of the world. Ody's breath was like a clock, it was like meaning. In the movies there are many ways to make blood appear—you can shoot it from a gun, you can snap a capsule between your teeth, you can put it under a charge on a pad strapped to your chest—but none of them break the skin. A small pool of blood slowly firmed and dried in the space between us. I did not touch him. I could not minister to him. Flecks of light caught in his hair, smearing the native blond to silver. His hand, the hand on his thigh, was mottled in the palm like a baby's, but pale; the blood sank into his body and rose to leave it, the blood escaped slowly, sighing out from his chest. And then the thought: was it a picture or did it happen: the boy lying on the bed, in a shabby house in Florida? What did I think then, standing by the white bed across from D'Nel Boyd, elegant in his black suit, his competence shining on his face like paint? Did I think the woman who stood beside him loved me? Did I think she would turn aside and return with me? I could not catch her when she fell; and when she lay before me the last time—days, weeks later—crooked in the bed, every cell of her body standing rigid and bursting, when she lay bent before me and I saw the veins in her sweet throat thicken and strain, saw her hands knotted like roots, her pointed feet tapping, tapping out a rhythm from a distant, terrifying world, why did I then press the knife into the soft flesh under her chin, and press in like someone probing for the hidden jewel until I felt the tip of the blade break through the thickets of flesh and cartilage and bone, into the soft center of the brain? Why did I press in, lifting her face on the blade, as if I might press in with my whole body, as if I might carve through her an opening I might sink through—into what? Where is love, then? In the ocean? In the earth? In the flesh that stirs and cries? Is it in the creatures? In the leaves? In stones? Is there God if God's not here? Why did Bess tell me once that if I wanted to find peace I must give alms? What then of those who have nothing to give? Is there simply dignity in breath, in simple breathing life—is this enough? How can anything matter if this is so? And must I—please answer this—must I—against evidence, against sense—love this murderous, self-destroying world?

Something in me fell. Something in me broke. I lay my head in Ody's lap, I lay my head in the blood, and I reached my arms around his waist, which was the small hard waist of an athlete, and I held on to him crying, sobbing. The sobs, as heavy as bodies themselves, tore out of my chest. I cried as his breath, as the life of him, dimmed, grew dim, and died.

Then there was only the silence of the living world. They—these men—stopped, but the world didn't stop, I didn't stop. In school the teacher said, *If you're not finished, you have to keep going.* I cried the tears out to the end, and, if the truth be known, on past the end. I didn't want to stop crying. All these human lives, all the hostages I'd taken, held the platform of my weeping up. I saw my father in his final bed, so ruined and helpless there, I saw my wives, the bonny women I had loved, my friends and peers, these feral movies and characters who peopled them, my killers and my dead, my hopeful, naive faces crushed by disasters they couldn't stop or evade; I saw my life and its long wandering, its strung web of journeying, like D'Nel's cable sculpture, hung on poles stretched across the continent; I saw St. Louis and the lumpy disintegrating houses, and the perpetual river; I saw Manhattan and its rainy, shining streets, its lovely stink like the hot, irrepressible stink of a great animal body; I saw my garage, the Lower East Side studio, its yellow arch like the opening of a cave; I saw the brightly polished rooms of Celest's ongoing creation, and then I saw, as if it were a face rising out of a bed of violets, out of the dimmed space of a movie, the face of my child, of Rachel, saw the long upper lip that was her mother's and the bright gray eyes that were mine, so skittish and curious. Once, in a thoughtless moment, dumbly, I told her that I hadn't had that day enough money in my pocket to pay for lunch, that I'd had to go without eating; her small, clear face, lifted to me as to sunlight, crumpled instantly, and tears sprang into her eyes, tears of pain for me and love. I grabbed her in my arms and held her close and pressed her wet, warm face against my neck; and the shame that burned in my face seemed to bear a stain that might be permanent. But as I thought this, as for a moment, through the body of the dead fisherman,

I held the body of my child in my arms, it came to me—the simple thought—that nothing was permanent, that life—the one we lived in and the one that streamed about us—knew no permanence at all, that it was only in the mind, in the jingo fantasy of the mind, that permanence, completion, if you will, existed. And this seemed right to me.

Later—I don't know how long it was—in Mexico, after I sailed the boat south and west, and burned it in a quiet cove, and swam ashore—later I was walking down a dusty street when I came on a small traveling carnival. The rusty creaking rides wove a glitter in the air and the bauchy music was festive. Lights and paper streamers hung among the peppertrees, and the crowds, the fathers and the mothers and the children, moved among the booths and rides with what seemed to me an air of lightness, of happiness. For a peso I bought a length of peeled sugarcane and chewed it as I walked the small provisional streets of the carnival, stopping here and there to look over the shoulder of some young wizard as he tossed a ring at a stake, or placed a centavo on a colored square to make his eager bet. Above us all, the Ferris wheel—a small rusty steel affair, half the lights of which had burned out—and the Tilt-a-Whirl revolved like the jeweled wheels of Maya in the clear night air. A little girl came up to me—a little girl somewhat older than my daughter, wearing a pale yellow dress with ruffles along the hem and at the ends of the sleeves—and she took my hand. For a while we walked around the carnival together, holding hands and laughing in our separate languages. I didn't mind when she asked me for money; I took what I had from my pockets and gave it to her. She ran to a booth nearby, bought a ticket, and as I watched her, leaning against a pole that supported a stand selling candied fruits, she climbed into one of the Ferris wheel's pastel cars. With a slight jerk the car rose swinging and carried her up into the night. As she rose, lifting above the heads of the crowd, above the canvas roofs, above the leafy trees strung with lights, I felt a thousand tiny explosions go off inside my heart. The ground rippled in waves, like a dark sea. The stars spun out of control. For one second everyone I loved on earth stood before me alive. As I reached to touch them—the faces, the hearts of love—the pale man beside me smiled.

ABOUT THE AUTHOR

CHARLIE SMITH was born in Moultrie, Georgia, in 1947. He attended schools and colleges in Georgia, New Hampshire, North Carolina, and Iowa. From 1968 to 1970 he worked as a schoolteacher and government adviser in the Mariana islands. He has made his living as a newspaper writer and editor, a businessman, a farmer, a laborer, and, for two years, as part-time secretary to the painter Myron Stout. Over the last twenty years he has traveled or lived in Micronesia, Great Britain, Greece, Italy, Turkey, Mexico, the Caribbean, Venezuela, Cape Cod, Arizona, North Carolina, and Georgia. He currently lives in New York City. His books of fiction include the novels *Canaan* and *Shine Hawk* and the forthcoming *Indigo Trilogy,* a collection of novellas. He has published two books of poems, *Red Roads,* selected for the National Poetry Series in 1987, and *Indistinguishable from the Darkness.* In 1984 he received the Aga Khan Prize from the *Paris Review* for his novella *Crystal River.*